K X

A FORBIDDEN PASSION

A squire's rebellious daughter, Katherine Miles's future is forever changed during a frantic chase through an English forest—when she is rescued from a pack of wild dogs by a civilized Cherokee "savage." The handsome "servant" of her fiancé John Fire Hawk has come from ~~...~~ to study the white ~~...~~ he looks into K~~...~~

A ~~...~~ ON

Hawk is ~~...sen,~~ the predestined defender of his people, learning the secrets of those he must someday fight. But his heart will not let him return to his homeland without this extraordinary woman. For passion burns like fire in their blood, as it propels Kate and Hawk across great waters to a new life in an unspoiled wilderness—where risk and rapture await them in the noble cause of freedom . . . and love.

JUDITH E. FRENCH

FIRE HAWK'S BRIDE

An Avon Romantic Treasure

AVON BOOKS ◆ NEW YORK

FIRE HAWK'S BRIDE is an original publication of Avon Books. This work has never before appeared in book form. This work is a novel. Any similarity to actual persons or events is purely coincidental.

AVON BOOKS
A division of
The Hearst Corporation
1350 Avenue of the Americas
New York, New York 10019

Copyright © 1997 by Judith E. French
Inside cover author photo by Theis Photography Ltd.
Published by arrangement with the author
Library of Congress Catalog Card Number: 96-96478
ISBN: 0-380-78745-8

First Avon Books Printing: January 1997

AVON TRADEMARK REG. U.S. PAT. OFF. AND IN OTHER COUNTRIES, MARCA REGISTRADA, HECHO EN U.S.A.

Printed in the U.S.A.

RA 10 9 8 7 6 5 4 3 2 1

For my son David and daughter Brenda
with love . . .

. . . Hurry to see your lady, like a stallion on the track, or like a falcon swooping down to its papyrus marsh. Heaven sends down the love of her as a flame falls in the hay.

Love Songs of the New Kingdom
c. 1550 B.C.

Prologue

Assateague Island
Mid-Atlantic coast of North America
Summer 1600

A golden bronze child parted the pine boughs and stared with wonder at the herd of wild horses grazing in the salt-grass meadow. The seven-year-old's obsidian eyes were almond-shaped; his thick, gleaming hair—as night-black as the ebony stallion's mane—hung loosely over his lean, straight back. His narrow, high-arched feet were bare; his only garment was a twist of braided leaves around his loins. Around his slim, graceful neck hung a miniature quiver of feathered darts, and in one small hand he clutched a reed blowgun.

He was a young Cherokee prince.

The horses were close enough for the boy to smell their rich, heady odor, near enough to see the long dark lashes around their huge, liquid eyes. "Oooh." A sigh escaped his lips and his heart thudded wildly. More than anything, he wanted to run to them, press his fingers against the soft hides and feel their warm breath on his face.

Nothing he had heard about the mystical crea-

1

tures had prepared him for their stunning majesty. They were as brightly colored as birds—one red and white, one painted with the hue of summer clouds, another as red as wild strawberries. But best of all was the herd leader, a mighty black warrior with a wide chest, proudly arched neck, and the fierce eyes of an eagle.

His cousin had told him that the horses were like giant dogs that ate human flesh, but they didn't look much like dogs, and they were eating grass. A bubble of joy swelled in his chest. It wasn't the first time Gar had lied.

The stallion's nostrils flared, and he tossed his head so that the ocean wind billowed through his streaming, ebony mane. His large brown eyes widened as his gaze raked the rolling dunes for the source of the man-scent wafting on the salt air. Snorting, he pawed the sand with one glistening front hoof, and corded muscles rippled like water beneath his glossy hide.

An aging bay mare, her belly swollen by an impending birth, paused in her grazing and nickered plaintively. Warily, the rest of the band raised their heads and sniffed the air.

Streamers of purple-gold light radiated from a pulsing orange sun, tingeing the sea with blue-green iridescence and burning away the mist from the edges of the meadow. Still the little prince stood motionless, committing every nicker, every movement of the horses to memory.

As he watched, he listened intently, identifying each sound . . . the eternal ebb and flow of the waves, the high-pitched cry of the seabirds, the restless snorts and whinnies of the herd.

Then another sound reached the child's consciousness, a shrill *kakeer–kakeer*. A faint smile crossed his lips as he recognized the hunting call of his spirit protector, the red-shouldered hawk. "Greetings, brother," he murmured, and glanced up to see the bird fold his wings and plunge toward the earth. Then an odd prickling at the nape of his neck warned him to look back at the black horse.

The stallion bellowed a warning squeal and snaked out his neck, baring long, ivory teeth as he stamped the grass, then broke into a thundering charge. The boy didn't move a muscle. Not when the horse skidded to a stop, and not when he became a terrifying specter rearing over the boy with flailing hooves, white-rimmed eyes, and blood red mouth.

No, you're not a dog, the child thought as he felt the animal's awesome life-force. *I don't know what you are, but you're not a dog . . . and you're beautiful.* Hot breath scalded his; foam from the horse's taut lips sprayed his bare chest; the stallion's angry bellow deafened him. Yet still he remained motionless, one hand extended, eyes dilated with wonder.

"Are you spirit or solid?" he murmured, staring into the huge brown eyes.

The animal reared again. His slashing forelegs missed the boy's temple by a hairsbreadth. The stallion gnashed his teeth, laid his ears flat to his head, and struck out with savage rage.

"Shh," the boy soothed. "Beautiful one, sea king."

The horse's gaze clouded with confusion, and he halted his attack. Gradually he grew calm.

A strong gust off the ocean blew the child's hair across his face. As if curious, the stallion plucked a lock between his lips and nibbled, tasting it. The

Cherokee boy continued to murmur softly, but his hand remained as still as the hot dune sand under his bare feet.

Equine eyes stared into human ones. The stallion twitched his ears, gave another snort, and lowered his head to brush the child's palm with a velvet muzzle.

The little prince thrilled to the sensation. "Soft as a new-hatched mallard duckling," he exclaimed softly.

Without warning, the horse threw up his head, wheeled, and dashed toward his band. The old mare broke into a rolling canter, splashing water to her withers; a half-grown filly galloped after her. The stallion nipped the rump of a gray, and the whole herd fled across a marshy meadow and vanished into a stand of pine at the farside.

Unwilling to break the magic, the boy sucked in a deep gulp of air. He was trembling now, and his eyes clouded with moisture. He swallowed and turned to see what had frightened the marvelous animal.

Plunging over a dune from his left came his Powhatan uncle, Iron Snake, his cousin Gar, and three tall Cherokee warriors, all armed with bows and arrows, spears, and knives.

"I'm all right!" the child shouted. He turned once more to stare at the meadow where the horses had grazed. No trace of the marvelous creatures remained . . . nothing but crushed grass and the lingering scent of the stallion in his head.

Then the men were all around him. His uncle grabbed his shoulders and shook him. "Didn't I warn you to stay away from the Spanish horses? You could have been killed."

He tried to speak, but his throat constricted and

no words would come. Shamed, he hung his head. And then a curious thing happened.

Gnarled fingers touched his chin and lifted it until he stared into the fierce eyes of the visiting Cherokee holy man, Painted Stick.

"We have waited for you for a long time," Painted Stick said. "You are the Chosen One of the Cherokee, the one our people have watched for."

"Impossible," his uncle scoffed. "The boy is not right in the head. He barely speaks."

"He didn't have the sense to be afraid of the stallion," Gar cried.

Painted Stick shook his head. "He belongs to us," he intoned. "His future has been determined for twice ten years. It only remained for the spirits to identify him."

"Surely this half-wit child cannot be . . ." Iron Snake began.

"Your eyes saw the Spanish horse as mine did," Painted Stick reminded him gently. "The animal could have killed him, but it did not. It is a sign, one we cannot—will not—ignore. His is a special path and a mission such as has been demanded from no Cherokee before him." He looked down. "Well, child? It will take a brave warrior to walk such a trail. Have you the courage?"

The boy nodded solemnly, and for once the thoughts that filled his head became words. "On my honor," he promised clearly, "whatever you ask, I will do, or I will die trying."

Chapter 1

County Kent, England
March 1620

A raw wind from the coast numbed Kate's hands and feet as she urged her hunter to jump the low thorn hedge. Her nose and cheeks were bright with cold, and her mare's breath came in great frosty clouds as they landed safely on the farside and galloped across the meadow.

Kate reined the horse to a canter and finally to a trot, circling a herd of sheep guarded by two black-and-white dogs. From the crest of a gently rolling hill, a shepherd boy waved and she waved back. It was the Sabbath day and few people were on the roads. Kate had neglected church at St. Anne's this morning to ride to Dobbin's Cross, twelve miles across the Downs.

Old Dame Agnes, her childhood nurse, was suffering a complaint of the joints and a reoccurring dropsy. The medicine, food, and coin Kate had taken to her would not hold back death, but they might ease the elderly woman's passing.

Kate had not been completely honest with her

mother. She'd pleaded a headache—which indeed she'd had, since it was near the onset of her menses. But had Kate mentioned either her condition or her plans to go to Dobbin's Cross, her mother would have forbidden the grooms to allow her access to the stables. Now that the deed was done, she'd confess her adventure and take whatever punishment Mother dealt out.

Kate hoped it would not mean another week in the sewing room. Squire's daughter or not, Kate had no hand for fine stitchery and never would. Had she been the son her father wished for, she could have been deliriously happy spending her life in the fields, the stables, and the sheepfolds. Instead, she was a twenty-two-year-old spinster, still and perhaps forever under her mother's watchful eye.

Kate glanced up at the cloudy sky. It was too gray to see the sun, but she guessed that the hour was later than she'd intended. If she were not home for afternoon tea, there would be hell to pay. The road was the safest way, but that led through the village and past St. Anne's. The town gossips would be certain to spy her riding boldly through the streets when she'd been too ill to attend services. They would tell the vicar, and there would be a second tizzy when he complained to her father.

So, she decided, it was best not to go by the road.

In that case, she could either ride around the village and cross the open fields and hedges as she had done this morning, or she could take the shortcut through Sir William's lands, a narrow, twisting track through Bramble Wood.

Touching her quirt lightly to her mare's rump, Kate reined the horse about and started for the forest route at a sharp trot. She didn't believe any of the nonsense about the forest being haunted or the tales of the murders and robberies that had supposedly occurred within the shadows of the ancient chestnut, oak, and beech trees. Kate prided herself on being a practical woman, one who didn't flinch at every owl's hoot or rustle of underbrush. Yet, Bramble Wood had a fey quality about it, a sense of timeless foreboding that never failed to raise the hairs on the back of her neck.

The wood was not so large as it had been in her childhood. Sir William's father had put his tenants to slashing and burning timber, extending his grazing land by at least a hundred acres. Even so, the trace through Bramble was a formidable one: the trees grew so thickly that branches intertwined overhead, shutting out the sun; the path was rutted, blocked by fallen logs and invaded by green briers and blackthorn. Deer, fox, and weasel roamed the tangle, and birds of prey nested in the thick canopy.

Kate's mare showed her displeasure by laying back her ears and dancing sideways as they entered the forest. "I don't like it any better than you do," Kate murmured to the skittish animal, "but the quicker through, the quicker you'll be snug in the stable with a scoop of heated oats to warm your belly."

The cold was intense in Bramble Wood. The trees blocked the wind, but the constant rattle of dry branches and the creak of limbs increased Kate's chill. She drew her cloak tighter around her and clicked to the horse, urging her forward. The air here seemed musty, heavy with the scents of mold and decaying logs.

The silence was unnerving. No birdcall broke the rustle of the leaves, no comforting sheep's baa or cow's lowing. An old ballad came to Kate's mind, and she found herself humming the tune, and finally singing the words to give herself courage.

Sisters dear, oh, there were three,
Each one fair as ever could be,
When they stepped from their mother's bower,
Each to pick a bonny flower.

They picked nay bloom but only one,
When up leaped an outlawed man,
He'd taken the eldest by her hand,
Turned her round and made her stand,

It's will ye be a robber's wife?
Or meet your end by this cruel knife?
Oh, strike me swift and strike me clean,
For never will I be an outlaw's queen.

He'd stabbed the eldest through the heart,
And laid her down where the roses part,
He'd seized the youngest by her sweet hand,
And turned her—

Kate's song died on her lips. She'd heard something, no, not heard—felt something, *someone*, watching her. Her mare pricked up her ears and lunged forward. The way ahead looked clear, so Kate loosened the rein and let the horse quicken her stride.

Gooseflesh rose on Kate's arms and her mouth felt suddenly dry. When she looked back, she saw nothing but shadowy tree trunks, heaps of dry leaves, and tangled undergrowth. *I'm being foolish,* she thought. The lane was empty before and behind her; the woods were too thick to hide any highwayman.

"A brigand would catch his waistcoat on a thorn tree and hang there until the crows finished him off," she told herself. But the uneasy feeling did not pass, and Kate leaned low over the mare's neck and pushed her into a loping canter. They'd not gone a hundred yards when Kate heard the long, drawn out baying of a hound.

The eerie howl echoed through the trees before a second dog's hunting cry joined the first. Sweat broke out on the horse's neck as she plunged down the forest trail; her long, slender legs pounded the damp earth, and her mane and tail streamed out behind her as she ran.

Suddenly, staying in the saddle became a feat for Kate. Low-hanging branches clawed at her face and cloak. Her hat caught on a snag and went flying, and her hair came all undone and tumbled around her shoulders.

Kate sucked in a deep breath and glanced back. Two gray shapes separated from the shadows and raced after her. "Go! Go!" she urged the mare. She'd heard tales of a roaming dog pack in the area; one of her father's tenant farmers had lost three sheep in a vicious attack only a week past. But her mare was fleet-footed. Kate was sure that they could outrun the dogs; and if they couldn't, she'd beat off the animals with her riding quirt until they turned to other game. Wild dogs were a menace, but not nearly as frightening as the unknown. Dogs, at least, were flesh and blood.

"Hiy!" she cried, and the mare responded with a burst of speed that made Kate seize a handful of the animal's mane.

Suddenly a fallen log loomed before them. Standing in front of the barrier were two more dogs; one was black, his head as massive as an oaken bucket, his back as high as a yearling calf. The second was a spotted hound, his teeth bared in a hungry snarl.

The mare caught sight of the beasts. She fought the bit and would have shied if Kate had not slashed down with her riding quirt. The horse took flight, soaring over dogs and barrier. Kate felt the shock as one of her mare's hooves struck something soft. A dog yipped, then let out a ferocious growl. Kate didn't twist around to see if she was being pursued; instead, she hung on tighter and laid the whip on in earnest.

The mare stumbled, regained her balance, and leaped ahead. The ground was swampy; puddles of standing water and mud made the way slick and treacherous. Another log lay half across the track. Her horse took that with room to spare. They splashed through a low spot and followed the hard right curve of the trail that doubled back beside a stagnant pond.

The hounds were still hot on her scent when two more crashed through the underbrush from the left. There was no more need to use the whip; her mare was running flat out, bit in her teeth, foam flying from her lips. Kate spied an overhanging limb ahead; clenching her eyes shut, she leaned low to avoid being knocked from the saddle.

Abruptly, hands closed around her and snatched her upward. She opened her eyes and screamed as she caught a glimpse of a man's copper-skinned face and two great slanting black eyes. "No! No!" she cried, striking out with both hands. Her legs tangled in her riding skirts, and she nearly toppled from the tree to the path below.

For an instant, the world turned upside down, and then a muscular arm locked around her waist, knocking the wind out of her. Before she could catch her breath to scream again, a sinewy giant in Lincoln green breeches tossed her over his shoulder, ran the length of the limb, and dropped her upright into the crotch of a tree.

Instinctively Kate wrapped her arms around the nearest secure branch. Her head spun, and the ground seemed a long way off. "Let me go!" she gasped. "Oh, please, let me go. Whatever you want, you can have. Just don't hurt—"

"Shhh!" the stranger ordered. "Be still. I will not hurt you." His words were faintly accented but clear, and she had no trouble understanding him. "Look below!" he said.

Kate groaned as a lean, red-eyed hound launched himself against the base of the tree. Another snarling cur joined him. The rest of the pack was closing in fast; their savage belling rang in Kate's ears.

Her heart hammered against her chest. She couldn't take her eyes off the vicious animal. "My— my mare," she stammered.

The black mastiff stood on his hind legs and flung himself against the tree trunk, jaws gnashing. Bloody claws raked the bark of the beech, and he flung his head from side to side, terrible in his rage.

"My horse! What happened to my horse?" Kate demanded.

"Fled from the forest by now. Without your weight, she flies like arrow from Welshman's bow." He admonished the dogs sharply in a language Kate had never heard.

"Are you a gypsy?" she asked. "Poacher or high-wayman?" She was quite light-headed. Her palms were sweating, and she was terrified that she'd faint and fall from her perch into the pack below. "I warn you, this is Sir William's land," she cried with more pluck than she felt. "He's the local magistrate. Any robbery here will land you in a hangman's tree."

The rogue's sloe eyes narrowed beneath granite brows as his gaze burned through her skin. His prominent cheekbones were as high and fierce as a Cossack's; his nose jutted as boldly as any Roman centurion's. And his hair . . . Kate swallowed the lump in her throat. His long glossy hair—gleaming black as a raven's wing—fell loose around shoulders that seemed too wide for any mortal to possess.

"Who are you?" she whispered.

Sensual lips softened in a face too exotic to be English.

"Are you . . ." Her mouth went dry as tingling sensations rippled through her body. "Are you an infidel?" she questioned breathlessly. "A Turk?"

He chuckled, revealing even, white teeth. "Infidel I am guilty of." His eyes glowed with an inner flame. "This brave is no Turk. I am Cherokee!"

"I don't know that word." She tore her eyes from him to glance down at the snapping dogs. "My father is a squire," she managed in a voice too throaty to be her own. "If you harm me—"

"Peace, little medicine woman. Fire Hawk does not make war on women. He saves your pale skin from the wild dogs."

"Medicine woman? What do you mean? I'm no midwife. You're mistaken. I'm the squire's daughter."

With the ease of a wild animal, the man crossed

14   JUDITH E. FRENCH

his legs and settled on the limb, giving no heed to his precarious position or the frenzied dogs still ringing the tree trunk. "Do not deny truth. Your eyes show the mark of spirits, of a powerful medicine woman. A shaman."

Kate averted her gaze as a hot flush crept up her face. "It's not my fault that I was born with one blue eye and one green," she protested. "But I'm not a witch. It's an affliction."

"Fire Hawk does not accuse you of black arts. He says only what is plain for all to see. He gives you the respect that those blessed by the Creator deserve."

"You must be crazy." She forced herself to meet those bottomless black eyes. "You must be a mad Russian or a Pole. The Polish are—"

"The English call me John Fire Hawk. Hawk is not Ruskie, not Pole. White men say that my people are Indian. My home is there." He pointed to the west. "Across the great salt sea."

She blinked and shook her head in disbelief. "A red man? From America?" True, his face and skin were darker than the sun could make them, and he did have a copper red sheen to his skin, but he looked nothing like the sketches of wild Indians she'd seen in her father's broadsheets.

"If you're an Indian, where are your feathers?" she demanded. "And why aren't you over there?" She waved vaguely toward the west.

"Hmmp." His sensual lips curved into a sardonic smile. "Fire Hawk often wonders the same question."

His blatant arrogance made her angry. "I don't believe you," she flung back. "I think you're a thieving gypsy. Gypsies are all terrible liars."

The amusement faded from his fierce eyes, which

grew as cold as frost. "Fire Hawk is a Cherokee. The Cherokee do not lie."

Fear made her giddy, but she wouldn't back down to this half-naked poacher. "You wouldn't admit it if you were a gypsy," she cried. "The last ones caught in Kent were tarred and feathered. Why should I believe you?"

"Fire Hawk has never spoken with a gypsy. Is it true they lie?"

Kate looked down at the snarling dogs again, not sure if she would be safer in their midst. "My father says they are born liars," she answered, not willing to be bested.

"I am sure that the English medicine woman knows many gypsy people."

"None," she admitted.

"Leni-Lenape are an Indian nation to the north of Cherokee land. For as long as the elders can remember, the Cherokee and the Lenape make war against each other. Many Cherokee say that the Lenape are cowards, but if so, why do the Lenape face us in battle like brave warriors? This man believes the Lenape must be brave. This man believes it is easy to say untrue words about a tribe who is different."

"Gypsies do steal," she protested. "Clothing, sheep—even horses. They poach game in forests that do not belong to them, and they're dirty. I've not spoken to any gypsies, but I've smelled them."

His forehead creased as he appeared to consider her statement. "A man who does not wash each day is proved a liar?"

"Don't be ridiculous. No men wash daily—nor women either." She couldn't believe she was sitting in a tree with a supposed wild Indian, discussing bathing of all things. Her mother would think it a scandal. Kate's fear was beginning to recede. This wild man was certainly touched in the head, but he seemed to be harmless. And he had saved her from the dogs. Almost.

A knot under her leg pressed into her flesh, and she squirmed to find a more comfortable spot without losing her balance. She looked at him sideways from under her lashes. He was most curious, this green-clad stranger. She was certain she'd never seen his like before.

He was not handsome. He was too exotic . . . too rough-hewn to be called handsome, wasn't he? But . . . She struggled to find the right word. Striking? Magnificent? It was impossible to think so long because he kept staring at her. His gaze was so intense that she imagined he could see through her clothing. Her breasts tingled as they swelled against the tight confines of her stays. "You must let me go," she whispered.

He glanced down at the milling dogs and shrugged. "We wait."

"My father will be looking for me. When my mare comes home without me, he'll become alarmed."

He placed a powerful hand on her shoulder, and she flinched as she felt the heat of his fingers burn through her clothing. "What is your name?"

She knew she should protest and throw off his hand, but the peculiar sensations that spiraled down her spine were more pleasant than threatening. "I'm not in the habit of giving my name to strange men or allowing them liberties," she protested. "A lady must be formally introduced. You will please . . ." She threw up her hand to push his away, and he laughed, a deep, warm sound that lulled her fears.

"This man is Fire Hawk That Hunts At Dawn, warrior of the Cherokee." He removed his hand, but not before he sensually brushed her fingers in the motion. "Below us are wild dogs. They do not tell me their names. Now we have formal introduction. You are?"

"Katherine," she replied, feeling foolish. "My name is Katherine Miles, but I am called Kate." She knotted her fingers into a fist, but she could not forget the shock of his touch.

"Kate."

The way he said her name made her skin prickle. She was still afraid of him, but her curiosity was nearly as strong as her urge to flee. She had a thousand questions she longed to ask him about America—if he really was a savage—but she forced herself to maintain an illusion of dignity. "If you will chase away the dogs, I can walk home," she murmured. "If you release me unharmed, I promise I won't tell anyone that you laid hands on me."

"You do not trust Fire Hawk."

She drew in a ragged breath. "Why should I? It's not every day that a . . . an Indian snatches me from my saddle and flings me into a tree." This was all so very strange that she began to wonder if she'd taken a fall from her horse, been knocked unconscious, and was dreaming all this. There was something very unreal about John Fire Hawk. A beam of sunlight piercing the canopy of leaves overhead shone directly on him, illuminating his features and casting a golden glow around him.

"You do not answer this man's questions about gypsies," he reminded her. "You say that they tell lies because they do not wash, but I lived among the Spanish Jesus fathers for eight winters. They never wash." He arched a black slash of a brow. "Most Englishmen stink too."

"My father bathes. He washes all over each fort-night in summer, and monthly in all but the dead of winter."

"I see."

"Gypsies do not bathe at all."

"Never?"

"How do I know?" She was fast losing whatever control she had. A few minutes more and she would dissolve into tears or hysterics. "I told you I'm not personally acquainted with any gypsies. I can only say what I've heard."

"Cherokee wash every day."

She glared at him as the impossibility of that statement sunk in. "Now I know you are spinning tales!" she declared. "Everyone knows that the winters in the New World are terrible."

"Ha!" He scoffed. "You know nothing about Cherokees. You know nothing about gypsies."

She felt as though she was about to dissolve into tears. "I'm telling the truth when I say my father will do something terrible to you if you don't release me," she managed.

"So." He nodded. "We wait no more." He made a quick, slashing move with his right palm, flashed her an enigmatic smile, and leaped down into the midst of the wild dogs.

Chapter 2

$\sim\!\!\curvearrowleft\!\!\curvearrowright\!\!\sim$

Kate choked back a cry of alarm, shut her eyes, and steeled herself for Hawk's screams as the feral pack began to tear him apart.

Nothing.

Astonished, she forced herself to look down. Instead of bloody carnage, she saw him crouched motionless, his face inches from the black mastiff's gaping jaws. The huge animal rumbled deep in his throat and uneasy growls rose from the pack as they moved in on their prey. Then Fire Hawk murmured to the mastiff in that same unfamiliar language that Kate had heard him use before.

The big, black dog froze. A spotted hound, hackles raised, dripping slaver from his bared, yellow teeth, slunk low to the earth and circled around behind the man.

"Behind you," Kate warned, purposefully keeping her voice low so as not to incite an attack.

Hawk gave no sign that he heard her. He extended his hand, palm down, toward the pack leader. For a second it looked to Kate as though the animal might ravage his arm. Instead the mastiff sniffed, gave a puppylike whine, and began to lick the man's fingers.

Slowly, as if he had all the time in the world, Hawk twisted to fix the hound behind him with a stern glance. Again he said something that Kate couldn't understand, and this time the command was stern. The hound didn't hesitate: his hackles relaxed, his ears perked up, and he began to wag his scarred tail.

"God's heart," she whispered hoarsely. The tiny hairs on her arms and neck prickled, and her throat constricted. "What manner of man are you?"

Hawk stood and looked up at her. His slow smile warmed her like a hearth fire on a chilly night. "They will not attack," he said. "You can come down now."

She considered the ten foot drop and shook her head.

"The dogs will not hurt you," he assured her. "Fire Hawk spoke to them."

"You spoke to the dogs? You calmed that blood-thirsty pack by talking to them?" She blinked several times, unable to continue that dangerous line of thinking. She'd just seen him exercise some unnatural power over the animals. She didn't believe in witchcraft, but what he'd done was impossible. Desperately seeking solid ground, she seized on her next conclusion. "You were poaching!" she accused. "You said you weren't a poacher."

"No," he corrected. "I said I am not gypsy."

Her nails bit into the crumbling tree bark. "The penalty for killing a deer is . . ." Realizing what she was saying, she let the rest of her sentence trail off. Was she mad? She was the sole witness to his crime. She had no intention of reporting him. Seeing him hanged was the last thing on her mind, though he mustn't realize that. He might fear she would tell, and he might decide that the only way to prevent that would be to do away with her.

"Just let me go home," she bargained. "I'll pretend I never saw you."

He ignored her and addressed the pack again. He clapped his hands sharply, and one by one the curs slunk into the shadows of the forest. "Have no fear," he said. "Come down. This man will take you home."

"Just go away," she answered. "I'll be fine."

He threw her a disbelieving look. "What if the dogs come back?"

She renewed her grip on the tree trunk. Now that Hawk wasn't so close, her own good sense was returning. "I think I'd rather take my chances with the dogs than with an avowed outlaw."

"You have leaves in your hair."

She turned her face away. It was easier to argue with him when he wasn't gazing into her eyes with that black devil stare. He was well named. A wild falcon had eyes like his, intelligent, wary and . . . Kate inhaled deeply. Fire Hawk's eyes were more than that, she admitted. There was something intensely sensual in his gaze, and that raw, carnal power called to a similar wildness in her own blood that both frightened and intrigued her.

"Have I done you any hurt?" he asked. "No? Then why do you fear me?"

"I'm not afraid," she lied.

"This man will bring his horse. I will come back. You can jump into Fire Hawk's arms and ride home on his horse, or you can stay in the tree all night."

"I'll have to think about it."

He grunted, then turned and sprinted away down the path.

* * *

Ahead of the dogs, Fire Hawk reached the place where he had hung the deer. Cupping his hands to his mouth, he uttered a call midway between a howl and a bark. That would bring the pack. The dogs were starving. They might as well have the meat. Sir William would have to content himself with mutton instead of venison at his table on the morrow.

With a slash of his knife, Hawk sliced through the leather thong that held the carcass off the ground. The deer tumbled to the thick-packed leaves, and for a long moment the Cherokee knelt beside the cooling body and offered a prayer for the creature's departing soul.

"You are old, brother, and your hair is turning white. Long have you reigned over this forest, and mighty are the bucks and does you have sired. But now your journey begins; this life is over, and a new one awaits. Forget the ache of aging joints and the pain of your shattered hind leg. Go in peace, brother, and graze on the sweet, green leaves that grow beyond the spirit river."

When Hawk rose to his feet, he felt a lifting of his own spirit and knew that his words had been heard. He smiled. It was good to hear Cherokee, even from his own lips. He had been too long away from his beloved mountains and the voices of his people.

To be the Chosen of the Cherokee was not easy. Many times, he had wondered if a mistake had been made—if the honor should have gone to another, more worthy.

He could not rid his head of the scent of the white medicine woman. She was not Cherokee. Her hair was the russet brown of a spotted fawn, not the gleaming black of a proper Indian woman. Kate's eyes were not the hue of earth; they were sky blue and lake green. Her skin was too pale, her mouth too wide and lips too full, her nose too thin. She possessed none of the beauty of his kind, yet in his heart he could not deny that she had captured his fancy in a way he had never known.

"By the roar of the *Thunderers*!" he vowed. "Have I fallen under the spell of this foreign woman?"

He had known other white-skinned females since he had been captured by the Spanish and carried across the sea, first to Spain and now to England. Some women had been of lowly station, others highborn and haughty, but all had been lusty and willing. He had eased his body with them and given joy in return, but none had touched his heart. Until today. . . .

"I would have been better to leave her to deal with the dogs herself," he muttered. But that would have been unthinkable. No Cherokee who wished to call himself a man could have left a defenseless woman in danger, not even an enemy woman. And Kate was not his enemy.

"She is the one," whispered the fading spirit of the deer.

"No," Hawk replied. She was not. She could not be. She was an obstacle in his path put there by *Ukenta*, the Great Snake, to keep him from fulfilling his mission. *Ukenta* was wily, and a beautiful woman was prime bait for a man far from his home and all things familiar.

Leaves fluttered in the still woods, and from high above the trees came the hunting cry of a falcon. Fire Hawk stiffened, feeling the presence of the unseen spirits around him.

"She is," sighed the oaks. "She is the one."

Fire Hawk turned away, rejecting the wisdom of the ancient trees, and began to make his way to the spot where he had tied his own horse. "Best to return her to her father's house and be rid of her," he muttered to a spotted dog that pushed through the underbrush. "Do you not agree?"

Whatever the hound thought, he gave no indication. Instead he followed his nose, breaking into a trot as he caught the scent of the deer's blood.

A quarter of an hour later, Kate found herself mounted astride a saddleless horse, clinging to Fire Hawk's waist with all her strength as the animal galloped headlong down a wooded slope. "If this beast trips, we'll both break our necks," Kate cried.

Hawk laughed. "His feet are sure. He will not fall."

Kate's skirts were bunched around her thighs like a hoyden's. Worse, her breasts jostled against Hawk's muscular back, and his clean, woodsy scent filled her head as her face pressed into his silken black hair.

She'd danced with men, even been kissed by a few, but never before did she have intimate contact with such a strange male. And never had she realized how powerful the aura of a virile man could be.

When Hawk had returned to the tree where she'd been stranded, he'd appeared larger and fiercer than she remembered. An odd-shaped bow and a quiver of arrows were slung over his shoulder, and a brightly decorated, sheathed knife hung from a leather loop around his neck. He looked to Kate exactly as she imagined a gypsy bandit must look, and she knew she'd have to be crazy to trust him.

"Are you afraid?" he dared, leading his bay horse under her perch in the branches.

Whispering a silent prayer, she held her breath and leaped into space. She was no lightweight, but he caught her in his arms as easily as if she'd been a child.

He vaulted onto the big, bareback gelding, then motioned for her to turn around so that he could lift her to ride pillion in front of him. She refused, unwilling to put herself in such a helpless arrangement. Chuckling, he guided the animal to a fallen log so that she could step onto it. Then, seizing her arm, he pulled her up so that she sat sideways behind him.

That arrangement lasted no farther than the length of a small boy's arrow shot. The horse broke into a trot; Kate lost her balance and slid off, landing soundly on her backside in the mud.

"Hurt?" he asked as he guided his mount back to where she lay.

"No." Her cheeks stilled burned when she remembered the amused twinkle in his eyes.

In truth, falling was her own fault. She'd been afraid to put her arms around his middle and had tried to hold on by grasping his shoulders. When he'd helped her mount again, with her astride behind him this time, she didn't make the same mistake twice.

She'd ridden farm horses bareback when she was young, but it had been many years since she'd felt the heat of a horse between her thighs. The thin silk breeches that covered her sex gave small protection, yet she offered thanks to the Almighty for the Italian grandmother who had brought to her mother's household the unusual costume of undergarments for women. Without any barrier between her private parts and the horse's hide, 'twould make for a most uncomfortable seat indeed!

Still, her bare legs came in contact with Fire Hawk's sinewy ones at every stride the bay took.

And between upper body and lower, she was plagued with the most troubling sensations. She closed her eyes and tried to think of anything but the laughing pagan giant in her arms. She'd not believed that a man could be so hard in so many places, yet move as gracefully as a willow in the wind.

Her heart simply would not stop racing. What she was doing was dangerous and terribly wrong. She was risking her maidenhead—even her life—by trusting this brigand. If her father caught her, she'd be locked away in a nunnery, and John Fire Hawk would be hanged before sunset.

The horse thundered toward a low stone wall. "Hold tight!" Hawk warned. He locked her hands in his and let out a whoop of joy as the gelding soared over the barrier. A grassy meadow fell away in front of them, and the animal continued to run faster and faster.

Excitement bubbled in Kate's chest, and she let her fears fly away in the wind. She ceased trying to comprehend John Fire Hawk and let the moment take her. Indian or gypsy, dream or reality, he was simply Hawk, and she could do no more than hold on and savor the thrill of this wild ride.

As they splashed through the stream and neared her father's grist mill, common sense replaced Kate's elation. "You must let me down now," she cried. "Please. I can walk from here. The farmyard is just beyond that bend in the lane."

To her relief, he reined in the horse. She let go of his waist and pushed herself back so that she slid down over the animal's rump. Instantly she pushed down her petticoats and skirt and tried to regain her dignity along with her balance.

"You will be safe here?" he asked brusquely.

"Yes, of course. I'll tell them I fell off my mare."

"You told me you do not lie."

"What kind of poacher are you?" she demanded. "You'll not last long if you can't learn to cover your tracks." She swallowed the lump rising in her throat. "I'll simply say I took a fall. That's true enough, isn't it?"

His steady gaze brought a fresh wave of uncertainty washing over her. "You have to go," she insisted, tearing her eyes away from the way his green suede breeches fit his thighs like a second skin and his wide shoulders strained his plain leather jerkin. "I won't tell on you. I promise."

"Beware of Bramble Wood, medicine woman." He brought a fist to his left breast, then extended it toward her, palm up, in a graceful gesture.

"Goodbye," she said shyly.

"The Cherokee have no word for farewell."

Kate hesitated for a moment and then blurted out, "Thank you for saving me from . . ." She took a breath. "Goodbye and Godspeed."

He inclined his head, dismissing her with the haughtiness of a royal prince.

Blushing, she turned and hurried toward the barnyard. When she looked back, he was gone. He'd ridden away so silently that she almost wondered if she'd dreamed him.

"Miss! Miss!"

Kate saw Edgar hurrying down the path toward her. Even at this distance, it was plain to see that the usually placid groom's weathered face was contorted with concern. "I'm here, Edgar," she called. Giving a final glance to see if Hawk was really gone, she gave her attention to her father's chief stable hand. "I took a spill . . ." she began.

"Your lady mother's in a fit." Edgar snatched off

his shapeless hat and tugged his thin forelock in a gesture of respect. "Up to 'e house with ye, Miss Kate. Squire's got important folk in t' hall. Sir William and his brother, Robert. Hurry, miss."

"My mare?" she demanded. "Is she all right?"

He nodded. "Right as rain. Come in not long ago, lookin' pleased with herself. I figured ye were walkin' home. I was comin' to look for ye when Sir William and his people rode up. Had to look after their mounts, I did. Couldn't trust that lazy Matt."

"You didn't tell Mother I was missing, did you?"

His faded blue eyes narrowed in scorn. "What? Tell the missus that Edgar let ye ride off alone? 'Twould mean my job, it would. Do I look the fool to you?"

"Don't worry, I'll tell her something."

"Ye ain't come to harm, has ye?" he asked.

"No, Edgar, I haven't come to harm."

"Best go in by the kitchen wing, Miss Kate. Squire wants to make a good show a'fore Sir William and his kin."

Kate laughed. "You don't think Father would approve of my greeting guests with no hat, my hair like a bird's nest, and my skirts covered with mud?"

"No, Miss Kate, I don't reckon the Squire would like that much at all."

Kate had barely reached the top step of the back servants' stairs when her mother, Eleanor, appeared on the landing. "There you are!" Eleanor said. "Your father called for you and Alice at half past the hour!"

"Sorry, Mother," she murmured. "I just . . ."

Eleanor pursed her lips and frowned. "No time for your excuses, my girl. To your room and make yourself presentable."

"No excuses, my girl," a high, childish voice

echoed, then broke into giggles. Two curly, taffy-colored heads popped around a corner of the upstairs hall.

"Presentable," chimed the second twin.

Eleanor clapped her hands. "To the nursery with the lot of you," she ordered crisply. "I've no time for your nonsense." She glanced back at Kate. "Well? Have you suddenly gone stone-deaf? Why are you standing there like a dunce? Alice is ready and waiting."

Kate drew a breath and tried to control her rising panic. "Why, Mother? What does Sir William want with us?" For an instant, she thought that someone had seen her in Bramble Wood with Hawk and told Sir William, but that wasn't possible. He'd been here when she arrived. "I don't understand."

Her mother uttered a sound of impatience, scooped up the small red-cheeked sister who had trailed Kate up the steps, and pushed her into the arms of the nearest maid. "It's past time for Emma's nap. And see that Nan and Betsy are settled with their Bible readings."

"Mother!" Nan protested. "We've not had our chocolate."

"It's Sunday," her twin wailed.

"If you're good, you may have the chocolate before bed." She pointed. "No. Not a word."

When her sisters were gone, Kate fixed her mother with a suspicious stare. "Does this have anything to do with a marriage arrangement? If it does, I'll not go down at all. I've no intentions of wedding—"

"In your room, if you please. I'll not provide a show for the servants."

Kate hurried down the narrow hallway and pushed open the door to her bedchamber. The room was large and sunny, despite the low ceilings and old-fashioned exposed beams. The oak floor sagged, sloping six inches from door to outer wall, and the oversized poster bed with its intricate headboard carving had served her mother's family for generations.

"Mother, I've no wish to marry a man I don't love," Kate replied, crossing to a casement window and peering out at the meadow below.

"Would you rather see us all spinsters?" Alice, setting her fists on her small hips, turned from the cracked mirror where she'd been struggling to adjust a perfect curl in front of her left ear. "You may be the oldest, but you'll not spoil this for me." Her lower lip protruded in a childish pout. "Father's arranged a splendid match."

"Not Sir William?" Kate shook her head. "I haven't exchanged a word with him since—"

"Not for you, for me," Alice declared, unable to conceal the triumph in her voice. "You're to wed William's brother."

"Robert?" Kate said.

Alice laughed prettily. "It's perfect, isn't it, sister? I'll have a title—Lady Bennett."

Kate looked at her mother. "Is she telling the truth?"

Eleanor nodded and folded her arms over her faded peach gown. "Your father wanted to tell you, but *someone* . . ."—she glared at Alice—"someone couldn't keep her mouth shut."

"This isn't fair," Kate answered. Not that she wasn't marrying Sir William—that would have been a disaster—but that she had to wed any man she hadn't chosen. "I won't do it. Robert's a rakehell! He's fathered half the bastards in the county."

"Hold your tongue, girl!" her mother scolded.

"Men do as men do, and it's not a woman's place to judge them."

"You shall wed Robert!" Alice cried. "Father's given his consent, and parson's coming to witness the betrothals this afternoon. Sir William's agreed to have us both without dowries. And a good thing too, considering the state of Father's finances."

"Alice!" Eleanor chided. "Mind your own unruly tongue." She followed Kate to the window and clasped her hand. "I know you've always said you'd not marry, but it's time you stopped acting the foolish chit and faced reality. You were the first child I bore that lived. We were so happy to have you that we've thoughtlessly indulged your fancies. I've spoiled you, and now you must pay the price."

"I don't love Robert Bennett, and I'll not become his wife."

"Love? What does love have to do with marriage?" Eleanor demanded. "Do you think I loved your father when we were betrothed? I'd not set eyes on him three times before we were churched. Marriage is a far more serious thing than a girl's fancy."

"She gets those ideas from the romances she reads," Alice put in. "Isolde and Tristram. Guinevere and Lancelot." She cupped her heart-shaped face in her hands. "Tragic lovers all," she taunted.

"Enough, Alice," Eleanor snapped. Her voice softened as she looked into Kate's eyes. "Daughter, listen to me. I wept for days when my father told me that I was to be married, but I curbed my foolish will and gave obedience to my parents' wishes. They knew what was best for me. The boy I pined for soon went blind of French pox. Respect and duty come first, and if you are lucky, love for your husband will follow as it did for me. At least Robert is no stranger. He has been your friend since you were a child."

"My friend, but not a man I wished to be bound to for all my life."

"Nevertheless, child, the decision has been made."

Kate turned her face away, determined not to be swayed by her mother's argument. "I don't want . . ."

But Eleanor refused to release her hand. "Look at me. There is more to this than your future." She sighed heavily. "Your father is a good man. He's been a doting father to all five of you girls. Never once has he blamed me for not providing him with a son. But facts are facts; Henry has never been particularly clever with money. His heart rules his head in all things. For years he's been borrowing from Sir William, a few guineas here, a few there. Now the debt is substantial, and wool prices are lower than ever."

"I am of age," Kate murmured stubbornly. "You can't force me to marry Robert Bennett. Let Alice have Sir William. I'll be content to stay at home and help you with the children."

"*Mo*-ther," Alice insisted.

"You know better than that," Eleanor said quietly. "You are the eldest. You must marry first. If you don't take a husband, your sisters must all remain spinsters."

"The twins are nine, and Emma only five," Kate argued. "I hardly think—"

"Sir William will forgive your father's debt," Eleanor said. "No one will drag you to the church in chains as my great-grandmother Mabel was dragged by her parents, but I do not believe you could be so selfish. Will you at least speak with Robert?"

"Please," Alice begged. "For Mother's sake?"

"For yours, you mean," Kate replied. But she couldn't help noticing the mending and the frayed cuffs on her mother's best go-to-church silk gown or the worry lines at the corners of her shrewd green eyes. "All right," she agreed reluctantly. "I'll talk to Robert, but I'm promising nothing."

"That's all I ask," Eleanor said, giving Kate a kiss on the cheek. "That and proper respect for your father and his guests. Hurry. Put on your blue brocade. I'll call Sarrie to help you fix your hair. We don't want to keep the gentlemen waiting."

"No," Kate answered softly, "we wouldn't want to do that." She closed her eyes and for a brief instant wished she was back in the tree with the Indian surrounded by wild dogs.

Chapter 3

⟨◦◦◦◦◦⟩

An hour later, Kate walked down the twisting garden path into the boxwood maze with Robert Bennett. Her composure was nearly lost, her cheeks burning from her father's stinging censure. She'd not refused the betrothal or caused a scene; she'd only told him that marrying was not something she wished to do without careful thought.

Sir William Bennett had laughed. "Now there's a novel thought," he proclaimed archly, "girls deciding who and when they will marry."

Her father had sputtered, then choked on his white Rhenish wine. Turning an angry shade of scarlet, he'd bellowed like a Jersey bull. "You'd best remember your place, you ungrateful jade! I am your father, and you shall wed when and whom I choose!"

For seconds the two of them had glared into each others' eyes, but before Kate could make the situation worse, Robert intervened. "Let us walk alone together and discuss this, Katie," he suggested, gently taking her arm. "This announcement was sudden, I'm sure. When you've had time to think about it, I believe you'll see the wisdom of your father's decision."

Mother, red-eyed and about to dissolve into tears, had draped a cape around her shoulders. Robert had led her to the long passageway and outside to the relative seclusion of the gardens. She had gone with him without another word, but although she held her tongue, she was far from composed.

Wisely, Robert sensed her indignation and didn't press her for conversation. He covered her cold silence with an easy flow of words, speaking of familiar topics such as the price of wool and the mildness of the past winter. She let him run on; she nodded in the right places, and pretended to give him her full attention while both knew her thoughts were tumbling like stray leaves down the crumbling brick walk.

In another month, the tulips would be bursting into bloom, and the lavender and rosemary would send out new leaves. Now there was a sense of suspended time, without even a birdcall to bring the garden alive. Even the fountain was dry, littered with a season's collection of dead grass and twigs. *Like me,* Kate thought. *I seem to be always waiting for something or someone in this life—but for what I cannot say.*

Her near disastrous ride through Bramble Wood seemed more dream than reality, not an actual event that had happened only hours ago. And John Fire Hawk—gypsy brigand or Indian—seemed even more a figment of her imagination.

"Doubtless this betrothal came as much of a shock to you as it did to me," Robert said smoothly, motioning her to an iron bench beside a high wall of boxwood. "William only told me of his plans last night."

His untarnished honesty broke her self-induced trance and she looked into his face. "Were you surprised at the match or surprised that you got stuck with the changling?" she asked as she sat down beside him and smoothed the wrinkles from her skirts.

Robert grinned. "Changling? You? You're hardly that, Katie. You've a fine figure for a woman and a level head on your shoulders." He chuckled. "Not to mention that odd sense of humor I've always appreciated."

She refused to be mollified so easily. "The village children called me changling enough times," she reminded him. "You heard them."

He nodded. "True enough, but the fault was not mine. I never joined in." Robert's eyes were blue, not the faded blue of old Edgar's, but the vivid blue of a summer sky. His slightly curly hair was the color of new-mown straw; it reflected dancing rays of pale sunlight. His forehead was high, his nose thin and straight, and his chin firm. He sported a small beard in court fashion that she wasn't certain she cared for, but she did think the small scar on his left cheekbone added to his dashing appearance.

Robert was no taller than average, but stocky with the muscular arms of a soldier and a well-turned leg that showed off to his advantage in his stylish garb. Many a local village girl had sighed over Robert Bennett as he rode past, but Kate had never been one of them.

"No," she admitted. "You didn't. If I recall correctly, you told my tormentors that I had one green eye and one blue because I was a twin who'd gotten mixed up with my twin sister in the womb."

He laughed. "Each of you got one of the other's eyes, when a gypsy witch cast a spell over you."

"But my twin mysteriously vanished, and my parents hid the secret," she finished.

"She was stolen by the gypsy witch to raise as an apprentice." Robert spread his palms dramatically.

Kate couldn't help smiling at him. "Once, you said it was a washerwoman who carried my twin out of the house in her laundry basket."

"Did I?" He shook his head. "I didn't remember that one. I'll admit I spun some wild tales in those days."

Her smile became a chuckle. "We did have fun, didn't we? Everything was simple when we were children."

"You had fun. You were more lad than girl. Skinned knees and knuckles. Ready for any dare. I was mightily embarrassed when you dressed up like a butcher's brat and entered the greased pig race at the May Day fair."

"You wouldn't have cared if you'd been the one to capture the pig instead of me," she reminded him.

"I would have got him if I hadn't slipped in the mud. It was mortifying to be beaten by a little girl," he admitted. "What were you then, ten?"

Warm memories bubbled up inside her as she remembered the stunned expression on her father's face and the cheering of the villagers when she appeared, hands outstretched, to accept the prize, covered with muck from the crown of her head to her bare feet. She'd spent three weeks in the sewing room for that trick, but the thrill of victory had been worth every minute of imprisonment.

"I remember that I was three years older but you were exactly my height," he went on. "I didn't dare pick a fight with you because I was afraid you'd be too much for me to handle. I didn't begin to grow until I was sixteen. My mother feared I'd end up a dwarf."

She smiled at him, remembering the plump

yellow-haired boy who hated to get his fine clothes dirty. But once Robert had taken the plunge and waded in, he was as rough as the blacksmith's son. "I was nine when I caught the pig," she said. "Ten the following year when Father let me go with him on the first autumn hunt. Remember my piebald pony? You were riding a beautiful gray. He must have been sixteen hands."

"Pony or not, you always managed to keep up with the lead riders until it came to the kill."

"I felt sorry for the fox," she said.

"That was my last hunt for years. Our tutor left and I went off to Eton, and from there into the military."

"I knew you always wanted to be a soldier, but Father said you were bound for the church."

"So my mother planned, but I'm too ambitious for a religious life. Like you, I have a boundless curiosity and a yen for action." He squeezed her hand, then raised it to his lips and kissed her knuckles.

She tried to pull free, but he held her. "Admit it, Katie," he soothed. "If you have to have a husband, I'm not a terrible catch, am I? We've been friends long enough to know all of each other's terrible secrets." He pushed back a stray curl from her face. "Besides, I'm handsome, good-natured, and I have all my own teeth."

"And modest," she teased, "always modest." He let go of her hand, and she edged away from him. She'd always been at ease with Robert because they were friends, but now . . . She tried to guess what he was thinking. Would he remain as good-natured if she married him, or would he become a demanding master, as most husbands did?

She wasn't entirely comfortable with his touch. Without wanting to, she found herself comparing

Robert unfavorably to Hawk. But that was madness. Her future lay with Robert. Any sensible maid would welcome his advances. Wouldn't she? she argued with herself.

"You're different, Katie," he observed. "I'm not sure what caused this change, but I find you gentler and more womanly. I think I like it."

"You've not changed a wit," she replied. "You're as arrogant as ever."

He shrugged. "Let brother William be modest. He has the money in our family."

"As sister Alice has the beauty in mine." Robert slid closer, and she moved away again. There was a slight sour odor about him that she found distasteful. He was wearing an expensive greatcoat with silver buttons, but it had obviously not been aired since it was last worn.

"Alice?"

She pushed aside her foolish thoughts and concentrated on what he was saying. "I'm sorry," she murmured. "Are you certain you wouldn't rather have her for a bride?"

"Alice?" He dismissed her sister with a grimace. "Not for me, thank you very much. Alice never appreciated my magic tricks."

"They were pretty awful."

He started to protest, then shrugged. "You leave little way out for a gentleman. If I tell you why I don't favor your sister, I'm insulting your family. If I admire her . . . her attributes, then I'm . . ."

"No gentleman?" she supplied.

"Exactly."

A sparrow hopped along the walk. She watched it, wondering how much, if anything, she could say without being disloyal to Alice. "She's not what she appears."

"I know she's not as she appears to William."

Kate flashed him a wary glance. "You haven't—"

"Known her in the biblical sense?" He shook his head. "No, I never have."

For a fraction of a second, she thought she read something in his eyes that contradicted his denial, but then he laughed and the expression was lost in his easy charm.

"I have heard rumors . . ." He trailed off. "This really isn't a suitable discussion for me to have with my betrothed."

"We aren't betrothed yet," she reminded him. "Alice is a light-skirts. You know it, I know it. Half the county must have *knowledge* of her antics. God's wounds! She's never been particularly secretive. She's been climbing into haymows with village lads since she was twelve. I'm surprised your brother doesn't see her for what she is."

"William sees only what he wishes to see. She's fair of face and sings a pretty hymn, therefore he thinks she must be saintly."

She nodded. "He's much like my father. Long ago, Father marked me as the hellion in our brood. Alice says what is expected of her and then does what she pleases without anyone noticing."

"Your misbehavior is hard to miss."

She sighed. "I do like you, Robert, but I don't love you—not in that way." She nibbled at her lower lip. "I can't imagine us . . ."

"Climbing between the sheets together?"

"Now who's blunt?"

"I'm a soldier, lass. I say what I think. It's why we'll make a good marriage. I need a wife to go to Virginia with William's company. He's offered me command of his guards. Think of it. A new land, new sights and smells! Where's your sense of adventure? This is your chance to be part of—"

"You'd take me with you to America?"

"What did I just say? You and Alice both, you're coming with us. William is establishing a new settlement on the James River in the Virginia Colony. There will be families, a real town."

Kate felt a shiver of excitement. Perhaps Robert was right. If she had to have a husband, why not him? Father and Mother would be eased of their financial burdens, Alice would be safely wed, and she—Kate—would have an opportunity to see more of the world than Kent.

"If it's the physical part of marriage that frightens you, leave that to me. I would be gentle with you, Katie," Robert said. "The pain of losing a maidenhead comes only once. After that, there is more pleasure in a husband's arms than an innocent maid can imagine."

"Have you ever known me to be a coward?" she asked. "It's not that; it's making a lifelong vow with a man who has fathered children by every—"

"Your father has done you no good to coddle you and let you run free as a spring lamb." Robert slipped his arm around her shoulder and pulled her close.

"Don't." She stiffened, but he tilted her chin with one finger and looked full into her face.

"Listen to me, Katie. What you accuse me of comes as natural as breathing to any full-blooded bachelor. After we are wed, I shall become the soul of propriety." He chuckled and pressed his lips against hers.

She gave a small sound of protest, then stopped struggling when he made no attempt to fondle her or to deepen the kiss. His caress was light and teasing, and she took it as such, returning his affection for an instant before withdrawing.

He winked at her. "You see, there are benefits to marriage that you've not reckoned with." He clasped her hands and rose to his feet. "Come. We'll tell William and your father that you're content to have me, and the parson can post the banns." He draped an arm around her shoulder. "You'll not have cause to regret this, Katie, I promise. I'll take good care of you in Virginia."

Virginia. She closed her eyes for an instant, trying to imagine her father's rambling brick and timber-framed house transported to the American wilderness. Virginia lay thousands of miles away, across an ocean. "If I go, I'll never see my mother again, will I?"

"Of course, you will. I've no intention of remaining in the New World. I'll make our fortune there. The ignorant savages are sitting on top of a wealth of gold and silver. The furs alone can make a man rich. We'll stay long enough to see William's little town established and then we'll sail back home as rich as Croesus."

"What makes you think the Indians will give up their treasures so easily?"

"*Hist*, honey." He covered her lips with three fingers. "You don't have the faintest idea what you're talking about. They are primitives. Godless, filthy, barbaric, perverted. Like lackwit children, they can be bribed with a few strings of worthless glass beads and a handful of hawk bells."

"Surely they have their own customs," she argued.

"None worthy of preservation. These red heathen sell their women like slaves—did you know that?"

And the English do not? she thought. *What's happening to me?* "Robert . . ."

"I will have William explain it to you," he said, patting her cheek. "He is better with theology than I am, and all this is naturally difficult for a woman to understand. Suffice it to say that the Lord has given America into our hands. It is our duty to convert the natives or destroy them, and make of the New World a civilized English colony."

"It seems so unfair."

He scoffed. "Hardly unfair. We offer the red men Christianity. What price would you put on their immortal souls?"

She didn't reply. His words had not completely convinced her, but his opinions echoed those of her father and his friends. Even the vicar preached the same doctrine from the pulpit. The vast stretches of North America were too precious to leave in the hands of primitive savages—that much must be true.

Still . . . Fire Hawk had said he was an Indian. And nothing about him had seemed childlike or unintelligent. The man had showed keen intelligence and raw courage in the face of danger. Could Robert be wrong about the Indians? Could they all be wrong?

Robert continued to carry the conversation, ignoring the doubts she had expressed. "Think of the fun we'll have and the stories we'll have to tell. When we're old, sitting in front of the fireplace with our feet propped up, drinking claret, we'll have something to look back on."

"You're right," she said. "If I stay here, what will I have to look forward to?" The alternative could be years of subservience to her mother and acting as an unpaid nurse to her younger sisters, if Father didn't force her into a worse marriage with some aging, pock-faced cleric.

Robert grinned. "I dare you."

"Yes," she said, suddenly coming to a decision. "I'll do it. I'll marry you." It was the sensible choice, the only choice. She pushed her fears to the darkest corners of her mind. "I will be honored to be your wife, Robert Bennett."

"You will?"

"Yes. I'll go across the sea with you and see the Indians." *See another Indian*, she thought. "And when I'm a gray-haired old woman, I won't wish I'd had the nerve to accept."

It was close to ten when Robert, William, and their accompanying attendants returned to Kenton, the small, fourteenth-century walled castle that the Bennett family had held claim to since Queen Elizabeth's reign. Built of crumbing Kent ragstone and once surrounded by a moat, Kenton's gray walls and old-fashioned square towers reared upward out of the sleepy tranquillity of rolling meadows. The village with its church, smithy, and gristmill lay less than a quarter mile to the west on a rise above the river, but Robert couldn't see a single light flickering.

"They're all abed in the village," he remarked to his brother William as they entered the castle courtyard on horseback.

"As we should be," William answered. "The Lord has blessed our endeavor this day. It is time to give thanks and to gather strength for tomorrow's challenges."

"You can give me some of that credit," Robert said. "Kate was dead set against marrying me. It took all my powers of persuasion to—"

William gave a snort of derision. "God's will and her father's. As usual, you are too willing to boast of your own accomplishments." He dismounted and tossed his horse's reins to a servant. "Katherine Miles would not have been my first choice for you, Robert. She is too forward, too rigid in her opinions to make a dutiful wife. But the difficulty of the ages of the girls made it necessary. I will expect you to mold her into an image of her sweet sister, Alice. And I will pray that God lends his—"

"I'm marrying the wench you chose for me," Robert said as he swung his leg over the saddle and motioned to the groom. "You've managed my life for years. Can't you have the good grace to let me control my own wife?"

"I wish it were so simple," William continued as they entered a narrow stone hallway and strode over the rusty grating of a murder hole, another of the ancient devices the castle's original owner had installed for defense against an invading army. "Katherine's behavior will reflect on the Bennett family name, and her shortcomings will be noted by all the women in the settlement. You must be strong, Robert. And you should not chafe under my guidance. You are the younger brother. It is my duty to instruct you, and even you must admit that you have been less than pious in the past. I simply will not stand for your whoring in Virginia."

"With a wife, I'll have no need to seek my pleasure elsewhere."

"That will remain to be seen, won't it?"

Robert clenched his teeth and kept pace beside his brother. Once William began his sermons, there was no stopping him.

"And you speak nonsense when you say I've managed your life," William intoned. "If I had, you'd not have gotten into as many scrapes or experienced so many failures. Where would you be if I hadn't sent men to rescue you from that Spanish prison?"

"I was glad enough to see your hired mercenaries," Robert admitted grudgingly. "But if I hadn't ended up in that hole, we'd not have John to help us establish relations with the savages in Virginia, would we? Where else would you find a member of the Indian nobility who speaks English—and Spanish and Latin—so well? You saved my life, but I may have saved your venture when I met John and convinced him to break out of prison with us."

William cleared his throat. "You have more faith in your heathen friend than I do, brother. A self-proclaimed prince of barbarians is no rock to build our fortunes on."

"I'm the one with the military experience. You've put me in charge of our soldiers, and I believe John will be a vital key in our security. And it hasn't hurt that I'm learning more of the Powhatan language every day."

"No, I agree with you there," William replied. He glanced toward the curving stone staircase. "Will you share my candlelight to our chambers?"

"No," Robert said. "I'm dry as dust. I'll have a tankard of ale before I turn in. You go ahead."

"There is much to do on the morrow," William reminded him.

"When have you seen me lie abed when the sun was high?"

"Nay, you speak truth there. You are no sluggard, but you too often miss morning devotions before we break our fast."

"Tend to your own soul, and I'll tend to mine."

His brother's mealymouthed bleating wore on

Robert's patience, and he wondered at his own willingness to be cooped up on a ship with William on the long voyage to America. Cursing under his breath, Robert snatched a candle from the housekeeper and made his way down a series of corridors to the kitchen wing.

If he was lucky, he might meet that young Welsh scullery maid in the passageway. He could have sent a servant to fetch her, but he enjoyed the hunt as much as the sport.

Damn, but he missed Joan. The woman had hips like a warhorse, but a man could lose himself in her curling black thatch. Too bad she'd gotten herself with child once too often, and William had married her to a tinker and sent her packing. The Welsh girl was young and nubile, but few sluts gave bumpy as good as Joan.

Finding the ale and a bit of cheese and bread but nothing more to tempt his palate, Robert went upstairs to his small chamber on the third floor of the east tower. There was no fire on the hearth and no lantern burned—the room, as black and still as death. Robert hesitated in the doorway and rested a hand on his dagger.

"John? Are you in there?" he called.

"Yes."

Robert lifted his own candle until the faint circle of light illuminated the tall figure at the open window. "Damnation, John! Close the friggin' shutters. This petrified heap of stone is cold as hell without you letting in a gale."

"It stinks in here."

"You always say that."

"It always stinks," Hawk replied.

Robert set his candlestick on a table, crossed to the window, and swung the shutters over the gap in the stones. He locked the latch and turned back to his friend. "You've got to stop creeping about like a ghost. Why couldn't you at least light a lantern? I might have taken you for a thief and slit your throat."

Hawk laughed softly. "This man likes the dark. He thinks better in the dark, when the wind brings a scent of the forest."

"Where were you today?" Robert threw up his open palms. "No, don't answer that. I'm better off if I don't know where you were, especially if you were hunting William's deer again."

"I watch the deer."

"You're saying you never shoot one?"

"Today I did shoot one. An old buck. His hind leg was broken. If I did not kill him, the dogs would have run him down and eaten him alive."

Robert made a sound of disapproval. "Why is it you always do what you're not supposed to, and then give an excuse for why you had to do it?"

"Hawk gives no excuse to you. He says only what he did."

"Try telling William that." Robert dropped into a leather high-back chair that had seen better days. "I would have liked to have you with me this afternoon. I went with my brother to Squire Henry Miles's home."

"So."

"You've heard?"

Hawk nodded.

"Servants' gossip?"

"My heart is troubled."

Robert frowned. "Need I remind you of your place in this household? You're my indentured servant."

"I made a bargain with you to return home. I

speak the tongue of the Powhatan. I can teach the English how to trade with the tribes. Fire Hawk is your friend, not your servant. A Cherokee is no man's servant."

"Ours is an unusual arrangement, I will admit," Robert said.

"We are friends."

"We are," Robert agreed, "but that doesn't give you the right to question my actions. William insists I have a wife to go to Virginia with him. He insists everyone have a wife so they won't go lusting after . . ."

"After Indian women," Fire Hawk finished.

"Exactly. Mixing Christian blood and heathen."

"I agree. I think that is not a good thing."

"So you should welcome my taking an English bride. It will keep me home nights."

"This woman is the wrong woman," Hawk said. "You would make her a bad husband. Choose another."

Robert stiffened. "What the hell are you talking about? How do you know anything about the woman I've decided to take to wife?"

"Each man, each woman has a totem," Hawk began. "Some spirit protectors are stronger than others. Kate's guide is powerful. She—"

"Enough!" Robert rose to his feet and took a few steps toward the Indian. "How dare you use my intended's Christian name? What do you know of her?"

Hawk shrugged. "That is not important. What is important is that you do not ruin her life by marrying her."

"Not another word, you arrogant savage. If it wasn't for me breaking you out of that Spanish prison, you'd be rotting in your grave by now."

"So? And what man stepped between you and the lance of that Spanish sergeant?"

Black fury filled Robert's chest. "Enough, I said! I could have you whipped like a dog."

"Do my words shatter your faith? Is it so weak that you cannot hear of another's beliefs?"

"My faith or lack of it is not a subject I discuss with my servants," he hissed. "And I'll hear no more of your heathen nonsense."

"This Kate with eyes of different color is not one of your bleating English sheep. Her will is strong. It will overpower yours."

"Damnation, John! My personal life is none of your affair. Get out of my sight before I'm forced to do something we'll both regret!"

Hawk walked past him to the door. "This I tell you, Robert. This marriage cannot be. You must stop it, or I will."

"Interfere and you'll never see America again. Do you hear me, you red bastard?"

But the Indian had vanished into the murky darkness of the passageway.

Robert slammed the heavy plank door shut and sank onto his bed, his head in his hands. "You take too much on yourself, John," he muttered. "You always did."

Chapter 4

A week later, Hawk lingered in the deep shadows of the stables and listened to the sounds of music and laughter drifting from Kate's house. The squire had invited half the county to celebrate the betrothal of his two daughters, and Robert had insisted that Fire Hawk come to tend the horses while he and William took part in the festivities.

It was unseasonably warm for March, and thick fog rose in patches off the damp earth. The crescent moon was hidden by heavy clouds, and servants' bobbing lanterns near the main entrance to the house emitted only feeble light. But the enveloping darkness of the barn held no terrors for Hawk; he preferred the solitude.

Robert was still smarting over Hawk's warning not to take Kate to wife, and the two men had hardly exchanged civil words since the disagreement. In truth, the Cherokee mused as he stroked the neck of Robert's gelding, things might never be the same between them again.

His friendship with Robert Bennett had begun when the two were thrown into the same cell in a Spanish prison. Sharing a single blanket and a loaf of moldy bread each day for months made men

51

comrades or enemies. The color of their skins had seemed to make small difference when both faced torture and execution, but since they'd arrived in England, Robert had showed a prejudice that Hawk found difficult to excuse.

He sighed and buried his face in the black horse's neck. The animal nickered and pressed close. Hawk inhaled the rich scent of the hunter and whispered to him softly in Cherokee.

Horses fascinated him as much today as they had when he'd caught sight of the first one as a child on Assateague Island. He'd been blessed with the gift of communication, not just with four-legged beasts, but with birds and insects as well. Even bees seemed to sense that he meant them no harm; he'd never been stung, not even when he robbed a wild honey tree. His love for animals was strong; but horses gave him the greatest joy, and he liked nothing better than to fly over the ground, clinging to a horse's mane.

"Will there ever be a place for your kind among the Cherokee?" he asked the gelding. "I will miss you when I return to my own land."

Usually being close to the horses calmed him. Tonight was different. He was troubled by the thought of the coming marriage between Robert and Kate. The little medicine woman with the strange eyes plagued his dreams and haunted his days. She was English, and whom she chose as a husband should not matter to a prince of the Cherokee nation. But it did. He had promised Robert that he would do all in his power to prevent the union, and so far he had not even spoken to Kate.

In the days following their clash, Robert had kept Hawk at his side. Two nights ago, Hawk had sneaked out of Kenton Castle in the darkest hours of the night and ridden here to Kate's father's house. For hours he had crouched in the garden staring at the casement windows and wondering which one opened on her sleeping chamber. But he had not climbed the walls, and he had not thrown pebbles at the small glass panes. At dawn, frustrated, he had stolen away as silently as he had come.

He did not deceive himself that his concern was for Robert's happiness, or even Kate's. She was a smoldering flame in his blood. He desired her in the way that a man wants a woman.

Only Kate. No other would do.

This very morning a comely washerwoman had beckoned him into her hut at the edge of the village. She had raised her skirts to display shapely bare legs, and she had promised him things that delight a man. But despite the pounding in his swollen loins, he had refused her favors.

"Kate," he whispered, saying aloud the name that had been echoing in his heart since he'd snatched her into that tree in Bramble Wood.

"John Fire Hawk?" a woman's voice answered— *her* voice.

He froze.

"Are you in here?"

"Kate?" His heart thundered in his chest.

For an instant her cloaked form was visible in the golden light of the lantern hanging from a hook outside over the stable door. His heart leaped in his chest. *Are you flesh and blood?* he wondered. *Or are you a spirit illusion that I've conjured up?*

She was too lovely, too full of life for any ghost. She was swathed head to ankles in a green hooded cloak, her cheeks were rosy red, and curls had escaped her cap to tumble around her oval face. Even the thick wool wrap could not hide the strength of a woman in her full flower or the graceful way she raised her hand to shield her eyes from the lantern glare. She pulled the door closed behind her, shrouding her erect form in darkness.

"Why do you come to this place?" he demanded.

"I . . . I just wanted to thank you," she murmured in the husky voice that made his blood surge hot. "For saving me from the dogs."

The darkness should have divided them, he thought. But it didn't. It pulled them closer together.

"It is wrong that you come," he said brusquely.

"This is my father's stable. It isn't your place to tell me where I can and can't go!"

He crossed the distance between them and put out his hand to touch her. His fingers brushed her cheek. How soft her skin was. She smelled of rosewater.

"Oh," she gasped.

He heard the fear in her words, and he was suddenly ashamed that he'd spoken to her so harshly. "Do not be afraid," he told her. An overpowering urge to protect her filled him, and he was more certain than ever that Robert would only hurt her.

"I'm not afraid of you."

He knew it wasn't the truth. He could sense her fright; he could feel the trembling of her spirit. "How did you know I would be here?" he asked.

"Robert. Robert told me."

Kate's words tumbled like bubbling water over a falls. Her voice soothed and agitated him at the same time. He felt a tightness in his chest and a heightened sensitivity along the surface of his skin. His heart thudded and he fought the sudden urge to throw her down into the clean straw . . . to taste her ripe, red mouth and feel the heat of her pale body.

"Robert told you to come to the stables in the dark to seek this man?" he asked coldly.

"No. He told me that his . . . his *Indian* was tending his horses. I knew it must be you. There could only be one John Fire Hawk in Kent."

He made a sound of disbelief. "You left your marriage ceremony to thank Hawk?"

"It's Alice's party more than mine." He was right, she thought, as shivers ran through her, making it difficult to keep her voice from showing just how terrified she really was. She shouldn't be here. She must be out of her mind to put herself at risk this way. If her father and Robert found out that she had come, they would be furious. Her reputation— perhaps even her betrothal—would be destroyed.

He echoed her misgivings. "Go. Quick."

"John—"

"To my people this man is *Fire Hawk Who Hunts At Dawn*."

"Fire Hawk Who—"

"Hawk."

"Hawk," she repeated.

"Why do you marry Robert Bennett?" he demanded.

It was so dark that she couldn't make out his face, but she felt his stature—his power. "My father—" she gasped, "My parents . . ." She drew in a breath and tried again. "Surely, among your people, marriage is . . ." She let her thought trail away. Hadn't Robert just told her that Indian wives were bought and sold like objects? How could she make Hawk understand without insulting him? "Here in England, a girl's father . . . at least those of my station . . . Arrangements are made."

"So. Cherokee elders make marriage too," he answered. "But not with a man like Robert Bennett. You will not do this." His English words were precise, each dropping like an icy stone.

"I have to wed him. I mean, I want to. My father knows—"

"Robert is my friend. I would not want him as a husband for my sister."

"Your sister? You mean you think of me as your sister?"

"No. For a Cherokee sister. Robert is no good—"

"Naturally not," she agreed. "A white man and a red—"

"Not the color of skin. Spirit. Robert is no good for a woman like you. You tell him you will make no marriage."

She shook her head. "You don't understand. Our betrothal has already been—"

"John?" An unfamiliar male voice interrupted her explanation. Hinges creaked as someone pushed open the barn door. "John?"

Before she could react, Hawk clamped a hand over her mouth and yanked her deeper into the shadows. His arms tightened around her as he crushed her against his chest. For an instant she was too startled to struggle, then anger spilled through her. "Let me go," she tried to cry, but no sound could pass that granitelike hand.

He leaned close and whispered in her ear. "Shhh."

Her heart pounded, and she felt a strange excitement begin in the pit of her belly and spread outward. He was standing so close that she could smell his clean, wild scent and hear the faint intake of his breathing.

"John! If you can hear me, there's food and drink at the kitchen door for the likes of us," the groom called. "Come if ye like or sit here and brood." Receding footsteps told Kate that the servant had gone.

"Let me free," she whispered as Hawk took his hand from her mouth. Her throat constricted; her knees turned to warm wax and she sagged against him. Her face was inches from his chest. She could feel the heat radiating from his heavily muscled arm, feel the solid wall of his chest, the length of his rock-hard legs.

"Kate."

The earth seemed to sway beneath her feet. She tilted her face up to his, parted her lips, and waited.

Waited for an eternity.

His lean fingers kneaded the hollow of her spine. She could not see him, but she could imagine the intensity of his black, devil gaze. She moaned softly as his fingers splayed across her exposed throat and threaded through her hair.

A curious tingling sensation ran along her skin as she murmured his name. "Hawk."

An eddy of warmth brushed her lips, and she drew in the sweet, male scent of his breath. She arched against him, and he lowered his head to nuzzle the curve of her throat.

Kate gasped as he nibbled her skin and then brushed her with the tip of his tongue. Her senses reeled, and she let her own fingers glide across his beardless jaw and stroke his hair. It was soft and silky.

"Please," she whispered. "I shouldn't . . ."

He raised his head and brought his mouth to hers.

For a heartbeat, he lingered there, letting her grow used to the feel of him. Then—ever so slowly and patiently—he began to tease her lips with feather-light caresses. Heat suffused her cheeks as her pulse quickened, and she raised on tiptoe to meet his tantalizing kiss.

His lips were firm and beguiling, his intimate nearness overwhelming. *This is wrong!* she thought. *I can't do this!* But the pressure of his mouth . . . the lingering sensuality of his touch were intoxicating.

She stopped struggling with herself and began to respond. Her arms tightened around his neck as she gave herself over to the incandescent pleasure of his ever deepening kiss. Time stopped. Nothing mattered but this man. Not Robert, not her parents, not even her reputation.

Without warning, he pulled away. She gasped and swayed. She would have fallen if he hadn't steadied her.

"Do you understand? Do this man's kisses make you understand why you can never marry Robert?"

"I'm sorry," she managed. "I shouldn't be here. I . . ." She couldn't finish. It was a lie. She wasn't sorry. Even now her heart was beating so fast that it made her feel faint. She had no shame. She wanted to kiss him like that again. She leaned toward him.

"Go," he said harshly.

"I didn't come here to let you kiss me."

"You came this place knowing I would."

"I didn't." She hadn't known; she'd secretly hoped. She'd dreamed of being held in his arms. "Please," she begged. "Don't make this harder than it is."

"You felt the magic between us from the first moment I pulled you into that tree. Does Hawk lie?"

She stepped out of his arms and touched her lips,

still warm from his caress. They ached to have him kiss her again. "You mustn't think I'm a whore," she said.

"No man will say so and live."

Tears welled in her eyes. March wind seeped through cracks in the barn walls. The barn was damp and chilly, but it felt warmer here with this dangerous man than in her father's house. "America is so far away. I'll need a friend. Please, Fire Hawk, be that friend," she pleaded.

"You will not marry Robert."

"If I say no to this marriage, I go against my mother's wishes, my father . . ."

"Look into your heart. Can you say Robert is the right husband for you?"

She uttered a small sound of distress. "My father is in debt to Robert's brother William. William wants to marry Alice, and Father won't allow it unless I take a husband first."

"Your father sells you in marriage."

"No, not selling in the way Indians do. This is an arrangement of—"

"Cherokee do not sell women."

"Robert said they do. He said—"

"A Cherokee man must buy his right into his wife's clan. He does not buy a wife. Cherokee women are free."

"Naturally English customs must be difficult for you—"

"English sell their daughters, not the Cherokee."

"No," she cried. "You have it all wrong." She would have turned and run from the barn, but he captured her hand and held it. His touch made her giddy, and the anger drained away. "No one has ever asked for me but Robert," she admitted. And the pain bit deep.

"Among Cherokee, that would not be true. Many would seek to become your husband."

"It is kind of you to say so," she replied. "But not even savages would want a woman such as me."

He chuckled. "There is much you do not understand about the Cherokee," he said in his deep, lilting voice. "Living among the Spanish and English, this Cherokee man see many things he would not have believed possible. I think the white men are barbarians, not the red man."

"I have to go. I can't stay here with you. Robert may be looking for me."

"Let Robert hunt for you. Come."

"Where are you taking me?"

"Trust me, English medicine woman."

"Robert will be—"

"You were having a good time with Robert?" Fire Hawk teased.

"No, I wasn't having a good time," she admitted. "But you must promise you'll not take liberties with me again."

"Liberties?"

Her cheeks flushed in the darkness. "You'll not try to kiss me."

"Hawk will not kiss you unless you beg me."

"Then you shall have a long wait."

He laughed. "So. We shall see."

She willed herself to put him in his place—to flee. But when he led her deeper into the stable, she followed without putting up a struggle.

"I see a carriage where a woman may sit without getting hay on her many skirts," he said.

"Grandfather's old coach, but . . ."

He stopped, and Kate heard the squeak of hinges as he swung open the door of the old conveyance.

"We can't . . ." she began.

His hands closed around her waist and lifted her up effortlessly. *How strong he is*, she thought as she settled onto the old leather seat and slid to the far corner.

Hawk took the bench across from her and closed the door. "Robert will not find you here."

The coach had not been used for years, but it was regularly cleaned by the stable boy. Kate and her sisters had pretended it was a playhouse, and she had often hidden here when her mother had scolded her. She should have been terrified to climb into this black, confined place with a wild Indian; instead the familiar scents of neat's-foot oil and old leather made her feel safe.

"You are a terrible servant," she ventured.

He chuckled. "So Robert says."

"If we are caught, he'll have you whipped."

"Not if Robert wants to live."

Kate's heart skipped a beat. "Don't talk like that."

"I am the *Chosen One* of the mighty Cherokee, a prince. No man can whip a Cherokee prince and live."

She swallowed the rising lump in her throat. "I did not know that Indians had kings and princes."

"My grandfather is the Powhatan. A great chief. When he waves his turkey feather fan, two thousand warriors take up their bows."

"Two thousand men is not so many for an army. Our English king—"

"Your English king is in London. In the land you call Virginia, two thousand braves in war paint are a great many."

"Your Cherokee live in Virginia?" She tried to imagine two thousand men like Fire Hawk. The thought was intriguing.

"The Cherokee lands lie west and south, in the

mountains. Powhatan lands lie near the sea. My father was Powhatan, a prince, the son of the Emperor Powhatan."

"Your father is a Powhatan prince? What is his name?"

"My father is dead. Among my people, it is considered bad luck to speak the name of the dead." He leaned close and whispered, "But we are far away from Powhatan country. His spirit may not roam so far. It might be that his name was War Club."

"And your mother?"

"War Club's father made a marriage of state for his son to seal a peace treaty between the Powhatan and the Cherokee. My mother is of high birth, high clan, as we say. Cherokee reckon descent through the mother's bloodline. As her son, I am Cherokee. My mother's people number many more than the Powhatan. We are stronger and claim vast hunting grounds."

"What colony?"

He grunted in derision. "No colony. The mountains-of-smoke are Cherokee and will always be Cherokee. They were given us by Creator. Not even the Iroquois dare challenge us for our land."

"Are your mountains beautiful?"

"The sky is bluer than the sea, the trees higher than your father's house. Rivers run cold and clear and the meadows shine green as jade. This man sees nothing in England to match them."

"I have heard of the Emperor Powhatan of Virginia. My father said that he has dozens of wives."

"Ten times ten." He laughed. "But not all at one time. He has many, many children. My father was conceived in the belly of the Emperor's favorite wife."

"So the old emperor must hold you very dear."

"He has never looked on Fire Hawk's face. My father died before I was born. My grandfather blamed my mother for his death."

Kate leaned forward with interest. "Your mother killed your father?"

He shrugged. "The Emperor Powhatan believed she put a curse on War Club and made his body sicken."

"Your grandfather thought your mother was a witch?"

"He thought so, but he dared not accuse her of witchcraft. The Powhatan people fear witches and kill them, but even the Emperor feared the Cherokee wrath. Instead of killing her, he gave my mother to my father's brother, Iron Snake."

"But she was innocent of witchcraft, wasn't she?" Kate insisted.

Hawk sniffed. "I never knew my father. People said he had a bad temper like Powhatan and Iron Snake. No man could beat my mother and live long enough for his hair to turn gray."

Kate drew in a ragged breath. There were so many questions she wished to ask about the New World, about the savages, about him. She didn't know where to begin. "So you grew up among the Powhatan?"

"Seven winters. Then spirits chose me and I journeyed to live among the Cherokee."

"And your mother?"

"I would not go without her. She was a good mother, and this man has great love for her. She is very beautiful, very strong." He chuckled. "It did not take her long to find a Cherokee husband."

"But I thought she was married to your father's brother."

"She was never Iron Snake's wife. She was his woman, his possession. You would call her . . ." He struggled for the word. "His concubine."

Kate was shocked. It proved how uncivilized Fire Hawk was, that he could talk so easily about what should be hidden for decency's sake. "I must get back," she insisted. "Please. Let me go. It will cause a scandal."

"If you wish."

"I do wish."

Still, another half hour slipped away before he helped her down from the coach. And another quarter hour passed before they could walk the length of the barn. Her questions surfaced one after another, and he answered them with wit and charm, telling her strange tales about endless flocks of giant pigeons that darkened the sky and great herds of wild cattlelike creatures that took days to pass.

A misty rain was falling as Kate stepped into the yard outside the barn door. "Stay," she whispered. "It would not do for any to see me with you."

"This man will walk you to the safety of the house."

"No, I'll go in by the garden door. It's far from the great hall, and no one will see me. I must go up to my room and fix my hair. My dress may be—"

"Hawk will take you to the garden door."

"No, Fire Hawk. You must not. It will put you in danger. I'm always wandering off. If I come in alone, Father will be angry, but he won't beat me."

"Strangers here; servants come with other guests. Not wise for a beautiful woman to . . ."

Beautiful. No man had ever said that before. Kate knew it wasn't true, but it sounded so sweet to her ears. "Please listen to reason," she said. "Stay here."

She lifted her skirts and started across the muddy yard.

He matched her step for step.

She hurried to the picket fence and opened the gate. "I'm all right," she whispered. "Just down this path past the dairy and . . ."

He swung the gate wide.

She led the way around the laundry and the dovecote. A lantern hung above the smokehouse door. The pale, yellow light cast shadows across the hard-packed ground. How tall he was, how broad. He wore the leather tunic and skintight Lincoln green breeches that she had seen in the forest. And when he walked, his steps were silent.

He paused as she fumbled with the latch at the small door that led into the old part of the house. "Remember," he said. "Break the betrothal. Robert is wrong for you."

"I can't," she said awkwardly. "I must be wed. Who would I marry, if not Robert?"

"Marry Fire Hawk That Hunts At Dawn."

"What?" She stared wide-eyed at him. "What did you say?"

"Marry this warrior," he answered without a trace of mockery. "Come with me to my mountains-of-smoke. Hawk will show you freedom. He will show you a life of—"

"Ad's flesh!" she cried. "Marry you? Are you mad?" Heart pounding, she ducked inside and slammed the door.

Icy reality drenched her as the enormity of her mistake settled in. She'd led him on, acted the strumpet. But marry an Indian? That was outrageous! She'd sooner wed the devil. Her last vestige of control broke and tears spilled down her cheeks.

Sobbing uncontrollably, she raced up the winding servants' stairs, hoping to reach the safety of her bedchamber before anyone saw her.

Chapter 5

❦

April sunshine poured through the lead casement windows of Kate's bedchamber, creating
a series of rainbows across the honey patina of the
old wooden floor. Kate stood stoically as their maid,
Sarrie, finished the final stitching on the bodice of
her yellow Kincob silk gown.

"There ye be, miss. Fine as any ye might have of
any London shop." The red-cheeked woman leaned
close and bit off a loose thread, then turned to Kate's
mother, Eleanor, for approval.

"Lovely work, Sarrie," she agreed. "You've done
wonders with that old gown of mine."

Sarrie beamed. "Good India silk, my lady. 'Twill
outlast us all if the moths don't get to it."

"You look beautiful, dear." Eleanor patted Kate's
cheek.

"Just like a princess," said her little sister Nan.

"Like a queen," corrected her twin.

Emma clapped her hands. "Me too!" the baby
cried. "Me be a bride too!" The twins howled with
laughter, and one stuck out her tongue at Emma.
Emma's laughter turned to howls of outrage. "She's
nasty!"

"Take Emma downstairs and tell cook to give her milk and gingerbread," Eleanor instructed Sarrie.

"Gingerbread? We want gingerbread too!" Nan shouted.

"All three of you, out!" Eleanor insisted. "Tell cook to cover their gowns with bibs. I'll not have them showing up in church looking like swineherds."

"Yes'm." Sarrie bobbed a hasty curtsy and shepherded her noisy charges out of the chamber.

Eleanor turned back to Kate. "Happy is the bride the sun shines on," she said.

I don't feel happy, Kate thought, folding her arms across her chest and hugging herself tightly. "This marriage has happened so quickly, it can't be fair to Robert for me to marry him when I still have doubts." *When I keep thinking about another man.*

Strain showed on her mother's face. "You can't back out now, on your wedding day. It would be a terrible insult to Robert and to Sir William. In time you'll see the wisdom of your father's decision, and you'll be content. Now, stop crushing your lovely gown. It will be your best dress for years to come. You don't want to spoil it today."

Kate's throat constricted and she felt as though she was going to be sick. She let her arms fall loosely at her sides, contenting herself with knotting her fists and pacing the uneven floor. "Doesn't it bother you at all, Mother?" she pleaded. "That I'm crossing the ocean to the colonies—that you may never see Alice or me again? Or that I may never be with you and Father and my little sisters on this side of heaven?"

She and her mother had never been close, but she knew that Eleanor loved her children in her own stern way. Surely she could understand Kate's unwillingness to leave home and family behind to go with a man who was practically a stranger.

Her mother's compassionate expression hardened. "Of course, it matters that you're going to America. What mother wouldn't weep at the loss of two daughters? But if you stay here, what do you expect? You'll be fortunate if you end up married to a tradesman. With five daughters and all his debts, what can your father do? Jack Talbot's youngest girl, Maude, had to be satisfied with a man nearly eighty and bedridden at that. Take Robert Bennett and thank God for him. He's young and fair, and he'll give you children. With you and Alice safely wed, your father and I may manage to eke out a small bridal portion for Nan and Betsy."

Kate hesitated, not certain how much to say to her mother. She could never tell her that she had met a wild man in the woods and later left her own betrothal party to seek him out and allow him to kiss her. She herself couldn't understand why she had done such a thing.

Moisture clouded Kate's eyes, and she blinked the rising tears away. She would not cry, despite the knot of pain that radiated through her head and chest. She wouldn't weep, she vowed. Her dignity was all she had left.

The sad thing was, she had been away from the betrothal celebration for over an hour without Robert missing her. When her mother did send Betsy upstairs to search, she'd been stretched on her bed. She'd complained of a headache, and although she had to return to the party, she'd suffered only a mild scolding from her father.

Kate looked into her mother's eyes, searching for some sign that she really cared about her happiness. *What would you say if I told you that I have feelings for a copper-skinned poacher?* she wondered. *If you knew what I let him do?*

But Kate couldn't say the words. There was no doubt as to what her mother's reaction would be if Kate confided in her. Fire Hawk would suffer dearly for her breech of decorum. He might even pay with his life.

"It is only natural that you have misgivings on this day," her mother said brusquely. "All brides do." She stepped close and unfastened the string of pearls at her throat. "I want you to have these. They came with your grandmother from Venice when she married your grandfather. She told me they once belonged to a Moorish princess."

"No," Kate answered, pushing her mother's hand away. "Save them for little Emma. She is the youngest. Alice has always coveted your pearls, and if I take them, it will be a point of contention between us."

Eleanor blanched. "You don't want them?"

Kate shook her head. "It's not that. They are exquisite, and I've always loved them. But Emma will be a beauty when she's grown. She never knew Grandmother Nicia. I did. Let them be my gift to my baby sister."

"If you're certain . . ."

"I am." She took her mother's hand. How delicate her fingers seemed; Kate could feel the bones easily through her flesh. She'd always thought of her mother as indestructible. Suddenly her heart went out to her. Eleanor was thirty-eight; she had married at fifteen, brought eleven children into the world and buried six. She had survived plague, small pox, and an attack by highwaymen that took the life of her favorite aunt. Now she was losing two more children to the New World. "Oh, Mother." She could not stop a single tear from escaping and running down her freshly powdered cheek.

"I want only what's best for you," Eleanor whispered.

"If I told you that there was another man, would that make a difference?"

Her mother gripped Kate's hands until the polished nails dug into her skin. "Have you been breeched? Have you given your maidenhead to—"

"No. No." Kate jerked away. "I never—"

"You swear on the Holy Book that you are a virgin?"

"Mother!"

Eleanor sniffed and looked relieved. "You're telling the truth. You were always the worse liar of my brood. Forget him, whoever he is. Never repeat those words to a living soul." She sighed heavily. "I once had romantic fancies about a hayward's son. They were soon forgotten when I married your father and put my childhood behind me. A woman's duties to her family come before personal choices. Wed Robert, and take comfort in the fact that you do not go to Virginia alone. You have a sister with you."

"Alice? Alice is poor comfort. Once she is Lady Bennett, she will treat me more like a servant than kin."

"I know that your sister is shallow, but underneath she has a good heart." Eleanor smoothed the front of her gown and started for the door. "I must see if Alice needs anything before we leave for the church. Will you come down with me?"

"No, not yet," Kate replied, rubbing her eyes. "I'd like to be alone."

"Just a few minutes then. We'll not keep Sir

William waiting at the altar. Alice's ceremony will take place first, due to her groom's position." She hesitated. "Ease your heart, Kate. You have an unruly nature, but you are full of grace. Your father and I love you dearly. We want only what's best for you. Robert will give you children, and it may be that your greatest happiness will be in motherhood. Mine has been."

"Mother?" Kate ran to her and hugged her. For a few seconds Eleanor returned the embrace, giving Kate the comfort she'd longed for so many times before. Then she stepped away.

"I'll pray for you, dear."

As her mother's footsteps receded down the hall, Kate glanced into her wavy reflection in the small mirror that hung over an old blanket chest. "Why?" Kate murmured. "Why must I always do everything the hard way?"

This should be the happiest time of her life. Instead she felt . . . "I don't know how I feel," she murmured aloud. Was it possible that her mother was right? That all brides had reservations on their wedding day?

Or was she simply spoiled—and jealous that Alice was wedding a knight and she a younger brother, as her father had said more than once?

William? Kate wrinkled her nose. She certainly didn't want him. She didn't envy Alice his soft, paunchy body or his yellowed horse teeth. And all his money and title couldn't make up for the fact that he was old enough to be Alice's father. No, envy did not make her reluctant to wed Robert.

She did not fool herself that marriage to Robert would be without problems. Men who chased after women as often as Robert did not become monks after they wed. Her father had always been such a man, and it had been her mother's lot in life to bear such burdens. But that alone would not keep Kate from doing her duty to her family.

Perhaps it was Grandmother Nicia's hot Italian blood that tortured her. Kate had been tempted by the devil in the barn, and he had found a willing leman. Hawk's kiss had caused carnal desires within her that any decent woman would suppress.

She rubbed her lower lip gingerly. If she closed her eyes, she could almost taste Hawk's mouth on hers.

A slight sound behind her made her turn toward the open window. She uttered a small sound of surprise.

Hawk leaned lazily against the window frame. An amused expression filled his fathomless black eyes, and a slight smile twisted his thin, sensual lips.

"Greetings, medicine woman," he said.

"What are you doing here?" she demanded. "You can't be here!"

He chuckled softly, a sound that made her heart quiver. "So?" He shrugged.

Ripples of numbness rolled over her. She took several deep breaths and stepped back, staring at him. Was he real? Or had she lain down on her bed, fallen asleep, and dreamed him? "Th-this is my wedding day," she stammered. "This is my bed-chamber. If they find you here, they will hang you."

He glanced at the old walnut four poster with the carved headboard and faded hangings and sniffed the air. "Yes, this is where you sleep," he agreed.

She shook her head, trying to make sense of this. She couldn't remember him being so tall, so broad, so magnificently male. He wore a sleeveless, fringed leather vest that exposed both muscular arms and left a vast expanse of bronzed chest bare. A silver engraved gorget encircled his powerful neck, and his raven black hair hung loose, nearly to his waist, with only a thin leather-wrapped braid on either side of his face to keep his gleaming locks in place. Two eagle feathers dangled from a silver clasp at the crown of his head, and two red stripes of ocher streaked his cheekbones.

Pagan! she thought. He looked like some pagan prince. Her room was too small and shabby to receive him, and she had the oddest thought that she should curtsy.

Shivers ran through her as she let her gaze flow down over his narrow waist, taking in the beaded leather knife sheath with its bone-handled weapon, and the curious doeskin bag that dangled beside it.

He wore a short leather kilt over his loins, and she glimpsed flashes of bare thigh between kilt and the curious fringed leather leggings that clung to his thewy legs. His shoes were soft leather, fringed, and beaded with strange barbaric designs. He stood motionless, completely relaxed, yet looking as though he could spring into action without warning.

Like he did when he jumped down among the wild dogs, she thought. Then she remembered her father's Irish wolfhounds. "How did you get past the watchdogs?" she demanded. "How did you climb up to my window without . . ."

He shook his head. "We have no time for useless talk. You cannot marry Robert."

She sighed. "You're right, I can't." It was a dream, she decided. Why else would she agree with him? If she were awake, she'd scream for her father.

He nodded. "Good."

But this wasn't a dream. Hawk had invaded her bedroom. She could smell the scent of the woods on him. "No, that's stupid," she whispered. "Of course, I shall marry Robert. I've given my word."

Hawk's eyes narrowed to black slits. "A woman's word is her bond. True. But a woman may change her mind. Tell Robert you belong to me."

"N-No," she stammered. "No, that isn't true. I know that what I did in the barn was wrong. I led you on—let you think . . ."

He took a step toward her.

"No, please. Stay away. You must understand." She retreated to a spot behind the table. "Fire Hawk, please, listen to me," she begged. She had to make him understand. If he didn't heed her, he would surely be seized and put to death.

"This man understands. You, my medicine woman. You do not understand."

"There is nothing between us. Nothing but a kiss," she corrected quickly. "It was my fault. You are a stranger here in England. I couldn't expect you to understand . . ." She took another breath and tried again. "There can be no *us*, Fire Hawk. The differences in our stations . . ." She trailed off. How could she explain that a squire's daughter—an Englishwoman, for God's sake—couldn't become the property of a red savage?

His brow wrinkled in concern. "You speak the truth. This man is a prince of the Powhatan and the Cherokee. You are only an Englishwoman. The tribal council elders will not like that. They will not want a prince to take a foreign commoner for his wife." He made a clicking sound with his tongue. "It will be hard but not impossible. This man will have to find a highborn Cherokee woman willing to challenge the council by adopting you. That would make you acceptable."

"Acceptable? Me?" He had it all wrong. *She* was the one of quality. *He* was an Indian—a bond servant. "I can't possibly become your wife," she said.

"Why not?"

"We are different."

He nodded. "A man and woman are different." The corner of his mouth tilted up. A languid grin spread over his face. "Among the Cherokee, we think it best that a man and woman marry, although I did know of—"

"I can't marry you, Fire Hawk," she insisted. "That's crazy. I don't love you. I don't even know you."

"You love Robert?"

"No, but I know him. We are both English and of the same class."

Hawk's smile vanished, and the air in the room took on a chill. "Robert's skin is white."

"Look at you," she said, pointing at him. "And look at me." She indicated her wedding gown.

He snorted in derision. "Yes, English women do wear foolish clothing. Too heavy and tight to run in. Too cumbersome to climb a tree, or ride a horse without sitting sideways. But Hawk will overlook your clothes. He will forgive your too-pale skin like goat milk, and your hair—which is the proper color for dying leaves but not for a human."

Her temper flared. "And my eyes?" she demanded. "What about my eyes? I suppose they aren't human either?"

"Hawk likes your eyes. Kate's eyes are the mark of one the Creator has chosen for great things."

"I don't love you."

"So." His face became a mask of polished stone.

"I . . . I care about you. I want to be your friend."

"You lie or you do not know own heart."

"As your friend, I don't want to see you die. Please." Tears stung her eyes. "You must go before someone sees you here."

"You still intend to marry Robert?"

She tried not to let her inner trembling show. "I must."

"It is a bad thing. If you do this, you will regret it. This marriage is wrong for Robert, wrong for you. You must listen to your spirit guide, medicine woman. Look into your heart. Listen with your soul, and you will make the right choice."

"My family . . ."

A flicker of emotion crossed his inscrutable face. "Shall I take you away, Kate? I can do that. I could take you back to the forest. Robert would never find you in Bramble Wood. Your father would not find you either."

"No." She lifted her head and stared straight into those ebony black eyes. "You told me that you were the Chosen One of the Cherokee. Chosen for what, Fire Hawk? Chosen to die needlessly for a woman who doesn't want you?"

Sadness flickered behind his fierce warrior's mask. "Hawk was sent by the Cherokee to learn of the Spanish—of the white men and sticks that speak like thunder. This man learns English ways too. I will take that knowledge to the Cherokee. Wisdom makes the greatest weapon. I will use it to defend the Cherokee mountains-of-smoke against all white man."

"But I am English too, Hawk. If the English are your enemies, then we are enemies."

"No," he said. "This man and Kate will never be enemies."

"You have your own duty," she reminded him. "If

you are this chosen one, then you must live to go back and tell your people about us. If you try to kidnap me, my father's men will come with guns and shoot you. What happens to me is none of your affair."

He shook his head. "You belong to me. The spirits say I will make you my wife. One day you see."

"You say that my eyes prove that I am special, that I have the ability to know what others can't?"

He nodded grudgingly.

"Then you must go, leave me to make my own decisions."

"Your own mistakes?"

"Maybe."

"Kate!" Nan's childish shriek filtered through the door. "Kate! Mother wants you down here now!"

Kate let out a ragged breath. "Please, Fire Hawk. Go. Trust me to do the right thing."

"You do not know Robert."

"Please." She shut her eyes, and when she opened them a minute later, she was alone in the room.

The church was so crowded that many guests were forced to stand along the walls; the common folk stood outside, peering through the open windows and door. Kate found it hard to breathe. Her head ached, and she still felt nauseous.

Alice, splendid in her rose satin gown with the deep rose underskirt, looked like a princess. Diamond earbobs winked in her ears, and an heirloom length of Irish lace covered her golden hair. Her dulcet replies to the minister's questions could hardly be heard by those in the first pews, and she kept her eyes modestly downcast.

Kate felt as though her legs and lower body were

carved of wood. Her stays were laced too tight, and her mother's best high-heeled slippers pinched her feet. Robert was a blur beside her; his possessive grip on her arm made her want to yank free and run out of the church.

A few feet behind her stood Fire Hawk. She couldn't see him, but she could feel his gaze burning through the back of her gown. His presence in all his barbaric attire had been Robert's idea.

As always, her betrothed liked a grand show, and those who might have concentrated their attention on Sir William and his bride couldn't take their eyes off Robert's party, which included a red savage in feathers and war paint.

Just a few more minutes, Kate thought. Soon she and Robert would exchange vows and her indecision would be over. Her reckless behavior with Hawk would be in the past, and she would belong to Robert so long as they both drew breath. As her mother had assured her, it would be for the best.

William lifted Alice's veil, and for an instant, Alice's gaze met Kate's. The look of greedy satisfaction was one Kate knew all too well. Then her view of Alice's face was blocked by Sir William as he kissed his bride. The newlyweds stepped back, and the minister motioned to Kate.

In her head, Kate heard Fire Hawk's words. *Listen to your spirit guide.* She glanced back over her shoulder at Robert, then past him to the Cherokee.

He smiled at her.

"I'm sorry," she murmured to Robert. "I can't do this." She stepped back, pulling free of his grasp.

Hawk laughed.

Robert threw up his hands to grab her. "Kate?"

She caught up the corner of her skirts and dashed around him.

"Kate, stop!" Robert bellowed.

She fled down the aisle, past her parent's pew, ignoring her mother's cries of alarm and pushed through the crowd of curious onlookers. She didn't stop until she burst out of the church and into the clear, clean air of the brilliant April afternoon.

Chapter 6

Virginia Colony, America
Autumn 1620

Seven months later, and far to the west in the place the English called Virginia, Fire Hawk Who Hunts At Dawn let fly an arrow and brought down a young deer with a single shot. He walked toward his quarry, but his thoughts were not on his hunting success. His mind dwelt on the past.

Hawk vividly remembered the triumphant expression on Kate's pale face as she fled the church and her would-be bridegroom. Hawk had not seen her since that day. She had remained with her family in England, and he had come home to fulfill his mission to the Cherokee. Hawk knew he should forget he had ever met her, yet . . . Strangely, the woman with hair like autumn leaves still held the power to twist his heart and make his throat constrict with emotion.

Kate had touched a chord deep inside him that no other woman, white or red, had ever done. If she were Cherokee or even Powhatan, he would have fought for her, claimed her as his own no matter the cost. But it was not to be; her place was with her own kind, and his path was ordained by the spirits. He accepted those truths as right and good. So why did thoughts of her hurt so much?

He shrugged and knelt by the fallen buck. Pushing Kate to the shadows of his mind, he whispered a prayer before sprinkling Indian tobacco over the deer's head. Then he drew out the arrow that had pierced the animal's heart and wiped it clean on the thick carpet of autumn leaves.

"For whom do you hunt, Cherokee?" called a taunting voice in Algonquian.

Hawk glanced up as his Powhatan cousin Gar stepped from the shelter of a scarred chestnut. Two seasoned braves flanked him, both men whom Hawk had seen in his uncle's village recently. The youngest hunter, hardly more than a boy, carried a string of ducks over one shoulder.

Gar puffed out his chest and strode haughtily to Hawk's side. Hawk ignored him and continued the task of field-dressing the buck.

"This is a Powhatan deer," Gar said loudly. "Have you shot it to share with us?"

"Greetings, Gar," Hawk replied. "Do you still draw breath?" he asked in the ritual greeting.

"Who dares to speak to me in the tongue of my fathers?" He made a show of peering down at Hawk. "What have we here? Is this a pet dog of the English white-eyes?"

The other two Powhatan snickered.

Tiny hairs rose on the back of Hawk's neck, and he fought to maintain his temper. The cold venom in Gar's eyes told him that his cousin was looking for trouble. Again.

Hawk had not seen Gar in the months since he'd returned to Virginia with Robert Bennett and the white settlers. The first time Hawk accompanied

Robert and a party of English soldiers to Hawk's uncle's village in midsummer, Gar had been absent on business for the Emperor. The second time Hawk visited the Powhatan, he'd believed that his cousin was in his *yi-hakan*, dwelling house, with his wives. Gar hadn't yet welcomed him as custom decreed. And although other braves told Hawk that his cousin was an important man in the Powhatan nation, Gar had never come with the delegations to trade at William's Hundred.

You should know Gar by now, Hawk's inner voice whispered. *Did you expect anything more, now that you are both grown to manhood?*

For the first seven winters of his life, Hawk had lived with his mother, Rainbow Basket, in a Powhatan village not far from this spot. His cousin Gar's cruel nature had made most of those years a struggle.

Hawk's father, War Club, favored son of the mighty Emperor Powhatan, died soon after Hawk's birth. According to custom, Rainbow Basket—a Cherokee noblewoman—should have had the freedom to return home to her people with her child. But the Emperor forbade it. His heart burned with hatred for his dead son's bride, and he yearned to offer her to his shaman as a sacrifice to the harvest gods.

Instead, fearing the wrath of the Cherokee if their daughter was executed, Powhatan had given Hawk's mother to another of his sons, Iron Snake. Iron Snake was *weroance*, or chief of a powerful coastal tribe, and father to Gar.

Rainbow Basket made no secret of her dislike for Iron Snake, but she was very beautiful, and he prized her above his other four wives. He wanted to have sons by her, but she never quickened with his seed. Gar's mother had been Iron Snake's favorite before he took Rainbow Basket to his bed, and her jealousy and ill will spread like a cancer through the Powhatan village.

Gar led the pack of older boys who scorned Hawk and refused to let him join in the children's games. Hawk had desperately wanted to be accepted by his peers, but Gar saw to it that he received only ridicule and rejection. In time, Hawk learned that tears brought more bullying, but it was a lesson that came at great cost.

"Turn your tears inward," his mother had whispered as she'd soothed his bruises. "Make strength from the hurt Gar flings against you. Grow to be a man greater than Gar shall ever be."

His cousin yanked him back into the present by kicking the hindquarter of the deer. "You would see Powhatan women and children starve to feed the English?" Gar's tongue lashed out with acrid scorn.

Hawk gritted his teeth. Even as a boy, Gar had been a master of sarcasm. It was his way to begin an attack with a false smile and a voice of reason, then grow increasingly hostile as he warmed to the battle. Today he had not even bothered with the smile.

But Gar's assaults had taught Hawk patience. When his cousin's ire whipped to a frenzy, he became careless. Deliberately, Hawk didn't answer. Instead he concentrated on preparing the deer to carry back to William's Hundred.

Because of Gar's constant persecution, Hawk had spent most of his time without the company of other children. He'd been shy and retiring—not speaking easily or often to anyone except his mother. She had poured all of her love and attention onto her only chick. She sang him to sleep at night, told him childhood stories of the Cherokee, and promised

him that someday she would find a way to take him
home.

Gar's mother fanned the fires of resentment
against Hawk and Rainbow Basket. She called Hawk
spoiled and Rainbow Basket an unfit mother. The
charges were untrue. Rainbow Basket often spent
hours fashioning her son a toy or preparing a
favorite dish, but she demanded respect, and she
would tolerate no disobedience or laziness.

Most of the time Hawk shadowed his mother's
footsteps, helping her gather nuts and berries, working beside her in the cornfields, or crouching nearby
and watching as she tanned and sewed animal skins
for clothes and moccasins. When Iron Snake demanded Rainbow Basket's attention, Hawk would
go into the forest alone.

There among the animals, he always felt at home.
He learned the song of each bird and the special
language of the fox and rabbit. With the wild
creatures, he never felt a stranger. They accepted
and trusted him. He could run barefoot through a
snake's den without fear that they would bite him.

The Powhatans saw these things and were afraid.
Gar's mother ventured that Hawk was not a normal
child but a changling, put here by forest ghosts to
bring harm to the village.

Rainbow Basket made light of the women's superstition and taunted them for believing such foolishness. But she went secretly to Iron Snake and
warned him that if harm should come to her son,
she would curse his wives and children with a
Spanish pox, so that no seed of his should live and
no Powhatan remember his name.

Hawk's mother kept him safe, but she couldn't
stop Gar from stomping to death a nest of starving
baby bluebirds that Hawk had found and tended, or

from strangling the fox pup that Hawk had tamed to
eat from his hand.

"Well? Are you a dog or a man?" Gar demanded.

Hawk laid his knife on the grass and regarded his
cousin. They had not seen each other since they
were boys, but Hawk would have recognized Gar
anywhere because of his close resemblance to Iron
Snake. Gar's eyes hadn't changed at all; they were
nearly hidden in the folds of his eyelids, as flat and
expressionless as those of an eel.

As was his father, Gar was thick and muscular—a
formidable figure of a man. His round moon-face
was unmarred by burns or old wounds, and his
sharp teeth were as hard and white as a shark's. His
chin and throat were thickly tattooed with purple
and black bands and long, pointed red darts, as
were his long, powerful legs and feet.

Gar's large skull was plucked bare except for a
strip of coarse blue-black hair that ran from the
center of his forehead to the nape of his neck. The
crest was trimmed to the length of a woman's hand,
stiffened with bear grease, and adorned with hawks'
claws and duck down. Two eagle feathers dangled
from a tuft at the back of his head.

Hawk decided that Gar looked every inch a
weroance's son, a fierce warrior who lusted to take
his father's staff of office, and a man who would not
hesitate to set Indian against Englishman if he could
gain by the bloodshed.

"This is a Powhatan buck. We will take it," Gar
snarled.

Hawk drove his knife into the ground beside his
cousin's foot. Surprised, Gar leaped back and his
face darkened in anger.

"Do you dare question my right?" the Powhatan
demanded. "You? The Englishman's dog? You who

plant corn like a woman and whine for your master's scraps?"

Gar's companions tensed.

Hawk retrieved his knife and carefully wiped the dirt from the steel blade. Then he rose to his feet and found to his great satisfaction that he was a good three-fingers taller than his cousin.

It was a childish glee, and he knew it. But Gar had always been bigger and stronger. Gar had taken what he wanted from Hawk, no matter how hard he'd fought to protect what was his. Now, that reign of terror had ended.

"My arrow brought down this buck," Hawk said. "And English trade-goods purchased my right to hunt on Powhatan ground."

"Paah!" Gar spat on the leaves. "A handful of beads and mirrors? A few yards of scarlet cloth?"

"Iron tools. Hoes, axes, scissors, and chisels. Your father's choice to accept or reject. He is still *weroance*, is he not?" Hawk kept his features immobile.

"My father grows old and soft."

"Since when has old age prevented a ruler from making decisions? My grandfather, the Emperor Powhatan, has hair as white as the breast of a goose, so I hear. But none challenge Powhatan. Or do they?"

"Speak not of the mighty Powhatan!" Gar snapped. "He is all wise, immortal, undefeated in battle, a stallion among his wives."

Hawk's eyes narrowed. "He is my grandfather as much as yours."

"So you have always said," Gar replied. "If your mother was as faithful as she was beautiful. But I have heard it whispered that she already carried you in her belly when she joined in marriage with my father's brother."

"Do not speak of my mother," Hawk warned. "Never speak of her again. And do not start what you cannot finish."

"Listen to him! The English dog roars like a cougar." Gar spat again at Hawk's feet. "Do you deny that the great Powhatan refused to lay eyes on you?"

Hawk's gut knotted. It was true that the Emperor's spite toward Rainbow Basket had extended to her son. Powhatan had threatened Hawk with death if he ever came in sight, because he believed that Rainbow Basket had poisoned his son.

So Hawk had never seen his grandfather. He had been cursed in his cradleboard, and the sentence had stretched for all the years of his childhood.

Among the Cherokee, Hawk would have had uncles and grandfathers to teach him to shoot a bow and arrow, to catch fish with his bare hands, and to track animals from the time he could walk. Among the Powhatan, he had only Rainbow Basket, and the bows she fashioned for him were weak and his arrows poorly fletched. His mother could show him the difference between moccasin flower and painted trillium, but she could not tell him how old a wolf's tracks were or show him how to use a blowgun. His mother was wise and brave and devoted, but she did not have a man's skills to teach.

Had Hawk been an orphan in the Powhatan camp—even a child born of another tribe and adopted into the village—many men would have willingly shared their hunting skills with him. But none would dare raise Powhatan's anger. All that Hawk learned in the seven years before he went to the Cherokee to live, he'd had to teach himself.

Hawk could never find it in his heart to forgive his grandfather, and he had vowed that he would never meet with the Emperor, even if the old man relented and asked for him. He held no hatred for the Powhatan, but neither would he forget the years of agony he'd suffered because of him.

"Do not think that your bellows will keep us from taking this deer if we want it," Gar said.

Hawk allowed himself a faint smile. "You can try."

Gar scowled. "Is this what the Chosen One of the Cherokee has become? A slave to the whites? One who obeys his masters without question?"

"The deer is mine." Hawk refused to let Gar anger him. He would fight if he had to, but he hoped it would not come to that. He wasn't afraid of Gar anymore, but he had not traveled to the ends of the world and back to shed the blood of his father's people. He had a greater mission. When his heart told him that the time was right—after he'd kept his bargain with Robert Bennett—he'd return to the Cherokee and fulfill the task he'd been born for. He would teach the Cherokee how to survive against the hordes of whites Hawk knew would someday pour across the sea.

His cousin scoffed, strutting for his men. "You would shed the blood of your kin to feed the greed of Englishmen?"

Hawk met his gaze without flinching.

"There are three of us," Gar warned.

So Gar had told him once before—the day Hawk had tried to prevent them from crushing his nest of baby birds. He had fought the three bigger boys in vain that long ago afternoon. He had kept fighting them even when his birds were dead, and he was choking on his own blood.

But Hawk was no longer a child and no longer afraid. He cradled the handle of his knife in his right hand. The blade was English steel and sharp enough to cut metal; it glittered in the sunshine. "True," Hawk admitted softly. "There are three of you, but you have but one life to lose, elder cousin."

Gar grabbed for the rawhide-wrapped haft of the stone war club that hung from his belt, but before he could drag it free, a sound as deep as thunder boomed through the forest.

"Can-non!" shouted one of the Powhatan braves. "The white soldiers fire the great balls of iron!"

Gar glanced toward his men and then back at Hawk.

"They may be shooting at our people!" the second warrior cried.

Another dull explosion echoed down the valley.

"I will settle with you later," Gar warned Hawk. Without another word, he raced after the others. The three Powhatans pounded into the forest with the intensity of hunting wolves, leaving Hawk alone with the deer.

"Later," he murmured. He too was troubled by the cannon blasts. He had heard the sounds and seen the cannon fired enough times to lose his fear of them, but he wondered whom Robert's soldiers were defending the settlement against.

In one swift motion, he swung the body of the deer over his shoulders. Then he balanced the weight and gathered up his bow and quiver. With a final thought for the spirit of the buck, he strode away from the blood-soaked grass and headed downhill toward the English town.

On the deck of the *Constant Lady*, Kate clung to the rail and stood on tiptoes to try and see the crude wooden palisade above the trees. Four months she had been at sea, not counting the two-day stop in

Santa Cruz in the Canaries or the week they'd anchored in the West Indies to take on fresh food and water. The *Constant Lady* had sailed from Dover in July; this was November, and Kate never wanted to set foot on a boat again.

Settlers and gentlemen jostled each other to catch sight of the William's Hundred landing. Kate hadn't seen her sister on deck, but surely, she thought, everyone else was here. In minutes they would all be going ashore, and Kate would have her first real look at Virginia.

Captain Gordon hadn't permitted anyone ashore in Jamestown who wasn't remaining there. Kate's first impression of the walled fort and scattered log huts on a spit of marshy land had been disheartening, and the colonists who crowded the wharf to demand news of home seemed less than prosperous. She hoped that Bennett's Hundred would be a more substantial settlement, but she felt that anything would be an improvement over the confides of the *Constant Lady*.

Even Robert's face would be a welcome one. She hoped he would forgive her for leaving him at the altar. She was still uncertain about becoming his bride, but she wanted them to be friends. She was genuinely sorry she'd shamed him and nearly prevented him from going to Virginia with William's expedition.

She had been the cause of a great scandal. Her father had been furious; her mother alternated between bouts of weeping and shouting. But Kate had held her ground, insisting that she wasn't refusing the match with Robert; she just wanted more time to make her decision. In the end, her father and William decided that she should accompany Alice to the New World as Robert's future wife. With her sister to act as chaperone, proprieties would be upheld, and once she was in Virginia, everyone was certain that she would soon agree to the wedding.

William, Robert, the soldiers, and most of the male settlers had sailed within days of Alice's wedding. It was William's intention that they should complete the fortification and put in a crop to help provide food for the coming winter. Alice, Kate, and those wives with small children were to come on another ship, arriving in midautumn.

Kate's heart leaped as cannon fire burst from a corner tower of the log palisade. The captain of the *Constant Lady* ordered his sailors to shoot off the ship's guns in answering salute. Crew and passengers cheered as the gates swung open and a company of soldiers marched out of the fort, accompanied by the stirring notes of fife and drum.

Kate clapped and wiggled with excitement. How could Alice miss this after coming so far to join her husband? That stout man in helmet and steel breastplates could be no one else but William, and the tall captain directing the troops could only be Robert. Her gaze swept past him and her pulse quickened as she scanned the shore for the copper-skinned figure she'd first met in Bramble Wood.

Then Kate heard Alice scolding her maid, Edwina. "Alice!" Kate called. "Here! You're going to miss it! Look! There's William come out to meet you!"

Alice pulled the netting of her broad-brimmed hat over her face. "Yes, yes, I'm coming. Watch my skirts," she snapped to Edwina.

"That's Robert!" Kate cried.

Alice swatted at a circling greenhead fly as she joined Kate at the railing. "Bugs. I knew Virginia would have bugs." She pursed her pretty mouth and uttered a soft French oath so low that only Kate could hear. "Better I had stayed in England, at William's ancestral home, then to come to this . . . this pigsty."

"Cheer up, Alice," Kate urged. "It won't be so bad. You know William likes his comforts. It's not as though they didn't come ahead to make everything right."

She wouldn't let Alice's cross temper ruin this day. Her sister was as arrogant and self-centered as ever, and traveling across the ocean in the same cabin had been awful. But today was the greatest adventure Kate had ever experienced. There would be new sights and sounds, new smells and experiences.

Kate shivered with excitement. The monotonous ocean voyage was behind them, and her future stretched before her as bright as all the vivid colors of the towering trees that lined the shore.

I am betrothed to Robert, she told herself once again as she twisted the heavy, gold betrothal ring on her middle finger. *I've given my word, and I've signed a legal agreement. I can't imagine the consequences of breaking that agreement. If I was sensible, I would marry him and forget my rebellious thoughts.*

Forget Hawk . . .

She sighed. In truth, she might never agree to marry Robert. But if she couldn't, she vowed to find someone suitable, someone she could love with all her heart.

Yes, I may decide to defy them all and choose my own husband, she thought recklessly. *And . . . and I might even claim part of this free Virginia land in my own right.*

And then she saw him.

Kate took a step back from the rail, her skin tingling.

It was Hawk. It could be no other man striding out

of the tall trees like a pagan prince, all sinewy bare chest, muscular arms, and scandalously unclothed bronze-colored legs. He wore nothing more than a brief fringed deerskin kilt and soft leather shoes. He carried a bow in one hand, and a dead deer was slung across his broad shoulders.

Kate gasped for breath.

Once she'd stood near a tree in a summer storm and a lightning bolt struck it. She'd not been injured, but the air had vibrated with an invisible force that drained her strength and made her giddy. She felt the same sensations now—the same loss of control.

"Hawk." Unconsciously her lips formed his name.

She'd tried to put him out of her head . . . told herself that he wouldn't be here when she arrived. Surely, she'd reasoned, he would have left William's Hundred to return to his beloved Cherokee in the faraway, misty mountains.

All her life, Kate had struggled against the rules. She'd not been content to accept the bonds that stifled women. She'd questioned authority and spoke when she should have held her tongue. But in spite of those faults, she'd never considered herself a fool.

Allowing Fire Hawk to become too familiar because he appealed to her wanton sexual nature was dangerous. His attraction was solely physical, and if her honor were impugned, she would lose everything. She would be disowned by her family, shunned by those of her class. For women alone without support, there were few options in England; here in Virginia, there would be none.

Had not her father reminded her that marriages were made for the common good rather than the selfish wishes of one woman? A gentle woman must submit to those whom God and law had placed over her.

She might dare to choose her own husband, so long as he was an Englishman of her own church and station. But she could never give her heart to a red savage. Such a sin would doom her soul to eternal damnation. She could not risk hellfire for Hawk's touch.

Cold reality swept over her. She must marry. If not Robert, then another, and quickly. The wild stirrings Hawk raised in her blood must be stifled.

She must marry someone of her own kind or burn.

Chapter 7

Half an hour later, Kate stopped short just inside the gates of the stockade and stared wide-eyed at the collection of crude stick-and-bark huts. Despite the beating of the drum, the smart ranks of soldiers standing at attention, and the excited waves and shouts of welcome from the settlers, Kate's heart sank. She'd expected more of William's Hundred. She certainly hadn't expected it to be this hot, and she hadn't been prepared for the wretched condition of the houses or the stench from the free-running swine and livestock.

Glimpsing Jamestown's rough structures from the deck of the *Constant Lady* a day earlier hadn't dispelled Kate's dream that William's Hundred would be a snug English village nestled against a green wall of impenetrable forest and wafted by cool river breezes. Now her foolish illusions dissolved in the face of stern reality.

"Sweet Je'su!" Alice hissed as she raised her skirts to avoid the clinging mud. "Are we supposed to live in one of these hen coops? Father wouldn't kennel his hunting dogs in such sties."

For once Kate agreed completely with her sister. William's Hundred bore no more likeness to an

English town than a feathered Indian bonnet did to a lady's beribboned hat.

The fort enclosing the settlement was laid out in a triangular shape. Palisade walls of upright logs sharpened to a point at the top were completed on two sides and capped with guard towers at the corners. The third wall bore a gap, closed with a shoulder-high fence of thorns and branches. Fire-blackened stumps littered the area between the houses; holes where trees had been yanked out by teams of oxen overflowed with slop. Not a single shade tree remained standing to shelter the dwellings from the cruel Virginia sun, and not one blade of grass hid the raw earth.

Sir William Bennett finished his official speech to the new arrivals and rushed to sweep off his hat and bow formally before his wife. Kate noted that William's face was badly sunburned beneath his powdered wig and that he was perspiring heavily. In his purple silk hose, silver-buckled high-heeled shoes, and satin coat of lavender, he looked oddly out of place in this wilderness.

"My lady," he began. "Lady Bennett. Dearest wife. Thank the good Lord for your safe passage. My heart is—"

"Praise God," Alice replied, cutting him off brusquely. "If you would show us to our apartments, kind husband. We are greatly wearied by the journey and near famished. The food aboard ship was terrible. If I never see another slice of salt pork, I will be well pleased."

Alice's lower lip quivered prettily. She was as pristine as if she'd just stepped from her dressing room. Her golden hair was curled beneath an elegant plumed hat, her puffed sleeves were tied with velvet ribbons, and the wide lace collar of her elegantly cut gown was as white as a swan's breast.

Alice, naturally, wasn't sweating. It was Kate's considered opinion that her sister didn't sweat, being much like a bitch dog in more ways than one.

"Of course, of course," Sir William sputtered. He had lost weight since coming to Virginia. His jowls sagged and his once-plump stomach no longer filled out his shirt and waistcoat.

Robert approached Kate and grinned. "Welcome to Virginia," he said, then bent and kissed her on each cheek. "You seem none the worse for the crossing. If anything, you're more beautiful than before."

She felt her cheeks grow warmer still. "Thank you, Robert," she replied. "You look as robust as an Indian yourself." She wiped her throat with a handkerchief and looked up at Robert through her lashes. He'd tanned almost as dark as Hawk, and he seemed as fit as she'd ever known him.

"We're a bit rough here, but don't judge us hastily," he warned. "William's planned well. This settlement will rival Jamestown in two years."

"Have you found your gold?" she asked.

In answer, he pulled a chain from under his ruffled shirtfront. A golden fish, the size of his thumbnail, dangled from the metal links. "I traded with a Powhatan prince for this, and I've seen more on their persons. I'll find the source, Kate. Damn me for a lackwit if I don't."

"I . . . I saw John Fire Hawk from the boat. I would have thought that he would be gone by now." Her mouth felt strangely dry, and she rushed on to cover her discomfort. "Back to his own tribe."

"Aye, he's spoken of it often enough. But we've need of John yet. He speaks the language of the Powhatan, and he's showed some of the farmers how best to plant in this climate. Mark you, Kate, we arrived too late to plant Indian corn this season, but we've cleared trees beyond the fort walls to raise grain next year. We did grow beans. Cabbages, turnips, and greens, as well. And John Hawk is a fine hunter. He brought us in a big buck today."

"I saw it," she murmured.

He grinned again. "There will be venison for dinner. Be glad of it. There's naught else but pork or fish. William would sooner slaughter a settler than one of his beef. He's saving them for breeding stock."

"Brother." Alice smiled and dipped a slight curtsy to Robert. "Surely you do not mean to keep us standing in the sun all afternoon."

"Nay, sister." He took her offered hand and lifted the back of it to his lips. "Virginia has never seen your like, lady. The two of you shine as do the sun and the moon."

Kate chuckled at the extravagant praise.

"Come then," Sir William called. "To the house. Lady Bennett is tired and in need of refreshment."

Alice looked around for her maid, then waved urgently when she caught sight of her talking to a young soldier. "Edwina, come here at once!" She offered her husband a gloved hand. "I can't tell you how difficult it was to come all this way from England with only two girls to wait on me. Foolish sluts, both of them."

Robert slipped his arm through Kate's and leaned close to whisper, "Methinks your sister's sweet disposition is unchanged."

Kate laughed. "If only you knew the half of it."

"If only you knew how much I've thought of you in the past months," Robert said. "Let us put our difficulties behind us, sweet."

"I'm sorry about spoiling the wedding . . ." she began.

"Past," he soothed. "Past and done. A maiden's nerves, nothing more. Only our future is important now. We belong together. Surely you realize that."

She let him talk on as they made their way through the mud and mire. Perhaps Robert was right; perhaps they should be wed. That would solve her immediate problems, get her out of her sister's household and her position as an unpaid servant, and put an end to her lusting after Hawk.

"Don't you agree, Kate?" he urged.

She nodded and murmured an answer in all the right places. *Can I bear a lifetime of this?* she wondered. *Or does Robert deserve a wife who would not question his boasting or doubt his ability?*

Try as she might, she couldn't keep her thoughts from racing back to Hawk as she had first seen him emerging from the forest. She wondered if he had seen her.

"If we post the bonds this week, we can be married by the first of December," Robert said.

"I cannot make a decision yet," she replied meekly. *I cannot wed you so soon,* she thought, *and maybe not ever.*

Sir William's house was no more than a cottage: a great room and parlor downstairs, and two loft chambers above. The house was floored with logs hewn flat on top on the bottom floor and rough-cut boards on the second. Chimneys of mud and stick stood at either end of the dwelling, providing heat for each room. Across from the entrance, in one corner of the great room, a small, closed staircase wound to the upper floor. The frame structure would have served for a coachman in England; in Virginia, it was a manse.

Once Alice had claimed the parlor as her own sitting-room bedchamber, and insisted that her bed-stead be brought from the ship's hold and set up, she became sweet and amiable. She charmed both her husband and Robert by listening attentively to their every word and laughing at their jest.

Robert was a perfect gentleman during supper, and Kate had to admit that the Indian corn bread, venison, and wild salad greens were far tastier than the ship's boring diet of dried peas and salt pork.

"We'll replace the shutters with glass windows. Two came on the ship," Sir William said. "I intend to add to the house in the spring," he assured his wife. "It's not what any of us are used to, I know."

"Your house was the first built," Robert explained. "Even before the church or the stockade walls went up, William had bondmen from Jamestown at work here."

"I've bargained for the craftsmen again in the spring," William said. "Once our crop of Indian corn is planted, we can improve our home."

"Surely that is an expense, is it not?" Alice asked. "What of the soldiers? Can't you use them to—"

Robert answered, "My guardsmen are needed to protect the settlers as they plow and put in their crops. I maintain constant patrols."

"My brother speaks of patrols, but his heart is in seeking the Indian gold mines," Sir William said, lifting his goblet for Edwina to refill with good Dutch wine.

Alice twittered. "Do you really believe there are treasures in Virginia?"

"Captain John Smith saw them with his own eyes before his return to England," Robert said. "The Spaniards have reaped untold riches from their natives—silver and gold and heathen idols set with precious stones. I mean to do the same."

As soon as darkness fell over the settlement, William and Alice hastened to the privacy of the parlor. Kate was left at the table with Robert, and he soon captured her hand in his.

"I have missed you sore," he said.

Kate sipped at her wine.

"I've waited so long for this day."

Through the chamber door, she could hear her sister giggling and the squeak of the bed frame. Kate pulled her hand free and rose. "I am very tired, Robert. I've had such a long journey . . ."

"I would like to bed you, Kate."

She shook her head firmly. "That's not what I had in mind."

"We are betrothed in the eyes of man and God," Robert argued. "I am a man of natural appetites, and I've been too long in this lonely place. Can you not take pity on a poor husband?"

"Not husband yet," she reminded him.

He took hold of her suddenly and yanked her against him. Before she could protest, he leaned down to kiss her. She twisted so that his mouth found only her cheek.

"How can you be so cruel?" he demanded. "Modesty in a woman is admirable, but we've been this path before." He raised her chin and kissed her full on the mouth.

She felt nothing.

"You are hard-hearted, Kate."

She placed her hands on his waistcoat and pushed him away. "I'll not be fondled like a serving wench at your whim."

He frowned. "It's obvious that you are tired and cranky. You disappoint me, sweet. But I've waited so long, I can wait a little longer." He squeezed her hand and lifted it to his lips.

She pulled her hand back.

"What ails you, girl? You belong to me. You have no right to deny me a simple kiss."

What began as simple annoyance became anger. "As I've told you, we are not yet wed," she told him. "This is no way to begin our reunion."

He flushed and his eyes took on a hard glint. "You quibble about details, woman. Ask any Bible-thumping cleric. A betrothed couple may have physical knowledge of each other without sinning. If you swell with my seed, our offspring would be legitimate."

"If I'd been ready for that, I would have taken my vows in the church, Robert."

He swore a soldier's oath. "Mark me, Katherine, I'll not be dandled at a woman's pleasure. You'll not make a fool of me a second time."

"Perhaps I was the fool," she flung back, "to think that we might make a marriage after all."

"Witch. I should have guessed what you were, with those different colored eyes. Your sister is what she is—but by God, she has a loving nature, for all her sharp tongue. Perhaps William got the best bargain after all."

"Perhaps he did." He took a step toward her, and she retreated until the table barred his way.

" 'Tis not all your fault," Robert said. "Your parents encouraged your willfulness, but we've no time for such foolishness here in Virginia. You'll come around."

Her temper flared, but she forced it to icy politeness. "Good night, Robert." She motioned to the open door. "Shall I have a servant show you out?"

He slammed the door so hard that the pewter plates rattled on the table.

When she was certain Robert wouldn't come back, Kate channeled her anger to clearing the table with quick, precise movements. "Edwina!" she called, summoning the maid.

Dirty bare feet and a soiled petticoat appeared at the top of the narrow staircase. "Miss?"

"Come down here, you worthless chit," Kate chided. "Wash your hands and finish cleaning up . . ." Hurt showed in Edwina's pale eyes, and Kate softened her tone. It was, after all, Robert who was the ass, not this witless girl. "Clean off the table and put the rest of the meat . . ." She stopped again, wondering where the meat should go to best keep it cool in this intolerable heat. "Hang it in the well. Is there a well?"

"Yes, miss, but t'girl in the next house told me nay to drink it. 'Tis muddy-like."

"I don't want you to put the meat in the water, just hang in above the water to keep it cool. When the room is readied, you may go up to bed."

"Lady Bennett won't be wantin' me no more this night?"

"I think not."

"Shall I bar the door, miss?"

"No, I'll do that. I want to step outside for a breath of air. It's stifling in here, don't you think?"

Edwina stood on one foot and rubbed her ankle with her other heel. Her freckled face was smudged with ashes, her hair braided untidily beneath a none-too-clean linen cap. "Never thought much about it, miss. Stifling? S'pose it is. I can go up to bed now, can I?"

"When you've finished here. Your room is under the eaves. You'll share it with Grace and any other female servants Sir William employs."

"At least t'floor be solid," Edwina replied, scratching an invisible itch between her breasts. "I'd not cross that bleedin' ocean again to save my soul."

Kate took the wine bottle, locked it in the cupboard beside the fireplace and slipped the key in her pocket. She would give it to Alice in the morning. Leaving Edwina with free access to spirits was never a wise decision. The wench was a perfect match for her mistress, as lacking in morals as a cat.

The smell of wood smoke and livestock hung heavy in the air as Kate stepped out into the still night. Overhead, a sprinkling of stars scattered across the velvet bowl of heaven. The moon had risen, but the light given off by the pale crescent was feeble, and Kate could hardly see two armlength's ahead of her.

Cautiously she made her way to the back of the house, feeling first the walls and then the top of the woven fence that encircled a lean-to storage shed. Somewhere she could hear a man's deep voice singing, and from another direction the wail of a baby. Closer, from the right, came the low nicker of a horse.

The air was warm and moist, rich with the heavy scents of manure and newly turned earth. The earth felt strangely alive under her feet. She inhaled deeply and spread her arms, trying to understand the magic of this wild Virginia.

Besotted with the myriad of new sensations and

the unwatered wine she'd consumed at supper, she laughed softly and spun around . . . into the arms of a man.

"Why did you come to this place?"

Fire Hawk's voice.

Kate trembled, but she had no strength to pull away. Fear and hope spiraled inside her. "Who are you to ask me such a question?"

"You should have stayed in England."

"And you should have gone to the Cherokee." It was too dark to make out his features, but she knew them in her heart. Oh, she knew them as she knew her own.

His powerful hands were on her shoulders. She should have been angry, but she wasn't. Instead she touched his cheek with trembling fingers. It was smooth, so smooth, without a trace of whiskers. "We are old friends, Hawk," she whispered. "We . . . shouldn't be arguing."

He released his grip and stepped back. "We are not friends, Kate Miles. You lie if you say we are friends."

Moisture threatened to well up in her eyes. She swallowed against the constriction in her throat. "I thought we were friends," she murmured.

"Have you forgotten that Hawk asked you to be his wife?"

"Yes, I know you said that, but . . ." She struggled for the right words with a tongue that seemed suddenly turned to clay. "You . . . didn't mean it, not really. You and I . . ."

"Are you my enemy?"

"Never." Her heart was racing. Her breaths came in ragged gulps. She wanted him to hold her.

"Better you were my enemy."

Weakness washed over her. "Why are you angry with me?" she asked. "*I* should be angry. You put my soul in peril."

He made no answer to that truth. Instead he said flatly, "You have come here to marry with Robert."

"You know that?"

"Today I learn this. Today. When all the time since we've parted, I believed you were safe from him. Robert, not Hawk, will destroy your soul. Robert is not a man worthy of you."

"Why aren't you gone from here?" she demanded, trying to turn the tide of battle. "You told me you had to go to your people. You said your whole life was a sacred mission to—"

"You are a greater danger to the Cherokee than Robert Bennett."

"Me?" She clung to the rough fence.

"You were sent to keep me from my task. Admit it. You are a shaman. The spirits have sent you here to bewitch me."

"I don't have the faintest idea what you're talking about," she protested. "I told you, I'm no witch."

"So you were just born with one eye of green and one of blue."

"Yes. Born to a Christian family, a family with whom I must keep faith."

"Knowing Robert for what he is, you still want to marry with him."

"Yes . . . no. I don't know what I want," she admitted.

"You crossed the sea to be his wife," Hawk accused.

"I didn't, not really. He thinks so, but . . . but I came to accompany my sister. I might not choose to wed Robert. I might marry another."

"An Englishman. A Christian."

"Of course an Englishman. Who else could I wed?"

"You are a fool, Kate Miles."

"Thank you," she replied, trying to keep from dissolving into tears. "Thank you, indeed. One man tonight has called me willful and cruel. Now you call me a dolt."

"I am the Chosen of the Cherokee. I will not be swayed from my mission by a woman's hips and follow-me eyes."

"What's wrong with my hips?" She let go of the post and balled her hands into tight fists beneath her apron. "And I do not have follow-me eyes."

"Did you come to meet Robert in the darkness?"

"No." Her defenses softened when she heard the husky catch in his voice. Hawk cared for her—she knew he did. She nibbled at her lower lip and admitted, "I sent Robert away because he kissed me against my will."

"And how long do you think to hold him off by words?"

"Stop. You've no right to ask these questions of me." She had vowed that Hawk would not confuse her priorities again, but when he was so close, it was impossible to think. She could smell him in the darkness. His scent was not like that of any other man; it was wild and clean and musky, and it filled her head with impossible thoughts. "You said you were not my friend," she managed, "so you have no right at all."

"This man is more than your friend," he answered. "And he will always be."

"No, you won't," she said. "I'll not let you bend me to your will any more than I'll let the rest of them."

"You will not?"

"I will not."

"We will see," he said softly. "Now go back to the house, and do not come out alone in the dark again. There are many men less patient than this man. You could be in danger."

"Not from you?"

"Never from me," he replied. And then he vanished into the mist, leaving her alone and shaken.

. . . And wishing with all her heart that he had kissed her.

Chapter 8

Kate slept until the sun was high the next morning, even though she had no proper bedstead, nothing but a straw-stuffed mattress on the floor. Still, she woke fully rested. It was the first time she'd slept in a room alone for months. She'd been fortunate that her father's house was large. Most women of her station shared a sleeping chamber with family members or servants, but time alone was always something Kate cherished.

She dressed quickly, taking care not to get splinters in her bare feet from the crudely hewn floorboards. The room was small with a single window and not a stitch of furnishing except the leather chest containing her personal belongings. Fortunately she'd brought her own chair, writing desk, linens, and bedstead aboard the *Constant Lady*. Once they were installed, she would ask William to have some pegs set into the wall so that she could hang her clothing.

"It's not home," she murmured, "but neither is it altogether unpleasant." She pushed open the wooden shutter and looked out over the rooftops and palisade wall to the looming forest beyond.

Robert had told her that the trees stretched on to

the far ends of the earth, without clearing or habitation. She wasn't sure she believed him. How was that possible? Even Indians must live somewhere. And Hawk had told her of sunny meadows strewn with wildflowers, towering mountains, and crystal-clear bubbling streams.

Robert told her only what was hearsay, she decided. Hawk had come from the misty southern mountains. His stories must be true and Robert's exaggeration. Still, she reasoned, the forest was formidable. Once on All Souls' Day, when she was a child, she had heard a traveling minstrel sing an old ballad about an enchanted forest.

> ". . . The wood where evil dwelled,
> And no Christian dared to tread.
> 'Twas the heart of darkness,
> Lair of sprite and spirit dread."

Kate shivered as the eerie tune played in her head. She and Alice had both suffered nightmares and clung together like babes, demanding that their nurse bring in a nightlight.

We were close then, she thought, before the little sisters were born, before Alice turned from a skinny mite to a raving beauty. . . . And before Alice realized how disappointed Father had been that she'd not been born a boy.

"It's not his fault," her mother had explained one afternoon when both Kate and Alice had been shouted at by Father for bringing a puppy into the hall. "I lost two boys before you were born alive and thriving. You were the proof that we could have a healthy child. He had it set in his mind that Alice would be the son and heir he needed. And when she wasn't, his dreams came to naught."

Alice had wept then, wept until she'd become sick and thrown up. After that, she had developed a fever and had come down with an ague that kept her abed for weeks and caused all her hair to fall out. When she began to recover, she was bald, petulant, and demanding.

When Kate brought the puppy to Alice's room, her sister screamed for her to get out. "Father wanted you and not me," Alice said. "I hate you!"

Mother said Alice was unwell and would get over it, but she never did. In time, Kate came to understand that she'd lost her best friend. They were still sisters and always would be, but things would never be the same between them again.

Alice's golden hair came in thick and curly. She grew a woman's breasts when Kate's were still flat as a boy's. Alice's hips were shapely, her legs dainty and well turned. Her eyes, framed with lush, dark lashes, were the exact color of bluebells. Alice's complexion was flawless, her tiny straight nose turned up just a little at the tip, and her pouting cheeks, a delicate rose.

Yes, Kate mused, Alice had been granted a woman's portion and then some. And she'd never hesitated to use her wiles to get anything or anyone she wanted.

Once, Kate had gone to ask the village blacksmith about lighter shoes for her mare when she'd caught Alice and Will Smith, bare-arsed in a shocking act of fornication. Both were as black as mummers from wallowing in the ashes near the forge, and sweet little Alice was whinnying like a horse as Will drove home his tool.

Now Alice's shy smiles and soft voice had bought her a knight and a lofty position in the new colony.

She was Lady Bennett and Sir William's darling. Kate wished him well. If she knew anything at all about her sister, Alice would lead William a merry chase.

Kate closed the shutter and fastened it with the leather tie. She finished tying her bodice and went downstairs to find the long table containing the remains of breakfast and her sister still abed.

"Kate! Is that you? Come here," Alice called. "Where is that slut Edwina? Has Grace come yet this morning?"

Kate picked up a corn cake from a plate and went to the parlor door. "Neither of them are in the house as far as I can tell."

Alice shoved her chamber pot under the bed and waved Kate into the room. Alice was stark naked. As far as Kate knew, Alice always slept naked. "Bring fresh water. My face feels like a tennis court. The sun here will make a hag of me in no time."

Her sister's belongings were strewn untidily around the room. One shoe lay near the door; the other was wedged between the bed frame and mattress. Her stockings hung over the back of a straight chair, and her petticoats were heaped on the windowsill. In contrast, Sir William's garments were stacked neatly in one corner.

"This house is impossible," Alice said, picking up an ivory-handled hairbrush. "No furnishings, no style. I wouldn't put a cow in such a stable."

"There is bread and ale on the table. And something that looks like dried fish. Are you hungry?" Kate asked. She always found it best to ignore Alice's complaints.

"William sweats like a pig. I won't have him in my chamber. It won't do at all. He can have your room.

Your things can go in the small room, under the eaves."

"And the servants? Where will they sleep?" Kate asked, trying to hold her temper. "That room won't have enough floor space left to put them there. Would you have me take them into my bed?"

"Bother." Alice tossed down the brush and sank back on the featherbed. "Put the maids wherever you wish, sister. You may have the running of the house—if you can call it a house—so long as you're here. You'll be making a match with Robert soon enough. He's hot for you. I saw that last night. You didn't give him a bit of honey after William and I retired, did you?"

"I did not."

"Anyway, Robert's building his own dwelling. You'll be queen of your own hearth soon enough." She sneezed. "I'll have a mug of that ale and some fish if you don't mind."

"I do mind," Kate replied. "Get it yourself." Snatching up another square of bread, Kate flung open the door and went out.

Alice's French imprecations colored the air, but Kate didn't care. Enough was enough! Now she would lose the small chamber she'd hoped to claim. It was unfair, and so very like Alice. She should have known what to expect under her sister's roof.

Kate had not gone a few steps from the house when she heard the sound of someone splitting wood. Behind the house, she found Hawk standing over a chopping block, axe in hand. A pile of neatly stacked logs rose beside him.

His back was to her. She stopped short, and once again the conviction washed over her that Hawk was more than an ordinary man. Naked but for moccasins and a strip of buckskin around his loins, he radiated an aura of royalty.

Long ago Father had taken them all to London. They stood in the pouring rain for nearly an hour, waiting for the king to pass by on horseback. Kate remembered seeing him as if it were yesterday. She'd cheered loudly when His Majesty rode into sight. He was ever so tall and stern and sat his saddle as straight as if his spine were made of steel. As the royal party drew near, her father lifted her onto his shoulders. For an instant, King James had stared straight at her. Then he'd ridden on, but she'd never forgotten his noble presence.

Fire Hawk had that same mystique.

Kate stood motionless, watching him, unable to take her eyes off the ripple of his back and thigh muscles as he swung the heavy ax. His red-gold skin glowed in the sunshine; his night black hair hung over one bulging shoulder in a single braid. His high-arched feet and shapely calves were as bare as his arms. With each mighty stroke he took, chips flew from the oak log balanced on the stump. And with each blow of the ax, her heart skipped a beat.

Abruptly Hawk plunged the ax head deep into the stump and turned to fix her with a magnetic stare so unnerving that it nearly caused her to turn and flee. But she stood where she was and gazed back at him. It was her first good look at him in full sunlight since she'd seen him the day of her wedding.

He looked older, harder. Every inch of fat had melted from his face, leaving his features sharply drawn and haunting. His dark, almond-shaped eyes burned with an inner flame; the outlines of his high-chiseled cheekbones and proud nose stood out as though hewn of granite.

Then the thin sensual lips curved into a faint

smile, and her heart fluttered like a trapped bird in her breast. "Kate." The slight curve of his mouth widened to a devilish grin. "Are you just rising from your bed? The day is half over."

"What time I get out of bed is none of your affair."

"Peevish too."

I do sound like Alice, she thought. Determined to maintain her dignity, she tried again. "Where can I find drinking water?" she asked. "There's none in the house, and the servants are gone."

"Servants? You need servants to find water?" His mouth pursed in silent disapproval, but she could not escape the thought that he was making fun of her.

"You forget that I am come new to this place. In my father's house, I would know where to find the well." She stiffened, refusing to allow him to chastise her.

"Cherokee women need no servants to carry their water."

"I'm sure." She made her tone cool. "I'm not a Cherokee woman."

"True."

She waited.

Hawk chuckled. "Come, Kate, I will show you a well of good water. There is one on the other side of the house, but the spirits of that water are sick. Too many people here. They dirty their houses by relieving themselves in cooking pots and throw the piss out the window."

Kate flushed. "English do not . . . not in cooking pots. They are chamber pots." She glanced around to see if anyone was nearby. "Don't you know anything? Chamber pots are used only for . . . for personal needs."

"Only a lazy man would piss in his house."

"Urinate," she corrected.

"That is what I said."

"You don't understand."

"This one understands that clean people, civilized people, do not do in their houses what should be done in a pit, away from the village. And the Cherokee never empty pots of urine onto other men's heads."

"Proper gentlemen do not talk of such things to ladies."

Hawk shrugged.

"The Cherokee and the Powhatan are not civilized," she said. "A civilized man would not go about unclad."

"Unclad." He smiled again and repeated the word. "Unclad." He motioned to his leather kilt and said something that she couldn't understand. "This is what Cherokee men wear," he explained. "It does not offend Cherokee women. Cherokee women are not easily impressed by men."

"Impressed? I'm not impressed. I'm merely telling you that I find your lack of proper attire . . . highly improper."

"Hawk thinks you look a long time at this man for one who does not like."

"Oh." Her embarrassment grew even greater. He must have known that she was watching him. "I didn't—" she began, but he cut her off.

"This man thinks you say what you do not mean. Hawk's body is as the Creator made it. If Kate finds fault, it is with His work."

"Englishmen cover themselves decently."

He scoffed. "Englishmen wrap their flesh in wool when the sun is hot. Fools. The heat of this land will kill them. The Creator means for a man's skin to breathe."

"Adam clothed himself in the garden of Eden when he ate of the apple and first learned of sin."

Hawk looked dubious. "If our bodies are meant to be smothered in garments, why are we not born with the pelt of the gray wolf?"

Kate shook her head. "I will not argue theology with you. Since you refuse to show me when the water can be found, I—"

"Hawk will show you. Come."

He walked past her to William's house and took a wooden bucket from a post. Unsure of what else to do, she followed him. He led her down a lane between another group of huts.

Two women leaned from an open doorway to watch her, and Kate heard her name being whispered. A group of soldiers looked their way, and a red-faced farmer leading an ox frowned at Hawk and doffed his hat to Kate as they walked past.

"You do not seem to have many friends here," Kate said.

Hawk made a sound of derision. "Your English settlers have little respect for red men. They think only of how to steal our land and corn supplies. And of hunting gold." He shrugged. "But they do not mind eating the fish that Hawk catches or the deer brought down by his arrow."

"You're different. Most people are afraid of those who are different," she replied softly.

Near the last dwelling on the street there was an open lot. A small wooden well-house stood alone on the bare earth. "This water is sweet," Hawk said. "There . . ." He pointed back toward the river. "Not good. This you can drink."

Kate waited for him to turn the crank and bring up the bucket, but he made no move to do so. Awkwardly she took hold of the handle and gave it a turn.

"Good," he said. He placed his strong fingers over hers, and she thrilled to his touch.

Why can't Robert make me feel this way? she thought. *Robert is my betrothed. Fire Hawk can't do anything but keep me from heaven's gates.* But she didn't withdraw her hands, and together they brought up the brimming bucket of water.

Keeping his hand on the handle, Hawk swung the pail over until it lodged firmly on the well-house rim. Kate picked up her bucket and held it as he poured water from the first container to the second, then lowered it to the ground.

Hawk plucked a gourd dipper from a hook, scooped up the cool liquid, and held it out to her. "Taste," he said.

She obeyed. The water was as sweet as he'd promised. Shyly, she handed back the cup.

Hawk refilled the gourd and drank deeply. Drops spilled over and trickled down his throat. Without thinking, Kate reached up and touched a bead of moisture with her fingertip.

Hawk stared at her over the top of the gourd and a shiver ran through her. How could such a simple thing as the sharing of a drink of water bring such a sense of intimacy?

"Why?" she asked.

"Why what?" His black eyes showed her nothing of his thoughts.

"Why do you make me so angry and then happy without doing anything?"

He shook his head, and warmth replaced his stony expression. "Happiness comes from here," he said, touching the place over his heart with his fist.

"This man cannot make you happy. You must find it within."

Kate held out her hands, and he poured water over them. She splashed some on her face. "That makes me happy," she said. "I'm so sick of bathing in salt water that I . . ."

She stopped, realizing that she was talking to Hawk about bathing, another intimacy that should be forbidden between them. She sat on the edge of the well and smoothed her skirts.

"This man is glad you are here, Kate."

She smiled at him. "I'm glad too."

"That does not make it right."

"Why do you care?"

"Hawk cares about your safety."

"Why wouldn't I be safe?"

"My cousin Gar is a powerful man among the Powhatan. He does not like the English. He cannot be trusted."

"I believe I heard Robert and William talking about him last night. Have you told Robert about your fears?"

"Robert seeks gold. Gar has promised it to him."

"Your cousin told you that?"

Hawk shook his head. "There is no friendship between this man and Gar. When I was a child, he hated me. I think he still hates me."

"Then how could you know what—"

"Robert told me. He thinks I know where these mines of gold can be found." He scoffed. "Have you seen the bauble Robert wears around his neck?"

"The gold piece? Yes," she answered. "He showed it to me."

"That amulet came from far away. Farther even than my mountains. It was traded to the Powhatan for the shell beads called peag or *wampum*. Other tribes value them highly."

"Are you telling me that there is no gold in Virginia?"

He made a clicking sound with his tongue. "Buried with the dead, worn around the throats of the living. No gold such as Robert seeks. Gar knows the English weakness, and he will stab at it until blood flows. I would not have you caught in the middle of a war between English and Powhatan."

Kate looked toward the forest and shivered despite the hot morning sun. Were there hostile Indians watching William's Hundred? Watching her?

She took a deep breath. "You and Robert have been together a long time. He should believe you if you're telling the truth."

"I think Robert trusts me no more than I trust Gar."

"Then why do you stay here? Why don't you go to your Cherokee and leave us and our problems behind?"

Hawk's eyes narrowed. "Robert took me from the Spanish prison. In return, I promised to help him. I have not kept my promise yet, but soon. Soon it will be finished between us. When my debt is paid, I go. And this man will not look back."

"I'll miss you when you're gone."

"Better we had never met. Better you had never come to Virginia." His features hardened. "I would still have you for my wife, Kate, but if you will not, I would have you on Gordon's ship sailing back to England."

"Stop saying that!" She turned her face away so that he couldn't see how upset those words made her. "I can't marry you, Hawk. It's impossible! The

English . . . my English could never accept you as my husband. And I would not risk hellfire and damnation to go and live in the woods with you."

"So you have said."

"You are a good man, Fire Hawk, but—"

"Katherine!" Robert's shout made her break off what she was saying. She turned to see her betrothed hurrying toward them. Judging from his expression, he was exceedingly irate.

"Robert." She rose to meet him.

"What do you think you're doing?" he demanded.

"Fetching water for . . ."

Robert swore a Spanish oath. "Your sister's been asking for you. She's afraid you've come to harm." He glared at Hawk. "It's unseemly for you to be alone with an English woman. You should have better sense."

"As should you," Kate retorted. "I'm getting a bucket of water, Robert, not hiding in a haystack with him. He was showing me where—"

"There are servants to carry water. William has two maids and three men to do such work. When did you ever do kitchen chores, woman?"

"Neither maid nor manservant could be found and I was thirsty," she replied hotly. "Surely I've not offended your honor by walking inside the town walls with your friend—"

"With my bond servant. My native bond servant."

Hawk's face took on a coldness Kate had not seen before. "Would you have me watch her drink from a dirty well?" Hawk asked Robert.

"Nonsense. All our wells are good," Robert insisted. "Carry this water back to the house, and see that you keep away from Mistress Miles unless you are attending me."

Kate looked at him, red-faced and sweating beneath his broad-brimmed felt hat, linen shirt, woolen doublet, breeches and hose, and high, heavy military boots. Suddenly what Hawk had said about the English and the way they dressed in the Virginia heat seemed eminently true. And regrettably, she began to snicker.

"I see nothing funny, Katherine."

Hawk turned and walked away.

"John! I told you to take this bucket to Sir William's house," Robert said.

"I'm afraid it must be me or you," Kate said, still giggling. "It appears your tame Indian is not as tame as you think."

"The insolent—"

"Please, Robert, be reasonable. We did nothing wrong. Now you've insulted him by calling him a servant and inferring that we—"

Robert took her arm. "I'll send a wench for the water, Katherine. And I trust you'll use better judgment next time."

Kate sighed. "You can hope so." She accompanied him without protest, but she paid little heed to what he was saying. Instead she mulled over what Hawk had told her about the Powhatan, Gar, and the danger that hung over the settlement. And she wondered—once again—why she had crossed the ocean to America.

Chapter 9

Hawk left the settlement and slipped into the trees. A soldier called after him, but he ignored the challenge. He needed to get the stench of William's Hundred out of his head. He desperately needed to be alone with his thoughts and to greet the dawn each morning with traditional Cherokee prayers.

How he had longed for this sky and this earth when he was a prisoner in Europe. And how much more did he long to see the face of his mother and his younger half brother and sister. He wanted to walk with the Cherokee holy man, Painted Stick, and listen to his words of wisdom. And he yearned to hear the voices of his own people again.

Since he could not be with the Cherokee now, he wanted to be by himself. Early on he'd learned that peace can be found amid the stillness of a forest or the glory of a rising sun. Hawk was not a man who needed the company of other men, least of all these crude English who were so different from his own kind.

. . . Except for Kate. She was not like the others, but it was best that he put distance between them as well. Nothing could come of the desire he had for her, nothing but unhappiness for both of them.

He had told Kate that he stayed at William's Hundred to fulfill his bargain with Robert Bennett, but that was only part of the truth. All his life, he'd followed the direction of an inner force. Now that voice was silent, and he knew that it was wrong to return to the misty mountains until he received the final command.

Was there something he had not learned? Was there some secret the English possessed that they had hidden from him? He'd studied their clumsy weapons, watched as white men cleaned and loaded their cannons and guns. He understood black powder, and he was certain he could aim and shoot one of the long muskets, even though he'd been forbidden to touch them. He could build a fire with flint and steel; he could use his magnifying glass to ignite a flame still faster. He had learned to read and to write a fair hand, and he could speak their tongue.

It was not the English soldiers or their fire sticks that he feared; it was the white man's way of looking at the world that would most threaten the Cherokee. To red men, the earth was mother. Each plant, each animal, each bird was formed by the Creator. A man was part of the Creator's plan; his life spirit was precious—but so was that of a tree, a blade of grass, or a turtle. Red men sought to live in harmony with nature; white men felt the need to control and even destroy the land and forests and rivers.

Not even the mighty Powhatan emperor could claim a section of creek or a meadow or the air above it. Yet the English built fences around plots of ground and said, "Do not set foot here on peril of your life."

Hawk had seen the poverty in Spain and England.

He had watched men die for a scrap of bread or a few feet of parched garden soil. There were thousands upon thousands who owned nothing but the rags on their backs. And once word trickled back of the richness of the Cherokee land, those penniless men would risk everything to try and take it for their own.

As Hawk left the clatter and smell of the English settlement behind him, his heart was eased. A great weight lifted off his shoulders as he strode among oak trees that had been acorns when his great-great-grandfather was born.

The woods was unnaturally silent. A light breeze stirred the treetops, and from time to time, a squirrel chattered or hopped from one branch to another. Most of the migrating birds had already begun their winter journey to the south. It was early for them to leave, Hawk mused. He wondered if the winter would be a particularly harsh one.

Food stocks at William's Hundred were low. It was Hawk's opinion that Robert's brother depended too much on goods brought by white ship's captains and on Powhatan promises. The Emperor Powhatan had agreed to trade corn for ax heads and knives, but Hawk had no more faith in his grandfather's cautious words of friendship than he did in the English. Hawk hoped that Robert's steel knives and axes would not be turned against him.

Hawk stopped and knelt on one knee to examine the tracks of a lame doe that had passed this way only minutes before. Curious, he followed the trail, and minutes later he came upon the deer drinking from a sinkhole just ahead. Hawk stood and watched her, but did not unsling his bow. He could not use so much meat, and he had no intention of returning to the settlement this day.

The doe was old and lean, graying around her mouth and ears. Her hip bones pushed against the scarred hide, and the hairs on her tail were thin and scraggly.

As Hawk gazed at the animal, she turned her head and stared directly at him. Her ears twitched and shot upright; her muscles tensed.

Peace, old mother, Hawk thought. *You need have no fear of me.*

The doe sniffed the air and blew droplets of water from her lips. Her eyes widened even further, and she took a hesitant step toward him.

Hawk stood motionless, hands outstretched.

The deer came closer, stepping daintily through the underbrush. Her long ears flicked nervously; her tail stiffened upright, fluttering like a white flag.

He held his breath as the doe kept coming. When she finally halted and uttered several short, grating coughs, she was not five arm's lengths away. Hawk could smell the musky scent of her, could detect the odor of wild onion on her breath.

Why do you come to me? Hawk asked silently of the deer. *Are you flesh or spirit?*

The doe spread her hind legs and passed a handful of earth brown pellets.

Hawk's eyes twinkled with amusement. *Real enough, old mother.* The faint smell of scat brushed his nostrils. *Do you carry a message for me?* He closed his eyes and tried to clear his mind of everything.

Kate's image filled his brain. He saw her as clearly as he had beheld her sitting on the edge of the well—the russet curls that escaped her linen cap to frame her oval face, the thumbnail she had bitten to the quick, and the reddened mosquito bite on her forehead. Suddenly, he ached for the sound of her laughter as a thirsty man aches for cool water.

When he'd left Kate behind in England, he'd missed her more than he would have thought possible. He missed her questions and her keen intelligence. He missed watching her many expressions and the graceful way she walked. Most of all, he missed the warm feeling he got in the pit of his stomach when she was near.

No matter how often he tried to block out thoughts of Kate and concentrate on the old doe's message, he could not help wondering how it would be to return to his lodge each day to find Kate waiting for him.

His wife . . . His chosen woman, not just for a night of passion, but his forever. What would it be like to have her as mother to his children? Kate . . . his eternal beloved.

Hawk's eyes snapped open. He was alone. The doe was gone, and he had no idea how long he'd stood there.

"Was that the message you brought me?" he murmured aloud. Was it possible that the spirits intended him to return to the Cherokee with an English wife?

"Go to the land of the white strangers and learn their ways," his Cherokee mentor, Painted Stick, had commanded. "Return with knowledge so that we may use their own evil against them—so that the Cherokee shall not vanish beneath the hooves of iron-clad horses as other tribes have done."

Excitement pounded in his blood. Bringing an English woman back to the Cherokee mountains was not part of his instructions, but taking a wife among the whites had not been forbidden. Was it implied, he wondered, or was his yearning for Kate clouding his judgment?

Then he clearly remembered one of his mother's favorite sayings. "Who better to know the ways of a fox than a vixen?" Women's wisdom, he mused, and this was an affair concerning a woman.

He crouched, sitting on his heels, and removed a tiny leather pouch from his medicine bag. Carefully he unrolled a strip of soft deerskin. Cradled within were a few strands of Kate's hair that he'd carried with him since the day he'd snatched her into the tree in Bramble Wood. Thoughtfully, he rubbed the token between his fingertips.

"Kate, Kate," he whispered. "Did my trail to you begin the first time I saw you, or was it always part of the great plan of the spirits, written in the clouds before either of us was born?"

Happiness seeped up from his belly and filled his chest. So great was the joy that he could not remain quiet. He leaped up and shouted her name. "I will have you, Kate!" he proclaimed to the silent forest. "Fight me, deny me, flee from me, but we shall be together. On my honor, I so swear. I will have you to wife, and I will warm your heart from English frost to Cherokee fire."

Two days passed without Hawk's returning to the settlement. Kate overheard William and Robert at breakfast, complaining about his absence.

"I don't entirely trust John Fire Hawk anymore," Robert said. "He's different since we landed. In England it was hard for me to keep him in his proper place; here it is impossible. He disobeyed a direct order before he ran off to the woods."

"I agree," William said, between bites of corn pudding. "I've never trusted him, and if, as you say, this Powhatan prince, Gar—"

"A striking man, this Gar. A prince, you say, husband?" Alice murmured. "Grace, more ale for Sir William," she ordered the serving wench.

Robert held out his cup and smiled at his sister-in-law. "Grandson of the Powhatan emperor himself."

William cleared his throat. "Not striking to my way of thinking. Naked savage. No different than any of the rest."

"But useful," Robert said. "Useful if he can show us where the gold mines are."

Grace crouched by the fireplace, turning the corn cakes, some of which were already starting to blacken.

Heat from the open hearth made the room stifling, but Kate lingered near the doorway, listening.

"Gar has promised to send some of his young men here to learn our language. He also asked if he could come to one of our worship services. I think you'll like him, and since his father is a chief, his goodwill should go a long way toward providing us with the support we need."

"I'll mention him to the minister. Christianizing our local Powhatan is vital."

"John told me that Gar was a cousin of some sort, but I don't believe there's any love lost between them."

William wiped his mouth with a napkin and belched. "We'll keep Hawk to translate until another is as proficient, but I won't have him coming and going from the fort to suit himself. It puts us all in danger."

Alice interrupted the conversation by pushing open her parlor door and calling for Edwina.

"She's not here," Kate said.

"Fetch the wench," Alice said. "I need my gown aired and pressed. I've nothing fit to be seen in."

"Grace can—" Kate began.

"I won't have Grace put a hand to my clothing," Alice declared. "I want Edwina."

"Edwina is working in the garden." William rose and kissed his wife on each cheek. I'm sorry you are distressed, my dear. Your Edwina is a farm lass and has experience with such matters. Each household must share in the labor, and it seemed wisest to send the girl. Robert insists we'll need the vegetables this winter."

Alice pouted. "I won't have Grace. Kate must fill in if Edwina is occupied. Sister—"

Kate ducked out of the open doorway. Robert followed her. "Kate, Alice wants you—"

"You tend to her," she called over her shoulder. Her sister had two maids; she had no intention of becoming a third. And she had no wish to speak with Robert after the chastising he'd given her when he'd caught her with Hawk at the well.

She wanted to get away from her sister's house and Alice's constant demands. And in so small a fort, the only place of solitude was the unfinished church.

Lifting her skirts above her ankles, Kate slogged through the muddy clearing that William called his town green. It had rained again in the night, and now the hot sun turned the settlement into a steam bath.

Kate tried to ignore the trickles of sweat that ran between her breasts. It could be no later than nine in the morning, and already the air was heavy and humid. Her garments clung to her body, making her skin itch until she'd scratched a welt from her elbow to her shoulder.

This was late November. If it was so hot now, she wondered what summer must be like. "Impossible to bear," she murmured. Buzzing swarms of green-head flies and mosquitoes descended on her head and assaulted every exposed inch of her skin.

Several large, unfriendly looking swine blocked her path. "Get away!" she warned, kicking at the nearest one. The hog snorted and bared yellow teeth. "Shoo," she shouted. The evil-tempered hog whirled and bit the nearest pig. That sow squealed, and piglets ran in all directions, scattering the chickens. The foolish birds left off scratching in the mud for scraps, squawked in panic, and flew into the air. One came down on the largest sow's back, and the pig charged away with a flapping rider. Kate laughed and trudged on through the puddles and muck.

On the opposite side of the square, men labored in the broiling heat to erect a log arsenal where weapons and gunpowder could be safely stored. It was Robert's plan that this armory would also provide a last source of protection for the settlers in case of Indian attack.

At the far end of the green, one of Robert's sergeant's drilled his two score, minus one of the soldiers. There had already been a casualty. A seasoned mercenary had taken one look at William's Hundred and deserted to God knows where.

The guardsmen looked even hotter than Kate felt. Her woolen gown and linen petticoats were bad enough, but the soldiers were equipped with steel breastplates and metal helmets. Their knee-high leather boots were heavy with clinging mud, and their muskets, swords, and powder horns added even more weight to their burdens.

Near the marching Englishmen stood three Indians staring in astonishment. The Powhatan wore nothing but a twist of skin around their hips, even less covering, it seemed to her, than Hawk wore. These braves were well-formed men with strong bodies and dusky skin. Their heads were shaved on one side and their coal black hair long on the other.

Then one Indian moved aside, and the smallest stepped forward. Kate caught only a glimpse before she turned her head away in shock. The young squaw wore only a brief leather skirt and a string of shell beads. Her small, brown breasts were completely exposed to the leers of the soldiers.

Kate's face flushed with embarrassment. The sight of a woman's body wasn't uncommon, but she wondered what manner of woman would appear half-naked in public and why William would allow such behavior inside the fort.

Quickly she hurried into the shadowy interior of the church. The log walls and shingled roof were complete, but Robert had told her that no services had been offered here yet.

The floor of the sanctuary was brick, brought as ballast in the hold of the ship that had carried the first group of settlers. The ceiling soared nearly three stories high. There were no pews, only a raised area at the end of the room where the minister would stand to deliver his sermon. A single lead-paned window high on an end wall gave the only light.

Kate tried to put the Indian woman from her mind. She'd come here to try and find a measure of peace . . . answers to the problems that troubled her. At home she had taken Sunday worship as part of her life. She'd never considered herself particularly pious, but she'd tried to obey the Commandments and live a life that would someday admit her to heaven.

Never in her childhood had she considered that she'd ever come to care for a man who was not of her religion. But Hawk was a good man. Could loving him be so terribly wrong?

For more than a hour she prayed. Then, still without answers to her dilemma, but strangely comforted by the peace of this quiet place that smelled of newly cut cedar shakes and white pine, she left the church and returned to her sister's house.

Neither maid was present when she opened the door and entered the great room. "Alice, are you here?" she called.

When there was no answer, she started for the steep staircase, then stopped short when she heard an odd mewing. Could it be a cat? Kate wondered. She'd seen no cats in the settlement. Then she heard the noise again.

"Eieee, eieee, ahh."

Kate realized that the strange sounds were coming from her sister's parlor. She hesitated. The next squeak was definitely that of a creaking bed frame. "Oh, that," Kate murmured.

Certain she'd intruded on an intimate interlude between husband and wife, Kate slipped off her shoes and moved quietly toward the entrance way. Leaving the two alone in the house, she felt, would be the only polite thing to do.

"Ahh, ohhh! Robert!" came her sister's voice through the bedchamber door.

Robert? Kate whirled around. *Robert?*

Alice whimpered. "Yes! Yes! Harder! Harder!"

"Can William do this for you?" Robert's voice was coarse with lust.

"Ahhh! Ahhh!"

Kate flung open the parlor door to see her sister and Robert swiving each other royally not ten feet from where she stood. Alice sprawled crossways on the poster bed, her yellow-gold hair hanging down and her naked legs thrashing in the air. Robert wore nothing but his high leather boots as he slammed his thin, purple organ rhythmically between Alice's thighs.

Kate noted that Robert's bare buttocks were fish-belly white. She burst into laughter.

Robert caught sight of her and froze in midthrust. His mouth fell open and he gasped.

"No! No!" Alice cried. "More! I want—" She saw Kate and screamed.

Robert clamped a hand over Alice's mouth, muffling all but the first squawk. "Shut up!" he hissed. "Will you bring the whole settlement?"

He leaped off the bed, yanking the sheet with him. Frantically he wrapped the linen covering around his rapidly shrinking member while Alice sat dumbfounded, staring at Kate.

"Katherine!" Robert babbled. "What are you . . . How . . . Not what this seems."

Alice's eyes clouded with fury, and she began to swear at both of them in French.

"Thank you," Kate said, still dissolved in giggles. "Thank you both. A more likelier pair of rogues would be hard to find this side of Newgate Prison."

"Kate, be reasonable," Robert begged. "You—"

"Devil take you both!" Kate tugged off her betrothal ring and flung it at his head. "Give this to your paramour. She deserves it far more than I."

"Kate—"

"We're finished, Robert," she cried.

Alice used up all of her French vocabulary and switched to Italian curses.

Still laughing, Kate dashed out the door into the

bright Virginia sunshine. "Thank you, God," she murmured. "You've answered my prayers and set me free."

Chapter 10

❦

Kate awoke the following morning to the sound of pebbles striking her bedchamber window. For a few seconds, she lay there, remembering the ugly scene she'd discovered yesterday—remembering how furious her sister had been.

Alice hadn't appeared at supper the night before, and she hadn't spoken a word to Kate. She hadn't wanted to remain in Alice's house, but there was no where else to go. She didn't want to tell William that she'd found his wife and her betrothed committing adultery, and no other household would take her in without a very embarrassing explanation.

The odd rattling noise came again.

Rubbing her eyes, Kate got up, stepped cautiously over the sleeping maids on the floor, and pushed open the wooden shutter.

"Who's out there?" she whispered. It was close to sunrise, but not light enough to make out the figure below.

"Come down," Hawk called to her.

"Is that you?" It was a foolish question. She knew it the moment it came from her lips, but she was only half-awake, and she wanted to be certain she wasn't dreaming. "What do you want?"

"This man is going fishing and wants company."

"Me?" It was a ridiculous suggestion. William had forbidden any of the women to leave the safety of the fort walls. Robert had forbidden her to be alone with Hawk again.

Slowly a smile spread over Kate's face as she realized that what Robert wanted would never again be her concern. "I'll be right down," she told Hawk.

She closed the shutter and swiftly pulled her plainest wool skirt, petticoat, and bodice from a hook on the wall. Luckily she slept in her shift and linen drawers.

Lacing up her stays in the darkness was a bother, but finding her stockings amid the clutter of the tiny room without waking Grace or Edwina was even harder. Still, she was sneaking down the stairs in two minutes, shoes in hand.

Hawk was waiting.

"How did you get into the fort?" she whispered. "The guards won't let anyone pass the gate at night." The morning air felt cool on her skin, and she shivered with excitement.

He held a finger over his lips.

Feeling much like a child on an adventure, Kate followed him. He led her to the side of the stockade wall that wasn't fully completed and helped her climb through a hole in the thorns and branches.

In the east, the sky was beginning to take on an amber hue. Fallen leaves crunched under her feet as she walked. Gradually the dark shapes around her became trees and branches. The air was cool with a crisp snap of autumn that she hadn't noticed inside the settlement.

Hawk didn't speak to her until they were a long way from William's Hundred. "I did not know if you

would come," he said softly. "They will be angry
when they find you are gone."

Kate shook her head. She didn't care what anyone
said. Coming away with Hawk was daring, heart-
stirring. It was fun . . . something she hadn't felt for
a long time.

"You aren't afraid of Robert?"

A chuckle escaped her lips. "Robert couldn't be
any angrier with me than he already is. I've broken
my engagement to him."

"This is true?"

"You should be happy. I'll never marry him.
Never!"

"Good."

"I came upon something I wasn't supposed to
see," she explained. She'd told no one, but Hawk was
different. "I found Robert and my sister together."

"Grinding corn?" he asked.

"No. They were . . ." Her cheeks grew warm as
she searched for ladylike words. "Intimate. Doing
what only man and wife should do." She hesitated.
"I laughed at them. Neither will ever forgive me."

Hawk's laughter was deep and merry. "As I said."
He gestured with his hands. "Grinding corn. He is
the pestle, she the—"

"I understand."

"It is not the first time."

Her surprise was greater than her embarrassment.
"It wasn't?"

"In England, your sister and Robert were . . .
together many times."

"They never! The dog! You knew? Why didn't you
tell me?"

He shrugged. "Would you believe Hawk?"

"Maybe not. But I believe you now." She exhaled

slowly. "William doesn't know. I wouldn't talk about what I saw, only to—"

"To this man."

She nodded. "You are my only friend here."

"More than friend," he reminded her.

Her heart fluttered. "Yes," she agreed. "We are more than friends." She stopped walking. "I would like us to be just friends today, friends fishing together."

The changes in her life were coming too fast. She had broken with Robert once and for all, but she wasn't ready to leap into the unknown . . . wasn't ready to consider it. She couldn't promise Hawk anything. Not yet. "Please, Hawk—"

"You are a cruel woman. This man wants to hold you in his arms and whisper love words into—"

"No. I don't want to hear that," she insisted. "I came to go fishing. That's all."

"Hard as a Mohawk."

She tried to smooth her confusion with brisk chatter. "If we're going to fish, where are our fishing poles?"

He pointed to a dugout canoe pulled up on the bank of a narrow stream. Kate didn't see any poles, but lying in the bottom of the narrow boat were coils of string and a three-pronged spear.

"I hope you remembered bait," she said.

"Into the boat, woman. You chatter like a squirrel."

His chiding was good-natured, and she took it as such. She climbed into the dugout and watched Hawk retrieve a paddle from beneath a pile of leaves. He pushed the craft off and stepped inside.

The current took them lazily downstream. There were no sounds but the morning songs of birds and the gentle swish of Hawk's paddle. Kate closed her eyes and let her fingers trail in the water.

"Do you fish for sturgeon?" Hawk teased.

"Will they bite?" She had no idea what a sturgeon was, but she snatched her hand back. Sighing, she looked around her. The stream was opening into a wider waterway, but there was no sign that any humans had ever passed this way before.

"Might," he teased.

Silently she watched the shore glide by. After a long time, the croak of a great blue heron broke the stillness. Startled by their passing, the stiltlike wading bird spread its wings and rose slowly into the air.

"Are you ever afraid of the forest?" Kate asked. The massive trees on either side of the river stretched to the sky; their branches intertwined and piled layer upon layer to block out the sun.

Hawk chuckled. "No. I am not afraid of the forest."

"I think I am."

"In London, I was afraid. Too many people, too much noise. The forest is my home."

"But not mine."

"You do not know that, Kate. This man will teach you the ways of this land. You will come to love it as I do."

"Perhaps." She felt an inner chill. The sunshine sparkled on the water, but a few yards away, the forest lay locked in shadow. Bears lived there. Wolves and furious wildcats. Snakes . . . She rubbed her face with her hands. She hated snakes. Even thinking about them made the hair rise on the back of her neck.

Hawk drew his paddle in and laid it carefully in the bottom of the dugout. Taking a coil of line, he lifted the hook for Kate to see.

"It has no curve," she protested. "How can you catch a fish with that?" Tied at the end of the string was a sliver of bone no thicker than a quill pen and the length of her little finger. The hook had a slight groove cut around the center and came to a point on both ends.

Hawk threaded a grub on to the hook, lowered it over the side, and handed the end of the line to Kate. "When a fish swallows the bait, the hook turns sideways in his belly. It will not come out until you cut it from the fish."

Kate grimaced. "Not very sporting."

"Fishing is not sporting, not for a Cherokee. Not for a Powhatan. Fish feed our families. And they will feed your people at William's Hundred as well."

"William and Robert are angry that you left the fort."

Hawk concentrated on baiting the second line.

"Where did you go?"

He lifted his head and gazed at her. "This man needed time to be alone. Robert does not behave like a friend."

"They don't trust you. I heard them say it. Robert thinks that man Gar will lead him to the gold mines."

"Gar will lead Robert to his grave."

"I don't think that—Oh! Oh!" she cried. Something tugged hard on her line. She snatched it up, and the force pulled harder. "Oh! I've got something! I've got a fish!"

Robert and William were both forgotten in the excitement of the moment. Kate had taken in half her line when a fish swallowed Hawk's bait. Laughing, she struggled to bring her fish in before Hawk landed his.

She gave a final yank and an enormous black fish

with whiskers flopped into the bottom of the dugout and then out over the other side. "I win," she cried.

"Does not count," Hawk said, hauling in his fish, another of the same kind but smaller. "Your fish must be in the boat."

"It was!" she said. "It just jumped out again. And mine was bigger." Laughing, she pulled the fish in again.

They caught five more catfish before the sun clouded over, and the wind began to blow. "We go back now," Hawk said.

"All right," she agreed. "I'm as wet as the fish, and I probably smell as bad."

One thumb burned where she'd snagged herself on a catfish spine, and she had fish guts on the hem of her skirt, but she didn't care. She was having a wonderful time. She looked at the fish with satisfaction.

Hawk smiled at her. "You do not look like an English lady now."

"Nor an Indian one either, I suppose."

"A woman with one green eye? How could she be Cherokee?"

She splashed water on him.

Hawk looked stricken. "This man brings a gift for you, and this is how you treat him."

"A gift? What? What do you have for me?"

He held out an ivory hairpin, delicately carved with a running leaf pattern and a exquisitely lifelike bird at the tip.

"Oooh," she gasped. "It's beautiful."

"Not so beautiful as a woman with hair like autumn leaves."

"My hair is like leaves?"

He smiled. "It is the color of leaves. Red, like an English fox, but not so bright. A Cherokee fox is gray. Gray is the proper color for a fox."

"You, sir, are quite opinionated for a barbarian," she teased. "But thank you." Her voice grew husky with emotion. "Thank you, Hawk, I'll cherish it forever." She looked up into his face. "But where did you get it? How?"

"On the ship, crossing the ocean. I traded with a sailor for the ivory. It comes from the teeth of a walrus, far to the north in the land of ice."

"And the carving?"

He smiled again. "This man did that for you."

"You're an artist. It's beautiful workmanship."

"True. Fire Hawk is a man of many talents."

"And modest," she teased, pushing the ivory pin into her hair. "Very modest."

"Very," he agreed, and they laughed together.

Mother, what would you think? Kate wondered. *Your daughter alone in the wilderness with a red man. You'd be certain my life was in danger, wouldn't you? . . . Certain the devil had tempted me to evil.*

But Kate had never felt safer in her life. It was a good feeling, and it made her warm and happy inside.

Her mother, her home in England, and her family seemed to belong to another lifetime. She missed them terribly, missed the house where she'd grown up, the food, the smells of the courtyard and the stables. Most of all, she missed her little sisters—the clatter of the twins' feet on the stairs and the sound of little Emma's tinkling laughter.

I'll never see any of them again, she thought. Unbidden, tears welled up in her eyes.

But before the sadness could overwhelm her, Hawk took hold of her hand. "It's dirty," she protested.

"A catfish spine carries poison." He lifted her thumb to his lips and sucked at the wound.

"It will be all right." She tried to pull away, but he held her. "R-Really," she stammered. Her heart raced, and she felt breathless, as though she'd been running in mud. *What is it about this man?* she thought. *He has only to touch me, and the world falls away from under my feet.*

"I should take you back now," he said. "I hear thunder."

"I don't hear anything."

He smiled. "You don't listen, but that will come. As will the rain."

"Yes," she agreed, "before the rain." *And before I say or do something rash*, she thought. *Something I won't be able to escape as easily as I did my betrothal to Robert.*

The breeze stiffened, and Kate's thoughts tumbled like the windblown leaves that cascaded through the air and bobbed along the surface of the water. What was it that she found in Hawk that she couldn't find in a man of her own kind? And why did his touch make her yearn for what she knew was forbidden between them?

Hawk's voice broke through her reverie. "I wanted to be with you this day. I do not know how many others we can share." He turned her hand over and kissed the faint purple vein on the other side of her wrist.

Sweet shivers spilled through her. "I don't want you to go away," she admitted. "I'll be alone if you go."

"Your heart is full of love," he replied. "If other English had your good heart, there would be no trouble between whites and Indians."

She shook her head. "There are many good white people."

He let her go and picked up his paddle. "I have not seen many good ones."

She cradled her hands in her lap. "Really. We are not bad. If you let us, we can bring your people much that you don't have."

"So? What do the English have that the Cherokee lack?"

"The true word of God," she replied.

He shrugged and dipped the tip of the paddle into the calm, dark water. "The Creator has many names. We worship Him in the way of our grandfathers."

"Pagan ways," she argued. "You have seen the churches and cathedrals of Europe. How can you compare Indian superstition to the true religion?"

"The Christian religion."

"Of course."

Muscles flowed under his copper-colored skin as he drove the paddle deep and thrust the dugout forward. Kate found herself studying his broad hands and strong, finely shaped fingers. *Good hands*, she thought. *Honest hands.*

"I read much of your Jesus among the Spanish priests," he said. "All that I read was good."

"But?"

"But what I see of Christians here is not good."

"How can you say that?" she protested.

"Both the Spanish and the English settlers have wronged the Indian people. They come illegally to steal our land."

"No, that's not true. William has a royal grant from the king."

Hawk scoffed. "The king of England? How can he give away Powhatan land? And if your king has the right to do that, then why cannot the Emperor Powhatan give away English land?"

Kate pursed her lips. Hawk was irrational. He was spoiling her day with arguments that confused her. She knew he must be wrong, but she couldn't explain. "We've done good things as well," she said. "We've brought metal and the wheel and—"

"Smallpox, measles, cholera. Until the whites came, we had no diseases that spread from camp to camp, wiping out whole tribes."

"I don't know about that," she said.

"This man does. He has seen the pox marks on the faces of Indian children and heard the weeping of survivors."

"It's not fair to blame us. No one is sick at William's Hundred."

"Not yet. Wait until winter comes and your food supplies run low."

"We have food."

He scoffed. "Your salt pork is spoiled. Your flour is weeviled, and your dried beans and peas moldy. William has already traded for many bushels of Indian corn. The Powhatan will not give away their winter stores."

"But I heard Robert tell William that—"

"Believe nothing that Robert says."

"You expect me to believe you," she countered.

His intense gaze pierced her with cold fire. "Has Hawk ever lied to you?"

"No," she answered. "You haven't."

"You must trust me."

That was what her father had said when he'd arranged for her betrothal to Robert, and what Robert had said when he pressed his suit. Once, Kate had given her trust easily, but no more. Now she must rely on her own judgment.

Her future and her life depended on it.

"Damn the fish!" Robert shouted when Kate and Hawk returned to William's Hundred. "How dare you run off into the woods with him?" He whirled on Hawk. "And how dare you to take an English-woman—my betrothed—into danger?"

Hawk ignored Robert's tirade and continued tossing the catfish onto the riverbank near the fort gate.

Kate tugged off her muddy cap. "You've no right to speak to me so," she replied mildly. "I will never be your wife. Our agreement is over. I've been fishing with a friend, and I'm perfectly safe." She started to walk past Robert, but he grabbed her arm and spun her roughly around.

"Never walk away from me when I'm talking to you, woman!" Robert thundered as he slapped her hard across the face.

Kate cried out in surprise and threw her hand up to stop another blow. He hit her a second time so hard that she stumbled backward onto the ground. "You bastard!" she cried. "I won't—"

Two soldiers stood between Hawk's dugout and Robert. Fire Hawk dove between them, slammed an elbow into each man's middle, and was on Robert before they could stop him. Both Hawk and Robert hit the ground and rolled, fists flying.

"Stop it! Stop it!" Kate shouted.

Robert's helmeted head struck the ground, and his pistol spun away across the grass. Blood gushed from his nose and his split lip. Hawk's fists blurred as they battered Robert's face and upper body. Robert fought back with ever weakening blows.

"Stop!" Kate repeated. "Please stop!"

More people were running from the fort. Two settlers tried to drag Hawk off Robert, but the Cherokee's hands were around Robert's throat and he paid no heed to the men striking him from behind. Robert's eyes gaped; his mouth opened and shut as he gasped for air.

Kate threw herself over Hawk's back and

pounded him with both fists. "Enough! Let him go, Hawk," she begged. "Don't kill him. Don't . . ."

Slowly her pleas seemed to penetrate his veil of savage fury. He loosened his grip on Robert, who fell back limply. As soon as Hawk began to rise, someone pulled Kate away and shoved her sprawling on hands and knees.

Cursing soldiers swarmed over Hawk, striking and kicking him. He struggled wildly, throwing off one and then another with almost superhuman strength.

Robert's breathing came in loud rasps. "You red bastard," he slurred, when he could suck in enough air to speak. "Shoot him!"

A mercenary in a stained leather jerkin slashed at Hawk with a sword. Kate screamed, but at the last instant, the Cherokee thrust one of his assailants into the path of the blade. The weapon pierced the soldier's arm, and he howled in pain. Hawk seized the weapon and cut a swathe of cold steel around him.

Rough hands yanked at Kate. She bit a hairy arm and twisted away. She fell to her knees and her fingers closed on the butt of Robert's Scottish snaphance pistol.

"Shoot, damn you!" Robert ordered. "Shoot the bastard!"

Kate scrambled to her feet and held out the gun with shaking hands. The muzzle wavered dangerously and came to rest aimed at Robert's head. "Let Hawk go!" she cried. "Let him go, or so help me God, I'll send you to hell, Robert!"

His face grayed to the hue of old tallow. "You're mad."

Kate cocked the pistol.

The ominous click of metal silenced the soldiers' clamor. Horrified, they stared at Kate.

"Let him go free," she said.

For what seemed an eternity, Robert stared into Kate's eyes, and then he nodded. "Release the prisoner."

From the corner of her eye, Kate saw a flash of bronze skin. His moccasins made no sound as he dashed for the safety of the trees. Still, Kate stood, holding the heavy weapon at arm's length while seconds passed.

"All right," Robert said. "The performance is over. Put down the gun, Katherine. Your red lover is gone."

A single tear rolled down her cheek. She felt nothing. She was numb and terrified.

William's stern voice broke through her stupor. "Give me the pistol, girl." His hands closed over hers as he pointed the weapon toward the ground.

She made no attempt to keep it as he removed it from her grasp. Her fingers were damp with sweat, so cramped that she could barely uncurl them.

Vaguely, she heard Robert swearing. He bore down on her, a hamlike fist raised, but William stepped between them.

"She tried to kill me!" Robert croaked.

He smelled of vomit and something else . . . Kate's gaze trailed down his breeches to linger on the dark stain at his crotch. She tried to keep from snickering as she realized that the brave captain had wet himself like a raw recruit at his first battle.

Robert's face flushed an angry puce. "She's ruined."

"Slut," a hard-faced soldier muttered.

"What's amiss?" demanded a stout woman hurrying through the gates. Her eyes widened as she spied Kate.

"The Indian, John Fire Hawk," whispered her husband.

"He attacked the captain's lady?" the woman demanded.

The minister, wig askew and stockings sagging, pushed through the throng. "Rape? She's been raped?" he demanded.

"No," Kate whispered. "Hawk's done nothing to me!"

"The less you say, the better for you, miss," William advised. He motioned toward the gate. "Home with you. Now."

"Send out a party at once," Robert commanded. "Find him. Shoot him on sight."

"Rape," the miller echoed.

Kate shook her head. "You're wrong. It was Robert who hit—"

"Take her away," William ordered two male servants, who appeared at his side. "Take her to Lady Bennett." He lowered his voice and murmured to Kate, "This will go ill for you."

"Robert hit me," Kate insisted. "It was all Robert's fault."

"My brother has every right to chastise you," William said. "You are his responsibility. Your father placed you in his charge."

"I don't care," she protested. "I will not wed him. And I will not be governed by him."

"Then be governed by me." William nodded to his servants. "Take her back to my house and keep her there."

"We must make an example of John Fire Hawk." Robert wiped a smear of blood from his chin. "If he gets away with this, it will set an example. The savages will murder us all in our beds."

"Find him, then," William said. "Find him, try him, and hang him. He is your bond servant. The law is clear. Striking his master warrants death."

Fear twisted in the pit of Kate's stomach. "William, please, you must listen to me," she begged.

"Get her out of here," William snapped.

No one heeded Kate's pleas, and she found no compassion in the eyes of the settlers as the men escorted her back to her sister's house. Whispers and scornful glances followed her as the news of the confrontation raced ahead.

The women were the worse.

"Red man's whore," one matron called after her.

"What can you expect?" cried a sour-faced serving wench. "Have you seen her eyes? She's in league with the devil. Naught but a witch."

"She'll bring us ill." The minister's wife made the sign against Satan. "Mark me well. We'll rue the day she set foot in William's Hundred."

Kate was beyond caring what insults they hurled or even what punishment William ordered for her. Her thoughts and prayers were with Hawk; her only fears, for his safety.

Run, she cried silently. Run . . . and never come back. Never!

And then the thought came that if he did save himself, she would never see him again. That certainty did what no threat of force by Robert or William could, and she was unable to hold back a flood of tears.

Chapter 11

Never had Kate known a Christmas day so bleak and cheerless: no gifts were exchanged, no one danced on William's muddy green, and the holiday dinner consisted of thin turtle soup and corn mush.

She toyed with her pewter spoon and stared absently at the bowl of congealing soup. William, Alice, and Robert conversed loudly, but she ignored them as they ignored her. She might have been a ghost at the table for all they cared. Even Edwina treated her as if she had committed a terrible sin.

The weeks since Hawk had fled the settlement had been particularly unpleasant ones for Kate. Robert had declared that he would not have a red man's leavings, and William had refused to listen to her version of what had happened the day she'd gone fishing with Hawk.

Kate missed him terribly. Without Hawk, there was nothing to hold her here in America. If William would give his consent, she would sail for England in the spring on the first ship that anchored in Virginia.

"Are you going to finish that soup?" Alice asked.

Kate pushed the bowl toward her sister. She was

still hungry, but Edwina had scorched the soup and the taste turned Kate's stomach.

Lack of food had become a pressing problem in the settlement. As Hawk had warned, the Powhatan had turned sullen, refusing to trade for corn when the English stores ran low. Angered by the Indian's betrayal, William had ordered two neighboring Powhatan villages burned and their grain stocks confiscated, but even that corn was gone. One by one, the settlement's breeding animals had been slain and eaten.

The oxen still lived, but their ribs showed, and they seemed more like caricatures of cattle than the strong beasts that had been carried from England. Robert set a guard over them both day and night to keep hungry settlers from killing them for the meat.

The beautiful horses were already dead. One broke a leg and had to be put down; the other had wandered into the forest and been found three weeks ago full of Powhatan arrows.

William had gone into a rage over the loss of the second horse. In retaliation Robert had seized the first Indian trader who came to the gates of William's Hundred. The gray-haired savage had protested that he was innocent, that he was not even a Powhatan, but a Nanticoke from the north.

The Indian was now a prisoner in the stocks. William had ordered him hanged, but in honor of Christ's birthday, Robert had decided to execute him on the morrow.

"An Indian is an Indian," Robert declared, raising his cup for more wine. "They must know the penalty for theft and wanton destruction of our goods."

Kate glanced up and caught William's eye. "Can't you spare his life?" she asked. "Beat him, if you must, but surely Christian charity calls for mercy. We don't even know if he's the one who killed the horse. Would he be foolish enough to come to our settlement if he'd slain the animal?"

"He might," Alice said. "This is men's business, none of yours, sister. The penalty for stealing in England is death. Why shouldn't it be the same in Virginia?"

"But no one stole the horse," Kate argued.

Robert scowled at her. "We need no advice from an Indian lover."

"You are as soft-hearted as your sister," William put in. "But Lady Bennett is right. Leave protecting of our settlement to those with experience."

Kate's throat constricted. The Nanticoke had come to trade. She was certain he wasn't the guilty one.

Robert wiped out his soup bowl with the last of his bread. "We'll have your paramour yet," he said. "John will come sneaking back and we'll seize him."

"No, you won't," she replied. "He's gone south to his people, where you'll never find him."

"Who would know better than you what he will do," Robert answered.

Kate raised her chin, refusing to be shamed by his insinuations. "I've told you before. I've done nothing to be ashamed of—unlike others."

Alice frowned. "I truly wish I could hold you innocent, sister, but you have shamed us all with your behavior."

"Let us not argue on Christmas Day," William soothed. "Your life is not over, Katherine. If you will but confess, your sins and—"

"I'll not have her to wife," Robert stated flatly. "I'll have no woman who'd put a gun to my head."

"No, not you, but perhaps another." William

smiled at Kate. "I've had inquiries from a James Butler of Jamestown."

"Mister Butler, the butcher? He lost his wife, did he not?" Alice asked sweetly. "Recently."

"Yes, in childbed," William said. "Leaving him with four small boys."

"I'll not be married off to a butcher," Kate protested. "I'm going home to England."

"Naturally you have funds to pay your passage," William said before draining his wine goblet.

"No, I don't, but my father will . . ."

Alice laid a dainty hand on Kate's arm. "Be reasonable, sister. Father won't want to pay to have you back. Then, of course, there would be the matter of his debt to Sir William."

"I'll not be bullied into a loveless marriage," Kate cried, leaping to her feet. "You may keep me a prisoner here, but you'll not force me to wed—not Robert and certainly not this Jamestown butcher." Her pewter goblet overturned, and dark red wine spilled onto the table, staining the Irish linen.

"We'll have no more of your tantrums, girl," William snapped. "Apologize to my brother and your sister and finish your dinner."

"She can't allow us even a measure of peace on Christ's day," Alice fretted. "Really, Katherine, you are impossible."

"Then I will take my leave of you," Kate retorted. "A Merry Christmas to you all. I'm sure you'll enjoy yourselves more if I'm not at the table to plague you." Ignoring William's command to return to the table, she grabbed her cloak from a peg by the door and wrapped it around her.

"Where do you think you're going?" Robert asked.

"To the church to pray. It is our Lord's birthday, is it not?" she replied.

"It's bitter cold out," Alice said. "Why not wait until—"

"Let her go." William nodded. "It is a holy day, and she may find wisdom in God's house. Pray for humility, child, that you may be guided to do what is right."

"Foolishness to go out in such weather," Robert grumbled. He snapped his fingers, and Grace hurried to refill his goblet with wine. "We'll find her frozen to death in the morning."

William chuckled. "Not likely. 'Tis only a short distance to the church." He motioned to Edwina. "Light a lantern for Mistress Miles. No need to go in the dark, girl," he said to Kate. "Say your prayers. God knows, you are in need of them."

Wind whipped around the corner of the house and buffeted Kate as she stepped out into the narrow lane. Her candle flickered and threatened to go out, but she sheltered it from the gust with her cloak. As William had said, the church was only a short walk, and she needed no light to find her way.

Needles of sleet drove against her exposed face, and she began to shiver, as much in anger as in cold. Life in William's Hundred was becoming impossible. How would she ever stand living in Alice's house until springtime?

I should have gone with Hawk when he asked me, she thought. Some nights, she would lay awake and torture herself with questions of *what if*. Could she be any more miserable if she had followed him into the forest than she was now?

Such musing was folly. Choosing Hawk as a husband was beyond possibility. She was a white woman, a Christian. Her birth had prepared her for life as a country squire's lady. It was unthinkable that she should run away with a pagan Cherokee.

Hawk might possess the power to stir her blood, but marriage was not founded on lust. Marriage for a gentlewoman must be an arrangement with a respectable man of her own class who would provide well for her and her children.

She should have remained in England and accepted the next suitor her parents offered. Instead she'd come to the colonies seeking adventure and a new life. But all she'd found was hunger and an aching heart.

Kate rounded the last corner and trudged across the green. The deep slush wet her shoes and stockings. A mixture of snow and hail had been falling all day and showed no signs of letting up.

Kate's stomach rumbled, reminding her that she was still hungry. *I should have eaten the soup*, she thought. What they would eat on the morrow, she didn't know. They would have had no soup with their corn mush if a large sea turtle hadn't mysteriously appeared on the front step on Christmas Eve. *Why couldn't it have been a leg of lamb?* she thought wistfully. She hated turtle soup.

Where was Hawk tonight? Was he warm? Had he eaten? Had he found his way home to his beloved mountains?

The soldiers' patrols had found no trace of him, but Kate wondered if the game, the turtles, and the strings of fish that had been left at William's kitchen door recently could have been Hawk's work.

Robert had asked the Powhatan, Gar, if any of his people had seen John Fire Hawk, but Gar insisted they had not. That was before Gar stopped coming to William's Hundred to trade and before Robert had burned the Indian village. Now there was no communication with the natives, and Robert claimed that a third village, farther up the James River, had been abandoned.

Kate hoped that Hawk was with the Cherokee. She'd prayed he was. He deserved to be happy. He deserved to find a good woman of his own kind, marry, and father children.

She clenched her eyes against the driving sleet. "I miss him," she whispered into the storm. "He was my only friend in this wild land." Unconsciously, she reached up to make certain her ivory hairpin was still safely tucked in her hair. Her fingertips traced the carving of the bird and rubbed the length of the smooth surface.

As beautiful as the keepsake was, she couldn't wear it where it could be seen; she had to hide it under her cap to avoid questions she didn't care to answer. Still, knowing her gift from Hawk was there comforted her, and it made her smile whenever she touched it.

At last she reached the church. Tugging open the heavy board-and-batten door against the force of the wind was difficult, but as soon as she stepped inside, she sighed with relief. Unheated and dark, the sanctuary still seemed a place of refuge.

The beeswax candle in her lantern emitted a warm circle of light in the pitch blackness. Kate held her hands over the wood-framed glass to ease the numbness in her fingers. The wind whistled through the rough, cedar shingles, and the sleet patted at the window, but inside, the church was very quiet. As always, the peace eased the aching in Kate's heart.

Abruptly a gust of wind hit her as the door swung open. Kate's lantern flared up and went out. "Who's there?" she cried. "Who is it?"

"Do not be afraid. It's me, Fire Hawk."

"Hawk?" Excitement surged through her. "What are you doing here? If Robert finds you—"

"Shhh." He laughed softly. "Robert could not find his man-spear on a foggy morning."

Hawk's footsteps came close, but he did not touch her.

Suddenly the church, which had been so cold, felt warmer. Kate pushed the hood to her cape. Her pulse was racing and she felt as if she could not stand still. "Merry Christmas," she whispered.

"And a Merry Christmas to you." He chuckled again, and the sound of his laughter heated the pit of her belly. "I've brought you a present."

"But . . . but you're not even a Christian."

"So we have determined."

Kate heard the strike of flint against steel and a spark flickered. Seconds later her candle glowed once more, and she saw that Hawk's rugged features were nearly hidden in a ruff of gray wolf's fur.

"A bitter night," he said.

"Yes. I can't understand this Virginia of yours. A few weeks ago I was roasting in the sun; now the water in my wash pitcher freezes solid in the night."

Hawk shrugged off his wolfskin wrap. She noticed that he wore high moccasins and fringed leather leggings of white buckskin. His chest was covered with a pale hunting shirt that hung to midthigh.

"It's a good thing my candle blew out," she murmured. "I would have taken you for a ghost." Then she remembered that the final wall of the fort had been finished a week ago, and that the settlement was heavily guarded at night. "How did you get inside the palisade?"

"A ghost can move where he wishes," Hawk

answered lightly. "But this man cannot stay long." He pulled a beaverskin muff from his hunting bag. "For you."

Kate took the butter-soft fur and cried out with delight. "It's wonderful," she said, examining the stitches. "How did you—"

"A Powhatan woman sewed it for me. When I saw the pelt, I thought it was the color of your hair."

She thrust her cold hands inside the muff. "Thank you. But . . ." She realized that she had nothing for him. "Oh, Hawk, I wish I'd thought to make you something, but I didn't know I would see you. I thought you'd gone away."

He chuckled. "This man will not go without you. And to see you smile is gift enough for me."

She looked away shyly. "It's dangerous here. They'll hang you if they catch you. They intend to hang an Indian tomorrow. He came here to trade and—"

"The Nanticoke, Turtle Digging. He is a good man, a trader among the tribes. He harms no one."

"Robert thinks he killed one of our horses."

Hawk shook his head. "Not even Robert is so stupid. Powhatan shot that horse. Some of my cousin's young men wanted to show their anger over the English fever that has sickened many of the people since first snowfall."

"They'll hang the Nanticoke anyhow. I don't think Robert cares who is guilty. He just wants to kill an Indian."

Hawk moved so close that she caught a whiff of tobacco and something else . . .

Kate sniffed. "What is that smell?" Saliva flooded her mouth. "Not roast beef?"

"Not roast beef." He dug into his bag again and

unrolled corn husks to reveal bread and slices of dark meat. "Try it," he said.

"It's not turtle, is it?"

"You didn't like my turtle?" He affected a pained expression. "I worked hard to find it for your Christmas meal."

Kate bit into the rich, juicy meat. Even cold, it was delicious. "It's wonderful too," she mumbled between bites. "What is it?"

"Bear."

"You should have brought the whole thing. I'm so sick of mush, I could—"

"Corn mush will keep even an English lady alive through winter if you have nothing else."

"Mmm." Kate devoured the last crumb and licked her fingers. "Thank you, Hawk. It was a terrible Christmas, and you made it memorable."

She reached for his hand, and he pulled her into his arms. His mouth lingered on hers, and they shared a kiss so sweet that she never wanted it to end.

When she drew back to take a breath, he cupped her chin in his hand and kissed the tip of her nose. "You must go back," he said. "You must go before anyone comes to look for you."

"But . . ." She didn't want to leave him. Frantically she searched for something to keep him just a little longer. "How did you know I would be here? I didn't know I—"

"This man watches your house in the night. If you had not come to the church, I would have had to find a way to go to your sleeping place, and that would not be as easy as getting into William's Hundred."

"Never do that!" she warned. "It's much too dangerous. Please don't. I don't know what I'd do if anything happened to you, Hawk. I couldn't stand it."

"Go now, Kate. And do not worry about this man. I am the Chosen One. English walls cannot hold me, and English bullets will not pierce my skin."

"Liar," she whispered. "Be careful, Hawk. Please, be careful."

He handed her the lantern. "Be certain that you make noise when you enter William's house," he advised. "And be very sure that all know you are there."

"Why?"

"What you do not know, you cannot be blamed for."

It was a puzzling statement that would cause Kate to lie awake wondering most of the night. Hawk was up to some mischief, of that she was certain.

And, she sighed sleepily, she could not be sure if Hawk's beaverskin muff or the memory of his kiss would keep her the warmest in the lonely days to come.

The following morning Robert's troops searched in vain for their condemned prisoner. The guards swore that no human had passed through the gates, and the night watch insisted that they had kept careful vigilance at the walls. The Nanticoke Indian had vanished without a trace, a deed that prompted the minister to hold a special church service to preach on the powers of Satan. Kate secretly rejoiced.

That night the temperature dropped and it began to snow. It snowed for two days and two nights. The ground was frozen so hard that when a soldier died at his post, they had to wrap his body in a blanket and put it in a storage shed until a late January thaw.

February was bitter cold. Snow fell until it reached the bottom of the windows. Every able-bodied man in the settlement searched out fallen trees in the forest for firewood. Kate kept busy preparing kettles of soup and distributing them to the women and children who came begging for something to eat.

Late in the month, a stray spark from a fireplace started a blaze that claimed three houses and threatened the powder store. A woman, Cassie Baldwin, was badly burned. Her passing added to the number of grave mounds beside the church; fourteen had died since cold weather had set in.

Next, a coughing sickness and ague spread throughout William's Hundred, sapping the strength of those who had survived the cruel winter. Both William and Alice were stricken, and Kate spent five nights sitting up with first one and then the other. Edwina fell prey to the illness, and there was no one to care for them all but Kate. She washed their linens, spooned broth into their mouths, and tried to keep the fires going in their fireplaces.

Robert was spared the illness, but he was useless around the sick. He spent hours maintaining order in the settlement and seeing that the dead were buried. The living kept watch against the Indian attack that many felt was imminent.

Robert's sentries had observed Indian boats on the river. The savages kept their distance from the shore, but the guards were certain that the log dugouts contained only men and not families, which meant that they were hunting or war parties. Shortly after that, five English woodcutters surprised two Powhatan field-dressing a deer. The English fired on the Indians, wounding one, and brought home the venison to a meat-hungry settlement. After that, the women of William's Hundred never went to the river for water without an armed escort.

It was a Sabbath morning in late March when Kate left the house with two empty buckets. The sun was warm on her face, and temperatures had been pleasant for most of a week. On the green, eight women gathered around a huge copper kettle of water suspended over an open fire. They laughed and exchanged gossip as they waited their turn to wash linen that had not seen water or lye soap since autumn.

During the winter, a raccoon had somehow fallen into the good well that Hawk had shown her. The animal's body befouled the water. And since so many families had been sick with fever, Kate was afraid to use one of the other wells inside William's Hundred. She had begun to bring water from the river as the other women did.

She loosened the ties of her wool cloak and inhaled deeply of the fresh air. Spring warmth and the newly budding trees lightened her mood. At home, Alice and William were both well enough to be cantankerous, and Edwina had taken over the cooking again. It seemed to Kate as though most of the illness had passed; she'd heard of no new cases of the ague in days.

Thank the Lord for that, she thought. *At times, I wondered if any of us would live to see the end of winter.*

Ruefully, she glanced down at her red, cracked hands and hopelessly stained skirt. Her mother would be scandalized. Not only did Alice treat her like a servant, but Kate was afraid she was beginning to look like one.

When Kate reached the gate, the sentry whistled for the nearest soldier to go with her to the river. Kate nodded to the man but didn't speak. His name was Donald, and he was a rough mercenary with crude manners and dirty hands. William said that Donald was the one who'd shot the Indian during the woodcutting incident. Kate had no wish to know him better.

They walked together in silence down the rutted path. The soldier carried his musket in the crook of his arm and stared warily at the surrounding trees. He stopped at the top of the rise while she continued on down to the water's edge.

To her surprise, Kate spied a cluster of bright blue wildflowers, springing from the muddy soil. Scattered among the delicate trumpet-shaped blooms were soft pink buds and broad green leaves, so exquisite that a lump rose in her throat. "Oh," she murmured. "Oh, how beautiful."

"Yes," came a husky whisper. "You are beautiful to this man."

Kate's eyes widened in surprise, but she held back the cry of joy that would have brought the soldier running.

Hawk. Her lips formed his name, but she uttered no sound. He flashed a boyish grin at her, and her heart fluttered in her breast.

Instinctively she glanced at her guard, but his back was to her and he was looking in the opposite direction.

Hawk nodded, ever so slightly, and locked his dark gaze with hers. Her knees went weak and it was suddenly hard to draw breath. *Oh, Hawk!* she thought fiercely. *What is this magic you possess that makes me witless when I'm near you?*

"Thank you for the game and fish you brought all winter," she said. "We would have starved without it."

"A warrior who does not provide for his woman is no man." He leaned lazily against a huge oak tree, arms folded across his chest, bow clasped in one hand. The tree trunk blocked the soldier's view, but Kate could see Hawk perfectly.

"I'm not your woman," she whispered.

He continued to stare at her with the black gaze that made her want to throw herself into his arms.

She picked up the bucket and took an angled route down to the water a few feet off the path, close enough to the tree to touch him. "What are you doing here?" she whispered. "It isn't safe. You must go at once."

"No, it is not safe. You must come with me."

Kate looked back over her shoulder. The soldier had leaned his weapon against a sapling and seemed to be fumbling with something at his waist. A stream of yellow liquid arced into the air. Normally she would have been incensed by the man's coarse behavior, but now she was grateful that his attention was focused elsewhere.

"Robert has ordered any Indian to be shot on sight," Kate whispered. "You mustn't be here."

Hawk's features hardened. "I have been with the Powhatan. My cousin and I have made a truce between us. But I have learned an evil thing. Gar will come, offering food. He will ask for peace between Powhatan and English."

"But that's a good thing," she replied softly. It was hard to think with Hawk standing so close. She couldn't take her eyes off him. How well he looked, how strong and healthy. His features showed none of the haggard strain of a winter spent without enough to eat. She wanted to reach out and take his hand . . . to feel the warmth of his touch.

"How I've missed you," she said. "Are you really here?" Sweet sparks of excitement danced along her spine.

His sensual lips firmed; for an instant, emotion flickered behind his black, devil eyes. "Gar sets a trap," he replied. "His word is useless. When he comes into your village, he will fall upon your men and slay them. He has vowed to kill every English man, woman and child."

Kate shuddered. "I have to warn the settlement."

"I have tried to reason with my uncle, Iron Snake, but he will not listen. He is old and sick, and Gar leads most of the young men."

"Isn't there anything you can do to stop it?" she whispered.

"I cannot help your people," he answered, so softly that she had to strain to hear his faintly lilting words. "Gar is my cousin. I am linked to the Powhatan by my father's blood. I warn you because I must, but in doing this, I break a bond of trust with the Powhatan that can never be mended."

"You must tell William. He might believe you."

Hawk sniffed, and his eyes narrowed dangerously. "Come with me. I will make you my wife, and I will love you all the days of your life. I will love you as no man has loved you."

"No." She took a step backward. "No. I can't go with you. I can't save myself and leave my people to die. I can't betray them."

"Why not? I betray the Powhatan for you."

"It's not the same thing."

His eyes clouded with sorrow. "For now we must follow different trails, heart of my heart. Go then. Warn Robert and William. Tell them of Gar's perfidy. But then come back to me, and we will flee together."

She shook her head. "I can't do that, Hawk. I wish I had the courage, but I don't."

"So." He slung his bow over his shoulder and extended a bronzed hand.

Kate ached to go with him. God, how she wanted to leave Alice, William, Robert, and the lot of them to their fate! Instead she turned and fled back up the incline.

"What? What did you see?" the mercenary demanded. He leveled his wheel-lock musket and whirled around, his eyes seeking a target.

Kate grabbed the barrel of the weapon and tugged. "Come! Quick!" she repeated. "I must see Sir William! I must see him now!"

She didn't look back, but she had no fear that Donald would glimpse Hawk. She knew that he was already gone, as swift as the wind and as invisible. Instead she grabbed up the hem of her skirts with one hand and yanked on the gun with the other. "Hurry." As she sprinted toward the walls, Donald ran cursing after her.

The sentries heard her shouts, and armed men gathered at the gate. Robert seized her shoulders as she dashed inside. "What's wrong?" he demanded.

"The Powhatan mean to trick us," she cried. "You must tell your brother. They will come with food, asking for peace, but it's a trap. They plan to murder us all."

"Give me that musket," Robert ordered Donald. Scrambling up into the gate tower, he surveyed the surrounding forest and clearing. "Have you seen anything moving out there?" he asked the sentries.

"Nothing, sir," a pox-faced soldier replied. "Not even a swivin' rabbit."

Robert climbed back down the ladder and took Kate's arm. "Explain yourself, mistress."

Nervous settlers gathered around them. "What is it?" one man called. "It's her again."

"What's she done now?" another cried.

A red-faced soldier hurried toward them. "What's happening?"

"Where did you get this information?" Robert peered angrily into her face.

"John Fire Hawk. He was there, by the river," Kate answered. "He told me."

"You, you, and you!" Robert pointed at three soldiers. "Search the area. If anything moves, shoot it."

"No," Kate protested. "You don't understand. John came to warn us about the Powhatan trap."

Two sentries eased the gate open far enough for the three soldiers to squeeze out.

"You can't shoot him," Kate cried. "He's a friend. He warned us."

"He's proved that friendship to me," Robert snapped. "He's a traitor, a runaway bond servant, as much our enemy as any other hostile."

Robert's left hand tightened on Kate's right shoulder, and he pulled her close. "Are you speaking truth, Katherine? Or are these more of your addled fancies? Did you really see John? Speak to him?"

"I did." She gazed into Robert's blue eyes. "The Powhatan leader, the man called Gar," she continued. "He means to massacre us."

"I trust none of the red bastards." Robert released her with a small shove. "And you . . ."—he lowered his voice so that only she could hear—"the woman I was once pledged to. I trust you even less."

"Hawk isn't your enemy," she said. A dull numbness spread through her limbs as she realized Robert thought she was lying. "He risked his life to come here. How can you reward him by . . ."

Robert scoffed. "And you believe his word?"

"I do," she answered.

Robert turned his stern gaze on Donald. "Did you see the runaway, John Fire Hawk, at the river?"

Daniel spat on the ground near Kate's skirt. "Nah, saw nothin' but her."

"Hawk was there," Kate insisted.

"For your sake, he'd better have been." Robert turned to his next in command. "Send out a half-dozen more men. If he's near the settlement, I want him. Dead or alive, I care not."

"No!" Kate cried.

Robert whirled on her, his face twisted with fury. "You are besotted with him, Katherine. How can you expect me to believe that you've seen and spoken to an Indian that no one else saw?"

Kate's stomach clenched into knots. She felt as though she was going to be sick. She'd thrown away her chance at happiness—perhaps her chance at life—for nothing. "Are you such a fool, Robert, that you would ignore Hawk's warning and believe a man like Gar?"

"If John Fire Hawk has information of an intended attack, why doesn't he come and tell me man to man?" Robert demanded.

"Because you'd hang him."

"You're damn right I would."

"And what if he's telling the truth, Robert?" she said. "What if the Powhatan do mean to massacre us?"

"Then we'll have to kill them first, won't we."

She shook her head in utter frustration. "Is that your only answer? Killing Indians?"

"Kill them or drive them away, it matters not to me," he replied. "There is no place for savages in this colony."

"I agree," she said softly. "The difference between us is that I see you and those who think like you as the worst savages of all."

Deliberately, Kate turned her back on him and walked away, back toward Alice's house. She would try to convince William of the truth of what Hawk had said. But in her heart, she was certain she would have no more success with her brother-in-law than she had had with Robert.

"Next time," she murmured under her breath, "next time you ask me, Hawk, I'll go with you. I swear I will. And to hell with all of them."

Chapter 12

Two and a half weeks after Kate had seen Hawk by the river, she knelt in the newly turned earth behind William's house and patiently planted a handful of tiny turnip seeds. A few feet away, Edwina leaned on a hoe. The maid's face was ashen, tinged with green. Her bony chin stuck out; her eyes were sunken and hollow-looking. Kate suspected the wench was carrying a child, but when and where she'd found time to get herself in that condition was beyond reason.

The sun shone warm on Kate's face; the sky was a brilliant robin's-egg blue, without a single cloud. How good it felt to be outdoors without layer upon layer of scratchy wool clothing. Today Kate wore only her workaday gown, with a man's leather vest over her bodice and a patched apron. She'd removed her good shoes and replaced them with a pair of wooden clogs.

As she bent over the precious seeds, Kate heard her stomach growl. She was hungry, as usual. She was always hungry. And the full coming of spring had done little to help the settlement's lack of food.

True, the Powhatan had left gifts of venison and corn near the front gate over the past two weeks, and they had brought a deer again last night. William had mentioned it at breakfast. The household would be assured a portion, but even that good meat would have to be rationed. Edwina did the cooking, but Kate was in charge of the kitchen stores. Left to her own, Edwina was so stupid that she would have squandered what meager supplies they had.

The thought of meat on the table made Kate's mouth water. She was so sick of the monotonous diet of mush. Still, she was terrified of the Powhatan's offers of friendship. She remembered Hawk's chilling warning that Gar meant to destroy the settlement. After that afternoon, Robert had forbidden her to leave the walled enclosure. Now Edwina fetched the water from the river, and Kate felt more a prisoner than ever before.

There had been bloodshed that day, but it was none of Hawk's doing. One of Robert's soldiers had fired upon another of his companions by mistake. The injured man had recovered, but many people, including Robert and William, blamed Kate for the accident.

Kate wasn't certain any of them believed she had seen Hawk, but she was relieved to see that Robert ordered his guards to keep close watch on the walls by day and night. And he insisted that hunting parties venturing out for game go under heavy escort.

Kate hoped Robert would maintain that vigilance as time passed. Hawk had told her that Gar meant to attack the settlement by guile; he hadn't said when. She knew Hawk would never lie to her. How he'd discovered the plot to attack William's Hundred didn't matter. If Hawk said the Powhatans intended war, it was true.

Robert continued to treat Kate with utter contempt. He barely acknowledged her when he dined with his brother and Alice, and since she couldn't abide the sight of him, that was fine with her. The situation here in William's Hundred had become unbearable, and the sooner she got away from it, the better.

Her future seemed to Kate a total void. She had no idea where she would go or what she would do. If only Hawk would come again, she would find a way to be strong and take the love he offered.

Bittersweet pain knifed through her heart as she summoned the image of his craggy face in her mind. Time might ease her loss, but she doubted she could ever forget Hawk or the feel of his mouth against hers.

Edwina interrupted Kate's reverie by gagging and dashing toward the midden heap to drop onto her knees and vomit. "Oh, Edwina," Kate said, rising and going to her. "Are you with child?"

The maid emptied the contents of her stomach amid a rush of weeping. "I am," she blubbered. "I am."

Kate exhaled slowly and untied her apron. Using the cleaner underside of the cloth, she wiped Edwina's mouth and chin. "Blow your nose," she said, then looked away as the wench blew between two fingers and rubbed them on her own skirt.

"I'm undone," Edwina wailed. "Sir William will see me in the stocks for certain."

"Dry your eyes," Kate said. "It's a baby that's coming. Surely worse has happened to us this past winter. We will speak to William. If your babe's father is unwed . . ." She fixed the girl with a stern gaze. "Is he married?" The thought that it might be William himself crossed her mind. "It's not . . ."

"Cain't tell you." Edwina sniffed loudly. "You'll hate me, do I tell."

"I won't hate you," Kate answered, forcing herself to be patient. "Sleeping with a man out of wedlock is a sin, but if William can arrange a marriage for you—"

"Won't." The maid began to cry again.

"Shhh, shhh," Kate murmured as she brushed a stray lock of hair from Edwina's face. "I'll speak for you. I promise. Just tell me who has done this, and I'll—"

"He tole me not to tell," she protested amid sobs. "He said no one would believe me."

"I'll believe you," Kate assured her.

"Nah, nah." Edwina groaned. "He will not marry with the likes of me. 'Tis, 'tis . . ." Her lower lip quivered. "'Tis Master Robert himself."

"Robert?" Anger spread through Kate, making it hard to speak with a normal tone of voice. "Robert did this to you?"

Edwina nodded. "He's good to me mostly, miss. He give me a penny once, and a ribbon. Lady Bennett said I stole the ribbon, but I didn't."

"I know you're not a thief."

"It were a pretty ribbon, miss. I never seen such—"

"Enough about the ribbon. Are you sure this is Robert's child?"

She shrugged. "Peers so to me, Miss Kate. Master Robert's jealous-like."

"He is the only man you—"

"Oh, they's lots of fellas, and they do speak sweet to a wench when—"

"When they want what you're supposed to keep for your husband," Kate finished. She shook her head in disapproval. "You've been foolish, Edwina, and now you're paying the price."

"Lady Bennett will have the hide off my back, she will. She said if I got a bun in my oven, she'd sell me to the savages." Edwina sniffed and wiped her nose again with the back of her hand. "She said they'd roast me over an open fire and eat me."

"If you'd not been so foolish, you'd not be in this fix, but no one is going to sell you to the Indians. If Robert is the father, he's to blame, but there's more than enough blame to go around. I'll speak to Sir William about—"

"Please, miss, don't make no more trouble for me than I already got," Edwina begged.

"That would be hard to do, wouldn't it?" Kate gathered up the dirty apron and pressed it back into Edwina's hands. "Wash yourself and go up to the loft and lie down until you feel better. I'll do what I can for you."

"But Lady Bennett will—"

"Lady Bennett is visiting with the minister's wife. She won't know." Kate stripped off the man's vest as she entered the relative coolness of Alice's great room. There she made herself presentable, donned her own shoes and stockings, and put on a clean linen cap and a good wool cloak.

William had forbidden her to leave the house and yard, but she didn't care. Edwina had served them well for all her faults, and it wasn't fair that she should pay full price for whoring with Robert. Kate would have enjoyed the satisfaction of publicly accusing him of seducing Edwina, but she knew it would do the serving wench no good. Going to Robert would be useless; Kate must see William at once.

The unspoken rules about conceiving a bastard child were quite clear. Many girls quickened before they went to the altar. The public sin was bearing a babe without a legal father. If Kate told William the truth, she was certain he would quietly arrange a decent marriage for the wench and provide her with a suitable bridal portion. William was stodgy, full of self-importance, and none too bright, but he was usually fair with his servants.

"Good day, Mistress Miles," called Dame Miller.

Kate nodded at the sour-faced woman and kept walking. Dame Miller's favorite occupation seemed to be spreading harmful gossip through the settlement. It would take her no time at all to tell the other wives that Kate, the Indian's lover, was up to something. Ignoring the whispers and stares of her neighbors, Kate hurried across the green toward the armory where William was usually to be found.

Today she didn't have to go that far. She'd barely entered the cross street when she heard the tattoo of a military drum.

A platoon of soldiers rounded the corner, and she saw Robert, William, and a group of Powhatans directly behind them, walking toward her. Quickly she stepped into an alley between a house and a stable.

Kate recognized the Indian called Gar at the head of a delegation, surrounded by wary soldiers. Robert was talking excitedly; his attention seemed focused on a shiny object suspended around the Powhatan leader's neck.

As Kate watched, Gar stepped from the shadow of a house into the bright sunlight. A golden disk as broad as her hand and covered with some sort of strange symbols glittered in the center of his chest.

"Gold," she heard a passing settler murmur to

another man. "The Indian's brought a bag of gold nuggets the size of pigeons' eggs to trade for beads and mirrors."

A cape of turkey feathers was draped over Gar's broad shoulders and fell to his ankles. Strings of purple shell beads hung around his throat and dangled from his ears. His moon face creased with friendship, and he laughed heartily as he pumped Robert's hand up and down in an overly animated handshake.

A score of plump Powhatan women, garbed from neck to ankle in robes and carrying strings of fish and ducks, accompanied their men. Kate stared at the stoic women in surprise. Why had the Powhatans brought their wives and daughters? Since trouble had begun between the English and Indians, only males had appeared at William's Hundred.

The number of braves that accompanied Gar was small, no more than seven or eight. In contrast to the women, they wore only twists of buckskin around their loins. None of the Indian men carried any weapons at all. One played a bone flute; another shook a strange rattle made of wood, leather, and deer hooves. All of the Powhatan men seemed to be in a holiday mood. They smiled and waved at the bystanders, and some even spoke a few words of English greetings to the settlers and their families, who spilled out of the houses to stare at them.

"Good days!" called a hard-faced brave with a crest of hair along the crown of his shaved head.

His dark-skinned companion grinned and shouted. "Friends!" The word came out sounding like *wrens* to Kate.

"English friend," repeated another man, a small, wiry brave with half of his face painted white.

Gar stopped and raised his hand. The Indian

squaws crowded close to their men. One girl's almond-shaped eyes darted nervously from side to side.

A strange prickling ran down Kate's spine. Something was wrong. She could almost smell danger in the air. "Robert!" she called out. "Robert, beware of—"

The Indian with the half white face uttered a war whoop and lunged for the nearest English soldier. The Powhatan women flung aside their robes to reveal hatchets, war clubs, and knives strapped between their naked, copper-colored breasts. One woman leaped forward and drove the point of a blade into Donald's belly. The mercenary gasped, staggered sideways, and fell to his knees, groaning.

A soldier fired his musket point-blank at the Indians. One squaw fell, but a Powhatan brave wrenched the gun from the guard's hands and bashed him over the head with the butt. The Indian women passed their deadly weapons to their men and darted back toward the gate.

Shrieks of pain echoed across the green. The soldiers greatly outnumbered the Indians, but the firearms were almost useless in hand-to-hand fighting. Gar had seized a terrible war club of bone and polished wood. He whirled it around his head, cutting down English soldiers. They fell like stalks of ripe corn before a reaper.

English women and children panicked and ran screaming. Some of their men entered the fray; others fled the terrible scene of carnage. Kate stood frozen, unable to move, staring in disbelief as a soldier stumbled toward her with a hatchet sticking out of his back.

Puffs of white smoke from the muskets rose in the air. Blood spilled into the mud and stained the new grass scarlet. Kate couldn't take her eyes off the soldier's face. He fell almost at her feet. His hands scrabbled in the dirt, and his fingers tightened on her ankle. "Help me," he gasped. "Help me."

You're beyond mortal help, she wanted to cry.

Instead, she threw herself over his prone body to protect him from the Powhatan brave who plunged after him. For a heartbeat, Kate gazed into the Indian's crazed face as he lifted his war club to finish off the Englishman.

It's Gar, she thought. The Powhatan chief was going to murder her. She tried to think of a prayer for impending death, but her mind went blank.

The awful weapon hung in the air for what seemed an eternity; then the Powhatan gave a howl of laughter and stayed the blow. With one fist, he knocked her aside. Straddling the soldier, he brought the war club down.

Kate heard the dull crunch of wood on bone as she lay sprawled in the mud. Without looking back, she scrambled to her feet. She was alive, shaken by Gar's blow, but not seriously hurt. She didn't know why Gar hadn't killed her; she did know that if she didn't do something fast, she'd be as dead as the soldier.

War whoops filled the air as more and more Indian warriors crowded the green and chased the fleeing English. Robert's soldiers were fighting gallantly, but now it was the English who were outnumbered. Vaguely, Kate realized that the squaws must have overcome the guards and opened the gates to the settlement.

"This way!" a settler shouted to Kate. "The armory. We can hold them off there."

But when she turned in that direction, her path was cut off by two screaming Powhatan braves. A shot rang out; one man tumbled backward, but the second kept running. Then from behind her, a mercenary appeared, and Englishman and Indian clashed in a violent struggle.

Clouds of smoke and bits of burning thatch drifted down. Something stung Kate's face, and it was suddenly hard to breathe.

She choked and rubbed her eyes. She was past being frightened. Instead she watched the mayhem around her with a strange detachment, as though it were a bad dream.

A hard hand closed on her shoulder and spun her around. Instinctively she threw up an arm to protect her head and screamed.

"Katherine! It's William!"

She blinked, hardly recognizing her brother-in-law with his face streaked with gunpowder and blood, his wig gone, and his clothing torn and filthy. "William?"

He shook her. "What's wrong with you?" he shouted. "Are you injured?"

"No. No," she stammered.

"Run! To the armory! Run for your life!" He reloaded his pistol and fired at an attacking Indian. The Powhatan brave clutched his midsection and staggered away as William methodically poured shot and powder into his weapon. "Go!" he ordered her. "Your sister is already there! I can't protect you. Save yourself!"

An Indian brave charged them from the left. William sidestepped his attacker and drove a fist into the side of the man's head. Another Powhatan challenged William with a knife. Across the churned grass and mud, a squaw thrust a burning brand into the church doorway.

"Fire!" an English voice croaked. "They're burning the houses!"

Kate waited to see no more. It would be impossible to cross the green without being killed, but if she could come around from the back . . . She began to run down the alley as smoke from torched roofs enveloped her.

A stout settler crashed into her, and she fell headlong into the mud. He cursed her, and she recognized the smoke-darkened face of Dame Miller's husband.

"Out of my way!" he cried, and bolted away.

The breeze whipped flames from the window of a dwelling to her right. A dog whined and ran past her, away from the fire. Her head reeled, and for an instant she wasn't sure where she was. She turned to look the way she'd come, and the figure of a Powhatan brave loomed up through the smoke.

"*Hi-yaaee!*" He hurled himself toward her, tomahawk in hand.

She took a breath and darted toward the burning building. Abruptly she collided with an immovable wall of solid flesh. She couldn't see his face, but knew he was an Indian. Terrified, she lashed out with her fists, beating at a massive chest with all her strength.

He shoved her aside. Kate rolled onto her back and watched the Powhatan's tomahawk descend toward her head. "Sweet Jesus," she gasped as she closed her eyes and prepared for death.

Instead she heard a sickening thud and the sound of a falling weight. Something soft fell across her legs, but the expected blow didn't come.

"Kate. Kate!"

Other words followed, spoken in a language she

couldn't understand. But she didn't need translation. "Hawk," she gasped. "Hawk?"

Strong arms swept her up and cradled her against
him. Coughing and struggling for air, she ground
her face against his bare chest, desperately seeking
shelter in his embrace.

"Shh, shh, you are safe now," he promised. "This
man will keep you safe."

Kate opened her eyes. The Powhatan warrior lay
sprawled on the ground in a river of blood. Hawk
stepped over his body. Carrying Kate through the
smoke, he strode forward.

"You killed him," Kate whispered hoarsely.

Hawk kept walking. "He tried to hurt you," he
answered grimly.

"Hawk, Hawk." She ran her finger over his neck
and cheek, reassuring herself that he was really
here. "I thought I'd never see you again."

"This man will always be here for you."

The fear drained away, and she was filled with
vibrant joy. She didn't question how or why Hawk
had found her. They were together and that was all
that mattered. His embrace gave her strength to face
her last minutes alive.

"I love you," she whispered to him. "I love you."
She could hear the steady beat of his heart, and it
seemed to her the most precious gift anyone had
ever given her.

Then a terrible heat flashed over her exposed skin,
and she closed her eyes and waited for the end.

Hawk glanced over his shoulder at the raging fire
behind them and the flames of a collapsed wall
ahead of him. Beyond the fallen timbers lay the
open green—and air that wasn't heavy with the
deadly smoke.

"I love you," he told Kate softly in Cherokee. His
heart was racing. If he failed, he would lose not only

his life but that of the woman in his arms. She trusted him, and he must be strong for her.

"Hold your breath," he ordered. And for the space of a heartbeat, he prayed that the Creator would grant him courage.

Long ago the Cherokee holy man, Painted Stick, had told Hawk a story about a shaman who could walk across a bed of red-hot coals without being burned. When Hawk had asked the elder how such a thing was possible, Painted Stick had laughed and said, "The trick is to think of crossing a frozen lake."

"Be right, old man," Hawk muttered as he summoned up an image of ice and snow in his mind. "Be right, or your chosen one will be as much a legend as that ancient shaman."

Steeling himself against the pain, Hawk leaped forward into the heart of the fiery logs that blocked the alley. Without hesitation, he plunged through the inferno. Waves of heat whirled around him, but he felt no pain.

He was thirty paces into the clearing when he stopped to crush the embers that had lodged in Kate's hair.

Shifting her weight to one shoulder, he brushed away the fiery cinders that clung to his own hair and burned into his shoulder, and sucked in the air his lungs cried out for.

Kate tensed in his arms, but did not open her eyes. He knew she was still conscious, trapped in a trance of fear, stunned by the sights and sounds she had endured.

For himself, he had experienced such violence before, both as a boy and again in Spain where he'd witnessed a frenzied mob ravaging a Jewish quarter. Once seen, such sights were not forgotten. They branded a man's soul, a woman's as well, he supposed. Some witnesses withered under the strain, retreating to places in their minds where suffering no longer mattered. Others had stronger spirits, and he hoped that Kate's was one of them.

Powhatan screams of triumph sounded shrill in his ears. A brave lunged at him brandishing a tomahawk. The blade was red with blood; bits of yellow hair clung to it. Hawk stared into his eyes. "I am not your enemy," he said in Algonquian, the Powhatan tongue. "You know me, Seven Tails. I am Fire Hawk Who Hunts At Dawn, grandson to the great Powhatan."

The warrior hesitated, and an expression of doubt clouded his features. "If you are one of us, why aren't you killing Englishmen?"

"This is not my fight, brother," Hawk replied softly.

"If it is not your fight, then hand over the woman," another voice called. Hawk's cousin Gar emerged from the smoke. "You cannot have it both ways. Either you claim our blood or you do not. Are you a coward that you cannot swing a battle-ax?"

Hawk ignored the insult to his honor. Gar knew better, but the killing madness churned in his blood, and he was not thinking reasonably. "I will kill no Englishmen who doesn't try to kill me."

Gar scowled. "Give me your prisoner. A man who will not fight deserves no reward from the bloodletting."

"She is mine," Hawk answered.

"Reason enough that I should have her," Gar flung back.

Hawk and his cousin were close enough to touch. He could see the sweat streaming down Gar's face, smell the blood on Gar's skin and clothing, taste the acrid bite of Gar's hatred.

The Powhatan lifted his war club. "I will have her, as I have had many things of yours, Chosen of the Cherokee." He laughed. "I will slay you and take her. She will groan and cry out with joy beneath my man's weapon this night."

Kate stirred in Hawk's arms. "Save yourself," she whispered hoarsely. "Put me down. I can stand." She thrust her hands against his chest. "Put me down."

He held her tightly against his body. How warm she was in his arms. How precious she seemed to him . . . how full of life in the midst of so much destruction. He looked into his cousin's face. "Stand aside, Gar."

"You are as witless as ever you were as a child," Gar muttered, switching to English.

"We are children no longer, cousin," Hawk warned.

Gar scoffed. "Think you I cannot order my men to seize you and this woman? I will have you stretched over a fire—the skin peeled from your body. I will have your stones cut away and fed to the camp dogs while your English whore watches."

Kate stiffened.

"*Whore* is not a Powhatan term, cousin," Hawk said so softly that even the warrior Seven Tails could not hear. "Have you taken the ways of the whites, that you lose respect for women? You have told me of the evils of the English. Do you take these evils for your own?"

"Let me go," Kate said. "I won't let you die for me, Hawk. They'll let you go if you give me up."

"I want no war between us, cousin," Hawk insisted. "There are other Englishwomen. Take your pick of them. This one is mine, and you must step over my body to have her."

"You are not Powhatan," Gar answered. "I owe you nothing."

Hawk saw a flicker of movement reflected in Gar's jet eyes, just as his cousin gave the order. "Kill him! Kill them both!"

Seven Tail's let out a whoop and swung his war club over his head.

Hawk threw Kate to the ground, snatched his knife from its sheath, and drove it into Seven Tails's middle. As he fell, Hawk snatched his war club and stopped Gar's charge with a blow to the ribs. Hawk heard the snap of bone, and his cousin groaned and sagged. Hawk grabbed him and swung him around, using Gar's body as a human shield against the attack of another Powhatan brave wielding a tomahawk.

The warrior's steel blade sliced through Gar's left biceps. Hawk locked an arm around his cousin's neck and bent his head at a dangerous angle. With his other hand, Hawk twisted Gar's left arm behind his back.

"To me!" Hawk shouted to Kate. She did not fail him. Scrambling up out of the mud, she snatched Gar's scalping knife from the sheath at his waist and held it menacingly in front of her as she took a position behind Hawk, guarding his back.

"I'll take the knife," he said. "Stay close." When she did as he bid her, he laid the blade along his cousin's throat. "Give the order that we may leave unharmed," Hawk murmured into Gar's ear.

Stunned and bleeding, Gar tensed against the knife. A trickle of new blood ran down his chest as the burnished steel cut through skin and flesh.

"Careful," Hawk warned. "You will not live to be *werowance* if you do not heed me, cousin."

"Kill me and my men will tear you apart," Gar hissed.

"But you won't be here to enjoy it, will you?" Hawk replied.

"We'll hunt you down. You'll never be safe!"

"You will give your word, as a leader of men, that there will be no vengeance against us. Speak, Gar, or you will join your ancestors in the bone temples sooner than you expected."

Warriors gathered around them, shouting angrily and waving their weapons. Hawk made out faces from his childhood, streaked with blood and smoke and twisted with savagery. He was ashamed and saddened for them. Gar had led them to this victory over the English, and it would be the beginning of the end for the Powhatan nation.

"Do you want him?" Hawk called out. "Have you not killed enough English today that your thirst for blood is eased? Let us pass, and I will not kill him." Hawk applied greater pressure to the knife and more blood flowed in a sheet down Gar's chest.

"Let him go," Gar croaked.

"Tell them that we are not to be followed," Hawk murmured into Gar's ear. "Tell them that I have your word as a war leader that there will be peace between us."

Gar did as he was told. Cries of protest rose from the other Powhatan. Hawk moved backward, a few steps at a time, toward the gate and the forest, Kate remaining close by his side.

"Stay here," Hawk commanded. "I will release Gar at the river."

"How do we know you tell the truth?" a warrior called Sturgeon demanded. "I say kill them."

"Does Sturgeon speak for your leader?" Hawk

shouted. "Does he want to see Gar die so that he can take his place?" He nudged Gar with his knee. "It seems that Sturgeon wishes you dead, cousin."

"Stay back," Gar said. "Fire Hawk's word is good. If he says he will let me go at the river, I believe him."

"You have heard your war chief," Hawk shouted. "You have done enough killing for one day."

Cautiously, Hawk, Kate, and Gar moved through the ruined streets and out the gate. Several hundred feet from the walled enclosure, Hawk pushed Gar down, grabbed Kate's hand, and ran toward the dugout he'd left hidden at the landing.

Gar screamed threats after them, but Hawk didn't look back. Half sliding, he dragged Kate to the water's edge and swept aside the leaf covering to reveal a small log boat. "Get in," he said.

She glanced back toward the burning settlement. "The others," she murmured. ". . . My sister . . . the children. Couldn't we take some of the children?"

He picked her up and dropped her into the dugout. From another pile of leaves he recovered a slender paddle, his hatchet, knife, hunting bag, and bow and arrows. Carrying them, he waded out into the river, pushing the boat into deeper water before getting in himself.

"What will happen to the children?" Kate asked.

"The Powhatan do not kill women and children," he said, keeping his eyes on the gate. He began to paddle as fast as he could, bending his back to the task, using all his strength to drive the dugout swiftly into the current.

"Where are we going?" she asked him.

"I will take you where it is safe."

"But where? Where is that?" Her pale face was

drawn and streaked with ashes. Her hair hung in wild disarray. "Jamestown?"

He did not answer. Behind them, screaming Powhatan warriors poured from the gate. Arrows flew through the air and splashed around them.

"Get down," he warned. "Make yourself as small a target as possible." He could not bear to lose her now. "Trust me," he said. "The Powhatan shall not have you. Now you are mine."

"Am I, truly?" She stared at him.

"I have taken you in war. From this day forth, you belong to me."

"You risked your life for me, but that—"

"It means you are mine," he repeated firmly.

"Your captive? Then you are no better than Gar."

He leaned low to avoid a Powhatan arrow that whizzed over the dugout. "Captive or wife," he answered. "It matters not to me which you choose. I will never let you go. I swear it on my honor. You are no longer English, you are Cherokee—and so you will remain, so long as you draw breath."

Then he shut his ears against her token protests and let joy fill his heart. Kate was his, and her eyes told him that it would be an easy task to win her heart. All he had to do was keep her safe until the Powhatan stopped looking for them, lead her home through hundreds of miles of enemy territory, and then convince his mother and the council members that he should keep her.

Chapter 13

When Kate opened her eyes, it was dark. For a moment, she was disoriented, unsure where she was. There was no sound but a faint swish of water and the far-off cry of an owl.

"You wake."

Hawk's voice. Suddenly everything came rushing back. She was in a dugout with him, and the small, splashing rhythm was the rise and fall of Hawk's paddle. She shivered. The sun had been bright when she'd drifted off, but now a chill settled over her bare arms and body. She ached and burned in so many places that she couldn't count them.

Kate couldn't guess how long she'd been asleep, and she didn't know if they were still in danger from the Powhatan war party. "Hawk." She spoke his name tentatively. They had argued before she'd stopped answering him. She'd not meant to sleep, but exhaustion and strain had taken their toll. Now they were alone, God knew where, and Hawk was all she had.

"Keep your words soft," he warned. "My Powhatan brothers hear well across water."

"Do you think they're all dead at William's Hundred?" she asked. She felt strangely hollow inside, detached, but she was glad to be alive and away from the horrors of the Indian attack.

The faces of Edwina, Alice, William, and Robert formed in her mind. She remembered William fighting fiercely. Sadness overwhelmed her as she pictured the smallest Dobson boy, a toddler, just learning to walk, and Faith Mathews, the young girl with the curly blond hair who sang so sweetly in church. She remembered them all, and wondered with a shudder which of them had fallen to Gar's bloody tomahawk.

She tried not to think of the screams . . . of the flames whipping through the houses where families crouched in terror, and she willed herself to push away the image of the wounded soldier she'd tried to protect.

"You slept a long time," Hawk said.

She rubbed the crick in her neck and concentrated on this moment. "Do you think anyone survived?"

"Many of the English men may be dead, if they fought and did not run."

"But you said the Powhatan wouldn't murder the children," she reminded him. "You told me that." Desperately she clung to some order, some reason in this madness.

He made a small sound that could have been compassion. "The Powhatan see no honor in taking the life of a child. Children are precious regardless of the color of their skin. They will be adopted into the tribe."

"And the women?"

"Most will be taken prisoner for slaves or wives."

She tried to picture Alice cleaning fish in an Indian hut, but the idea was too preposterous. She had never liked Alice, but she'd always loved her.

They were sisters, despite Alice's shortcomings, bound forever by blood and family loyalty.

"You must take me to Jamestown. If the Powhatan attacked William's Hundred, they may raid other settlements. We must warn—"

"I betrayed my father's people to warn yours. This man will do no more for the English." He kept his voice low as he had ordered her, but softness could not hide his anger.

"But you must!" she insisted. "Gar could use the same trick to get inside Jamestown."

"No. I leave the English to reap what they have sown."

"You would let them all die?"

"I would keep you safe."

She swallowed. "I never thought I was a coward," she admitted. "But I was terrified, I ran. Why weren't you afraid?"

He chuckled. "A man who tells you he does not fear death is a fool or a liar."

"But you came for me," she said. "You risked your life for mine. I've no right to ask you to risk it again for the people at Jamestown."

"I am the Chosen of the Cherokee nation," he replied softly. "If I meet death in fulfilling my mission, there will be no dishonor in it. But if I throw my life away, my people may die with me. Not just a few families or a clan, but our entire nation."

"You do think highly of yourself, Fire Hawk."

Again came the deep chuckle, so faint that it might have been a rustle of tree branches along the riverbank. "I do," he agreed. "In that, you speak truth, woman. But I have good reason. Have you ever seen a man to match me?"

"Why, you arrogant . . ." she began, then broke off when she realized he was teasing her. "How can you jest when such terrible things are happening around us?"

"Not so terrible," he corrected her. "The Powhatan are far behind us. We are alive and whole, and I have in my mind a place of safety to take you."

"I shouldn't want to go to a place of safety. I should insist you take me to the nearest English settlement. I do insist."

"You think I will let you get away from me so easily?"

She shook her head. "I don't want to leave you, Hawk, not now anyway. But my conscience tells me that I must try to help the English settlers. If any die when I could have helped them, I will—"

He made a quick motion with his hand. "I told you Gar would deceive Robert and attack William's Hundred, did I not?"

"Yes, you did, but—"

"And you told your English men?"

"Yes. I did. You knew I would."

He shrugged. "What good did it do? Stupid men will not listen."

"We can try."

"I should have stolen you away from William's Hundred. Instead I told you of Gar's plans. I wounded my own spirit and ignored common sense. I will not do so again."

"Stubborn. You're stubborn." She knew it was useless to argue with him now. She would wait and try to reason with him at a better time. "Where are you taking me?"

"There is an island this man remembers from his childhood, an island of wild horses. The Powhatan told me that those who lived there died of the white man's pox ten winters ago. They believe the island is haunted by the ghosts of the dead."

"And if I refuse to go to your island?"

"It is not your choice. You belong to me now. I do not fear the dead or the English pox. The Powhatan will search for us everywhere, but we will be as invisible as ghosts. And when Gar's people have forgotten us, we will cross their lands to the mountains of the Cherokee, you and I together."

"I've not said I'll be with you forever, Hawk, only for a while. I'm not ready to decide forever."

"You have no choice in the matter," he answered. "As I told you, you are in my world now. I, Fire Hawk Who Hunts At Dawn, have decided. So." His tone took on an edge of polished steel. "We will speak of this no more."

Still physically and emotionally exhausted, Kate fell asleep and drifted off once more.

In her dream, she woke to find herself lying on a beach. It was night, and a full moon cast a golden glow upon sand and water. She rose to her feet and looked around. She could see no sign of Hawk.

"Where are you?" she cried into the darkness. She could not remember how she had come here or why. She knew only that she could not bear to be alone.

Her hair hung loose to her waist, and she wore nothing but her shift. "Hawk!" she called. Her voice echoed over the water. "Hawk . . . Hawk . . ."

Then a shape appeared in the water. As she watched, Hawk's head and broad shoulders broke the surface. He stood and beckoned to her.

The moonlight gleamed on his wet skin. Droplets ran down his bare throat and over his naked chest and belly. She could not take her eyes off him.

"*Come,*" *he said.*

She stepped into the waves. The surf swirled around her knees and rushed up to her thighs. Heat throbbed in the pit of her stomach. Her breasts tingled; the soft linen of her only garment seemed too harsh for her tender nipples.

"*Kate.*"

The sound of her name on his lips sent ripples of excitement through her veins. She moistened her dry lips with her tongue.

"*You knew this would happen,*" *he said softly. First he took a step toward her, then she took a step toward him.*

Cold waves lapped over her hips. The rise and fall of the sea thundered in her ears. And then Hawk laid an open palm against her throat. She moaned as his fingers trailed down to caress her breast through the thin barrier of linen. "*Hawk,*" *she whispered. Twining her hands in his long, dark hair, she pulled his head down until their lips met.*

His mouth was warm against hers.

"*Come with me and be my love,*" *he said.*

Laughing, he drew her down into the water. She thought the waves would be cold. Instead the ocean water was warm . . . so warm . . .

"Kate?"

She clung to him, unwilling to let go of the magic.

"Kate?"

Her lashes fluttered against her cheeks. Hawk was no longer in her arms. She reached out to catch him and draw him back, but her fingers touched the hard wooden side of the dugout.

"You're dreaming," Hawk said.

She sighed.

"Wake up."

Shimmering waves of sunlight bouncing off the

water warmed Kate's cheeks. Slowly she shook off the stupor of night and looked around her. She was still in the boat, still fully clothed.

"You cried out in your sleep," Hawk said, resting his paddle against the side of the dugout. "Are you ill?"

"No." Disoriented, she rubbed her eyes. When she looked again, she saw that there was no land in sight. "Are we at sea?" she cried.

"Yes," he answered.

The shocking sensuality of her dream flooded her mind, and she turned her head so that he could not see her face. A dream. She had dreamed things such as no innocent maiden should imagine.

"You are all right?" Hawk asked.

"Yes, I'm fine," she lied. Her breasts still felt too tight against her stays. Her body still throbbed with an ache she didn't know how to ease.

"Good." He began to paddle again, as steadily as he had since they'd fled the muddy banks of William's Hundred.

Did he never tire? Images of her dream floated behind her eyelids. It had seemed so real. She glanced back at Hawk, hoping he could not read her mind and know what lewd thoughts possessed her. . . . Hoping he would not guess that her thighs still bore the dampness of her desire.

Slowly her dream faded and her present discomfort pushed all other thoughts from her head.

She was cold and damp, and she couldn't remember when she'd eaten last. Water pooled in the bottom of the dugout and soaked her garments. Her legs were cramped and stiff, and her head ached.

"Good morning," Hawk said.

"I can't see the shore."

Hawk lifted the paddle and pointed to her left.

"There. If you listen close, you can hear the breakers."

"I'm hungry and . . ." She felt her neck and cheeks flush. "I have to . . ." Her bladder reminded her of just how long she had crouched in this frail little boat. "Please, Hawk . . ."

"When the sun burns away the mist, I will watch for cook fires. If there are none, we will land. There may be Powhatan camped here. I can't take the chance of being sighted."

She nodded. "I understand." She could endure a little discomfort if it meant their safety. For now she would be grateful that they were alive and able to feel the heat of the sun on their faces.

Seabirds swirled around them in endless flocks. Shrieking and crying plaintively, they dove to the surface of the sea, then wheeled upward, fish clutched in their beaks. The air smelled of salt and seaweed and land. She couldn't see the shore yet, but she could imagine it . . . glistening white beach and towering forests.

Yet when the tree line first appeared, the terrain was not what she'd expected. They were much closer than she'd guessed; she could make out the shapes of shrubs and wind-scoured pines. The meandering ribbon of sand binding earth and sea was pristine white, but narrower than she'd thought it would be, and the breakers were scarcely waist high.

Once Hawk satisfied himself that there were no villages along this stretch of beach, he turned the bow of the dugout toward shore. When the water grew shallow, he leaped out and pulled the boat onto solid ground. Kate took his extended hand and climbed out to stand on shaky legs.

There were even more birds on shore than on the water. Tiny brown and white sandpipers, yellow-legged plovers, and dozens of colorful russet, black, and white birds with bright orange legs, which Kate had never seen before, fluttered and pecked, and ran up and down the beach. Gulls dove overhead, and sand crabs scampered along the water's edge. All of the birds and crabs seemed completely oblivious to their human visitors.

"They aren't afraid of us," Kate observed.

"No." Hawk motioned to her to remain where she was. "Wait for me," he ordered. He slipped his quiver of arrows over his shoulder, picked up his bow, and moved into the tangled morass of scrub pine and beach plums.

Kate looked longingly at the sea. She'd not realized how thirsty she was, but even she knew that drinking salt water could bring death. Minutes passed. Her need to relieve herself grew steadily more urgent. Finally she dashed for the shelter of the nearest tree and pushed her way under the low-hanging boughs.

When Hawk returned nearly an hour later, Kate was sitting on the sand beside the dugout. "We are alone here," he pronounced. "I found fresh water, but first we must hide the dugout. Up the beach is a small inlet. We'll leave the boat there."

"You didn't bring any of that water back, did you?" she asked.

He smiled. "Soon, Kate."

"Soon," she grumbled, taking hold of the side of the dugout and helping him push it back into the surf.

As he'd promised, the narrow gut leading to a saltwater pond was close. Hawk paddled, then poled the boat into a covering of marsh grass. To reach solid land, Kate had to wade knee-deep through the cold water and mud, and thread her way through a tangle of reeds.

Marsh gave way to sandy soil and pines. Hawk quickly found a game trail and led her along the twisting path to a windfall, where storms had uprooted large trees. "We are nearly there," he said.

Kate didn't answer. A blister on her heel burned like fire, her skirts were wet to her waist, and she felt as though she'd been washed through a mill race. Every inch of her body hurt, and she knew she must be near death from thirst and starvation. Still she didn't complain; she wouldn't have him think she was a milk sop. Gritting her teeth, she forced herself to put one foot in front of the other and follow him.

Then a whiff of something wonderful caught her attention. She stopped and sniffed the air. Yes, she was positive. Her mouth moistened with anticipation. "Food?" she asked in disbelief. "Is that chicken I smell cooking? You wonderful, wonderful man!"

Hawk raised a branch of holly, and Kate ducked under it. Ahead she saw a small clearing with a pool and a campfire. A spit over the fire held what could only be pigeons or small fowl. Kate's stomach rumbled noisily, but as hungry as she was, she needed water more. "Can I drink from this?"

"The water is good," he replied.

She ran to the edge of the mossy-edged pool and dropped to her knees, scooping up the water with her hands. Most ran back through her fingers, but enough was left to wet her lips. The liquid was clear and cold, the sweetest water she'd ever tasted. She savored every drop, then dipped her hands to her elbows, letting the fresh water wash away the salt and soothe her burned skin.

Hawk squatted beside her. He rinsed his hands

and made a cup with his clasped palms for her to drink from. "Sip slowly," he said.

"It seems you're always finding me water," she said, remembering the well in William's Hundred.

"You are water to my lips," he said.

Once again, her lips brushed his fingers, and the same delicious sensation raced through her. She raised her head and looked full into his eyes. For a long second, neither stirred, and then she drew in a jagged breath. "I think I love you," she murmured. "I know I do." She clenched her fingers into fists to stop their trembling, but nothing could prevent the fluttering of her heart.

She had always thought of Hawk as a big man, but never so large and imposing as here in this endless forest. Knowing that she was completely at his mercy should have frightened her. She was treading on a sheen of ice so thin that the slightest misstep would send her plunging into a chasm. But all she could think of was how gracefully he moved and how much she wanted to seek comfort in the safety of his strong embrace.

. . . And how much she wanted to kiss him.

This time she acted on her impulse. Flinging her arms around his neck, she raised her mouth to caress his. Slowly, tenderly, she brushed his lips, lingering, savoring the taste of him.

He held her tightly in his arms, accepting, giving, but letting her change the kiss from gentle to passionate. And when his lips parted, it was Kate who dared to venture beyond, exploring the taste and texture of him.

"Hawk," she murmured. "Oh, Hawk."

One kiss melted into another; now it was Hawk who guided, showing her the unknown path that led to swirling, giddy delights.

Finally she broke the embrace and pulled back, breathless and laughing. "You k-kiss . . . good," she stammered, unable to find words to express her happiness.

His thin, sensual lips turned up in a smile so sweet that she found it hard to breathe. "This man is glad he pleases you."

"You do," she whispered. "You please me very much."

He laughed. "Come. Eat. Rest. You have shown much courage."

"For a woman?" she dared.

His eyes flashed with warm amusement. "As great as a Cherokee woman," he agreed, taking her by the hand and pulling her to her feet.

"Tell me that's pigeon cooking," she begged him.

"It's pigeon," he agreed. "If I'd had more time, I could have—"

"This is fine," she said. "Wonderful. I'm starving." She held out her hands to the fire. "I just want to be warm and dry."

Hawk removed a bird from the spit and waved it in the air to cool it. "Don't touch it. It's too hot. You'll burn yourself." He broke off a section of the breast and held it to her lips. "Taste," he said.

"Give it to me," she said. "I can . . ."

He laughed. "Open your mouth."

Obediently, she did. The outside of the meat was crunchy brown, the inside moist and white. She devoured bite after bite from his fingers, then paused and closed her eyes, enjoying the feel of the fire and the good meat in her belly.

Hawk squatted beside her, patiently feeding her as though it was the most natural thing in the world. And she let him. She didn't know why, but in some odd way, it felt right. She found herself chuckling with him.

"Do you know how long it's been since I've had pigeon?" she said. "Ages, months. Not since Twelfth Day, more than a year ago. And it was tough, not like this."

"You need to eat," he said. "You are too thin."

"I am not!"

"A man likes a woman to be soft, to have more meat on her bones," he teased. "The English settlers do not feed their women."

She got up and went back to the pool for another drink, breaking the spell. "There was nothing to eat," she said, remembering the starving time with a shudder. "Corn mush. *Uggh*. I'm sick of mush." She splashed water on her face.

Hawk licked his fingertips and began to eat. Even without dishes, without a single utensil, it came to Kate that he made far less mess than Robert or William did.

"Ducks and geese blacken the skies," Hawk observed. "Fish swim in the water. The forest teems with game. Why are the English such fools that they starve amid the Creator's plenty?"

Kate returned to sit beside him. She found a cushiony spot of thick moss and curled her legs under her. "Robert sent men out to hunt. He led foraging parties himself. They couldn't find . . ."

Hawk frowned. "He searched more for yellow metal than for deer. And when they killed meat, they left half to rot, taking only the best pieces. Among the Cherokee and the Powhatan, everything is used. Hooves, hide, even the brain for tanning. The English and the Spanish talk much of sin. To kill a living thing and waste it, that is sin."

"You're not being fair," she argued gently. "It wasn't safe to go far from the settlement walls. The Powhatan turned against us."

"The river lay at your door. Robert could not fish through the ice or net crabs from the mud? He could not send his men to dig clams from the great bay or set snares for rabbits? Paahh." Hawk made a sound of disgust. "In England, William Bennett would have known more than to build his house in a swamp. Here, his people die of fever and bad water."

"No one knew—" she began.

"This man knew," he replied softly. "I told William that many people would die if he did not move his village. Swamp brings evil. Belly rot and running bowels. Even the weasel knows enough to drink clean water." He dug in the coals of the fire and produced several roots as long as her finger and several times as thick. When they had cooled, he brushed the ashes off and offered her one. "Eat," he said.

"What are they?"

"Ground nuts."

She did as he instructed. The taste was bland, but not unpleasant. When she'd finished, she reached for more of the pigeon.

Hawk shook his head. "No more," he said. "Later. Eat too much and you will sicken. Rest now. I will find us wood to keep the fire burning all night and grass to weave a blanket."

She laughed. "Grass? You'll make me a blanket of grass?"

"Wait and see, wife of the beautiful eyes. This man has promised to keep you safe and he will. I will show you such wonders that your heart will leap in your breast. You have seen nothing of this land but sorrow. Hawk will show you why men die for this earth."

"I'm grateful," she whispered huskily. "More grateful than you'll ever know. And I do love you. Can't it be enough that we're together, here and now. I can't promise to be your wife. I don't know if I can go away with you forever."

"You will," he said.

"As much as I love you, I need to know that I've done the right thing for my people. I have to know what happened to my sister, to Robert and . . ."

He dismissed her with a sharp shrug. "Wait for me. Do not leave the fire."

"I must be honest with you, Hawk. I'm afraid of your wilderness. At least, I'd be afraid if you weren't here with me. I'd be lying if I said I'm ready to marry you."

"Do as I say."

"I will, but—"

He cut her off brusquely. "Do not let the fire die out." Snatching up his bow and quiver of arrows, he turned his back on her and strode away.

"Hawk, you can't just . . ." Her voice trailed off as he moved into the trees, leaving her alone in the clearing. "It's not that easy for me to give up my old life," she murmured. "I wish it was, but it's not."

Kate edged closer to the fire and let the heat soak into her. She stood up and removed her tattered skirt and one petticoat. Her shift, bodice, and remaining petticoat covered her enough for decency's sake. If she was lucky, she could dry her skirt and outer petticoat before Hawk returned.

Mother wouldn't approve. But mother wouldn't approve of her catching pneumonia in her wet things and dying either. Tomorrow would be time enough to reason with Hawk and convince him to try and warn Jamestown. For now she would make the best of this time they had together.

She broke off another pigeon wing and nibbled on it. It was beautiful here, she decided, glancing around. The pool was as clear as a mirror; she could see the white sand bottom and fish swimming lazily in the depths. Deep green moss framed the water; on the far side grew a cluster of pink and white lady's slippers.

She was too far away to hear the sea, but the forest echoed with the chatter of squirrels and the rat-ta-tat-tat of woodpeckers. A chorus of birdsong surrounded her; and now and then, she caught a flash of a red cardinal through the verdant green of the pine needles and new-grown leaves. This could be Eden. And Hawk and I could be the first man and the first woman in all the world.

Kate laughed out loud. She was here, an ocean away from England and all she'd ever known. This was a harsh world of violence, blood, and smoke. But she was happy as she had never been before. At least she could be, if Hawk would stop pressing her to marry him.

She would clutch this happiness to her heart, she vowed. She would know what it was to love and be loved by a man, if only for a little while.

"I will," she whispered, and repeated the promise in a firmer voice. "I'll be Hawk's woman. And for a few days or weeks, I'll accept this gift of paradise. . . . If it costs me my immortal soul, I'm willing to pay the price."

Chapter 14

~~~~~oOo~~~~~

Early the next morning, Kate lay face down in the tall grass and peered through the foliage at a gray fox and her three kits playing beside a fallen log. The baby foxes were adorable balls of fur with eyes as black as currants. They were so fat that they waddled when they walked and lost their balance when they attempted to run. Yipping and barking, the kits rolled and tumbled, wrestling with each other, chewing on their mother's nose and chasing their own tails. It was all Kate could do to keep from giving away her hiding place by laughing.

"Be still," Hawk had warned her before he led her to the spot where the vixen had brought her little ones up out of their burrow into the warm sunshine. "The slightest noise will alert the mother."

"I'm not the one talking," she whispered.

"This fox is an old lady," Hawk told Kate. "She's crippled and bears scars of an old battle along her sides and hindquarters. I think she fought a wildcat or a wolf long ago. She had a hard life, this *tsu'`lă*. This may be her last litter of young."

"*Tsu'`lă*." She tried to imitate what she assumed must be the Indian word for fox.

He smiled and nodded. "This man will make Cherokee of you yet."

Kate shook her head and looked back at the vixen and her babies. They had not argued this morning, and she wanted to keep him in a good humor so that she could ask him again about going to Jamestown to warn the English.

He hadn't stayed away long the night before. And when he returned, it had been with an armful of soft pine boughs to make a bed for her. He'd kept watch through the night while she slept. It was proof of her trust in him that she could lie beside him in this wild forest and sleep.

He hadn't touched her, not in the way a man touches a woman, and she wondered why. Now that she'd made up her mind to have him, she wanted to make love to him. She just didn't know how to tell him.

This morning, she'd awakened early enough to watch him greet the morning sunrise with prayers in the Cherokee tongue and outstretched arms. He wore nothing but his loin covering and moccasins.

"Do you worship the sun?" she asked when he finished the ritual.

Hawk chuckled. "Who do you believe made the sun?"

"The Lord God."

"Yes." Hawk nodded. "The Creator set the sun in the heavens. The Cherokee believe that Sun and Moon are His lights to guide us. Our stories tell us that Sun is a young woman and Moon is her brother. I give thanks, not to them, but to the One who created them and all the world."

"I didn't mean to insult you," she said.

"You have not." He grinned at her. "Today I will build you a proper wigwam."

"Could you feed me first? I'm starving."

"Would you like fish? Or wild strawberries?"

"Both, please. I am awfully hungry."

He sighed. "I can see that hunting for you will be no easy task. But you must learn to find food for yourself. I'll show you where you can pick the berries while I see about spearing some fish in the surf."

As he led her toward the glade where the strawberries grew, he saw the tracks of the fox. "This fresh spoor is from a vixen," he had explained. "She may have young. Wait here while I go and see. Don't make any noise."

In minutes, Hawk returned. "She's close, and she does have little ones. Follow me and do as I do. The breeze will cover our movements. The wind is coming off the ocean, and we're approaching from the land side. The scents come from the foxes to us."

Hawk had been right. They'd crept within a few yards of the vixen and watched for nearly an hour. Kate was so fascinated, she forgot that she was hungry.

The biggest of the fox kits padded toward her hiding spot. The tiny animal was so precious that she wanted to reach out and pick him up and cuddle him.

"Sssh," Hawk warned.

The bright-eyed little fox leaped into the air and pounced on a blue-jay feather. He tumbled over, still clutching his prize, and growled in a high-pitched baby voice. Then the mother uttered a low sound, and her offspring trotted back to paw her belly in search of a teat. After a short struggle, he wiggled in between the other kits and began to nurse vigorously.

Kate smiled. How sweet the forest smelled.

Hawk's hand on the curve of her spine warmed her skin. Giddy sensations like swirling thistle filled her breast, and her heartbeat quickened when his breath brushed her ear.

Slowly he leaned closer. She tried to maintain her composure, but her fingers flexed in the grass, and she had to struggle to breathe normally.

"Do you tire of watching?" he whispered.

"No." How could she? The grass had never been so many shades of vivid green until Hawk had taught her how to see them. The sky had never seemed so blue or the trailing puffs of clouds so white. She could not glimpse the ocean from where she lay, but she knew it was reflecting the heavens, an azure expanse of glory, frosted with peaks of sugared foam.

The earth beneath her seemed as alive as every blade of grass and each brilliant leaf. If she closed her eyes, she could imagine that she could feel the slow, steady beating of a great heart. She had never imagined that such peace existed, or that the forest and marshland could play such music.

At home, in England, she had often listened to the wind playing through the shingles of the house or blowing through the wheat fields. Here, the wind had a thousand voices, and the stillness of the island gave her the quiet to hear them all. This morning, she had heard the deep sighing of the sea breeze through the cattails and the marsh grass, and when she'd waded into the surf, the gusts over the water whistled a lilting tune. Now, high above, in the treetop canopy of oak and chestnut, a rustling melody played. There was something magical here. Either the island was enchanted or she was bewitched by Hawk. Perhaps both. . . .

She felt the heat of his gaze, looked up hesitantly,

and smiled at him. Hawk inched backward in the grass. Instinctively she knew that he wanted her to do the same. Quietly they moved away from the foxes. When they were far enough away not to frighten the animals, Hawk stood up and pulled her to her feet.

"Thank you," she murmured with tears in her eyes. "Thank you for showing me." And then, without realizing what she was about to do, she stood on tiptoe and kissed him lightly on the lips.

He returned her kiss. She stepped back, breathless, her pulse racing, and smiled up at him. He cocked his head slightly, meeting her smile with one of his own.

"Your mouth is as sweet as any ripe berry," he said.

Her body still tingled, and the taste of his mouth lingered on her lips. Wide-eyed, she lifted her chin and waited for him to kiss her again.

"Shall I find something for you to eat now?"

"I think I'd rather kiss you," she replied boldly.

Satisfaction glowed in his features, and his eyes twinkled as he trailed a fingertip down her cheekbone.

Kate shivered and drew in a long breath. Now, she thought. Now, he will take me. Here, in the woods.

She was terrified and eager, and she wanted so much for him to tell her what she should do. She was glad that she'd never known another man . . . glad that he would be the first.

His gaze burned through the fabric of her clothing.

"Hawk," she whispered. "I . . ."

His smile made her heart skip a beat. She would have done anything to have him keep smiling at her like that.

"It is warm," he said. "It is the custom for a Cherokee to bathe before he eats. Will you swim with me?"

"Swim?" she echoed. Suddenly shy, she cast her gaze to the ground. "The ocean water is too cold to swim," she finished lamely.

"Not for Hawk." Turning quickly, he caught her hand and began to move down the trail toward the beach. Not certain what else to do, she followed without protest.

"This man will miss the sea when he returns to the mountains of his people," he said as he neared the water.

Kate stopped abruptly when he released her hand. Hawk shrugged off his hunting bag and dropped his bow and arrows. She looked away as he untied his buckskin loin covering. Surely he didn't intend to strip naked in front of her. She heard a splash and couldn't help glancing back to see him thigh deep in the water. For an instant, she caught a flash of taut, copper-colored buttocks, and then he dove.

Kate flushed from the roots of her hair to her toes, not because Hawk had gone into the water without a stitch on, but because she couldn't resist looking.

When he broke the surface, he was laughing at her. "Come," he called. "Why do you fear me?"

Kate sat stubbornly on the sand. "I'm not afraid of you," she replied. If he expected her to demean herself like some dockside slut by taking off all of her clothes in broad daylight, he was mistaken.

"Coward," he teased.

She glanced down at her hand, which he'd held so protectively as they'd followed the deer trail. She hated to admit that she'd wanted him to go on touching her.

Tentatively, she looked back at him and felt all of her resistance drain away. How beautiful he was! His high cheekbones and strong jaw seemed sculpted to match the raw splendor of this wild land. When he laughed and shook his head, water streamed from the gleaming black hair that hung across his broad shoulders. Droplets of salt-spray rolled down his muscular chest and arms.

Surely God had never made a human more perfect in form and feature. When she had first met Hawk in Bramble Wood, he had seemed dark-skinned. Now, his red-gold hue seemed right for a man, and she could not picture Robert without thinking him pale and sickly in comparison.

"Are you ashamed of your body?" Hawk asked. "You know that this man would cut off his own right hand before he would cause you harm." He dove under again and swam farther out, beyond the chest-high breakers.

Kate kicked at the beach with her heel, digging a hole in the damp sand. She wanted to throw off her clothes and join him in the blue water, but her conscience troubled her.

Yes, she had been prepared to lie with him, but the thought of swimming naked was terrifying. Surely to do so would be a terrible sin. No respectable English lady of quality would consider bearing her naked body to a man in the daytime, would she? Indian women might go about in a state of scandalous undress, but she could not. Could she?

Something moved under Kate's foot, and she jumped back. As she stared into the depression in the sand, a small, hard-shelled creature the size and shape of a walnut appeared, then began to burrow into the damp earth. Kate picked it up and examined it with wonder. Multiple legs peddled wildly, but the odd little crustacean made no attempt to bite her.

"Go on," she said, lowering it to the ground. The sand flea vanished from sight in seconds. Kate brushed off her hands and stood up. As far as she could see on either side, the beach was empty of any human.

"An English lady wouldn't go into the water with Hawk," she murmured aloud. But then, an English lady wouldn't have touched the little sand bug either. And what lady would ever have seen or appreciated the beauty of the birds or the foxes?

"I do," she said, and began to laugh at her own foolishness. What did it matter what was proper? She was alone on an island with Hawk. Who would know what she did here? If she did get back to Jamestown, her reputation would be ruined anyway. Everyone would think the worst of her, that she had committed fornication with an Indian.

Kate covered her mouth with her hands and giggled. Wasn't that what she had every intention of doing?

"It is good to hear you laugh."

"It's good to laugh."

"Come in and swim with me."

"I can't," she answered.

"Coward!"

"I can't swim."

He chuckled. "This man will teach you." He waded toward her and held out his hand. "You will come."

"I'm afraid," she admitted.

"You? Never," he shouted. "You have the heart of a panther."

"A panther?" Boldly, she tugged at the laces of her bodice. Next she removed her skirt and petticoats, and finally her shoes and stockings, leaving her in nothing but her shift and stays. The sun felt warm on her bare skin. The heat seeped through her body, giving her strength.

What was she afraid of? she thought with giddy abandon. Didn't she come to the New World for adventure? She loved him, didn't she? And she trusted him. More than anyone in the world. Shutting her eyes, she undid her stays and let them fall, then yanked the shift over her head.

"I'm coming," she said. She opened her eyes, ran down to the water's edge, and hesitated as the incoming tide swirled around her ankles. The sea was cold, but not as cold as she'd expected. Her heart hammered in her chest, and she felt her nipples pucker into tight buds. Her cheeks burned, but she would not back down from the challenge. "Don't let me drown," she called to Hawk.

"This man will protect you." He couldn't take his eyes off her as she walked toward him. Her gleaming hair, the color of autumn leaves, hung in one thick braid over her shoulder. Her small, firm breasts were as white as the sand beach; her belly was flat, and her hips were as shapely as any he had seen. Ocean foam washed over her knees, splashing up to drench her naked thighs and cover the russet curls above her woman's cleft.

His heart leaped in his breast. He wanted nothing more than to sweep her into his arms and carry her back to the beach. His blood pulsed at the thought of throwing her onto the warm sand and filling her with his desire.

Kate's face paled as she waded deeper. Water surged over the rise of her breasts. Hawk's groin tightened as he thought how sweet those breasts would taste.

Kissing a lover's breast, suckling them as an infant might—those things were not part of Cherokee or Powhatan custom. A Spanish flower girl had taught him the joys of laving a woman's swollen nipple with his tongue, then drawing the hard bud between his lips until her body stirred with desire.

Hawk groaned with wanting as he watched Kate come to him. She was untouched; the proof of that innocence shone in her eyes. It would be for him to teach her the joys of what could be between a man and woman.

Night after night since the first day he'd laid eyes on her, he'd dreamed of sleeping beside her, listening to her breathing, inhaling deeply of her scent mingled with his. No Powhatan torture could tear at his vitals the way keeping Kate at arm's length had done.

Last night had been the most difficult. He'd wanted desperately to mold her body against his, to feel her writhe beneath him . . . to know the rapture that joining with this special woman would bring.

But it would not be enough to have Kate for a few nights or even a few moons' pleasure. She must be his forever, his wife, his mate. His for this life and beyond! And for that, he had to wait until her need for him flared as hot and enduring as his for her.

A lifetime of hunting had taught him patience. Kate was the greatest prize he had ever sought, and he would not risk losing her for the physical satisfaction that rushing her into a sexual union would bring.

His instincts told him that the time was right.

Go slowly, he reminded himself, as she stood before him with her damp hair all undone and her eyes full of trust and hope. Go slowly with this woman, if it kills you.

And it might, he thought as he smiled at her. "So," he murmured, "you do not know how to swim."

"No."

He heard the quaver in her voice, knew her vulnerability, and willed himself to self control. "This man will teach you," he promised huskily. "All you need to know . . ."

Chapter 15

"**H**awk!" Kate twisted in his grasp and clenched her hands around his neck. The sheer panic in her voice ripped his gut. Instantly his muscles tensed, and he scanned the water around them for danger.

An enormous gray shadow with a high dorsal fin knifed through the waves toward them. "Be still," he urged Kate, recognizing their visitor. "Don't frighten him."

"Don't frighten him?" she echoed.

Hawk chuckled, realizing how good it felt to have her clinging to him, pressing her unclad body to his in a way that he'd only dreamed about before. "Not shark," he soothed. "In your language, dolphin. He will not hurt us."

The mammal slowed and raised his long beaked snout, drifting by them, fixing them with a curious gaze. Hawk slipped an arm around Kate's waist. She slid down his hip until she was partially behind him. "A dolphin?" she asked.

"Stand still," Hawk warned. "Absolutely still." His own ragged breathing was not from fear of the dolphin but from Kate's intimacy. Reluctantly he broke the spell, detaching himself from her tight grasp. Taking a deep breath, he slid down into the water, eyes wide and searching. Suddenly, the dolphin loomed up in his line of vision. *Welcome, brother,* Hawk thought.

The dolphin answered with a high-pitched whistle, and the sleek body passed close enough to touch. Nearly ten feet long, his striped back was so dark as to be almost black. His belly lightened to a creamy gray that extended up under his throat to surround his eyes with a gleaming white mask.

How majestic he is, Hawk thought. *A prince of the deep. I see you.* He did not speak aloud, but formed the respectful greeting in his mind and willed the dolphin to understand.

Uttering a series of squeaks and hisses, the dolphin circled. *Asgi'na.*

Hawk absorbed the single thought in the same manner that he heard the speech of other animals. Their words came to him more as image than as sound, loud and clear, edged in silver. Nodding respectfully, Hawk echoed the name in his head. *Asgi'na.*

A black fin moved in what seemed to Hawk a salute, and the dolphin swam swiftly away.

Hawk stood up on the sandy bottom and glanced back at Kate. The water was lapping against her chin, but his head and shoulders were well above the gentle waves. "Are you all right?" he asked.

She nodded. Her eyes were no longer glazed with fear. She trusted him. He knew it, and the thought warmed his heart. She was a quick pupil. During the short space of time it had taken the sun to move a handspan across heaven's bowl, Kate was already learning to hold her breath and swim under water.

He had touched her and held her, but only in a

proper manner for teaching her how to become accustomed to the water. He had not let his hands stray to her breasts or his fingers delve between her thighs, no matter how difficult that had been. Only patience and a hunter's caution would win his greatest prize, Kate's heart and loyalty.

"Will it come back?" she asked.

Hawk could see that she was shivering in the wind, but she made no complaint. She was brave, this pale-hued woman with eyes of unnatural color. "The dolphin is a he, and his name is *Asgi'na*. It means ghost in Cherokee." He shrugged. "This man cannot tell you what the dolphin means to do."

She fixed him with a disbelieving stare. "His name is Ghost. How do you know that?"

"He told me."

"The . . . the *dolphin* told you his name? It talked to you?"

Hawk shrugged again. "Not as you talk, my medicine woman. *Asgi'na* has his own language. He is much more intelligent than a dog or a horse." He chuckled. "More so than many English, this man would say."

"A fish?" She wrapped her arms around her bare shoulders. "You are a great spinner of tales, Hawk, or you are the witch you accused me of being."

He stared at her. "Think you a doe has no thought? Or the mother fox we watched with her young? Do you not understand that she loves her little ones as a woman does? We are all living things, created by One."

Her mood became somber, and she averted her eyes. "I'm cold. I'm going in." But before she could move, *Asgi'na* leaped out of the water a short distance away. Kate gasped and splashed over to Hawk's side. "He's back!"

"See." Hawk pointed to the spray arcing in the air over the dolphin. "He breathes air as a man does."

Kate laughed and clapped her hands as the animal spun into the air and scooted along the surface with two thirds of his body above the water. Then he made a final hop and dove deep before vaulting to an unbelievable height above the waves. With a burst of squeaking chatter, the creature sliced the depths and swam directly toward them again.

"Oh, he's coming . . ." Kate broke off as *Asgi'na* circled them, opening his mouth to reveal white cone-shaped teeth. Kate backed up until she reached Hawk. "Will it bite?" she whispered.

"No." Hawk smiled down at her. "This man thinks he is laughing at us. I do not think he has ever seen a female dolphin who cannot swim."

"I'm not a dolphin," she protested.

"A fish, then," he teased. "A fish who cannot swim."

Asgi'na nosed forward cautiously.

"Welcome brother," Hawk said. Without thinking, he made the handsign that the Cherokee used to speak with other tribesmen from the great plains to the west.

The dolphin made a deep clicking sound.

His one eye that Hawk could see revealed an eager warmth and a keen intelligence. "We mean you no harm," he said to the animal.

"Be careful," Kate whispered.

"*Asgi'na* will not hurt us," Hawk answered softly. "He is only afraid that you might mean hurt for him."

"Never! He's beautiful, but—"

"Think that," Hawk told her. "Hold that in your mind. Stay here unless I call you." Pushing off with

his feet, he glided to within a few arms' lengths of
Asgi'na. Treading water, Hawk hung suspended,
waiting for the dolphin to make up his mind.

Seconds passed, and then the animal flexed his
tail and passed by. Still Hawk waited, clearing his
mind of all but the feeling of brotherhood and
complete acceptance. The dolphin circled him, and
then he felt the gentle nudge of *Asgi'na*'s snout on
his back.

Turning slowly, Hawk extended an open palm.
The dolphin rubbed against it. Water streamed from
the animal's blowhole, and he rolled over, present-
ing his belly. Hawk stroked the powerful snout and
head, then trailed his fingers along the great body to
scratch his exposed stomach area. *Asgi'na* chattered
excitedly and quivered all over like a happy puppy.

Hawk pressed his hand against the rubbery surface of the smooth skin and felt the dolphin's life
force touch his.

"Friends," Hawk said.

Asgi'na gave a flick of his powerful tail and turned
over but made no attempt to swim away. When he
banged against Hawk's hip, Hawk patted the creature's back and skimmed the area around the dolphin's blowhole.

"He will not hurt us, Kate. Come," Hawk called.
He kept his eyes on *Asgi'na;* he knew Kate's curiosity
and sense of daring would not let her miss the
chance to touch the dolphin.

She did not disappoint him.

The dolphin showed no alarm as Kate waded to
Hawk's side. He wiggled and chirped as though
extending a welcome to her.

Kate's hand trembled as she reached out. "May
I?" she asked.

Asgi'na clicked.

"Oh," Kate exclaimed as her fingers brushed the dolphin's skin. "He's wonderful."

The animal slapped the water with his tail and looked expectantly at Hawk.

"What is it, brother? What do you want me to do?" Hawk asked.

The dolphin nudged him again.

"Be careful," Kate murmured.

"It is all right." Tentatively Hawk rested his weight against the dolphin's back.

Asgi'na let out a high-pitched squeak.

"He promises not to hurt me," he said to Kate. Taking hold of *Asgi'na's* dorsal fin, Hawk let himself float.

The dolphin gave an excited whistle and swam slowly for a few yards. Hawk glanced back at Kate's face, transfixed by wonder. Then he took a quick breath as he felt the dolphin dip under the waves. *Asgi'na's* powerful muscles thrust them effortlessly along the ocean bottom. Hawk held his breath and opened his eyes, thrilled by the sensation.

The floor of the ocean was a hazy line of sand, the world above gleaming blue that lightened to gold. Fish darted past, and once he saw the thick shape of what could only be a slow-gliding ray.

Hawk's lungs strained. He had used all his air. If the dolphin didn't surface soon, he would have to let go and swim for the top. But the urge to hang on and share the dolphin's kingdom was great. A ringing in Hawk's head became incessant, and he knew that if he didn't break free now, it would soon be too late.

Abruptly the dolphin rose toward the light above. Together Hawk and *Asgi'na* surged up through the waves into the sunshine. The animal leaped high out of the water. Hawk gasped for breath even as he lost his grip and fell. He went under and came up swimming. When he cleared his eyes and looked around, *Asgi'na* was gone.

To his left, a school of tiny bait fish skittered along the crest of a wave. He turned and looked for Kate, but before he could locate her, *Asgi'na*'s snout bumped his legs. "Back, are you, brother?" Hawk said.

The dolphin slid alongside him, dipping one fin in invitation. Then he rolled back the skin over his teeth and whistled through them much as a horse might whinny.

"All right, my friend," Hawk agreed, taking another deep breath. "But my lungs are not so great as yours." He grasped the dolphin's dorsal fin and was slowly pulled along as *Asgi'na* swam back to where Kate was waiting.

"I was frightened," she cried. "You went under and didn't come up."

"He knows," Hawk replied. "This man does not understand how, but *Asgi'na* knows that I am not a creature of the sea and cannot hold my breath as long as he does."

The dolphin glided to Kate and hung in the water, nearly motionless.

"Would he let me ride him?" she asked.

For an instant, Hawk was tempted to forbid her to try, but then he saw the eagerness in her eyes and nodded. "Only a few paces," he said. "You cannot swim."

"I can," she protested. "A little."

"If he dives, let go at once," he ordered.

There was no need to caution her. When she took hold of *Asgi'na*'s fin, the great animal swam gently in circles, remaining in the shallow water, almost as if he comprehended how helpless she was.

"Oh," she murmured. "Oh, you beautiful thing."

When the dolphin brought her back to Hawk, Kate slid off and jumped into his arms. "Thank you! Thank you, Hawk!" she cried.

He caught her and crushed her tightly against him, bringing his mouth down to hers. The banked fires in his loins flared, and he kissed her with all the fierce longing that he'd kept chained for so many moons. She tasted of sea salt and a sweetness that he had not dreamed existed.

Her eyes were wide; they flared with inner heat. She clung to him and made a small sound low in her throat as their kiss deepened. Slowly, tentatively, they explored each other.

How soft her lips are, he thought. *Made for a man to kiss.* He traced the lower curve of her mouth with the tip of his tongue. With a sigh, her lashes fluttered and closed, and she opened to him. Her body molded to his; he could feel the soft swell of her breasts, the length of her legs beneath the water, and the heat of her belly against his hardening spear.

Her scent filled his head and he groaned. Her head tipped back; her unbound hair floated on the surface of the sea, but their kiss went on and on. Tongues touched and twined. Intense sensations of pleasure knifed through him again and again.

He slid his fingers down to cup her breast, and she gasped. He tore his mouth away and leaned down to kiss her throat and the top of her shoulder.

She trembled and her fingernails lightly scraped his skin. "Hawk." It was almost a breath, so soft, so faint, he nearly missed it. "Oh, Hawk." Her eyes flew open and she laughed.

This time it was Kate who sought his lips. This

time the trail was familiar. She tilted her head and welcomed his tongue.

He sunk back into the waves, pulling her with him. For a few seconds, she lay full-length on top of him. His stiffened rod nudged the apex of her thighs and she jerked away. His loins felt as though they were on fire.

"I didn't mean . . ." she began. But that was a lie. Another minute, another second, and she would be a maid no longer. She wanted him as he wanted her. She wanted his mouth on hers and his hands on her breasts. She desperately wanted to get closer . . . closer to him.

Abruptly, the intensity of her yearning frightened her. "No!" she cried.

"Kate," he rasped.

"I can't." She turned, tripped, and fell into the water. When her feet found the solid sand beneath her, she stood up and splashed away. "Thank you for the dolphin," she said, but her words were lost in the crash of the surf.

Scrambling through the waves, she ran up the beach and snatched up her clothing. She did not look back. Instead she dashed into the shelter of the trees.

Later, when she'd run until her heart was pounding, she stopped long enough to pull the sandy shift over her damp body. She stepped on a shell and gasped. "Ouch." She hadn't taken the time to gather up her shoes and stockings, and her feet were bare.

She twisted the water out of her hair and pushed stray strands away from her face. Her pulse was still racing.

What had she done?

But the memory of those shared kisses was greater

than the shame at running away. She wished she'd hadn't broken off the embrace . . . that she'd remained in Hawk's arms and become a woman, no matter the cost.

"I love him," she whispered into the canopy of pine branches that closed over her head. "I do. I love him."

What had happened had not been Hawk's fault. It had been hers. She had thrown herself into his arms. She had welcomed his kisses . . . had kissed him back as passionately. She placed a hand over her breast. The nipple was still hard and aching, and she wondered how it would have felt to have Hawk kiss her breast and suckle it.

Curious heat swirled in the pit of her stomach. She could not forget the feel of his arms around her, or the sense of loss at being parted from him.

The day had been a dream, from the joy of the foxes Hawk had given her, to the sea and the wild dolphin that had let them touch and swim with it. Hawk's embrace had been the only possible conclusion to such a day, but her foolish maiden's fear had ruined it.

Kate sunk to the ground and hugged her arms tightly against her. She was not a child. She was a woman long past the age of wedding and having babes of her own.

"I do love Hawk. If I am damned for it, so be it."

She fell silent, stunned by her own conclusion. And then, it seemed to her as though the weight of a leaden cloak slipped off her shoulders.

Her memories of the time she and Hawk had spent together flickered behind her eyelids. She saw Hawk saving her from the wild dogs in Bramble Wood, coming to her bedchamber in her father's house on the night before her near wedding to Robert, and teaching her to fish.

Here on this enchanted island, he was introducing her to the ways of the wilderness, pointing out the birds and animals, showing her where to find food and how to keep herself warm and dry. She heard his laughter in her mind's eye, and saw the strength of character in his proud face.

Hawk's skin was reddish gold, his hair was as black as Satan's anvil, but his blood was the same color as hers. His heart she could not see, but if any man's was pure, Hawk's must be. Who else could talk to the wild beasts and have them heed his words? Who else could summon a dolphin from the ocean depths for her to ride upon?

He was gentle and bold, utterly courageous and completely honest. He was learned; he spoke Spanish, English, and at least two Native tongues. Indian savage, the white men called him, but this noble prince of the forest was more gentleman than most who bore the title.

Hawk was all these things, and he had declared his love for her. How had she been such a fool as not to see what lay within her reach? What waited for her in Jamestown or even in England? What man had she ever met to match the one who had asked her to become his wife?

She looked around her, suddenly realizing that she did not recognize the spot and could no longer hear the sea. In a little while, the sun would begin to go down. She might wander here in the forest until darkness closed over her.

For a short time, shivers of uncertainty ran down her spine. But then she stood erect and shaded her eyes to see where the sun stood. That way was west, and if she went in the opposite direction, she would reach the ocean. "I'm not lost," she whispered. "I'm not."

And if she was, Hawk would come and rescue her.

She began to walk faster, heedless of the briers that scratched her legs and bruised her feet. Suddenly she needed to see Hawk, to be back in his arms, to seize the time they had together in this paradise.

But the beach was farther than she thought, and shadows began to lengthen across the forest floor. Time and time again, she was forced to backtrack and circle around tangled scrub and storm-fallen trees. And when she found a clearing, it was not the sea as she supposed, but a grassy meadow that she didn't recognize.

She parted the branches and began to step out onto the thick green carpet when she heard the chilling, drawn-out howl of a wolf. Fear washed over her in an icy wave, and the hair rose on the back of her neck. Frantically she looked around for a tree with a branch low enough to climb. When the wolf's cry came again, Kate inhaled sharply and bolted for the nearest hemlock.

Chapter 16

Kate climbed as high in the tree as she could. The earth was a long way below. Then she noticed that the birds had stopped calling to one another, and there was no sound in the forest but her own ragged breathing. A twig snapped. Her stomach plummeted, and the acrid taste of fear filled her mouth.

"Is that a panther I see hidden in those branches?" Hawk called.

"Watch out!" she shouted. "There's a wolf! I heard it . . ."

Hawk placed his hands on either side of his mouth and imitated a wolf's howl.

"You! It was you!" She began to slide down the tree. "You scared me half to death! When I get hold of you, you'll wish you—" Her grip loosened and she tumbled the rest of the way down. Hawk caught her and they both toppled onto the soft grass.

Kate's anger dissolved in his laughter, and when he kissed the tip of her nose and her chin and eyelids, she began to giggle.

"That was rotten," she declared.

He rolled over so that he was stretched full-length

on his back with her on top of him. "I am your prisoner," he said.

"It would serve you right if I'd had a bow and arrows and shot at you." Unconsciously she moistened her lips. It was hard to remember how his jest had aggravated her when they were chest to chest and thigh to thigh, and her insides were fluttering with giddiness. "It wasn't a bit funny."

"There are no wolves on this island." He grinned wickedly. "Have we seen wolf tracks?"

"No." She shook her head. "But it was still a mean trick." She drew in another breath. Not even the threat of a wolf had made her tremble so much as the intimate touch of this man.

"Wolves prefer venison to human flesh." He angled an arm behind his head and rested against it. "Unless they are starving, they run from the scent of people."

"How was I supposed to know that? All the wolves I've ever heard of—"

"English wolves, not our wolves," he corrected. "A wolf mates for life—did you know that?"

"I don't much care what they do," she said as she got to her knees beside him and scrambled up. "How did you find me?" She forced her tone to near normal. She must pretend that goosebumps weren't rising on her arms or that standing so close aroused forbidden thoughts in her mind.

He chuckled. "A child could trail you. I would have come sooner, but I found an injured red-tailed hawk and stopped to care for her wound." He pulled her shoes from his hunting bag. "Put these on," he ordered.

"A hawk? How could a hawk be injured?" She

sat down and quickly pulled on her stockings and
her stiff leather shoes. Her heart was still racing.

"I'm not sure. She may have fought with an eagle
or a bobcat. One of the hawk's wings is torn and she
lost much blood. I took her to our camp and bound
her wound with the inner bark of cedar." He rose
and caught her by the hand. "I'm sorry I frightened
you," he apologized. "It was not such a good joke,
after all. You did right to climb a tree." His eyes
narrowed. "Forgive me."

"Not just yet." He did not let go of her hand; she
was acutely conscious of the warmth of his fingers
entwined with hers.

"Will it die? The hawk?"

"The hawk is my totem."

His thumb made small circles on her palm. She
found herself concentrating on the tingly sensation
of his touch instead of what he was saying.

"The spirits meant for me to find her. I think she
will live. But we must hunt for her until she can fly
again."

Twilight had fallen over the meadow; the birds
and animals were strangely hushed. Beyond the
pond, an osprey rose into the air, his powerful wings
and body all grace and beauty against the rose sky
of a fading sunset.

Hawk tugged on Kate's hand, and she followed
him without protest along the edge of the clearing.
She placed her feet as he did, and when she looked
back over her shoulder she could see no sign of their
passing in the grass.

The breeze shifted, bringing the scent of nursing
foals and fresh grass. Kate thought she could taste
the bite of salt on her tongue. "We're going toward
the ocean," she said.

Hawk nodded in approval. "For an English-woman you learn quick."

She laughed. How long had it been since she had been a proper Englishwoman? Before she'd gone riding through Bramble Wood? Or had she ever fit into the pattern she was born to? Had every footstep she'd ever taken led her to this virile, copper-skinned giant, who strode through his wilderness kingdom with regal nobility?

Kate let her gaze stray to Hawk. He was as clothed as he was likely to be in the warm air of May. His gleaming hair hung over bare shoulders and brushed the long, sinewy muscles of his arms. A copper band encircled one biceps. A twist of butter-soft leather covered his loins. With every stride, she caught glimpses of hard thighs and long, powerful legs. On his slim feet were moccasins, higher than her shoes, but adorned with intricate beading in vivid red, green, and yellow floral designs.

A sheathed knife hung on a leather band around his neck; a bow and quiver of arrows was slung carelessly over his far shoulder. And around his strong throat, he wore the silver gorget she had seen in the church the day she'd almost wed Robert.

It came to her mind that Hawk was finely dressed for a stroll through the forest, and she was about to ask him why when they reached the top of a scrub-strewn sand dune and he pointed to the sea. "You were not lost," he said. "You would have found your way back to camp." His jet black eyes glowed with pride. "You are a child of earth, Kate. Listen and she will speak to you. Always." He gestured gracefully toward the wide expanse of rolling waves and luminous, curved horizon.

Her heart fluttered with excitement at the sheer beauty of the view. No matter how many times she saw the ocean at the end of a day, she was still spellbound. The tide was coming in; row after row of white-capped waves crested, rolled in to claim the sand and then recede, ebbing gently in the dwindling light. The blue of afternoon's sea had darkened to jet, and the sky in the east turned from hazy purple to gray. A single sea gull floated over the surface of the water, trailing eerie drawn-out laughter.

She let go of Hawk's hand and ran down the dune and across the beach to the waterline with all the enthusiasm of a child. The sun's warmth still pulsed in the white sand, delighting her senses. She waded in to the surf until the cool waves washed around her ankles. Her heart drank in the beauty of the day's end as she inhaled deeply of the clear, clean air.

"Kate."

She turned slowly to see him standing at the water's edge. He held out a hand to her. "Kate?"

"The water isn't cold." She tried to cover her inner turmoil with ordinary words, but shivers of hot and cold danced under her too-tight skin.

"I have been patient a long time. How long will you make me wait?" he asked her.

"For what?" Surely that voice belonged to someone else. Her speech had never been so husky . . . so breathy.

"You know what I have waited for."

"Do I?" Laughing, she took a step toward him, then whirled and dashed down the beach, running until her hair came untied and her eyes watered from the wind. She left the child behind her and became a woman, a woman very certain of the spark she had ignited in her mate.

Hawk's footfalls thudded on the sand behind her,

and the knowledge that he was close behind her made her run all the faster.

What had begun in fun became a race in earnest. All her defenses fell away, and she knew that Hawk was right. They had waited long enough for what must inevitably be. Fear of the unknown lent her speed. She fled down the hard-packed sand as though the hounds of Bramble Wood were on her heels once more.

She did not know how long she ran, but when she stumbled, he caught her. Twisting in his embrace, she flung her arms around his neck and kissed him full on the mouth.

Hawk's answering kiss destroyed whatever lucid thought remained. Gone was the gentle lover. His hands were hard, his mouth plundering.

She did not care. She wanted him. Wanted him with all the fury of a lifetime of pent-up emotion. Needed him with an instinct so overwhelmingly powerful it drowned all else but desire.

Vaguely she was aware that he swept her up in his arms and carried her, but her immediate urgency was his mouth on hers and the heady, weightless feeling that tumbled her through space and time without reason. She wanted him . . . wanted all of him. She needed to feel his weight pressing her down, yearned to have his hands touching her naked body, his lips grazing her aching breasts.

Yearning swept through her with the force of an ocean storm; each shattering kiss drew her farther and farther into the whirling vortex.

And then he was laying her down. "No," she protested breathlessly. She clung to him, arching her back and rubbing her hips against his hard tumescence.

"Shh, shh," he whispered. "I will not leave you. Never again."

She felt the brush of soft fur beneath her bare legs and thighs and realized that Hawk had laid her on a blanket of beaver pelts. "You knew," she gasped. "You planned this."

"I did," he admitted. "And I dressed in all my finery for you on this—our true wedding night."

He skimmed the neckline of her bodice with his fingertips, leaving a blaze of fire. Suddenly she was hot all over, and the shift that had been so soft against her skin was rough and scratchy. She felt her breasts swell even more and her sensitive nipples rub against the linen material.

"Take it off," she begged him.

He untied her bodice and stays and cupped her breast through the thin shift. A rainbow tremor rocked her body.

She seized the fastening of her overskirt and began to undo it. "I want it off," she murmured. "Petticoats . . . everything. I want to feel you against my skin."

In answer, he kissed the place his palm had warmed. Then, chuckling softly, he helped her remove her garments and slip the shift over her head, leaving her naked in the first flickers of moonlight. "Say the words and I will stop," he said.

But she could not, and he knew it. Instead she caught his callused hand in hers and drew it down to cover her breast again. "Love me," she begged him. "Love me."

"For all my life," he promised. "Forever."

Speak not to me of forever, she thought. I'm not ready to think of forever. "Tonight," she murmured. "Love me tonight."

Could this be her body? How had it been possible to live in this skin, this flesh and never know the existence of these marvelous sensations?

His fingertips skimmed over the curves and hollows of her body. Her hips and belly knew the familiar caress of his touch. Hawk's skin was smooth against hers. A lock of his hair fell forward and brushed her throat and cheek, and he smelled of pine and the sea.

Kate stared up at him in wonder. His head and shoulders were illuminated by the glow of light reflecting off the ocean. His face was hidden in shadow as he removed his loincloth and tossed it aside, leaving him wearing nothing but his pride and the silver gorget.

"Sweet Kate," he said. "This man has wanted you since first I saw you, long ago, in England."

He kissed her lips, her eyelids, and the hollow beneath her ear. He trailed moist, passionate kisses down her neck, and then blazed a path along the ridge of her collarbone. His long, lean fingers stroked her breasts and teased her nipples to hard, tight nubs. And he leaned so close that she could feel the warmth of his breath and whispered love words in her ear.

"You are so beautiful," he rasped. "Touch me."

He lowered his head to nibble at her breast, and then to trace a circle around the nipple with the tip of his tongue and draw the swollen nubbin between his lips.

Her breathing came harsher as the delicious sensations washed over her, and the heat in her loins grew hotter. She tossed her head from side to side and dug her fingers into his back.

"Touch me here," he ordered. Capturing one

hand in his, he guided her fingertips to his manhood. And in her brazen shamelessness, she stroked the length of him and made sharp moans in her throat.

How could a man be so hard and yet so silken? And how could so much power lie waiting for a woman to set it free?

His hands were doing wonderful things. His fingers tangled in her nether curls and dipped lower to tease her moist folds.

"Oh," she cried aloud.

He kissed her mouth with slow, sensual deliberation, and then one long, lean finger slipped inside her. The resulting spasm took her by surprise, and she thrust her hips to take him still deeper.

He found her nipple with his lips and suckled until she writhed and bucked against him. Her need grew ever stronger. She could not bear the exquisite torture of his touch, and she would die if he stopped. "Please," she cried. "Please."

"Do you want this?" he demanded.

"Yes . . . yes," she sobbed.

"As this man wants you," he answered, sliding two fingers into her cleft.

Shocks of pleasure rolled through her, each one growing larger. "Now," she cried. "Now!"

"Now!" he thundered. There was no hesitation, no fumbling.

And when he parted her thighs and slid deep into her wet, throbbing cleft, she felt no pain, only glory. She cried out once more, and then surrendered to the sweet, wild giving and taking that echoed the crashing of the ocean waves.

With each surge, she rose higher, lost in the churning mist and eternal pull of a sea of emotion. . . . Until at last, when she was certain she would burst and shatter into a million shards of moonlight, she reached the crest of a final peak and found the star-burst of release.

"Yes? Yes?" Hawk urged.

"Yes," she whispered. "Yes."

She felt him drive deep inside her, once, twice, and yet a third time. And he too gave a cry of exultation. She felt him shudder as tremors of passion shook his body.

Gradually Hawk's breathing slowed and he sighed, long and contentedly. Then he held her, cradling her in his arms and kissing the tears from her cheeks. "It will not hurt again," he promised.

"You didn't hurt me," she assured him. She should feel shame, but she didn't. She'd never felt such happiness, such a sense of belonging. "I have never been with a man," she began, "but I felt no pain."

He laughed. "Love is good between us. You do not need to tell me. This man knows that he was the first for you, but it would not matter if he was not. I do not claim you before this night, only from this night on. You are mine, Kate, and Hawk is yours."

She shut her eyes and swallowed the lump in her throat. "I can't promise you next month or next year. Here, now, I'm with you, all of me."

She didn't want to think of tomorrow. All she wished for was the chance to savor the miraculous thing that had occurred between them . . . the act that still sent echoes of warm pleasure through her blood.

"I never knew that it could be like that . . . between a man and a woman," she admitted.

He took her hand and pressed her palm against

his so that each fingertip touched. "Do you feel the spirit leap between us?"

Her heart skipped a beat. She did feel it. "I think so," she admitted.

Slowly, tenderly, he kissed her lips. "Fire Hawk That Hunts At Dawn will love you forever," he said. "I chose you for my mate, my wife, my friend. While you live, this man will take no other woman in love or in lust."

"Don't say that," she said. "You don't know what might come between us, what might—"

"No man born of woman will come between us," he replied. "I have pledged my life to the service of the Cherokee, but after that promise comes the one I give to you. My heart beats for you alone. If I prove false, may the Thunderers strike out my eyes with lightning bolts and crows feast upon my withered staff."

"Shh, shh," she cautioned, stilling his lips with two fingers. "No talk about withering." And she laughed softly.

"You think what this man says is funny? Hawk does not make a joke. Is serious, this oath." He touched the spot over his heart. "Such an oath cannot be taken back. It means that you come before my mother." He kissed her again, so sweetly that she felt light-headed. "If you and my mother were drowning and this man could save only one, it must be you."

"I don't want you to let your mother drown to save me," she answered. She felt as though she were caught in an ocean current too powerful to fight against . . . as if she were being swept into a whirlpool.

He made a small sound of amusement and sat up.

"The mother of Hawk Who Hunts At Dawn swims like an otter. I do not think such a thing would come to pass. But if it did, you must come first."

She closed her fingers over his and brought them to her lips. She brushed her cheek against the back of his hand and then kissed each knuckle in turn. "You have ruined me," she teased. "No white man will have me to wife now that I have lain with you."

"No man, red or white, shall have you while Hawk lives," he replied. The intensity in his voice made her shiver. Suddenly she needed to break this serious mood. "Can we swim?" she asked him. "Now? In the moonlight?"

"If that is your desire, wife of my heart." He stood and tugged her to her feet. "But I warn you, it will be colder than by day."

"I think I am warm enough to risk it."

Hand in hand, they walked across the beach and waded into the surf. Kate gasped at the first shock of the water temperature, but before she could turn back, Hawk picked her up, walked a few strides, and tossed her into a wave.

She screamed as water closed over her head. But as soon as her feet touched bottom, she leaped up and looked around for him. Strangely, she was alone. "Hawk?" she called. Seconds passed, and she wondered where he could have gone. The first chilling doubts rose in her mind. "Hawk?"

Then strong hands seized her around the legs, and she screamed in earnest as he lifted her high up onto his shoulders.

"Put me down!" she cried, half in anger, half in amusement. "I was afraid a shark had eaten you. Put me down!"

"Down?" He shifted her weight as if to throw her again.

"No!" she protested. "Not like that!" She locked her arms around his neck. "If I go under, you go under."

"Ah. My panther woman has claws. So be it." He flung himself backward, and both went in with a splash.

This time Hawk caught her before she hit bottom and pulled her up with him. She wrapped her legs around his waist and kissed him. He wound the fingers of one hand in her hair and clasped her bare buttocks with the other.

She thought she'd remembered how sweet his caresses were. But as he filled her mouth with his thrusting tongue, and she reveled in the velvet texture of their meeting, she realized that she had much to learn of the art of kissing. And as they clung together, she forgot the cool air and the dark water, and thought only of the man who held her so close.

And slowly, slowly, she began to slide down his powerful, wet body, until she rested on that which had given her so much pleasure. Hawk was hard and throbbing, and it seemed the most natural thing in the world to open to his love.

They came together as true and pure as any wild creatures in the silvery moonlight, and her cries of ecstasy, mingling with his, rolled across the black water to be lost on the endless sea.

Time stood still. Kate had no idea how long they made love amid the breaking waves, but finally, Hawk carried her back onto shore to the place where they had left their clothes and blanket.

He laid her down on the bed of furs and began to towel her dry with the soft pelts. She lay there, eyes closed, satiated and exhausted but utterly content.

"When dawn comes, will you regret what we have

done?" he asked as he stretched beside her and pulled a section of the blanket over them both.

"Never," she said. Moonlight gleamed on the silver gorget at his throat.

"It warms this man's heart to know that you came to him willingly."

"And if I hadn't?" she asked sleepily. She snuggled closer to his solid heat. "Would you have taken advantage of me?"

He slipped an arm under her and she lay her head on his chest. "I did," he murmured huskily. "I brought you away from your people to this place where you could learn what a fine man Hawk is. And where I could teach you to bathe daily as a good Cherokee woman should."

She refused to let his teasing distract her. "That's not what I mean." She opened her eyes and looked into his face. "Would you . . ." She searched for the right words, not wanting to insult his honor. She knew he was not a man for rape, but there were many shades of gray between black and white. "If I had resisted, would you still have made love to me?"

"Then it would not be love, would it, my Kate? Love is never forced."

"Not all men think that way."

"Hawk is not all men. Hawk is the Chosen One." He nuzzled her hair. "Sleep while you can, for if you keep twisting against me, my man spear may—"

"No more," she protested.

"Never?" His deep chuckle made a golden glow around her heart.

"Well, maybe not never," she conceded.

"Tomorrow?"

She groaned daintily.

He traced her lower lip with his finger. "Tomorrow," he repeated.

"Perhaps." She closed her eyes and listened to the steady rise and fall of his breathing.

"Sunrise?" he murmured.

She giggled. "What have I started?"

"This was the beginning, Kate of my soul. I will take you to the mountains-of-smoke, where the streams run clear and cold, and where the valleys teem with game. I will show you clouds white as snow and a sky bluer than you have ever dreamed of seeing."

"Ummm," she murmured. She must make him understand that she'd never promised to go to the land of the Cherokee with him. Tomorrow she would make him see that here on this island might be all they could have and that they must make the best of this brief, precious gift.

She was too sleepy to think straight tonight. She loved him, and she would never be sorry that she had given herself body and soul. Tomorrow . . .

Chapter 17

$\sim$ $\cap$ $\cap$ $\sim$

Telling Hawk that she hadn't meant that she
would marry him was no easier the following
morning when she woke in his arms in the gray mist
of dawn. In truth, Kate found it hard to mention the
subject when his slightest touch, the quickest glance,
brought them together in a fever of scorching passion.

They made love in the darkest hours of the night,
in crisp May mornings when the dew was heavy on
the grass, and in the full heat of the afternoon sun.
Hawk was a generous and powerful lover. He taught
her delights that she had only heard whispered
about, and Kate found that she had a natural zest for
that which made the greatest pleasures between a
man and a woman.

There was no pretense between them, no concern
as to who should approach whom. Sometimes their
mating was hot and frenzied, other times tender or
even playful. Never had she been so happy; never
had she seen him laugh so much or lose his natural
reserve so often.

They swam in the ocean the morning after she
had given him her maidenhead and the morning
after that. Amid the caresses and the teasing, he

taught her to swim, and often the beautiful dolphin *Asgi'na* swam with them. Other dolphins appeared, but although one or two would come close to Hawk, Kate was never able to ride their backs as she did *Asgi'na's*.

On the third day, Hawk began building a small wigwam for them in the clearing by the spring. He framed the hut with saplings and covered the walls with layers of reed and bark matting. Hawk showed Kate how to weave the reeds together to make panels, and she worked at that task while he dug a fire pit and constructed a low platform approximately three feet wide around the inside of the walls. Together, they gathered pine boughs to cushion their bed.

It took four days to finish the wigwam. "I could have done it in two if I'd had a Cherokee woman to help me," he grumbled.

Kate only laughed. She was so happy with the house that she refused to pay any attention to his teasing. As much as she'd enjoyed sleeping on the beach, it felt good to know they'd have a roof over their heads if it rained. The wigwam was only nine feet from side to side, almost the same size as the playhouse she and Alice had had as children, but the snug walls made her feel safe at night.

"A door," she insisted. "You must make me a proper door."

"For that we'll need a deerskin. I don't suppose you know how to cure one? Actually, we'll need more than one hide."

Kate grimaced. "No, I don't know how to cure hides."

"You'll learn."

She gave him a dubious look.

"We need other things as well," he murmured.

The following day, they took the dugout north to trade for supplies with Nanticoke Indians. Hawk paddled for two days, stopping only long enough to sleep on the beach at night. When at last they saw the smoke of campfires, he halted and left Kate in the trees while he went on alone.

"I'll be back as soon as I can," he promised. "Stay out of sight."

She waited for hours, but when he finally returned, the boat was loaded with tanned deer hides, cooking utensils, and Indian clothing for her: a woman's doeskin dress, leggings, and beautiful beaded moccasins.

"I'm not wearing those," she protested when he insisted she change out of her English garments and shoes.

"You will," he replied. "Your shoes could cost you your life. Any Indian finding your footprints would know that you were white. And if a Powhatan sees you, he will know by your skirts that you are English."

"I like my own things."

"You will put them on, Kate, or this man will put them on you."

It was their first argument since they'd made love, but Hawk won. Sadly, she watched as he dug a hole and buried her things on the beach.

They returned to their own island, and Hawk used the soft hides to cover the bed of pine needles and to make an entrance covering that Kate could tie shut at night.

"It won't keep out a bear," Hawk warned her.

"It might."

The door went a long way toward soothing Kate's

injured feelings. And she had to admit that the soft, loose doeskin dress and moccasins were more comfortable than her English clothing.

After a few days, she came to appreciate the freedom of movement Indian garments allowed. Picking strawberries and beach plums would have been difficult in her tight stays and petticoats. Fishing, crabbing, and digging for clams along the tidemark would have been nigh impossible.

Each dawn, as soon as Hawk finished his prayers, the two of them prepared the morning meal together. It was a constant wonder to Kate how much food he could find for them in this wilderness.

Some days Hawk set snares for rabbits; those they grilled over the fire or baked in coals in a covering of mud. Wild turkeys were plentiful, the meat tender and delicious. Hawk brought them down at night, killing them with stones flung by hand. Twice, he shot a deer. Some of the venison they ate fresh, but most Hawk cut into thin strips and smoked, as he did the excess fish.

"Nothing must be wasted," he warned Kate. "That is the first law of our Creator. The deer and rabbit are our brothers. We kill when we must to live, but we do not squander what gifts the Creator has given us."

Usually breakfast consisted of fresh grilled fish that Hawk had speared in the surf and flat patties of Indian bread he'd taught her to make from the cornmeal he'd traded for with the Nanticokes.

Hawk didn't care if he ate salt or not, but Kate was used to seasoning her dishes. She added salt water and crushed strawberries to the corn cakes, creating a dish that looked rather odd but tasted wonderful. He teased her about needing salt, but she noticed that he ate more of her bread than he did his own traditional corn cakes.

It seemed to her that there were never enough hours in the day. Besides making love and gathering food, they spent long periods watching the young foxes grow and observing the other animals and birds.

From time to time, Hawk would take Kate to see the wild horses that roamed the island. She marveled at the shaggy mares and colts that grazed the swampy meadows or galloped into the surf to rid themselves of flies under the vigilant eyes of their herd stallions. There were blacks, grays, chestnuts, bays, and even spotted animals amid the several bands. Kate's favorite was a gray mare with a black mane and tail that ran with a black stallion. The mare, she named Seafoam; her dashing mate became Ebony.

"Never get too close to the herds," Hawk cautioned. "The mares are fierce in defense of their foals, and the stallions are always unpredictable."

He didn't have to worry about her forgetting the danger. She loved the wild horses, but the powerful kicks and bared teeth she witnessed were enough to make her wary. Despite his own warnings, Hawk seemed to have no fear of the horses or any other animal. She had seen him pass close enough to a wild mare to touch her. The horse hadn't shied away, but continued to eat. She gave Hawk no more than a curious glance.

"Why aren't the horses afraid of you?" Kate asked. "Why don't the squirrels or the other small animals run from you? And why do birds light within arm's reach? They aren't that trusting with me, no matter how still I sit."

Hawk's only answer was a shrug, but his dark eyes glowed with a hidden secret, and Kate couldn't help remembering the wild pack of dogs in Bramble Wood.

"You are different than most men," she concluded. And he was. He could move through the forest with the grace of a buck, vanish like the early morning mist, or suddenly appear beside her without making a sound.

"I am different." He flashed a fleeting smile. "I am the Chosen."

Never were Hawk's strange powers more apparent than when the two of them were caring for the injured red-tailed hawk he'd found.

The bird was a magnificent creature about twenty inches tall with a brown head and white throat, and nearly white belly. The underside of her tail and wings were banded with brown stripes, and her eyes were large and clear. Hawk told Kate that the red-tail possessed great intelligence, and so it seemed to Kate as she looked into the yellow-rimmed eyes.

From the first, the bird allowed Hawk to approach her and offer bits of raw meat on the end of a stick. He wove a cage of reeds and named her Starlady.

"Her wing heals quickly. See how bright and clear her eyes are," he said. "This man hopes that Starlady will be able to fly again when she recovers her strength. She is young and strong. As she gets older, the underpart of her tail feathers will turn to red. Then all may recognize her kind and tell them from other hawks."

For long periods, Hawk would sit and talk to Starlady, telling the bird Cherokee stories and legends. Sometimes he chanted in his own tongue and sang songs that Kate couldn't understand. She guessed that the stories were really for her, but in a strange way, Hawk's voice seemed to calm the bird.

Eventually Hawk was able to fasten a thong to the bird's leg and carry the hawk perched on a leather cuff on his forearm.

Kate found the wild hawk fascinating, but even if the bird hadn't been a source of unending interest, the man caring for Starlady would have held her spellbound.

She had always believed that once a man had what he wanted from a woman, he showed her less attention. This was far from true with Hawk. He courted her both day and night, bringing her handfuls of wildflowers, carving wooden trinkets for her hair, and playing for her on a flute he fashioned of reeds.

Each morning when she awoke, she would find a small gift in her moccasins. The presents were always different; a tiny woven basket of pine needles filled with sweet strawberries, a cardinal's red feather, or a beautiful shell.

"Where do you find these things?" she demanded one morning as she cradled a hummingbird nest in the palm of her hand. The nest was smaller than a copper shilling and bore shards of minute eggshell. "When do you find them?"

Hawk smiled at her as he wrapped his loin covering around his hips. "This man? This man knows nothing of what you speak," he teased. "Perhaps a wood ghost brings the treasures."

"A wood ghost?"

"It is possible, isn't it, Starlady?" he asked the red-tail. It had rained the night before, and Hawk had sunk a post into the ground inside the wigwam so that Starlady would not be helpless in the thunderstorm.

"And I suppose a wood ghost brought the necklace of blue shells I found in my moccasin yesterday morning," she said.

"Possibly."

"When I saw you drilling holes in a blue shell down by the beach two days ago?"

His dark eyes narrowed. "One shell does not a necklace make."

"I don't believe you." She flung herself on him and hugged him, reveling in his woodsy scent and the warm taste of his mouth. "I love my necklace and the hummingbird nest," she murmured between kisses. "But where did you find it?"

"A woman who wishes to find hummingbird nests for herself must learn to look and listen," he said.

"I do look. I've looked until my eyes are sore, but I see trees and birds and earth and sky."

"And horses," he said. "You do see horses."

"But not hummingbird nests."

"In time you will," he promised.

The next morning, after a storm had whipped the surf to thunder, Kate discovered an odd-shaped bottle of blue glass that she guessed had once graced a Spanish captain's table. But no matter how hard she tried, she could not get Hawk to admit that it was he who was leaving the keepsakes.

Everyday when the weather permitted, Hawk took Kate into the woods. He pointed out the difference in the signs left by squirrel, weasel, and muskrat. He taught her to build snares and fish traps. He even showed her how to build a fire, using flint and steel. He could make fire with his bowstring and several pieces of wood, but that was such a time-consuming task that Kate refused to try to learn.

"I'll let you tend to that chore," she said. Once she had perfected her ability to gather the proper tinder and firewood and start a campfire with flint and steel, he showed her the thick magnifying glass he carried in his hunting bag.

"Where did you get that?" she demanded. "And what do you intend to do with it?"

"I traded with a sailor. And if you will watch, my impatient one, you will see what magic this glass can make."

Eyes twinkling with mischief, he crouched in the noonday sun and held the glass over a tiny pile of cedar shavings. In seconds, the tinder began to smoke and finally burst into flames.

"Fire? If you can make a fire so easily, why have you been rubbing twigs together?"

He chuckled. "The glass only works in sunlight. And if you had known I had it, you would not have learned the proper way." He stamped out the infant fire. "Now you know two ways. Fire can be the only thing that stands between you and death, and I would not have you ignorant."

Unless the wind was strong from the land toward the sea, they kept no fire in the daytime. They made a new one each night when the smoke would not rise in a column and reveal their presence to anyone passing the island by dugout.

"Gar will not give up hunting us," Hawk told her. "I killed his men and my cousin has a long memory. I do not want us to fall into his hands."

Kate didn't worry about the Powhatans and tried not to think about the English. She knew it was too late to warn Jamestown now. Either her countrymen had been spared an attack by the Powhatan, been attacked and survived, or they'd died. She didn't

want to think of her own future either; she refused
to consider what would become of her if she didn't
go to the Cherokee as Hawk's wife.

If she was to have only this precious time with
Hawk, she must live each day without fear or
apprehension. Each sunrise was a new memory to
stitch into her quilt of happiness, and she could not
bear to let go of Hawk and this island until she had
stored up a lifetime of joy.

The one concern that she could not banish was
that she might conceive a child. She had been
innocent of sexual matters, but she was not a fool. A
child of mixed blood, English and Cherokee, would
surely be despised by both races.

One afternoon, after a particularly satisfying epi-
sode of lovemaking, as they lay side by side on a bed
of wild strawberries in a sheltered clearing, she
revealed this fear to Hawk.

He listened gravely, then raised her hand to his
lips and kissed the pulse at her wrist. "Think you
that our blood is not the same color?" he asked.

"Skin or blood, it makes no difference to me what
color you are," she replied passionately. "You are
the finest man I've ever known." It was hard to
speak her thoughts when his touch sent shivers
through her veins. "For myself, I can endure whatever comes, but I could not bear for a babe of ours to
be condemned for what we have done."

Hawk raised himself on one elbow and fixed her
with his piercing gaze. His mouth was stained with
wild strawberries and a berry leaf clung in his hair.
"This man was a child unwanted among the Powhatan. I know the ache of waiting to be called to join a
game of ball when even the smallest have been
asked. I have heard the whispers behind my moth-

er's back and seen the scorn on old men's faces when they looked at me. My own grandfather, the mighty Powhatan, emperor of the Powhatan nation, hated me so much that he would not look upon my face."

Hawk's eyes were dry, his features as hard as if carved of granite. He would allow himself no pity for the abused child he had once been, but Kate was not so disciplined. Her throat constricted and tears welled up to trickle down her cheeks.

"Then you know what I fear," she murmured, flinging herself across his chest. Both were as naked as the day they had been born, yet she felt no shame. She wrapped her arms around his neck and brought her face close to his. "I love you," she whispered. "You know that I love you, but . . ."

He pulled her head down and kissed her mouth tenderly, then sat up and wiped away a tear. "I do not tell you these things to make you weep, only so that you will know I would have care for a son or daughter of my loins." His smile was faint, fleeting. "I will not give you a child, Kate. Not yet. I would not be so foolish."

She pushed away and stared at him in bewilderment. "What do you mean? You won't? I could be pregnant even now. I could have . . ."

He shook his head. "No, heart of my heart. When autumn winds paint the leaves to gold and scarlet, you will be as slender as you are today. I intend to bring you to the Cherokee as my bride. It will be enough for my mother to accept that, without concern for a coming grandchild."

"Your mother? What does your mother have to do with this?" she demanded. Hawk had mentioned his mother, of course, and she knew that he was fond of her. But she hadn't supposed he would put such stock in what she thought of his choice in a bride.

Not that she intended to go with him, Kate reminded herself indignantly. She didn't. But if she had been willing, then why should he—of all men—be concerned about his mother?

Kate reached for the shirt Hawk had fashioned for her and wrapped it around her waist. Her fringed doeskin vest was lying on the other side of Hawk, and as she tried to crawl around him to reach it, he caught her.

"Do not be angry with me," he teased. "I speak the truth. Cherokee women have great power. A man who does not respect his mother or his sisters is useless. Who would want him for a husband? If he had no regard for the women of his clan, how could he respect a wife?"

"You did not tell me I would have to please your mother." She turned her face away from him. "Give me my vest. The sun is hot. I don't want to be burned."

He chuckled. "I could shade you from the sun."

"You've already done that." She tried to frown, then realized she didn't want to quarrel with him. "Please," she said. "My vest?"

He handed it to her and she quickly donned it and laced up the front. As May had turned to June, the weather had grown hotter than Kate could have imagined. She'd found the deerskin dress too warm. In response, Hawk had supplied these garments, so soft and light they might have been a second skin, but clothing that would see her locked in the stocks for a public disgrace had any Englishmen spied her in them.

Her fingers and knees were stained with red from the berries. The basket Hawk had woven for her lay empty on its side. They had quickly lost a desire to gather strawberries. Instead they had eaten them, thrown a few at each other, and ended . . . Kate laughed merrily and heat rose in her cheeks as she remembered where and how they had shared the sweet fruit and what scandalously brazen places she had kissed him.

Hawk retrieved his loincloth and put it on. "You will not swell with child," he said. "Since we reached this place, I have given you leaves of . . ." He searched for the English word. "Medicine. In your food."

"You've poisoned me?"

He laughed. "Among the Cherokee, we do not have children unless we want them. This man also eats, but not of the same leaves. For a man, it is the root of the . . ." He shrugged. "Know only that Hawk could never harm you, Kate. When you stop eating the medicine, we can make a child."

"I've never heard of such a thing."

"Trust me. I will never hurt you."

"Doesn't every maid hear such a tale from the man who wishes to take her virtue?" She grew solemn. "I do trust you, Hawk. But what we have together here can't last. It's wonderful and precious to me, but one day we must return to our own people."

He fixed her with a soulful look. "You are my people, Kate. Do you not remember what I told you? You are mine, and this man will never let you go."

"You care for Starlady, but when the time comes, you'll let her go."

He nodded. "I will. But you are not a bird. You are a woman, and your place is—"

"At your beck and call?"

"At my side," he answered quietly. "The years

that I spent among the whites have taught me much, but you know more. The knowledge you bring to the Cherokee will be worth twice mine."

"What makes you think I will go with you?"

He smiled at her. "I trust you. Your love is as pure as spring water. You will come, and you will learn to care for the Cherokee as I do."

"You expect me to betray my own kind?"

"Our children will be Cherokee."

She sighed and turned back toward camp. There seemed to be no way to make him understand how she felt. She loved him more than life itself. But marriage and a lifetime among strange Indians might be more than she could promise.

She wished she could convince him to stay here on this magical island with her. She could imagine herself living here for years, watching the horses, listening to the crash of waves and the cries of the seabirds.

Hawk spoke her language. He had lived among the English. He knew her ways. The Cherokee did not. They might laugh at her clumsy attempts to speak and understand the Indian tongue. They might ridicule her for not knowing how to cure a deerskin or prepare dried fish. They might hate her for the color of her skin.

Here, Hawk was hers. But among his own kind, who was to say that he would not tire of her as her own grandfather had tired of her Italian grandmother. She had come to England as a merry young bride, but she had never been accepted by her husband's family. She had remained a stranger in a far-off land, to her dying day.

Here on the island, the forest was not nearly as frightening as it had been, but Kate could not imagine the endless valleys and the high mountains of Hawk's Cherokee home. What if she felt smothered by the folds of the smoky hills? What if she never came to love Hawk's land or his people?

But how could she bear to leave him? And if she did, where would she go?

In mid-June, heavy rains fell. For several days, Kate and Hawk remained close to the shelter. He taught her a gambling game played with a turtle shell and colored stones, and she told him stories of her family and childhood.

"It was Father's greatest disappointment that he had only girls," she said. "Mother said that he would have been a better squire if he'd had tall sons to help bear his burdens."

"Among the Cherokee, girl children are welcomed," Hawk told her. "Women are the heart and conscience of a nation."

"So you keep telling me," she replied, "but what would happen to me if I did go with you to the Cherokee and your mother hated me on sight? What if she rejected me as a daughter-in-law?"

He laughed. "She probably will, at first. But my mother is a woman of uncommonly good sense. She will come to see your value."

"But what if she didn't? What then?"

"Then I would take you away to a hidden valley and live with you alone." He seized her by the waist and lifted her, twirling 'round and 'round inside the small wigwam until her head spun.

"Stop!" she protested. "You're making me dizzy."

"This man wants you dizzy," he answered. "Dizzy with love for him." He'd pulled her close and kissed her.

It was impossible to remain serious when Hawk

was in such a mood. Kate found herself laughing
and joining in his merry antics.

"Do you know the Cherokee rain dance?" he
asked between kisses.

"No. I've never heard of such a thing."

"I shall teach you." He drew a finger slowly along
the neckline of her vest.

"Is this another plot to get me out of my clothes?"

"Trust me," he teased. "Close your eyes and do
not open them."

"Is this a game or a dance?" She did not care. A
rainbow of colored lights spun behind her closed
eyes, and delicious shivers ran from the crown of her
head to her toes. Obediently, she waited while his
strong, lean fingers moved lightly along the surface
of her skin, leaving a path of tingling sensation
wherever he touched her.

Already waves of heat radiated outward from her
loins, and her sense of hearing and smell became
more acute. She could hear the patter of raindrops
against the outer shell of the hut and the faint rustle
of leaves swaying in the wind. The wigwam held a
dozen odors; pine, leather, cedar, and mint mingled
and swirled around one another, but the strongest
was Hawk's scent, clean and bold and virile.

She caught his hand and brought it to her lips.

"No fair," he admonished. "You must keep still."
Chuckling, he tugged at the ties that held her
doeskin vest together, then slowly pushed the soft
leather off her bare shoulder and kissed her there.

She shivered. "I thought this was a dance."

"Shhh." Still laughing, he repeated the same
gesture on her left shoulder. When her vest tumbled
to the floor, he began to tease the strings at her
waist.

Kate gasped as Hawk slid her skirt down over her hips and knelt in front of her. She felt his warm breath on her midriff. When he kissed her belly, she uttered a soft moan.

It was harder to keep her balance as his caresses moved lower. His hands brushed over her hips, and her skirt slid over her knees and ankles. Hawk's breath stirred her curls and she shivered with delight. "I think I like this dance," she murmured.

Then she felt a new sensation. Startled by the light tickle, she opened her eyes a crack.

"No cheating," he reminded her.

A feather . . . small and white and downy. She had caught a glimpse of it as he brought it to her naked breast. "Hawk . . ."

"Shhh." His voice was like the touch of the feather, so faint. Kate felt moisture pool in the depths of her woman's cleft.

Hawk brushed the feather across her nipples and under the curve of her breasts. She inhaled deeply as he painted a ribbon of invisible fire down to her belly button and still lower. With infinite patience, he tortured the inner surface of her thighs and down her legs to the back of her knees.

"Monster," she accused him. The heat had spread through her veins and bones. She trembled harder; each breath became a struggle. And all the while her mind created lustful images that swirled and clashed and flared on the back of her eyelids.

Then, suddenly, when she thought she couldn't stand another second of his teasing, he seized her by the hand and pulled her outside into the pouring rain. Her eyes flew open and she stared at him. "Have you gone mad?" she demanded.

"No, my Kate. Trust me. Put your hands so." He guided her fingers to press against his, hand to hand. "Close your eyes," he reminded her. "Our hands must keep touching."

And so, she stood naked in the rain, eyes closed, hands bonded to his while he led her through the steps of an ancient, erotic dance. He touched her and withdrew, over and over again. First cheeks, then breasts, and finally thighs. There was no music but the warm rain, and the drumming that echoed through her head came not from some Indian instrument, but from the pounding of her own blood in her veins.

Without the freedom of her hands, she was forced to find other ways to share the passion that possessed her. Tongues and lips and teeth could give pleasure, and as the dance gathered strength from the storm, she found herself on her knees in the wet grass rubbing her face against Hawk's throbbing tumescence and kissing the length of him without shame or question.

His shuddering groans fired her own desire as she reveled in the power she had not known she possessed. Slowly, tantalizingly, she tasted and laved his erect phallus, finally drawing him into her mouth and suckling until she felt tremors seize him.

With a groan, he pulled away, still keeping his palms and fingers pressed against hers. "There is more than that, my heart," he rasped above the melody of the wind.

It was her turn to stand, and his to explore. But she was not so strong. As Hawk's mouth touched her most intimately, spasms of sexual culmination rocked her body. Her hands fell away from his; her knees went weak, and she would have fallen if he hadn't caught her.

"Hawk! Hawk!" she cried. "I . . ."

"Shhh," he soothed, laughing despite the rain

running down his face. "Shhh." He carried her into the wigwam and wrapped her in furs, then lit a fire and crawled into the warm nest beside her.

"I'm sorry," she said. "I couldn't wait. I just . . ."

He pulled her close against him. "There will be other dances, light of my soul," he whispered.

"But I . . ." She hid her face against his chest. "I wanted to give you . . ."

"You did, my precious. You have given this man more than you know." He rolled her onto her back and brushed the damp hair away from her face, then kissed her lips with great tenderness.

"I am as much a barbarian as you," she murmured. Afterglow still coursed through her body, and she savored it. "I am completely and utterly a wanton."

"Yes," he agreed, kissing the tip of her nose. "A great compliment to a Cherokee woman."

"But I'm not a Cherokee woman," she wailed.

"I'll overlook that," he teased, "considering your skill at dancing."

"Hmmm." She curled against him and closed her eyes, remembering.

"It was a successful rain dance," he said.

She opened one eye. "And will it rain even more?"

"No. That was a dance to stop the rain. Tomorrow will be bright and clear. You will see."

"Mmmm-hmmm," she muttered. "And is there a dance to make rain?"

"Oh, yes." He chuckled, a warm deep sound that made her heart skip a beat. "And if the sun shines, I'll teach you that one tomorrow."

Chapter 18

Kate closed her eyes as she heard the twang of Hawk's bowstring. She didn't need to look to know that his arrow had brought down the yearling deer; if Hawk drew his bow, he hit his target. She turned her back as he sprinted away to the place of the kill. She could imagine him standing over the fallen animal, offering his prayer of thanks to the animal's spirit.

At home in England, she'd never thought of how succulent beef roasts or lamb chops appeared on her father's dinner table. She'd enjoyed the meat without considering that a beast had to die so that she might eat. Here on the island, it was harder to keep that barrier between her desire for venison or wild turkey and her regret for the killing of a beautiful creature.

"Kate!" Hawk called. "Come and help me."

Taking a deep breath, she did as he bid her. When she reached the spot, she tried to avoid looking at the glazed eyes of the dead deer. "I know you have to do this, but it's hard for me," she said. "Don't you ever feel that you're betraying the animals when they come to you?"

He shook his head and continued skinning the

265

young buck. "I do not use the power of the Chosen on those I must kill," he explained patiently. "I never forget that an animal's life force is as strong as my own."

"But you shot it. And this one didn't have a broken leg like the last. This one was—"

"We needed meat. I do not kill for sport as the English do. I am a man and a hunter. I would not take a doe unless I was starving. I do not choose a buck in the prime of his mating years. I killed this one quick with a single arrow. He will not suffer the pain of slow starvation or the gradual wasting of old age. The spirit of this deer will be born again into a new fawn."

She nibbled on her bottom lip. "We could live on fish."

"Is the life of a fish less precious than this buck? Or a blade of grass that the deer rips up?" He shrugged. "I am only a man. I do not know the mind of the Creator. I do not know why we hunt the deer, and the deer does not hunt us. I accept my place in the circle of life and try not to waste any of Mother Earth's blessings."

She met his gaze, then averted her eyes. "You make me feel foolish."

"Never foolish, Kate. Your heart is full of compassion." He wiped his fingers clean on the grass and lifted her chin. "Go back to the camp. I will finish here. You can learn to skin a deer another time."

She nodded. "If you really don't mind."

"Go. Gather some of those mushrooms I showed you on the way, at the edge of the meadow where the yellow flowers grow. Pick only those you recognize. Some mushrooms are poison and can kill with a taste."

"I know where they are," she assured him. "And you've taught me which are which. There are groundnuts there too. I want to dig some of those. They're good with venison."

"You won't get lost?"

She laughed and threw a pinecone at him. "I won't get lost. A babe could find her way to the spot."

Kate loved that meadow. Often the stallion she called Ebony grazed there with his mares and their young. There was a freshwater pond in the center of the field where she and Hawk sometimes swam.

Besides, she wanted to get back to the wigwam ahead of him so that she'd have time to start the evening meal and still be able to work on the moccasins she was sewing as a surprise for him. She'd taken apart a pair of his old ones to make a pattern, and she was nearly finished.

Oddly, she felt no fear as she hurried away from Hawk into this stretch of forest. At home she would have hesitated about going into a woods on foot, but here there were no traveling tinkers, no beggars, and no highwaymen. There was nothing to alarm her but an occasional snake, and those were mostly harmless. Hawk had pointed out a poisonous water moccasin one day when they were crossing the marsh in the dugout. She'd not overcome her dislike for snakes; those she would never feel pity for as she did the deer.

Today she saw no snakes, nothing but the usual rainbow of birds, a harmless box turtle, and a small rabbit. She found the well-trod game trail that led to the meadow and was soon on her hands and knees gathering mushrooms.

Then, without warning, the earth vibrated. When she looked around to see what had caused the strange sensation, a herd of horses thundered across the clearing, then wheeled past her in a solid mass, manes and tails flying behind them.

A gray mare with a black mane and tail shied off and galloped toward the spot where Kate knelt. She suspected this might be Seafoam, but the horse was moving so fast that she couldn't tell.

Hot on the mare's heels charged the black stallion, ears laid back against his sleek head, teeth bared. The mare squealed and lashed out at him with her hind hooves. The stallion pounded down on her, trumpeting a challenge. He crowded close to her side and bit her viciously on the neck.

The gray mare twisted and snapped at him. As she turned, Kate got a better look at her; she was certain now that it was Seafoam.

Kate's throat constricted, and a trickle of sweat ran down her neck. She dropped the mushrooms and clenched her hands into tight fists. She was frightened of the stallion's violent behavior, but she didn't want to attract his attention by running back to the forest. Instead she crouched on the grass and watched the primeval drama being played out in front of her.

Ebony reared and threw back his head. His black mane whipped in the wind, and his eyes flashed with savage light. Seafoam spun on her hind legs and tried to escape in another direction, but the stallion cut her off and threw his massive weight across her back. The mare staggered and her hindquarters buckled. The other horses scattered across the meadow.

The black's teeth closed on Seafoam's withers and bright red stained the beautiful silver coat. The mare scrambled up and stood trembling from nose to rump. White froth trickled from her open mouth, and her eyes rolled back in her head.

He'll kill her, Kate thought. She held her breath, afraid to move a muscle for fear the stallion would notice her and run her down with those iron hooves.

"He will not kill her," Hawk said, answering her unspoken question with uncanny accuracy.

Kate whirled at the sound of his voice. How had he crossed the open space to her side without her seeing or hearing him? "What are you?" she whispered, "a wood ghost?"

"Shhh," he whispered. "It is not safe." He caught her by the shoulder and pressed her down in the tall grass. "Watch."

The mare whinnied frantically, her shrill plea drowned in the black's thunderous scream.

The heat of Hawk's hand burned through Kate's deerskin vest into the small of her back. Tremors of fear and uncertainty washed through her. She wanted to break away to run as the mare had run from the stallion, but Hawk's harsh whisper in her ear held her motionless.

"See," he hissed. "See how he claims what is his."

Kate's eyes widened in shock. Her stomach plummeted, and the acrid taste of fear filled her mouth as she watched the stallion cover the mare in a wild, frenzied consummation.

Her father had kept horses, but she'd never been permitted near the stables when studs were brought to the mares. The squire had considered his unmarried daughters too delicate to be present during breeding.

How could she know that a stallion's organ was so huge or that he could be so savagely male? How could she know that the air would be charged with the force of that untamed mating?

She covered her face with her hands, but that

could not shut out the squeals of the stallion or the high-pitched whinny of the gray mare. Tears clouded Kate's eyes, and she began to shiver uncontrollably.

"Shh, shh," Hawk murmured. "Do not cry. Look there. The gray one is unharmed."

Tentatively she uncovered her eyes. Stud and mare stood side by side, both streaked with lather. Seafoam's neck arched and she nibbled at the stallion's nose.

Kate stared in confusion. Minutes ago, Ebony had been the violent aggressor, the gray the victim. Now the mare seemed to be in control. Ebony snorted and shook his head, while Seafoam skittered around him playfully. Finally when she appeared to tire of teasing him, she pranced delicately toward the pond and the stallion followed.

Hawk waited until the horses splashed knee-deep into the water and stood contentedly with heads touching, before he took Kate's hand and rose to his feet. "Come," he said. "He will not charge us now."

She took a deep breath. She couldn't get the erotic violence of what she'd just witnessed out of her mind. Her chest felt as though a heavy stone was crushing it, and her balance was off.

"Kate."

For an instant, her gaze met Hawk's, and she read the hot desire in his eyes. The thought lanced through her that he might throw her to the ground and ravish her here and now, but then she saw control settle over his features. His shoulders tensed and he motioned toward the woods line.

"Come," he said. "It is warm. We must wash the meat and cool it in the sea. What we don't want to cook at once must be sliced and dried, lest it go bad."

He had left the venison and the hide only a few yards inside the trees. Now Hawk retrieved the meat and started back toward the sea. Kate followed his purposeful strides in silence.

Hawk had never been less than tender with her. Their lovemaking had sometimes been quick and hot, but she had never felt threatened. She had glimpsed something in his eyes in the meadow that hinted at a depth of untamed wildness in him to match the stallion's. It frightened and intrigued her. Somehow, the sandy island soil under her feet didn't feel as solid.

Kate smelled the ocean when Hawk suddenly stopped and motioned her to crouch down. He shrugged the load off his back, and pointed to the sky, where a flock of terns had swirled above them.

"Stay here," he ordered. In seconds he was gone, melting into the low pine shrub without a sound.

Kate's heart raced. What had alerted Hawk? He'd seemed alarmed by the terns, but their behavior seemed ordinary to her. They were flighty, and even a single pelican could send them into shrieking panic.

Minutes passed. A mosquito buzzed around Kate's head. Her legs cramped, and she shifted onto her knees. An ant began to trek over her bare leg. Still she waited.

I'll count to five hundred, she thought. *If he hasn't come back by then, I'll go after him and see what's wrong.* She wondered if she should return to the wigwam. She wasn't sure she'd put the moccasins away, and she wanted to be certain he didn't see them before they were finished.

Abruptly, Hawk parted a low-hanging bough to her left and motioned to her. "Quickly," he hissed. "Follow me."

"What is it?" she demanded. "What's wrong?"

"Powhatan. They come by sea. Two score of boats, perhaps a hundred warriors."

"How? Why?" She went numb with fear.

"There is no time, Kate. Courage." He turned and darted down the game trail. She followed him, running. There were several hundred yards from the spot where she'd waited when she realized that he hadn't brought the venison.

"Hawk," she called. "The deer."

He turned and put a finger to his lips, then ran on. She was breathless when they reached the camp. He took a blanket, the fire kit, and his blowgun and thrust them into her arms. "Take this," he ordered. "We'll reach the dugout, if we can."

Kate grabbed the moccasins, a bag of meal, and the knife Hawk had given her. "Are you sure they know we're here?" she asked.

"They know. Only warriors come. No families. They'd have women with them if they were on a peaceful mission." He went to Starlady's cage and opened the door. The bird hopped onto his bare wrist, her talons drawing blood as she clutched tightly. He gave no indication that he felt the pain. He stroked her back lightly with two fingers, then took his knife and sawed through the leather band around her leg. Starlady hissed and stretched her neck.

"Fly free," he said, raising his arm.

The hawk tensed and gave a sharp cry. She leaped up, flapped several times, and soared up over the treetops.

Gooseflesh rose on Kate's arms as she watched the bird fly away. "Goodbye, Starlady," she whispered. "Godspeed."

"May the South Wind lend you strength," Hawk

said. He snatched the strips of dried fish from the rack and thrust them into his hunting bag. "We go."

"Maybe they don't know we're here," Kate said. "Maybe they're fishing or—"

"They come for us."

"How do you know?"

"Trust me," he answered.

She should have been terrified, but strangely, she wasn't. She was with Hawk, and she had faith that he would outwit or outfight his opponents.

"God keep us," she murmured. God keep Hawk safe. If he were safe, she would be.

Together they raced toward the gut where Hawk's dugout lay hidden under a mat of reeds, but when they were still a distance away, Hawk stopped and signaled her to wait.

"Let me come with you. I can help," she said.

"Stay, woman!"

She started to argue, then realized he was gone.

"Wood ghost," she muttered. The overhanging branches hadn't even swayed when he'd vanished into them.

This time he was back in minutes. She knew by his expression that the news wasn't good.

"Gar's braves have found the boat," he said. "They lie in wait for us." Swiftly he led her through a grove of cedar trees and along a high sandy ridge.

"Where are we going?" she asked when he stopped long enough for her to catch her breath. She noticed that Hawk had a long cut running down the side of his arm. "You're hurt!"

"It's nothing."

"You fought with the Powhatan?"

He shrugged. "There are marshes on the bay side of the island. We may find a place to hide where they can't find us."

They slid down a bank and followed a deer trail to the edge of a meadow. "Come!" Hawk commanded. Seizing her hand, he leaped into the clearing. Beyond the open grass was a thicket. Stickers scratched Kate's arms and legs and tangled in her hair, but Hawk didn't pause until they were deep inside the tangle.

Then she heard the first echo of drums and a long, drawn-out sound that resembled the notes of a horn. Kate looked to Hawk for an explanation.

"They hunt us as they drive the deer," he said. "Many men, much noise."

"What is that?" she asked as the horn blasted again.

"A conch shell."

"What do we do?"

"Wait." He encircled her with his arm and pulled her to rest against him.

Above them came the *keer–keer–keer* of a red-tailed hawk. Kate looked up, but she couldn't see the bird. "Is that Starlady? She'll give us away."

Hawk shaded his eyes from the sun, but the bird was gone. "Perhaps she comes to show us a way," he said. "The Hawk Spirit is strong. Starlady may be a messenger."

On hands and knees, he crawled out of the undergrowth. Kate followed close behind him. When they could stand again, she looked for any sign of the bird, but she saw nothing except blue sky and gray clouds to the east.

Not clouds, she realized with a start. Smoke. The first scent of burning wood and grass drifted on the wind. "A fire?" She pointed. "But why?"

"If Gar cannot track us, he thinks to burn us out."

"Burn the woods? He can't do that!" She thought frantically of the deer, rabbits, and birds. "And the horses? What of the horses?" she cried. "I'll kill him myself if he hurts those horses!"

Twigs snapped to her right, and Kate twisted around to see a doe and her fawn emerge from the trees and flee across a marshy stretch of ground. A gray fox broke from cover and vanished in the tall grass.

"The horses will survive," Hawk said softly. "The stallion will take the herd into the surf."

"How do you know that?"

"It is what I would do." He squeezed her hand. "He is wise, the one you call Ebony. He will care for his mares."

Kate swallowed. The column of smoke thickened. Another rose to the left. The rumble of drums grew louder, and a man's shout echoed from the meadow.

"Run!" Hawk said.

Two Powhatan men broke from a coppice of willows.

"Go!" Hawk cried.

Kate began to run. An arrow drove into the grass just ahead of her. She stopped short and looked back. The first brave staggered back, clutching an arrow protruding from the center of his chest. The second drew his bow and took aim at Hawk.

For an instant, the two men looked hard into each others' faces, then both let fly. Hawk twisted sideways and his opponent's arrow missed his hip by inches. The Powhatan took Hawk's missile through the throat. He fell with a strangled gasp.

Kate felt faint. She lowered her head and tried to breathe normally, but the meadow seemed to spin slowly around her.

Hawk ran to the men and retrieved not only his own arrows, but those filling the Powhatan's quivers. He also recovered a second bow and brought it back to Kate. "Carry this for me," he said. "But if I'm killed, make no attempt to fight them. Throw down the bow. You're a woman. You should be safe."

She shook her head in disbelief. "They were trying to kill me then. That arrow . . ."

"Missed." He took her arm and pushed her toward the nearest shelter, a fallen log. They climbed over the top and crouched down behind it.

Kate's fingers and toes felt numb. She had just seen two men killed violently by the man who'd held her close and cared for her for months in this lonely place. He'd killed to protect her, as he'd done at the attack on William's Hundred, and given the chance, she would kill to protect him. She fingered the little knife she'd tucked into her belt. "Did you know them?"

He nodded. "The first was Otter Swimming. The man I shot in the neck has a wife and infant son. I think his name is Stands In Fire."

She took in another deep breath and slowly let it out. "I'll never become used to it . . . the killing," she murmured. "In England, I never—"

Hawk's voice hardened. "In your country I saw men's bones hanging in iron cages at the crossroads, and I watched soldiers cut a boy's hand off for stealing a loaf of bread."

"Criminals."

"The boy had but ten winters."

She looked away. "The laws against stealing are harsh, I know." She rubbed at a bit of moss on the log. "What do the Cherokee do with thieves?"

"We banish them," he answered, scanning the woods line with his fierce gaze. "No man or woman will speak with them or share food. A thief is dead to us."

"But won't they just go to steal from someone else?"

"There!"

Off to the left, a brave's silhouette appeared briefly, then another and another. Each man carried a torch. Kate shivered. "We're going to die here, aren't we?" she said as she watched the Powhatans fire the grass and underbrush.

"We are not dead yet."

The breeze blew toward them, carrying with it dense smoke and bits of burning chaff. "If I lose you, I may as well be dead," she whispered.

She could not believe that the magic of the island was being so abruptly destroyed . . . that what she'd found with Hawk might be lost forever in minutes. Suddenly nothing mattered but her love for him. "If we get out of this, I'll go with you to your Cherokee," she promised. "I'll go with you and never look back." Tears clouded her vision, and she dashed them away.

For a few seconds, his eyes lingered on her and the hint of a smile tugged at the corner of his mouth. "I will hold you to this promise, my Kate."

She nodded, coughing. "I know you will." The smoke burned her eyes, and they began to tear.

The threat of being burned alive should have made her even more frightened, but the fear had passed. She could think of nothing but the love she and Hawk had shared. How could she have been so stupid? If she'd agreed earlier, perhaps they could have escaped to his beautiful mountains.

She wanted to throw herself into his arms, to feel his mouth crushing hers. . . . But there was no time and Hawk expected her to meet whatever came without hysterics. *Have courage*, he had told her. She must. . . .

Hawk pointed to the stretch of open marsh behind them. "See," he said. "That small rise . . . that tussock of earth and reeds."

Kate nodded. The area he indicated was no more than a dozen feet across. "Swim out to that island and hide in the reeds," he ordered. "The fire will not reach you there. I'll try to draw Gar's warriors away."

"No," she said. "That's crazy. I won't leave you." By now a thick wall of acrid smoke hid them from the Powhatan, but Kate could hear the warriors' taunting cries. "You can't kill yourself for me," she argued. "I won't let you."

Hawk stood and seized her around the waist and ran back toward the water. "Hold your breath," he said. "I'm going to throw you in, so you'll leave no trail on the muddy bank."

"I love you," she cried. Her heart was beating like a drum as he tossed her high into the air. She came down with a splash, went under, and surfaced sputtering. She wanted desperately to go back and stand beside him, but she knew it was too late. Trying not to think of snakes in the murky water, she swam to the tiny island and crawled up into the reeds. Wiping water from her eyes, she parted the foliage and looked back for Hawk.

He raised a hand in salute and notched an arrow in his bowstring. Then a thick fog of smoke drifted over him, and she could see him no more.

She waited, listening. Two ducks flew overhead. Something wiggled under her knee. She suppressed the desire to cry out and shrank back. A fiddler crab burrowed out of the muddy thatch and scampered down to the water's edge.

Kate pulled the dripping pack off her back. Her deerskin blanket was wet, her only food was soaked through, and she'd lost most of the darts for Hawk's blowgun. She pulled off the single moccasin she had left and flung it down beside her.

No-see-ums, tiny biting insects so small as to be almost invisible, buzzed around her head, crawling into her eyes and nose. She slapped at them frantically, wondering if dodging a forest fire would have been better than this.

The grass on the bank of the marsh crackled and sputtered. Small fires sparked from others, but the wind had shifted. The smoke blew back toward the Powhatan line. Kate strained to catch sight of what was happening.

She heard water ripple, and a dark head appeared above the surface. She almost screamed, then saw that it was Hawk. He waded up onto solid ground and crawled into the weeds beside her.

"Hawk!" She kept her voice low, but nothing could keep her hands off him. She hugged him and kissed his face, his hair, his smoke-smudged face. "I thought you were dead," she whispered.

"I had to kill another warrior."

His voice echoed with hollow aching.

"Someone you knew?"

He shook his head. "A stranger, but still a Powhatan." He dropped the strap of his hunting bag around Kate's neck. "Keep this safe for me. My gorget is in there and my magnifying glass."

"We're about to be murdered and you're worrying about your possessions?"

"I've carried them a long way. I don't intend to lose them now."

Hawk's eyes clouded with doubt, an emotion she had never read there before. "Are you hurt?" Kate asked him.

He nodded.

"Where?" Frantically she began to inspect his body for serious injury.

"No." He pushed her hands away. "This man's ache is here." He lightly touched the spot over his heart. "I have failed you, Kate, failed you and the Cherokee."

"Don't say that!" She cradled his face in her hands and looked deep into his eyes. "You haven't failed us, Hawk. No man could do more than you've done."

"But not enough." His proud shoulders slumped. "I am not worthy of you . . . not worthy of the trust my people put in me. And for my weakness, the Cherokee will go the way of the Powhatan. We shall scatter like thistle down in the wind until the day comes that none who walk the earth will remember a mighty nation once lived."

"Stop that!" she cried. "Stop it!" Her fingers knotted in his damp hair. "I won't let you talk that way!" She shook him fiercely. "Who chose you? Painted Stick? The holy man? Did he choose you?"

Hawk shook his head. "The spirits . . ." Muscles strained along his throat as he swallowed. "The Spirit of the Hawk chose me."

"And now you doubt the wisdom of that choice?" she demanded. "You doubt this Hawk Spirit?"

"No . . ." He blinked and looked at her like a man waking from sleep. "I doubt myself—not the spirits. Not Painted Stick."

"You cannot shed the burden so easily." Her touch became gentle as she stroked his face again. "Trust in the Creator, Hawk. Put your trust in Him. He knows what we can never know. Stay true to him, and he will never desert you or your Cherokee people."

"Oh, woman," he whispered hoarsely. "You are stronger than this man could ever be." For a second, moisture gleamed in Hawk's dark eyes, and then a grim smile twisted his lips. "The spirits were right when they picked you," he said. Then he leaned close and kissed her tenderly.

She clung to him as tears wet her cheeks. "I love you," she said. "No matter what comes."

He thrust her away and fixed her gaze with his. "If I die, you must complete my mission," he said. "If this man cannot go to the Cherokee, you must."

"I will," she promised.

A shadow passed over the tussock. Kate looked up to see a hawk flying overhead. "Is it Starlady?" The underside of the bird's tail still showed the speckled black and white of an immature red-tail.

Keer-Keer-Keer! the bird shrieked. She dove low over their heads and then rose to a height of twenty feet and circled.

Armed braves gathered on the charred grass beside the water. One, taller than his comrades, raised a fist and shouted in the Indian tongue. Kate recognized him as Gar.

"What does he say?" she begged Hawk.

"He wants us to surrender."

"The hawk gave us away," she murmured.

He nodded. "You told me to trust in the Hawk Spirit. She must have her reasons." He stood. "Will you promise to spare the woman's life?" he demanded in English.

"Have you forgotten your father's language?" Gar shouted back. "I promise you a quick death. Nothing more."

Keer-Keer-Keer! Starlady made a final sweep over the Powhatans. A brave lifted his bow, but another shoved the weapon from his hand. Then the young hawk soared high and away with powerful strokes of her wings.

"She's all right, isn't she?" Kate whispered.

"Yes," Hawk agreed. "We gave her time to heal."

"Lay down your weapons!" Gar shouted.

Hawk stared across the water at his cousin. "And if I do not?"

"I will give your woman to the shaman for an offering."

"What does he mean?" Kate asked. "Give me to who?"

"I want your word, cousin. Word of a Powhatan prince, one to another. I want her life spared."

Kate looked up at Hawk. "Don't trust him. We can swim! Hide in the swamp!"

"Make up your mind," Gar threatened. "The shaman will crush her head with a stone, or he will cut her throat."

"Enough, cousin," Hawk answered. "Give me your word that she will be returned to Jamestown."

"Alive and returned?" The Powhatan laughed. "You think me a fool? Death for her or life as my slave. Choose."

Hawk nodded. "We surrender."

Chapter 19

Kate stared around her as the procession of fierce warriors and captives marched into the Powhatan village. Until today, she'd not seen an Indian camp, and she was amazed at how many houses and people it contained. They had passed acres of burn-and-slash cleared corn fields as their captors had paddled up river from the bay in their dugouts. Kate's first view of the town had been from the water, but Gar had ordered his men to land their boats a good half-mile beyond the settlement.

Once on solid ground, a Powhatan brave had tied Kate's wrists together and looped a braided leather rope around her neck. Hawk had been cruelly bound since their surrender. Now Gar commanded that his men strip Hawk of his clothing, armband, and earrings. Barefooted, face and chest smeared with ashes, and hands trussed behind his neck, Hawk was forced to drag a heavy log by a line secured around his waist.

After her capture, the Powhatan had harried her through the woods and thrust her into a boat between four braves. No one had hurt her, but neither had anyone spoken to her in the hours it took to cross the bay. She had seen Hawk and known that he was alive, but he was a prisoner in another dugout, too far away to make eye contact or to exchange words. Kate could do nothing but pray silently and fervently for him.

Gar had ordered his men to make camp. A young brave with a burn scar on his cheek had tied her to a tree for the night. She was given no blanket or protection from flies and mosquitoes, and she was forced to watch the Powhatan grilling and eating fish without being offered so much as a bite.

She should have been terrified. Instead she was furious. What right had Gar to attack William's Hundred and to murder innocents who had never done him harm? And what right had he to come after Hawk? . . . To set fire to the island and threaten the birds and animals? She had never been a vengeful person, but if she could have gotten free and put her hands on a knife, she would have cheerfully driven it through his heart.

Hawk had not had the luxury of sitting upright lashed to a tree. The Powhatan had spread-eagled him and secured his wrists and ankles to stakes driven in the ground. Sometime in the night, it rained, and Kate, wet and miserable, wept for him.

All through that night, Kate thought of Hawk and the weeks and months they'd spent together. When they'd been together on the island, she'd believed that she loved him as much as a woman could love a man. But now that she faced losing him, she knew that the depths of her passion for him ran deeper than she'd dreamed possible.

Her parents had betrothed her to a man she didn't love, a man who proved how bad a husband he would have made for her. Robert had betrayed her, and Alice cared only for her own needs. No one in all the world loved Kate as Hawk did. In the face of his devotion—what did it matter if he was Cherokee?

Kate had always believed herself to be a strong woman, but she knew now that she was weak. She'd wanted Hawk's love without having to pay the price. She'd been content to let others make decisions about her life for her. Even in the Virginia Colony, she'd hesitated, remaining under a treacherous sister's roof rather than courageously making a life for herself.

She had much to regret, and she only hoped she'd have a chance to make right what she'd done wrong.

Now, this morning, in the full glare of the sun, Gar led his triumphant war party into his father's town to the delight of the excited tribespeople. The warriors had painted their faces and bodies and oiled their hair. Many were tattooed all over, and they used the paint to accentuate their strange designs.

Gar had stiffened the bristling crest on his head with animal fat, and he'd adorned himself with spirals, stripes, and dots of red, yellow, and black pigment. He'd also fastened Hawk's silver gorget around his neck and tied his cousin's magnifying glass on a cord at his hip. On his feet, he wore quill-worked moccasins; around his midsection, he'd draped a fringed skirt of cougar skin, complete with tail dangling behind him. Hawk's earrings had been added to Gar's own of cougar teeth. A round, iridescent shell nose-ring completed his finery.

Kate's mouth was dry and tasted of salt. She'd not had anything to eat in over twenty-four hours. At dawn, when she'd gotten back into the dugout, she'd pretended to slip. She'd let herself fall into the river and tried to drink, but the water had been brackish, and she'd had to spit it out. She was so thirsty that her lips were beginning to crack, and she felt weak and dizzy. But deep inside, she still burned with righteous anger, and that fury lent her the strength to keep walking and to hold her head high.

Cheering men, women, and children stood on either side of what seemed to be the main road into town. Drums pounded, and one of the warriors played a flute. A short barrel of a man in a bearskin headdress had appeared from between the houses. His face was covered with a straw mask, and he carried a staff topped with a stuffed crow in one hand and a gourd rattle in the other. The bear man danced back and forth in front of Gar, who walked straight and tall, giving no sign that he saw the costumed performer.

The pathway wound in and around clusters of wigwams and household gardens where corn, beans, pumpkins, squash, and Indian tobacco flourished. Small brown-and-white short-haired dogs barked and darted through the rhythmically clapping onlookers. Naked children stared wide-eyed. Old people cackled or whispered loudly, pointing at Kate and Hawk. Young women, clad in short skirts and moccasins, giggled together and cast shy glances at the strutting warriors.

The Indian houses were much alike, framed of poles and oblong in shape with arched, rounded roofs. Reeds, bark, and mats of grass or rushes covered the outside. There were no windows; instead, the mat side-coverings were rolled up to let in air and sunlight. Through the wide entrance opening at one end, Kate could see sleeping benches like those Hawk had made for their hut. There seemed to be no other furniture. Some houses had a smoke hole in the center of the roof and a fire pit in the dirt floor, but most cooking looked to be done outside beside the drying racks. Kate also saw round huts that were storage sheds or granaries.

Around the exterior of the main village ran a stockade of pointed stakes twelve to fourteen feet high and spaced so closely together that not even a child could squeeze through. Some wigwams were erected outside this protective wall, but all of the larger structures were within. None of the houses were arranged in any order; rather they were scattered here and there, either alone or in groups of two or three. Among the wigwams grew trees; some bore fruit or nuts. Turkeys and wild ducks picked at bugs in the gardens, and a pet crow wearing a leg band perched on a post outside one hut.

The village was neat and tidy. The center street was dusty but swept clean of leaves and debris. And the stench of manure and human waste that had permeated William's Hundred was noticeably absent in the Powhatan camp.

The red-brown faces seemed more curious than hostile. Their skin color ranged from pale honey to dark russet, but most were healthy-looking with good teeth and clear eyes. The children were especially attractive and seemed well cared for.

Then, in the midst of the copper figures, Kate noticed a fair woman with light hair. Stunned, she stopped short. Edwina! It was Alice's maid, not bare-breasted as the Indian women were, but wearing some sort of grass wrap which left one shoulder exposed, but covered her from chest to knees.

Edwina—large with her advancing pregnancy—gaped fish-mouthed, then raised a hand to wave timidly at Kate. The brave leading Kate by the rope turned back, frowned, and gave a sharp tug on Kate's collar. The jerk hurt her neck, and she hurried to keep pace with the others.

But the pain could not dampen her joy. If Edwina was alive, perhaps her sister and other English-women and children were too. Maybe Gar had told the truth, and he didn't mean to murder her. And if she lived, surely Hawk would live as well.

Hawk's cousin led his triumphant war party into a clearing in the center of the village and halted amid a flourish of drumbeats. At one end stood two large houses, each at least thirty feet long. The one on the left had the mats along one side rolled up so that Kate could see the people gathered inside.

Because of the respect Gar and the warriors of-fered him, there was no doubt in Kate's mind that the gray-haired man lying propped up on the sleep-ing platform and surrounded by women was a person of great importance. Hawk had mentioned that Gar's father, Iron Snake, was *weroance* of Gar's village, and that he was in failing health.

When Gar knelt and touched the earth with his head, then rose and embraced the invalid, Kate was certain the feeble man must be Iron Snake. The aging chief wore a mantle of feathers and an old-fashioned Spanish helmet. One side of the *weroance*'s drawn face sagged; his left eye drooped, and his left arm was drawn up close to his body in an unnatural position. The fingers of his left hand were heavy with rings, but they curled into a grotesque claw. The width of his chest and the muscular tone of his good side proved that Iron Snake had once been a warrior of strength; now he was a twisted shell of a man.

Someone shoved Hawk to a spot near her. She glanced sideways at him. His face and arms were bruised. Dried blood stained his body, but he squared his shoulders and took an arrogant stance. They had stripped and beat him to shame him

before the Powhatan, but he wore his naked body
with dignity and grace. She was never so proud of
him as she was in that moment. *I love you*, she
mouthed silently. Hawk's courage gave her the
strength to stand firm and unflinching.

Hawk did not return her declaration of love, but
his eyes glittered with affection.

"I want to be your wife," she whispered.

He nodded. "You will be."

"Pray, God," she answered.

"That is my uncle, Iron Snake." He glanced
toward the gray-haired man in the feathered cloak.

The *weroance* raised a finger, and a plump woman
hurried to fill a gourd with liquid. She handed it to a
tall, haughty matron who held the container to Iron
Snake's mouth. He took a sip and motioned with his
head to his son. The woman held the gourd for Gar
to drink.

"Gar's mother," Hawk said. "The Lady Squash
Pollen."

The aging chief wiped his mouth and spoke in
Powhatan at length, his voice thin and reedy.

"Iron Snake welcomes his son," Hawk translated
quietly for Kate.

Gar replied, speaking for several minutes in a
loud, boastful manner. He waved his arms dramatically, performing more—Kate felt—for the Powhatan people than for his father.

"What's going to happen to us?" Kate asked
Hawk. Her knees felt weak, but she wouldn't give
Gar the satisfaction of knowing he'd frightened her.

Hawk didn't answer her. When his cousin paused,
Hawk spoke directly to his uncle in a deep, clear
voice. "I greet you, son of the Emperor Powhatan,"
he said in English. "Do you draw breath, brother of
my father?"

A ripple of whispers passed among the villagers. The warriors' faces remained expressionless.

"Does my uncle still wear the mantle of power in this place?" Hawk continued.

The *weroance* looked at the prisoner for what seemed to Kate like a lifetime, then he said, "My son, Alligator Gar, claims that you have betrayed the Powhatan to the English, and murdered our warriors."

Gar clapped his hands and a group of braves entered the clearing bearing the bodies of the men Hawk had slain on the island. Several women screamed. One young matron threw herself on the ground in front of the procession in an agony of public grieving and heaped handfuls of dirt on her head.

After a period of confusion, Gar clapped again, and the deceased were carried away, followed by their wailing relatives.

"My father fed and clothed this man," Gar shouted. "My father treated him like a son. I say Fire Hawk That Hunts At Dawn is a traitor and thief. A traitor for killing those who carry the blood of his father. A thief for taking that white woman I claimed for my own. Fire Hawk should die like a criminal, bound and thrown alive into a fire pit."

"What say you?" Iron Snake demanded of Hawk.

"That I have killed Powhatan is the first true words my cousin speaks." Hawk spat into the dust. "He calls me a traitor, yet he betrayed the English. He calls me thief, yet he wears my belongings in his ears and around his throat. He says that I have betrayed the Powhatan, when he used false words of friendship to enter the English camp."

"And the English woman, Hawk That Hunts At Dawn? Did you steal the woman from Gar?"

"She is my wife, mighty Iron Snake. Would I be less than my father's son—than your nephew—if I let Gar take what is mine?"

The *weroance* frowned. "Give Hawk That Hunts At Dawn what is his," he ordered.

Gar glared at Hawk with seething malevolence. A muscle twitched along his jawline, and sweat broke out on his chest, but he ripped Hawk's earrings out of his ears and tore the silver gorget from his throat. When he would have thrown them into the dust at Hawk's feet, his father growled an order. With shaking hands, Gar approached Hawk and draped the gorget around his neck.

"My cousin can keep the earrings," Hawk said. "They look better on him."

A few people laughed, and Gar's face darkened with rage. He whirled on his father. "I do not accept his claim to the woman," he shouted. "Hawk lies when he says she is his wife. She is only an English captive, and worth nothing. But I will surrender my right to her, if he will do the same." His hands closed around the spear that leaned against the *weroance*'s couch.

Kate bit her bottom lip to keep from weeping with fear. The air was charged with energy. At any second, she felt as though Gar might drive the obsidian spear-point through Hawk's heart.

"Do you agree?" Iron Snake demanded. His voice was growing weaker; speaking was obviously a struggle. He began to choke, and Squash Pollen again offered him liquid from the gourd.

Hawk shook his head. "This Englishwoman must be returned to the English at Jamestown."

"No!" Kate shouted. "I am his wife. I stay with my husband."

Gar gestured toward his father. "Do you see? This

licker of English boots—this murdering traitor—
tells our *weroance* what he must do! Does a dead
man make law among the Powhatan?"

Gar's mother leaned close to Iron Snake and
whispered in his ear. Lady Squash Pollen had a
wide nose, and she was weighed down with necklaces of blue and white shell beads.

"The favored wife," Hawk murmured to Kate.
"No friend of mine."

Iron Snake nodded. He looked at Hawk and
smiled crookedly. "My brother's son wishes to give
orders here," he croaked. "He may command where
the Englishwoman goes. To Gar's lodge or to Crow-
Eyes, our shaman. What say you, Fire Hawk That
Hunts At Dawn? Shall she breed up grandsons for
me, or shall her blood soak the cornfields?"

"Give her to me!" the man in the bear head
shouted. He danced a circle around Kate and shook
his rattle in her face. "A sacrifice so that the corn will
grow tall and the pumpkins fat!"

"Well, cousin?" Gar demanded, lifting the spear
high. "My father the great *weroance* has spoken. Will
it be life or death for this woman?"

Kate looked at Hawk. Gar's English was only a
little better than his father's but plain enough for her
to comprehend. "You go straight to hell!" she
shouted at Gar.

"This man wants her to live!" The words were
ripped from Hawk's throat.

"No!" Kate protested. "I'm staying with you!" But
the man who held her rope was already pulling her
away.

Hawk's gaze locked with hers. "Go with him," he
said. "For me."

"Bastard!" she screamed at Gar. "I'll never be

yours. Never!" The brave shoved her, and she went down on her knees.

"You chose for the woman," the *weroance* declared. "Now my son will choose for you."

"I give him to Crow-Eyes!" Gar shouted. "A sacrifice! He shed the blood of Powhatans. Now his blood shall flow!"

Vaguely, Kate was aware that the man had forced her to her feet. She tried to shut out the words—tried not to hear the cries of approval from the Powhatan. Her eyes were dry; her legs and feet seemed made of wood. She was numb all over, too numb to feel the pain. . . . Too numb to accept the finality of Hawk's death sentence.

Children jeered. Someone threw a clod of dirt at her. Kate stumbled on. Angry faces, wigwams, barking dogs swirled around her, and still she felt nothing at all. Then the warrior seized her arm and hauled her away, out of the bright sunshine and into the cool interior of a wigwam. He dropped the end of the rope and thrust her forward. She tripped on the rope and went sprawling face-down on a rug of woven reeds.

Stunned, she lay there for a moment with her eyes shut. When she heard familiar laughter, she raised her head and stared into her sister's taunting face.

Chapter 20

decorative flourish

"**G**et up off the floor," Alice chided. "You look foolish lying there." She glanced up at the scar-faced warrior, clapped her hands sharply, and said something in the Indian tongue. The Powhatan scowled and backed out of the entranceway.

Alice rose from the sleeping bench where she'd been sitting and motioned to someone in the shadows. "Edwina, untie her." She pursed her lips and then looked thoughtful. "You're not going to do something stupid, are you sister? Like try and run away?"

"Where would I run?" Kate asked.

Alice nodded and Edwina knelt beside Kate and untied her bonds. Rubbing her aching wrists, she got to her feet.

"I saw Edwina before, but not you," Kate said. "I'm glad you're alive, both of you."

Alice embraced her with genuine emotion. "I feared you were dead as well. Have you been off with that Cherokee all this time?"

Kate returned the hug and kissed her sister's cheek. "Yes, I have."

Alice sniffed. "For all that we have spent a lifetime despising each other, it warms my heart to see you."

"Me too," Kate admitted. She glanced nervously around the spacious dwelling. There were no Powhatan in sight, men or women. "Is it safe to talk?" she whispered. "Are we being watched?"

Her sister stepped back and shrugged. "I don't know. I doubt it. Any who carry tales about me should watch their backs." She snapped her fingers. "Edwina! What are you waiting for, girl? Finish slicing those vegetables. My husband will expect hot food when he comes."

"Your husband?" Kate shook her head in disbelief. Alice was behaving as though she were in her own manor house. "William's here? He's not dead?"

Alice made a face. "Not William, you silly goose." She glanced around the wigwam with its hanging baskets and heaps of furs. She chuckled. "Can you imagine William here? Hanging his precious sword over my sleeping platform? Not William—Gar. My new husband."

Kate wasn't certain she'd heard correctly. "Gar?" Not the same Gar who'd condemned the man she loved to a horrible death! Not even Alice could welcome such a villain to her bed.

Her sister waved a dainty, ringed hand. "Naturally, Gar. He's the son of the *weroance*, and a great man in his own right." She winked slyly. "In more ways than one. I've never known a man so well endowed or with so much stamina."

"You're Gar's wife?" Kate's insides clenched, and she continued to rub her wrists. The numbness was fading, leaving shooting pains in their place; but the pain meant life in her hands, and she welcomed it. It balanced the anguish within—the throbbing ache that thoughts of losing Hawk caused her, an agony deeper than anything she'd ever experienced.

"Did someone hit you in the head with a war club? You're not usually so slow-witted."

Kate ignored Alice's sarcasm. "The war chief captured you during the attack on William's Hundred?" She eyed her younger sister with fresh suspicion.

Alice was neatly dressed in an English wool bodice and skirt, with beaded and quill-worked moccasins. Her ears were newly pierced with a second set of holes; strings of wampum—the blue and white beads the Powhatan prized so highly— dangled from them. More rare wampum encircled her throat, and her blond hair was braided into a single plait that hung down her back in the fashion of Powhatan wives. She looked more like an honored guest than an abused captive.

"My husband has four wives," Alice said mildly, "but he's smitten with me. He loves my yellow hair. Only Winter Reed, the wife who has children by him, has her own house, but it's not as large or fine as mine."

Kate swayed and dropped down on the sleeping platform to keep from falling. She was ill-prepared to deal with Alice's boasting. "You're with him by choice?" she asked, hoping that she'd misunderstood her sister's position in Gar's household.

It was too shadowy inside the wigwam to see if Alice's cheeks colored or not. "I wasn't at first," she admitted. "In a manner of speaking, he was quite forceful. I was . . ." She broke off and glared at Edwina. "Go finish your chores. I won't have your ears lapping up every word I say."

"Yes, ma'am." Edwina gathered up her baskets and knife and waddled from the lodge.

"She's lazy as ever," Alice said. "Gar wants to give her to one of his braves once she's dropped the brat. I'd let him, but none of the other squaws understand enough English to do as I tell them, and my Powhatan vocabulary is scant." She sat beside Kate and took her hand. "Don't stare at me so. You're no one to judge. You've been alone with that Cherokee on that island. You've probably got a bun in your oven now. Have you thought of that? A little red-skinned bastard. That would ruin Mother's day, wouldn't it? God knows she always expected it from me."

Alice's hand was cold and waxy. There was no comfort in it. "William is dead, then," Kate replied. *As Hawk soon will be*, she thought. *As I will be before I let Gar touch me.*

"Dead? William? Why so? Not so far as I know." Alice made a disapproving sound with her lips. "If the water or the mosquitoes in Jamestown haven't killed him, or he hasn't burst his gut by overeating, he's whole enough."

Kate pulled back her hand. "I thought—"

"The wind carried the fire away from the armory. William, Robert, and most of the surviving soldiers took shelter there and fired on the Powhatan with their muskets."

"But you were in the armory," Kate said. "William told me that you'd taken refuge—"

"I should have been there," Alice corrected. "I went home for my jewels. Gar captured me as I started to run back."

"And the others? What of the settlers?"

Alice sighed. "The Powhatan took only one man prisoner. Jack Brick. When Gar began to lose too many warriors, he retreated."

"What happened to Jack Brick?" Kate asked, although she didn't really want to know.

Alice shrugged. "They handed him over to old Crow-Eyes. He's the shaman here—sort of a cross between a barber surgeon and a pagan priest. When he was done with Jack . . ." She grimaced. "He died slowly and unpleasantly. Crow-Eyes is a decidedly bad man."

"The women and children? What happened to them?" Kate asked.

"Some were killed in the fire. Most reached the armory. A few were taken prisoner. The oldest Miller girl is here; she's taken a Powhatan husband as well. Janet Bolton has done the same. She has her little boy, Dickon, with her. The captured children were all adopted by Indian families or traded back to the English at Jamestown."

"If William's alive, why didn't he trade for you? Wouldn't Gar give you up?" Kate asked.

Her sister smiled. "He suits me, and I suit him. I carry his child." She patted her belly. "With all his grunting and poking, William couldn't plant a babe in my womb, but Gar did the first time he lay with me. He's a fine figure of a man."

"Alice, are you mad? This is difficult to believe, even of you. Gar is a savage murderer."

"Nonsense. You must stop looking at everything from the English point of view. Gar is only defending his people and his land. He's strong, Kate, the strongest man I've ever known." She chuckled. "We're very much alike, the two of us. We know what we want."

"And you don't care what you do to get it?"

Alice stiffened. "You'd be wiser to keep a decent tongue in your head. Iron Snake may be *weroance*, but Gar rules here. His father grows weaker by the day. And when my husband becomes chief, I—"

"Gar may favor you now, sister, but what will he do if you make a cuckold of him as you did William."

"I'm not the complete fool you think," Alice assured her. "I won't risk my life by lying with other men. Why should I, when I have the best lover in my own bed?"

Kate shivered and crossed her arms over her chest. She closed her eyes and tried to regain her composure. For a long space they sat in silence, then Kate opened her eyes and confided, "Gar wants this Crow-Eyes to put Hawk to death."

"Yes, he does. He hates him. Gar sees your Hawk as a threat to his power among the Powhatan."

"Gar is afraid of Hawk?" Kate asked.

"It's all that *chosen* business. Gar didn't say too much to me, but I gather the Powhatan think of Hawk as some kind of magician. He's the old emperor's grandson as much as Gar is. The men aren't supposed to inherit political titles from the male line, but Gar says things are changing fast. He believes he can become *weroance* here."

"Iron Snake gave Hawk to Crow-Eyes to do with as he wishes," Kate explained.

"Then your Cherokee will most likely have his skull crushed with a rock. In honor of some corn god or another." Alice laid a sympathetic hand on Kate's arm. "It's a quick death, the women tell me."

"It's barbaric."

Alice toyed with one of her earrings, sliding the string of wampum back and forth to ease the tension on her ear. "What do you expect?" She dropped her voice to a whisper. "Crow-Eyes is a warlock, a male witch. People are afraid of him, and it pleases him to keep them so. With the *weroance* so ill, Gar says Crow-Eyes has forgotten his place."

Kate swallowed her pride. "Please, Alice. If you have any love in your heart for me, you've got to save Hawk's life. For me."

"That may be impossible. Gar needs to keep the shaman as his ally if he wants to be elected *weroance* when his father dies. My loyalty lies with Gar and his needs."

"Won't you try?"

"You've lived with me long enough to know I do what profits me, Kate," Alice answered matter-of-factly. "Fire Hawk has been a thorn under Gar's skin since they were children. Why should I endanger myself to intercede for you?"

"You're my sister. We share the same blood. You owe me something."

"I owe you nothing, Kate. Nothing."

"Lady?"

Kate turned to see Edwina standing in the entranceway.

"Lady, there is something you should know," the maid said timidly.

"Well! Out with it! What should I know?"

Edwina bobbed an awkward curtsy. " 'Tis best said in private."

"I've no patience for your whining. Speak or be gone. I'm talking with my sister," Alice snapped.

" 'Tis just . . . just. . . . Winter Reed said that the master Gar wishes to take Mistress Kathryn to wife. She said he fancies havin' sisters in t'same bed at t'same time."

Alice swore a foul oath, grabbed up a gourd dipper, and hurled it at Edwina. The wench squeaked and fled, and Alice whirled on Kate. "Is it true? Do you mean to lie with my husband?" She raised a hand to deliver a slap.

Kate backed away. It was on the tip of her tongue to remind her sister that she'd not shied from futtering Robert, but common sense won over spite. "I'll not do it. I swear on my soul, Alice. I'd sooner sleep with that bastard Crow-Eyes."

"That might be arranged!" Alice balled her fingers into a fist and dropped her arm to her side. "You'll not have Gar. He's mine."

Yours and three other women's. The thought formed in Kate's mind, but she didn't speak it. Instead she forced herself to calm down so she could reason with Alice. "All the more reason for you to help me escape."

"Escape?" Alice scoffed. "You are a fool. Where are you? Do you have the faintest idea? Which way is Jamestown? North or south? You wouldn't last . . ."

Outside the wigwam, a woman shrieked. Other cries filled the air. Alice pushed past Kate to the doorway. "What's amiss?" she demanded.

A dog howled and yipped, then his baying was cut off sharply. There was a moment of silence and Kate could hear female wails of lamenting. A drum began to beat, dull, vibrating booms echoed through the village.

Kate ran to the entrance and looked out. A young brave ran past, blood streaming from long cuts on his arms. *An attack?* Kate wondered. But the drum didn't sound as if the Powhatan were in danger; it emitted a timeless message of mourning. Was it Hawk?

"Edwina?" Alice called.

A gray-haired woman hobbled by, her face darkened with ashes. Chunks had been cut from her hair, and her dress was torn. Tears streamed down her old face.

"That's Gar's aunt, Oyster Catcher," Alice said. "There's only one thing that could cause her to weep." She looked full into Kate's face and smiled. "The old *weroance* is dead."

At the first drumbeat, Hawk knew that his uncle had died. Gar would be the most likely candidate for *weroance*. He had coveted the position for many years. There was another man with the right bloodline, but he was lame and had never been strong enough to gather a following of young warriors.

Hawk's next thoughts were of Kate. If Gar became chief, he would have the power to protect her, but she would probably never get back to her own people. Hawk hoped she didn't blame him for choosing Gar rather than Crow-Eyes. He wasn't certain Kate understood that the shaman required human sacrifices to maintain his own position in the tribe.

Rarely were the Powhatan offered up to the spirits of earth and storm. Hawk could remember only one such killing in his childhood, but during the past winter, Gar had told him of three. One victim was English, another a newborn child with extra fingers and toes, and a third, a captured enemy from the Mohawk people to the north.

Hawk didn't think it was meant for him to end his days bleeding out his life force into the earth of a Powhatan cornfield. But if the Creator allowed it to happen, he knew it must be for some greater purpose. He had received no message from beyond. And until he did, he would scheme to foil Crow-Eyes and his cousin, and rescue Kate.

But Hawk had to admit that he was not in the best position to escape. Four warriors had dragged him to the center of the dance ground and bound him, wrists and ankles, between two posts with his arms over his head. He was trussed so tightly that he could barely move.

Crow-Eyes had ordered that Hawk be garbed as befitted a messenger to the spirits. With his own hands, the shaman had tied Hawk's silver gorget in place, wrapped a white fringed loin-covering around his waist, and draped a beautiful mantle of snow white fox skin over his shoulders, fastening it with a copper pin.

Then he'd summoned Gar's mother to help him. Squash Pollen had clamped incised copper bands around Hawk's arms and painted his face in a diagonal pattern, half-black and half-white. She'd woven a crown of white beads and bird wings, and shaved part of his hair in the Powhatan fashion. The remaining hair was knotted and pinned below his left ear; then she'd settled the headdress on his brow and secured it firmly in place.

Finally Squash Pollen had dressed Hawk in elk-hide leggings and moccasins, and laid at his feet his bow, quiver, and personal belongings.

"You should have been drowned at birth," Gar's mother hissed. He, whose name we can no longer speak, who was once my husband, was weak. Your mother begged for your life and he spared it."

"Do you hate me so, Aunt?" he asked her.

She spat at his feet and hurried away.

Hawk exhaled softly. It was chilling to realize that her malevolence toward him ran so deep.

More and more people were crowding into the village center to view the dead *weroance*. The shaman had propped Iron Snake up in a sitting position and painted his face for war. The women had dressed the chief in his finest garments and covered his staring eyes with shells.

Gar had left his father's side long enough to blacken his face with ashes and rend his clothing; but Hawk noticed that he had donned a regal crown of deer antlers and copper disks. Now he'd returned with armed warriors on either side of him.

With Iron Snake's sudden death, the reins of control had shifted to his cousin. Hawk wondered whether Crow-Eyes would continue to exert the power he had when Iron Snake was *weroance*. Hawk noticed that the shaman kept his distance from Gar.

The sound of drumming grew louder as other drummers joined the first. Some of the women draped blankets over their heads and began to dance in a wide, undulating circle. One grizzled, old warrior began to boast of the brave deeds of the deceased *weroance* while onlookers chanted a soft background of song. Hawk expected them to go on like this all night. At sunrise, he supposed Crow-Eyes intended to murder him as a climax to the festivities, but Hawk had no intention of remaining here until dawn.

Near the large wigwam where the *weroance* lay, a woman had built a fire. Now other men and women began to toss jewelry, furs, weapons, and items of value into it, providing their lost leader with necessary goods for his journey to the land of the dead.

For the most part, the dancers and the other Powhatan men and women ignored Hawk. The few who did catch his eye soon turned away. Too many of them had known him as a child. He had eaten with them and shared the dangers and joys of day to day life. His mother might have been a Cherokee, but his father had been one of them, and their confusion showed in their shamed expressions.

Then he recognized Kate's sister, Alice, coming onto the dance ground. Women moved back to let her through as she walked quickly by. She didn't stop until she reached Gar's side. He smiled at her and motioned to a seat nearby.

"Hawk!"

Kate hurried toward him.

"How did you get loose?" he asked her. "Never mind. Stay away." It wasn't safe for the Powhatan to associate her with him. She had too narrowly missed being offered up to the corn in his place. "Go to your sister," he said. "She may be able to protect you."

Kate threw her arms around him and hugged him.

"No!" he protested, but his heart raced at her courage. "Do as I say," he ordered her harshly. "Leave me."

"Never." She looked up into his eyes. "Promises can't be broken. Didn't you tell me that?"

"Go." The tears rolling down her cheek were nearly his undoing. He swallowed against the lump in his throat. What jest of the spirits was this, that they would give him his heart's desire only to snatch it away?

"I don't care," she cried. She cupped his cheek in her trembling palm. "I love you, Hawk. I'll never love another like I do you. I swear it."

The drumming stopped. Hawk snapped his head around to stare at his cousin. Gar had left the dead man's side and was striding toward Hawk and Kate. Hawk strained at the leather ties until sweat beaded his forehead, but the ropes did not break.

Gar shouted an order in Powhatan, and two men

lunged forward to seize Kate. She made no attempt to fight them. She kept looking at Hawk.

"I'll never take another husband," she exclaimed. "Never."

Gar stopped a few yards away. "This woman!" he shouted. "She wishes to feed the worms with my cousin. What say you? Shall she join him?"

Hawk's gut clenched, but he forced himself to gaze threateningly into Gar's eyes. "Harm her and you die," he vowed.

"What will you do to me?" the Powhatan demanded. "You will be dead."

"Dead or alive, I will have you," Hawk said softly. "The far side of the River of Souls shall not hold me. You will never sleep another night or rise to the touch of a woman if you shed a single drop of her blood. I . . ."

He heard a faint *keer-keer-keer* sound, and broke off. Looking up, he saw a single hawk feather drifting down. A shadow passed over the stakes, the familiar silhouette of a red-tailed hawk. "Starlady," he whispered.

Gar pointed at the bird circling overhead. "Shoot it!" he shouted to his warriors.

But no man raised a bow. The Powhatan began to murmur among themselves. One drummer missed his beat, and the dancers halted in their tracks.

Kate gazed at the hawk. "See!" she shouted. "Even the birds of the air obey his call."

"An omen," an elder ventured.

"See the Hawk Spirit who comes to the Chosen One of the Cherokee," said another.

The hawk made one final pass, then her powerful wings lifted her up. Soon, she was no more than a black speck against the azure sky.

"Ha!" Gar folded his arm. "Your Hawk Spirit has

been frightened away. My Fish Spirit is stronger."
He glanced at Kate. "My father has ordered that this
woman go to my lodge and give him grandsons," he
said loudly, still speaking his own language. "But
my heart is heavy. I cannot take her to my bed while
I weep for the loss of our *weroance*. I will give her to
my father to comfort his journey."

Kate looked at Hawk in alarm. She couldn't
understand what Gar was saying, but her face
showed her fear.

In that instant, Hawk would have gladly traded
the rest of his life for the chance to shelter her from
Gar's evil. But he could do nothing, and he would
not translate such words. Instead he fixed his rage
on his cousin. "You will regret this," he said in
Algonquian.

Gar only laughed. "Garb her in pearls and fine
furs," he said. "She shall be my father's last bride.
And she shall go with him on his final journey."

"Not one drop of her blood," Hawk whispered
hoarsely.

"Not a single drop, cousin," Gar replied
smoothly. "I shall strangle her with my own hands."

Chapter 21

Kate lay on her side in the pitch-black wigwam within an arm's length of Iron Snake's stiffening body. Her hands were tied behind her back so tightly that she feared she would never regain use of them. She had never feared the dead, but being alone in the night with a corpse made her skin crawl.

In the hours following the *weroance*'s death, Kate had suffered more than her share of indignities. A group of women—her sister among them—had dragged her to a low hut filled with hot rocks, stripped her naked, steamed and scraped her skin with shells, and thrown her into the river.

Kate had fought her tormentors, landing at least one good blow to Alice's face. She hoped she'd broken her sister's pretty turned-up nose. Kate had put up a good struggle, but she'd been one against many, and they had overpowered her.

From the riverbank, they'd carried her—kicking and sputtering—out of the swift current to her sister's house. There Edwina had brushed and combed her hair, and braided strings of purple wampum into it. Then two Indian women had dressed her in a skirt and cape of white fawn-skin and weighed her down with beads and copper jewelry.

Edwina had sobbed when Kate demanded what this all meant, but the maid had been too afraid of Alice to answer her questions. Her treacherous sister, swearing and clutching a wet cloth to her swollen nose, had been no help at all.

Squaws had set plates of meat, Indian bread, and vegetables in front of her, but Kate had no appetite. The only thing she would accept from them was a drink of water.

A procession of Powhatan women had escorted her to the dead chief's house in the early hours of the evening. The ceremonial fires burned high, and the reed covering on the side of the wigwam facing the dance ground had been lowered. Kate had strained to catch glimpses of Hawk, still tied between the upright posts amid the dancing and speech-making, and the fact that he still lived gave her hope.

Eventually, in the darkest hours before dawn, the flames had died to glowing embers, and the Powhatan had ceased their mourning and retreated in twos and threes to their homes. The remaining women trussed her like a roasting chicken and left her alone with the dead body of the old *weroance*.

The night passed slowly. Kate trembled from exhaustion, but she could not sleep a wink. She heard each rustle of thatch, each stir of wind and scratch of branch against the outer walls of the wigwam. Her emotions ranged from terror to anger, and finally to acceptance of whatever fate morning would bring.

She thought lovingly of her home in England, her parents, and her precious, younger sisters with their never-ending mischief—of the dimple on little Emma's right cheek and the freckles spattering the twins' fair faces.

She remembered the way the birds sang outside her bedroom window on a May morning, and the sound of rain patting against the windowpanes in gray November. She remembered lying on her belly in her father's barn loft, with a newborn kitten in her lap and the sweet scent of hay all around her, watching the shimmering purple sunset over Maiden Hill.

But most of all, she thought of Hawk. . . .

She remembered the taste of his mouth and the smell of his hair. She relived each embrace and the feel of his arms around her as he filled her with his love. She remembered their shared laughter, the dolphin he'd summoned up for her to ride, the wild horses, and a thousand bright images of sun and sand.

"I came to Virginia for adventure," she murmured softly into the inky blackness, "and if I die tomorrow, I won't regret a moment of it."

Her heart skipped a beat as she heard a tiny snap outside the side wall of the wigwam. It sounded like a twig breaking underfoot, and she strained to listen.

There was another ominous scrape. Faint . . . so faint she wondered if she'd really heard it, or simply summoned the footstep from a nightmare.

Heat flashed under her skin, followed by a wave of icy cold. Her heart hammered in her breast. Could it be Hawk? Had he gotten loose and come to save her?

The silence was as terrifying as the sound, but within seconds, she heard a dull thud. The warrior standing guard outside the entrance groaned and

fell heavily against the reeds. Kate heard the scrape
of the skin cover being pushed aside.

Her breath caught in her throat.

"Kate?"

It was not Hawk's voice but another she knew all
too well. "Alice?"

"Shhh. Will you have Gar's men down on us?"
Her sister crept close. She smelled of cedar bark and
Indian tobacco.

"Why are you here?"

"Hush! I didn't bash that brave over the head with
a chunk of firewood to have you give us away with
your yammering."

"Have you come to taunt me?" Kate asked.

"Why do you think I'm here, you fool? I've come
to cut you free."

Kate sucked in a mouthful of air. Alice's presence
made no sense. "I thought you hated me."

"'Tis true you're nought but trouble," her sister
agreed. "My nose is twice its size. If it's broken, I'll
regret coming here to my dying day." She put her
smooth hand on Kate's wrists. "Don't move. I don't
want to cut you." She began to saw at the leather ties
with a knife.

"Why, then?"

"Live men have need of wives, not dead ones.
They mean to marry you to Iron Snake and send you
to the grave with him."

Kate exhaled sharply.

"No need to carry on like Edwina. It's true we've
never been close, but I have my own position to
consider. I'm setting you free."

"I didn't think you cared what happened to me.
I'll never forget this."

Alice ignored her gratitude. "Swim the river and

follow it to the bay," she said curtly. "Then go south. If you're lucky, you'll find the English."

One thong parted.

"You've put your own life in danger for me. If anyone finds out that you let me go—"

"They'd bury me in your place," Alice finished. "But I'll not let them find out." She chuckled. "As you said, we are sisters when all's said and done."

"They'll know someone freed me."

Alice sniffed. "They're a superstitious lot. I've brought a few hawk feathers to leave behind. They'll think that blasted spirit bird came and released you."

"You know I'll try and save Hawk . . ."

"You'd be smarter to save your own skin, but what you do once I let you— There! That's the last of it. Now your feet."

Kate wiggled her fingers and rubbed the pins-and-needles sensation from her hands. "Come with us."

"Me? Are you completely mad?" Alice made a sound of derision. "Why would I go with you? I have a husband I care for—as much as I can care for any of them. I'm well treated, and I'm going to be a mother. There'd be nothing for me in Jamestown with a half-breed child. What would you have me do, sister, abandon it?"

"No, of course not, but—"

"But nothing. A cat will care for her kittens, and I pride myself in having the morals of a cat. I want to be a mother. Can you believe that?" Alice severed the last rope. "Goodbye, Kate. I'm going back to bed with my husband. He drank himself into a stupor last night on some kind of black, stinking herb brew. He'll never know I left his side." She thrust the knife handle into Kate's hand.

"Thank you," she said. She reached out to hug her sister, but Alice moved away.

"No need for either of us to stoop to foolishness. Go with God. And if you get caught, tell them a giant hawk bit through your ropes. Say a word of anything else, and I'll kill you myself."

A thick fog had moved in from the river, hiding the stars. Without moonlight, Kate could only feel her way across the open ground to the place where Hawk had been tied. She found the stake at last by stumbling into it.

He didn't make a sound.

"Hawk," she whispered. "It's me." She put out her hand and found his left leg, then began to cut through the leather ties.

His muscles tensed. "Kate?"

The mist was so heavy that moisture dripped down her face and arms and made her shiver. Nearby, she could hear someone snoring. Other than that, there was nothing but the occasional hoot of an owl and the dry *ch'crrrr* of a cicada as it burrowed out of its fragile shell.

Hawk's foot came free, and she found his other ankle. Her pulse pounded in her head, and her breathing came fast and sharp.

The blade squeaked against the leather, and the sound seemed to shriek into the night. When that leg was loose, she realized that Hawk's arms were over his head, too high for her to reach.

"What am I going to do?" she whispered. "How do I . . ."

On the far side of the village, a dog began to bark furiously. A musket blasted, and then another. A woman screamed, and guns began to fire in rapid succession.

"Hawk, what's happening?" Kate cried.

"English guns. White men are attacking the village. Get down."

"I have to get you free!" She threw her arms around his neck, braced her foot against his knee, and stretched to cut through the remaining thongs binding his hands.

"Climb higher," he urged.

More screams echoed through the town, followed by a dog's drawn out howl of agony. Warriors sprang from the wigwams shouting alarms. More dogs barked. Women ran with wailing babies.

Off to the right, flames flared against the sky. The heavy scent of smoke enveloped Kate. "No!" she cried. "Not again!" Memories of the burning of William's Hundred turned her blood to ice water.

"Hurry!" Hawk urged.

Desperately, she hacked at the leather thongs.

People rushed past them in the fog. A gun roared, and a child shrieked in pain. Hoofbeats pounded across the open ground. A shrouded figure on horseback loomed in the mist.

Fire spat from the muzzle of a wheel-lock musket. A lead ball slammed into the post near Kate's head. Splinters of wood sprayed her as Hawk twisted sideways, throwing her to the ground.

She hit the hard-packed earth on hands and knees, rolled, and scrambled up almost under the rearing horse's hooves. "Stop!" she yelled. "Don't shoot!"

A dazed toddler wandered out of the blackness. The baby saw the horse and stumbled backward. The horseman dug his heels into his mount's sides, and the animal rose on his hind legs, iron-shod hooves churning over the child's head.

Kate screamed and lunged forward, snatching up the tot and flinging both of them away from the flying hooves.

A woman called frantically in Powhatan. "Tottopottomoy!"

"Here!" Kate shouted.

Wailing, the little boy threw out his arms. The woman grabbed him from Kate and ran.

"Kate!"

It was Robert's voice. Robert was the horseman. She knew that if he saw Hawk he'd kill him. She had to draw Robert away.

"Robert!" She saw a faint glow of a dying campfire and backed away toward that source of light. "It's Kate," she cried. "Don't shoot me."

When she was close enough to see the outline of the fire pit, she circled it. "Over here!"

Robert urged his mount forward. A warrior dove out of the fleeing throng and swung a hatchet at him. Robert blocked the attack with his musket barrel, then smashed the gun butt into the Indian's face, felling him instantly.

An Englishman ran across the open space with a torch and hurled the flaming brand onto the roof of Iron Snake's wigwam. Then a Powhatan warrior rounded the hut with a drawn bow. His first arrow caught the Englishman in the shoulder. He cried out and retreated into the darkness.

The brave's second arrow pierced Robert's horse's neck. The gelding squealed in pain; his front legs folded under him, and he pitched forward.

Robert tumbled off.

The brave aimed his third arrow at Robert, but before he could let loose the shaft, a white man in a helmet appeared and engaged him in hand-to-hand combat.

Before Robert could get to his feet, a woman ran past the thrashing horse. Robert grabbed her ankle, and she fell on her face.

Kate saw the gleam of steel as Robert snaked a knife from the sheath at his belt. "No!" she screamed. "Don't!" The kicking horse lay between her and the struggle. She ran toward Robert, staying well clear of the injured animal.

The woman tried to crawl away. As she pushed herself up on her hands, Robert seized her by the hair and yanked her head back.

In the shadowy light Kate saw the girl's face. "No, Robert! Don't do it. It's Edwina!" She threw herself at him as he plunged the blade down.

White-hot rage flashed through Hawk when he heard Kate scream. He'd strained against the braided leather bonds until sweat streamed down his body and his wrists ran with his own blood. Now the primitive urge to defend the woman he loved lent him superhuman strength. The rawhide rope on his left arm snapped. With a final surge of power he tore loose from the right restraint and bent to snatch up his weapons and his hunting bag.

He heard Kate shout Robert's name and ran in that direction. He nearly tripped over a white man and an Indian brave rolling on the ground with their hands at each others' throats.

Leaping over them, Hawk knocked aside another Englishman in padded armor who was aiming a crossbow at a Powhatan woman. "Kate?" Hawk shouted.

The armored man loosed his iron quarrel at Hawk. The arrow flew over his head.

"Kate!" he called again.

She did not answer. Heart pounding, he skirted the downed horse and saw Kate kneeling with her arms around Edwina. The English maid sobbed hysterically.

Robert turned and stared at Hawk. "You!" He leveled his wheel-lock musket point-blank at Hawk.

"No!" Kate cried. "Don't shoot him." She shoved Edwina aside and snatched up Robert's pistol from the ground.

"I warned you, John," Robert said brusquely. "If you'd remembered your place, I wouldn't have to do this."

Hawk stood motionless. He had an arrow notched in his bowstring, but he knew that Robert's bullet would move with the speed of a striking eagle.

"I have your pistol," Kate said. "Let him go, Robert. I don't want to kill you."

Robert glanced at her and sneered. "You don't have the guts to pull that trigger. Now watch your red lover die." He looked back at Hawk and fired the musket.

Pistol and musket roared in the same instant. Hawk threw himself to the ground, but Robert seemed to sense Kate's intent to shoot at the last instant. Robert jerked off his shot, and the musket ball went high.

Kate's shot was dead on.

The bullet tore into Robert's side, wounding him mortally. He crumbled to the ground, eyes staring, mouth gasping for breath. A thin red line of blood trickled from his mouth. A torrent spilled down his waistcoat.

"You killed 'em," Edwina wailed. "You killed the father of me babe. You'll hang for it."

Hawk seized Kate and pulled her into his arms. The warmth of her sent shivers of joy through his veins. "You killed him for me," he said in Cherokee.

Kate lay her head against his chest and sobbed.

"Come," he cautioned. "The fighting goes on. We must go while we can."

"Master Robert's dead!" the maid wailed. "I'll tell Sir William who killed him. I swear I will."

Hawk could not resist kissing Kate once, hard on the mouth. The taste of her was sweeter than wild honey, and his blood coursed fiercely through his veins.

Another wigwam burst into flames. He swept Kate up into his arms and began to run through the burning village with her. Sparks flew around their heads. Everywhere men struggled, and bodies— both red and white—lay sprawled like broken dolls across the ground.

"This is madness," Kate cried. "Can't they see how wrong this hating is?"

In the flare of the firelight, Hawk saw William Bennett drive the point of his sword into the shaman's belly. Crow-Eyes staggered and went down on one knee. Bennett yanked out his weapon and brought the flat edge of the steel down across the back of Crow-Eyes's neck.

Two Englishmen appeared in front of them. One was pouring black powder into the barrel of his firing piece. The other man swore a foul oath and, swinging his broadax, charged at Hawk.

Hawk thrust Kate to the ground and dropped his bow and quiver. Sidestepping the soldier with the ax, Hawk wrested the terrible weapon away. Without slowing his attack, he lunged at the gunman and battered the musket from his hands.

"No more killing!" Kate screamed.

The soldier leaped onto Hawk's back. Hawk bent and twisted, slamming the white man onto the earth. He groaned and lay stunned. Hawk threatened the remaining man with the ax, and the settler turned and fled into the night.

Another musket ball whizzed over Hawk's head. He retrieved his bow and arrows, grabbed Kate's hand, and they ran for the forest.

As they reached the tree line, a dozen Powhatan warriors materialized out of the shadows to bar their way. "Who are you?" one called.

"Gar? Is that you?" Hawk answered.

"I should have killed you when I had the chance," his cousin replied. "I should do it now."

Hawk raised his bow and stepped in front of Kate, guarding her with his body. "I will not kill easily. Will you waste time arguing with me while your women and children are being murdered?"

"You run from a fight again—as you did before."

"The English are not my enemy," Hawk said. "Shoot if you must, but my first arrow goes into your heart, cousin."

"Give me the white woman, and I'll let you pass."

"Who is it?" Kate asked. "What are they saying?"

"I told him that you belong to me," Gar said, switching to English.

"My sister Alice! Did she escape the village?"

To Hawk's surprise, Gar answered her. "My wives are all safe."

"Tell her I love her," Kate said.

"Tell her yourself."

"Gar's wives are safe," Hawk said to the other warriors in Powhatan. "What of yours? What of your mothers and sisters? Will you risk death at my hands instead of fighting the English?"

"Spotted Bark will not!" a young warrior cried. He ran past Hawk toward the village. A second man followed him, and then a third and a fourth.

"Go, Gar!" Hawk taunted. "Lead them, or you will never be *weroance* in your father's place!"

"Another time, then, Hawk."

"Another time, Gar."

"You will never reach your mountains-of-smoke alive," Gar threatened. "I'll hunt you down. I swear it." He uttered a chilling war cry and bounded after his braves.

"What did he say?" Kate demanded.

Hawk lowered his bow and put an arm around her shoulders. "Shall I tell you that he wished us safe journey to the land of the Cherokee?"

"Tell me the truth."

"The truth is that the sun will soon rise over the sea. Gar will hunt English now, but when he rests to lick his wounds, he will hunt us."

"Then we had best put space between us, hadn't we?" she said.

"For an Englishwoman, you show great wisdom." Taking her hand in his, he led her into the shelter of the trees, and they ran until they could no longer hear the roar of muskets or the war whoops of the angry Powhatan.

Chapter 22

Foothills of the Blue Ridge Mountains

Kate supposed it was now midsummer, but she couldn't have guessed the date to within a fortnight. The days and nights since she and Hawk had fled the coast and the Powhatan village jumbled together in her mind. She hadn't imagined that a country could be so big or so wild.

They had crossed endless forests, more streams than she could count on both hands, and at least three rivers. Some bodies of water flowed gently toward the Atlantic; others boiled and tumbled, churned white rapids and cold, black currents. They had waded marshes and climbed hills, traversed ravines on fallen logs, and navigated rock-strewn gullies. They'd slept in brief snatches and risen to walk again in the first iridescent shadows of dawn or the light of a benevolent moon.

Hawk had found food for them on the march. Kate patched their moccasins and made new ones from his leggings when they shredded to tatters. "I sewed you a pair of moccasins on the island," she explained. "As a surprise. But I lost them when the Powhatan chased us."

Hawk eyed the clumsy skin shoes Kate had fashioned for him. "They'll do, but I hope my mother doesn't see them. She won't think much of your sewing ability."

"Beggars cannot be choosers." Kate frowned. "And not even your mother could sew moccasins without a proper needle."

"Didn't I make you one of bone?"

"Rabbit bone. And it's not as good as the Nanticoke needles I had on the island."

"When we reach the Cherokee," he promised, "you shall have the best sewing kit available."

"I'd better."

He accepted her playful scolding without becoming insulted. Since Kate had shot Robert to save his life, she'd become more than the woman he had to protect and care for. Kate had become his partner.

It was Hawk's job to find fresh water each day. Together they made the night camp, taking turns standing watch while the other slept.

Hawk teased, coaxed, and grew stern, but always he kept them moving west, hour after hour. They'd walked in the heat of the sun and in pouring rain. And by the grace of God and Hawk's skill as a woodsman, they'd kept two jumps ahead of the Powhatan war party that remained hot on their heels after weeks of travel.

There were three of them now. On the second day after the attack on Iron Snake's town, the red-tail had found them. Starlady had swooped down out of the treetops to land on Hawk's shoulder.

"Now you come," he'd teased. "You could have helped me if you'd made a good showing in front of the weaselly Powhatan shaman. You're a coward."

But Kate couldn't miss the warm glow of affection in his eyes as he stroked Starlady's feathered back and carefully examined the wing that had once crippled her . . . or that his powerful hands were as gentle as a spring rain when they cradled the hawk.

"Nearly as good as new," he pronounced. "She's a bit thin, but she's hunting for herself now. She doesn't need us anymore."

It was obvious to Kate that Starlady thought otherwise. The young hawk would fly off at her own whim during the day, but when dusk fell, she returned every evening to perch on Hawk's arm.

"Now I have another mouth to feed," he pretended to complain.

But it was often Starlady who brought them rabbits, ducks, and squirrels. Once she dropped a dead rodent at Hawk's feet. To Kate's relief, Hawk flashed her a mischievous grin and returned that dubious prize to the bird.

Rarely did she and Hawk have the luxury of a fire to cook game. Hawk would risk a campfire in the rain or when they'd found shelter in a cave or rock overhang, but usually he was afraid that the smoke or the light from the flames would draw enemies.

On those days and nights, they made do with roots, berries, raw greens, and fish. Kate had hated eating the uncooked trout the first time, but Hawk had sliced the filets thin and wrapped them in the crisp leaves of mountain sorrel. The acidic, but not unpleasant taste of the plant had made the fish palatable. As the days passed, Kate also found groundnut tubers, wild onions, and cattail shoots, to add to their diet.

The farther they traveled toward the setting sun, the freer Kate felt. Each day was fresh and exciting; each dawn brought new wonders. She was too proud to admit to being too tired or stiff to rise and continue the journey when Hawk gave the order.

"You do well for being English," he said. "When your legs gain strength, we will cover more ground."

"What do you mean, when I'm stronger?" Kate protested. "We must have walked twenty miles yesterday. And most of it was uphill."

He laughed. "A Cherokee warrior can run from the southern-most corner of our territory to the Great Lakes in the Iroquois land to the north in five days."

"How far is that?"

Hawk shrugged. "At this rate, it would take us weeks to walk it."

She fell in behind him, and for a long time they walked in companionable silence. It was impossible for Kate not to notice the ripple of muscles across his broad back and his rock-hard thighs as he strode along.

Not even the beauty of the forests or the flash of brightly colored songbirds could draw her attention from Hawk's lean and well-formed buttocks, moving beneath the supple leather of his loin covering.

Kate had always considered herself a fine judge of men's backsides, and Hawk's would make a crone leap from her deathbed and dance for joy. His muscular legs were long and his arms sinewy. In the full heat of summer, his copper skin tanned to a darker hue, making the whites of his jet black, almond-shaped eyes and the gleam of his strong, perfect teeth even more beautiful in contrast.

Hawk placed each moccasin-clad foot on earth, or tree, or rock with grace and elegance. His movements flowed like water. He made no more sound than a stag when he passed, and he left few tracks behind. Watching Hawk walk through the forest was like listening to beautiful music; sometimes it seemed so sweet to Kate that it brought tears to her eyes.

Hawk was powerfully male, yet tender and constantly protective of her. He carried his bow, quiver, tomahawk, knife, hunting bag, and whatever food they had. They had no blanket, and the only clothes they possessed were those they wore. At night Kate slept in the circle of his arms, and by day she walked in his tall shadow.

And often when she woke in morning light, she found a spray of wild flowers by her hand. Once, he left a single bluebird feather, tucked in a spray of wild-cherry blossoms.

"Why are you so good to me?" she asked.

He looked back at her in disbelief. "You are my heart's blood," he murmured. Then he smiled, a smile that lit his haunting eyes with inner fire and made her giddy with happiness.

She drew in a heady breath. "You are one of a kind."

"Of course," he answered solemnly. "I am the Chosen."

To that, she could only nod. In the months since she'd known Hawk, she'd come to believe that he was truly something more than a mortal man. The thought was dangerous, mind-boggling; and because she couldn't understand it, she accepted him as he was and did not question how or why such a thing was possible.

In all ways but one, she had never been closer to Hawk. He was kind, and funny, and wise. He never tired, and he never complained when she could not keep up with his heroic pace. But he'd not made love to her since they left the island.

"I cannot," he explained on the second day after they'd fled the Powhatan village. "I want you as much as ever—perhaps more. But I cannot relax my vigilance. We are pursued by the Powhatan. A Cherokee warrior does not share the pleasures of the mat with his wife while on the war trail."

"But I want you," she insisted. "Couldn't we—"

"No. We cannot." He shook his head. "Patience, my love. The Cherokee believe it builds character."

"Going without the one you desire?"

"No." He laughed. "Waiting for that which you want most."

Nothing she could say would sway him in this matter.

During this forced celibacy, her own intimate need for him had grown. At the oddest times, she found herself tantalized by erotic images. Her pulse-beat quickened, and she flushed when Hawk looked at her. Her nipples swelled if he took her hand to help her over a rough stretch of ground. She found herself entranced by the fluid swing of his black hair when he walked ahead of her, and it was all she could do to keep from quickening her step and reaching up to run her fingers through it.

She became acutely aware of his voice; Hawk had only to speak her name in the most ordinary way to set her insides quivering. And his scent intrigued her, coiling in the recesses of her mind to tantalize her. Hawk's smell was totally unlike that of any other man, white or Indian. He gave off a musky odor, intensely clean, yet woodsy and elemental . . . and eternally male.

By day sensual desires plagued her, and even at night, she found no peace. Repeatedly she dreamed of having Hawk make passionate love to her. So real were her sleeping fantasies that she often woke to find herself wantonly damp between the thighs.

To her shame, Kate also found herself remembering the raw and terrifying coupling of mare and stallion she had seen on the island. Try as she might, she could not rid herself of the sight, sounds, and smell of that awesome mating.

Eventually her need for Hawk grew so great that she lost her appetite and grew edgy and irritable. For two days, Hawk appeared not to notice her change of mood, but by midmorning on the following day, he told her that they would camp early and rest.

They had just reached the banks of a shallow stream, and Kate had assumed that they would wade across and keep going. "Why are we stopping?"

"I've just told you," he answered mildly. "I've driven you too hard. Your eyes are heavy. This man thinks that you did not sleep well."

Kate looked longingly at the winding creek. Trees grew so thickly on either side that their branches intertwined, forming a verdant canopy that nearly shut out the sky. Here and there a ray of sunlight sparkled through, caressing the surface of the water with a multitude of shimmering, diamond facets.

The stream called out to her with whispering fairy voices. They'd walked over rough terrain since daybreak, and she was hot and sweaty, despite her practical attire. Resting here to bathe would be a luxury. Kate sighed and leaned down to dip her hand in the clear, cool water. "Could we?" she asked. "Is it safe?"

"Yes . . . and no," Hawk said. "We've seen no Powhatan sign for days. And this man worries about you. We will stop and take our chances."

"Mmmm." She pulled off her moccasins and waded in, walking carefully on the rocky creek bottom. The stones were round and smooth, mostly fist-sized and larger. Tiny silver fish darted away; some brushed the tops of her feet and ankles, tickling her, and she laughed.

"We'll camp on the farside," Hawk said. "There, by that fallen tree." As he spoke, Starlady flew ahead and perched on a gnarled branch.

The water was cold, but not so cold that it numbed Kate's legs. Her hair felt oily and she wanted to wash it. She knelt and untied the single long braid that hung down her neck, then shook her tresses loose around her shoulders.

"Wait," Hawk said. "I picked some flowers of the sweet-pepper bush yesterday. It will make a lather for your hair." He dug in his hunting bag and produced a handful of crushed blossoms wrapped in soft folds of deerskin. Smiling, he held them out to her. "Have I offended you, Kate, that you suddenly wash with your clothes on?"

She felt the heat of a flush tint her cheeks. Shyly, she looked away from him. "I thought only to do my hair," she began, then realized how foolish her lie must seem. Self-consciously, she pulled off her vest and skirt and tossed them onto the far bank. "Are you satisfied?" She swallowed, trying to dissolve the constriction in her throat, at a loss to know why she was so upset.

Had it been so long since they'd consummated their love that she was suddenly shy? She nibbled at her lower lip, wishing he would take her in his arms and trail his fingers along the curve of her throat. She wanted him to kiss her in a way that made the earth shift beneath her feet. But she wanted him to reach for her first.

"Kate!"

She glanced back. "What?"

"You did not hear me?" He laughed. "Your thoughts are far away. I asked you to come here." He pointed to a curve of the creek, where the water pooled deep and slow moving, out of the main current.

She did as he bade her, steeling herself to be so close to him without responding to his naked masculinity. He led the way, his lean, bare buttocks clearly revealed in the dappling shadows.

Kate's mouth went dry. Flashes of heat scorched her skin. *Make love to me,* she cried inwardly. *Please love me.*

But when she reached his side, he simply motioned her to dip her hair in the water. Resolved, she dropped to her knees and lowered her head.

Hawk rubbed the bits of sweet-pepper flowers between his hands and began to rub them into Kate's hair. She closed her eyes, wishing he would slip a hand down to cup her breast or caress the small of her back with his lean, hard fingers.

When her hair was clean, Hawk scooped up handfuls of sand from the creekbed to scour his arms and chest. Kate lay back, floating, letting the cool water drift over her and trying not to look at the swell of his chest or the curve of his hips as he bathed.

Finally the cold seeped through to her bones, and her teeth began to chatter. "I'm freezing," she complained.

Hawk ducked under a final time and splashed up onto the bank. "Come," he said, offering her a hand. She took it, and the grip of his fingers sent shivers of excitement racing under her skin.

Bordering the stream was a sheltered glade of lush clover sprinkled with yellow, blue, and pink wildflowers. Kate stretched out in the sun, letting the heat and the soft, springy bed under her dry her damp skin and hair. As soon as she lay down, she felt the tension drain from her body. The earth seemed to infuse her with peace and strength. She closed her eyes and cleared her mind of everything.

"Rest," Hawk murmured. "I'll make a fire and catch us some fish for a hot meal."

Bees droned lazily, and a faint breeze whispered through the leaves. The glade was sweet with the scents of new grass and flowers, and Kate slept as she had not done in days.

She awoke to the delicious odor of grilling trout. She sat up and rubbed her eyes sleepily. "Is it ready?" she called. "I'm hungry enough to eat oak bark."

"Stay there. I'll bring it to you."

She sighed and yawned, letting her eyes drift shut for just a minute. When she opened them, Hawk was sitting beside her with a plate of woven leaves in his lap. Arranged on the leaves were golden brown filets of fish and wild strawberries. "Oh," she said. "Where did you get those? I love—"

Hawk popped a ripe berry into her mouth.

"Ummm." She reached for a bit of fish, but he shook his head. Instead he crumbled a filet and put a small piece between his lips. Then he leaned close and offered her the fish.

As she took it, their mouths brushed. "What are you doing?" she asked. Heat stabbed to the pit of her belly. It was hard to talk with the delicious bite of trout in her mouth and harder still to sound nonchalant when her lips tingled, and her unclad breasts were so close to his naked chest.

He chuckled and fed her another berry. Trembling, she caught the tip of his finger and held it between her teeth. Before she could stop herself, she licked his fingertip with her tongue.

"Kate."

Heat coiled and spiraled within her. Breathlessly, she nibbled his finger, then drew it into her mouth and suckled it wickedly. The plate slipped sideways and the fish and berries tumbled into the grass. Hawk tilted her head back and ground his mouth against hers.

She moaned and locked her arms around his neck. Hawk's answering groan was tinder to her flame. White-hot threads of fire spun and shot through her. "Hawk . . . Hawk," she whispered between searing kisses.

His hands were all over her. And wherever he caressed her, her flesh sizzled; the heat of him assailed her in waves. She fell back onto the crushed grass, pulling him down on top of her. The hard tumescence throbbing between them told her more than words how much he wanted her.

Greedily, she arched against him, thrusting her hips to meet his ardent striving. His hair brushed her cheek, and she inhaled deeply of its clean, damp scent. She caught a lock and brought it to her lips. "I love your hair," she whispered.

"I love all of you."

Kate's heart thudded wildly. She had waited so long for this. Now the happiness was almost too great to bear. She cried out in pleasure as he found her nipple and gently tugged at the aching bud.

"You are mine," he said. "Mine and no other man's."

Intense need licked up her belly and consumed her breasts. She wanted—needed—his mouth, his tongue, the nip of his teeth. For an instant the image of the mating stallion and mare flashed in her mind.

See how he claims what is his, Hawk had said. His words echoed in her brain.

Desire thrummed through Kate's veins.

"Claim what is yours!" she urged him.

Sparks billowed between them as their limbs entwined, and he continued to nuzzle and kiss and lick her bare skin. Her skin felt as though it was on fire and only he could put out the flames. She wanted him with a greater urgency than she ever had before.

She couldn't get enough of his hands—or of touching him. He was satin over granite—tender, yet as wild as the black stallion.

"Love me!" she cried aloud. She traced the hard swell of his muscular chest and let her fingers linger on his nipples until they hardened into tight buttons.

Hawk's sharp teeth closed on the tender skin of her shoulder. He bit down . . . not to cause pain, but to fan her incandescent hunger.

Kate's breath came in quick, shuddering gasps. "Please." She moaned. Fire raged in the moist folds between her legs. "Oh, please . . ."

He laughed and lifted his head, gazing at her with such intense desire that silver tremors radiated through her heated flesh.

"I love you," she whispered.

"And this man loves you." Slowly, ever so slowly, Hawk branded a line of fiery kisses along her collarbone. He circled the aureole of her breast with the pad of his thumb then teased her nipple until she squirmed against him, making tiny whimpers in her throat.

"Now! Now!" she demanded.

He bent his head and kissed her breasts, first one

and then the other. He moistened each nipple with his tongue and laved them until she writhed in pleasure. Then he slipped his hand down over her belly and ran his fingers through her curls, all the while suckling at her breasts.

She moaned, tossing her head from side to side and scraping her nails down his naked back.

"Yes . . . yes," he rasped.

Kate bucked against him, and his warm breath stirred her damp fleece. "Oh, oh."

"A soft spot for this man to lay his head," he teased. He wandered lower, and Kate whimpered at the joy. His fingers probed gently, then harder as she opened to him.

"Kate," he said. She met his heavy-lidded gaze. "We have not eaten of the medicine that will prevent a child," he warned her. "I can pleasure you without—"

"No!" she cried. "I want you! All of you! Now."

He knelt between her raised knees, and she felt the first sweet caress of his hot flesh.

"Yes . . ." she gasped as he entered her, full and hard.

She arched to meet him, and he drove deep within her, whipping her passion to a fever pitch with each mighty thrust. Like flames whipped by high winds, their mutual ecstasy became a conflagration that built higher and higher until Kate thought she would burn to cinders.

And when the first wave of glorious culmination spilled through her, she cried out Hawk's name and clung to him, and they rode the crest of the wildfire to the edge of heaven and back.

Afterward he held her for a long time without speaking. Finally he broke the tender silence. "I may have given you a child this day," he said, looking deeply into her eyes.

"I want your child. I want to feel my womb swelling with life." She sighed. "I never wanted to have a babe before, but I do now."

"A Cherokee child?"

"Yes." She lay her head on his chest.

"Was it worth the waiting?" he teased.

"Yes . . . yes!" She sighed. "I should have enough character now for ten Cherokee women."

He kissed her cheeks and eyelids. His lips tickled and she laughed.

"A hundred times I wanted you, my Kate—a hundred times. I wanted to fill you with my love more than I wanted to eat or drink. But I was afraid that if I did, Gar would fall upon us."

"I'm sure he's turned back to his own country by now."

"This has all been his country. That of the mighty Powhatan emperor, at least."

"Your grandfather." She wrapped her fingers around his hand and brought it to her cheek, savoring the feel of him. Her happiness was too great for words. She was content to lie here, arms and legs entwined, beating heart to beating heart.

"My father's father. He was never grandfather to me. My mother's father is Touch the Clouds. You will love him. He is wise and funny and—"

"It has been many years since you've seen him. Are you so certain he still lives?"

"Touch The Clouds lives. He and Painted Stick taught me what it was to be a man. If my grandfather had crossed over to the spirit land, my heart would know."

She sighed and burrowed closer. "When will we reach Cherokee land?"

"Soon." He kissed the corners of her mouth. "You are my undoing, Kate. I have broken a great law to love you here. You drain my strength and make me forget my first duty to keep you safe. The spirits will punish me for what I have done."

She made a small sound of amusement. "Surely even your spirits know what it is to be in love," she answered lightly. "You are strong enough for three men. If you were any mightier, you'd kill me."

"Never." He caressed her lips with his. "I am . . ."

Starlady's sharp *keer-keer-keer* shattered the peace of the shady glade. Hawk's muscles tensed and he rolled away from her, leaping to his feet and reaching for his bow in one swift motion. He snatched an arrow from his quiver and notched it on the bowstring. But before he could let it fly, Kate saw a flash of color from the trees.

To her horror, an arrow sped through the air and pierced Hawk's shoulder with such force that it stuck out of his back. He staggered, braced himself, and let fly a returning shaft.

In the blink of an eye, another iron-tipped arrow sunk into Hawk's thigh. His second shaft flew true, striking his unseen assailant. Kate heard a groan and then the sound of snapping bushes and a body falling.

Hawk fought to stand upright as he readied a third arrow. "Get dressed," he ordered. "Quickly." His bronze face drained of color, turning a sickly hue. Both terrible wounds seeped blood.

Kate glanced back at the trees as she wrapped her skirt around her and put on her vest. Icy dread crawled through her; Hawk was badly hurt, maybe dying. If another attack came, she would stand no

chance. She grabbed up his hunting pack and tomahawk and ran to his side. "Are there more of them?"

"Only one. For now. He's down, dead or
wounded. If there were more, I'd be dead." He
handed her his bow, then using both hands, he
grasped hold of the arrow in the fleshy part of his leg
and snapped the wooden shaft close to the wound.

Kate uttered a faint whimper. Tiny black particles
danced in front of her eyes, and the ground seemed
to sink under her feet.

Hawk's pale face was as expressionless as if it were
carved in stone, but his eyes dilated from pain. Blood
ran from the hole around the arrow shaft and
drenched his leg.

"My loin covering." He motioned for her to wrap
the leather garment around his waist.

Against his protests, Kate took a length of rawhide
cord from his hunting bag and knotted it around his
thigh above the injury. "Loosen that every few
minutes," she said. "We need to get that arrowhead
out of—"

"No time," he said. His face and his lips were
waxen, his breathing slow and carefully measured.

"Don't die on me," she begged him. "Please don't
die."

He dropped the feathered end of the broken arrow
in his hunting bag. Gritting his teeth, he sat down on
the ground and took several deep breaths, then thrust
a fold of leather between his teeth.

"No," Kate whispered as he put his hands on the
arrow that transfixed his shoulder. "Let me cut it."

He shook his head, closed his eyes, and broke the
second shaft. He made no sound, but his breath
hissed, and he slumped forward into her arms for
nearly a minute.

"Hawk!" Her pain at the thought of losing him was as deep and agonizing as what he must be suffering. The hurting cut to her core and left her dazed.

"No." He pushed her hand away. "I'm all right."

"You're not all right. You're flesh and blood, Hawk—a man, not a—"

"I need you."

She steeled herself. "What do you want me to do?" But she already knew.

"Pull it out," he ordered.

"Sweet Jesus." If the shaft broke off inside Hawk's shoulder it would turn gangrenous, and he would die a hideous death. She nodded. Her hands were slippery with sweat as she moved to his back and grasped the arrow just behind the barbed, triangular head.

"Now," he said. "Slow. Pull."

Tears scalded her eyes, but she threw her weight against the arrow. Nothing happened. She kept pulling, and then the shaft began to move. Blood stained his back and her hands, but she knew she mustn't stop.

Starlady screamed a drawn out *keeer* and fluttered down to strut back and forth beside them in an agitated manner.

"Please," Kate prayed aloud. "Please, God." The last of the hickory shaft slid out. More blood gushed from the hole.

"Fetch moss from the creek bank," Hawk rasped. With great effort, he rose to his feet.

"No," she argued. "You must lie down and let me—"

"Do as I tell you, woman!"

She looked into his eyes, wondering if the shock and loss of blood had affected his reason. When he fixed her with a black stare, she pulled on her moccasins and ran to the water.

There she gathered a handful of thick, blue-green moss and returned to his side. Hawk was still losing blood, but not as fast as he had been.

He gave her only a minute or two, and then he stiffened. "I must go and see who shot at us," he said. "If it is Gar or one of his Powhatan warriors, I have to know."

"I can do it."

Hawk shook his head. "Too dangerous. He might be playing opossum. Waiting for us to come close."

"You're not strong enough to walk."

"I must be. Stay here while I look."

His tone was hard. Against her better judgment, Kate gathered up the remainder of their belongings, including the rest of the cooked fish. If they had to run for their lives, they would need food.

Moments before, she had been completely lost in Hawk's embrace, and she had talked of having his baby. Now he might be dying. The green boughs closed around him as he entered the woods, and she tried to keep from shaking.

Sickening guilt washed over her. If they had kept going instead of stopping to bathe and eat and make love, the Powhatan might never have found them. If Hawk died, it would be her fault.

What had he said? *The spirits will punish me . . .*

They already had.

Hawk appeared again at the edge of the clearing. "We go," he said. He whistled to Starlady, and she flew up.

"Did you find the man who shot you?"

"A Powhatan. Dead. His name was Wolf Trapper." Hawk swayed slightly. "He was probably a scout for Gar."

"You can't walk," she said, going to him.

"I can walk." He straightened his shoulders and took several steps toward her.

"Lean on me."

His voice took on a steel edge. "I can walk."

Leaving the creek, they crossed the glade where they had made love and entered the tall trees on the farside. Starlady flew overhead. They had gone no more than a few hundred yards when Kate heard the bloodthirsty whoop of Powhatan war cries.

"They have found their dead scout," Hawk said. He took her hand and began to run. With each step he took, more blood flowed from his two wounds.

"You can't do this," Kate protested. "You'll bleed to death."

"If Gar catches us, we'll both die."

Abruptly, just ahead, Kate saw a brown, furry shape run from behind a tree. Hawk saw it at the same time, staggered, and pulled her close.

A wide-eyed bear cub peered at them for a second, squealed, and raised up on its hind legs.

Relief turned Kate's knees to jelly. "It's just a baby," she cried.

And then a mountain of fur and teeth rose out of the bushes, and the trees echoed with the furious roar of an enraged mother grizzly.

Chapter 23

"Don't move," Hawk whispered. "Don't make a sound. Don't even breathe."

The world stopped. For a flash of time, Kate's mind seemed to freeze. Colors, scents, and sounds intensified a hundredfold. And then, with infinite slowness, life went on around her.

The bear kept rising up and up. Kate had never imagined that an animal could be so large or have so many teeth. She caught her first whiff of the grizzly and her stomach clenched as the stench of musk and rotten meat enveloped her.

She thought she was standing perfectly still, as motionless as the ancient trees surrounding them, but Hawk must have sensed her panic because his eyes sparked a warning. "If you run, she'll charge."

The grizzly's eyes were small and black; her mouth gaped wide, filled with razor-sharped fangs. Her red tongue lolled above a dripping mass of white slobber, and the curving ivory-colored claws on each massive paw were as long as Kate's fingers.

The bear would smell the blood on Hawk. No matter what they did, she'd attack. Not even a musket ball could stop such a ferocious beast.

Kate sucked in a jagged breath. One or both of them would die. If she died, Hawk would mourn her, but if he was lost, then everything the Cherokee had done to save themselves would be lost as well.

He is the Chosen One. The truth rang through her conscious thought with the clarity of a crystal bell.

Suddenly Kate knew what she must do. She must sacrifice her own life for Hawk's. Uttering a loud scream, she whirled and ran back the way they had come.

The bear let out a tremendous growl. When Kate looked over her shoulder, she saw Hawk standing between her and the grizzly. He had dropped his bow, and his hands were outstretched, palm up, in an attitude of prayer.

"No!" She was so shocked that she stopped in her tracks—but not before she saw the war-painted faces of the Powhatans swarming down upon her.

"Hawk!" she screamed. "No!" Denial ripped from her throat. "You, bear!" she shouted. "Here! Come get me, bear!" She turned and would have run back to die by Hawk's side if Gar hadn't seized her arm and held her fast.

She struggled wildly.

The Powhatan war chief clamped a hard hand over her mouth and yanked her roughly against him. He twisted her around so that they were both facing the irate grizzly and Hawk's back.

Kate's breath caught in her throat.

The man she loved stood motionless, speaking to the bear in Cherokee. His tone was soft, soothing, and although Kate could not understand the words, she instinctively knew he was telling the animal that he meant her and her cub no harm.

The beast dropped onto all fours. Her savage snarl ripped through the trees as she charged Fire Hawk.

Kate screamed.

The shriek of a plunging red-tailed hawk mingled with that of the grizzly. Starlady shot through the branches and struck at the bear's head with outstretched talons.

The bear reared up and swatted at the red-tail with her front paws. Starlady attacked the grizzly's head in a frenzied blur of wings and beak. Enraged, the bear snapped at the hawk with curved, yellow fangs.

"Run!" Kate shouted to Fire Hawk. "Run!"

But he didn't move a muscle.

Abruptly Starlady broke off the assault and flew up to perch on a branch high above the bear's reach. The grizzly turned her attention to the man standing only a few paces away.

The bear opened her mouth and roared a challenge.

"Hawk!" Kate shrieked.

Still on her hind legs, the grizzly lumbered toward him. She towered over him, her eyes glowing with unholy fire.

Kate knew that one of those ivory-tipped claws could rip a man's head off with a single blow. She wanted to shut her eyes . . . shut out the horror that she knew was coming, but she couldn't. "Do something!" she screamed at Gar. "Shoot it! Save him!"

"If he is the Chosen, let his spirits save him," Gar said.

The bear's massive paw descended over Fire Hawk's head. Kate's knees buckled. As she sagged forward, Gar let her fall. She went down on her knees in the deep grass, with no strength to rise, no will to keep fighting.

But when the bear's paw struck Hawk, her claws did not rip through his flesh and bone. Instead the grizzly batted him aside with an almost affectionate slap and dropped onto all fours. Her pig eyes fixed on Gar, and she charged.

"Stay still!" Hawk shouted to Kate as the Powhatan broke and ran.

Nearly hidden where she crouched in the grass, she was too terrified to move in any case. The stench of the grizzly filled her head as the beast pounded past her in hot pursuit of Gar and his warriors.

The Powhatan prince fired off one arrow before he turned and fled. Gar's iron-tipped shaft buried in the bear's neck, but she snapped it off with one blow of her paw and never missed a stride. She brought Gar down on the second leap.

Hawk reached Kate in a heartbeat and covered her with his body. "Shh," he whispered urgently. "Stay still." She shut her eyes and tried not to hear Gar's death shrieks or the awful crunch of bone that followed.

When Kate opened her eyes again, the grizzly was standing over them, his mouth and neck stained with red.

"Go in peace," Hawk said in the Cherokee tongue. To her amazement, Kate understood the words.

The bear grunted and reared up on her hind legs to sniff the air. Starlady swooped off the tree limb and dove into the brush. Seconds later the grizzly cub bleated in pain. The mother bear twisted around and tore through the bushes at lightning speed.

Kate heard a final warning snarl as mother and cub bolted off through the woods amid the crackle and crunch of breaking underbrush.

Starlady returned to her perch and snapped her proud head to and fro, surveying the scene with glittering black eyes before beginning to preen her mussed feathers.

"Is it gone?" Kate asked.

"The bear is gone."

Hawk fought his way to his feet. Blood soaked his loin covering and body. His eyes were shadowed with pain, his voice gravelly but unwavering.

As Kate stood up, she saw that the Powhatan braves were returning to the spot where Gar lay. Her heart thudded in her chest. She and Hawk had escaped death from the bear, but they were still in danger. In this last minute, she wanted to tell Hawk how much she loved him . . . and that she wasn't a coward. She'd not run from the bear to escape, but to save him.

A grizzled Powhatan warrior looked down at Gar's bloody remains and then raised his head to gaze solemnly at them. "I see you, Fire Hawk Who Hunts At Dawn," he said. The aging warrior's hair was nearly white, pulled to one side in the young men's Powhatan fashion. His face was lined with wrinkles, the slits of his eyes nearly hidden in the folds of his lids.

"I see you, Walking Fish," Hawk replied.

"Your grandfather should have kept you."

Hawk said nothing.

His arrow wounds were bleeding again. Kate knew it was an effort for Hawk to stay on his feet, but he gave no outward indication that he was badly injured.

Walking Fish came closer. "Your grandfather, the Emperor Powhatan, was wrong to turn his back on you," he said. "You are the Chosen. When the bear and the red-tail know you, who are we to challenge the Cherokee spirits?" He sighed heavily. "We followed Iron Snake and Gar when it would have been wiser to heed the wishes of the spirits. You were born to us, and we did not realize what power you possessed."

"Whatever this man has been given, it is for the greater good, not for my own will," Hawk answered softly.

Walking Fish shrugged. "Now the Powhatan will know the wrath of the spirits. We will wither, while our brothers, the Cherokee will prosper. Sire many sons, Fire Hawk That Hunts At Dawn, so that the blood of our people will not be entirely lost."

"I will try, Walking Fish."

The grizzled warrior pursed his narrow lips. "I am certain that you will." For a heartbeat, a smile lit his faded eyes, and then he motioned to the remaining Powhatans. "Put down your weapons," he commanded. "This is Cherokee land. Our blood feud is ended. We came seeking justice, but we have found it with Gar's life instead. It is his death, not yours, that is payment in full for the deaths of our warriors."

Hawk extended his hand in the universal sign of peace. "Take my cousin's body home, Walking Fish, so that he may be buried with the honor due a Powhatan prince."

"So be it," Walking Fish said.

Hawk stood until the Powhatans vanished in the forest, then he leaned against a tree and sank slowly to the ground. "You should have obeyed my orders," he whispered to Kate. "That grizzly could have killed you."

"And not you?"

"It was not my day to die."

"No?" She knelt beside him, too shaken to cry. An eerie cold seized her, and she began to shiver. "Oh, Hawk, don't die," she begged him. "I don't want to live without you."

He forced a smile. "You risked your life for me . . . to draw away the bear." He nodded. "I know."

She laid her hand on his forehead. The air was warm, but Hawk's flesh felt chilled. "What can I do?" she asked. "Tell me what to do."

"Go and fetch my mother."

"What?" She snatched back her hand. "If you think I'm leaving you—"

"You will help me back to the creek," he gasped. "But I cannot go on. *You* must."

"Go where?" She stood and turned around. The trackless forest looked the same in every direction. "Go where? How far? I can't do it."

"You must." He swallowed and drew in another slow breath. "Follow the sun until you come to a long valley. Then turn south. Keep the sun at your left in the morning and on your right at night. Camp before dusk and build a big fire."

"You expect me to find Cherokees?"

"I expect them to find you."

"And your mother? You want me to bring your mother?"

"She is a healer, very powerful. If any can cut out this arrowhead and heal my wounds, it will be Rainbow Basket."

"I can try to treat your injuries," she said. "Let me—"

"Go, Kate. Swiftly. I feel the strength ebbing from my body with each breath. My shoulder is not so bad, but the second arrowhead carried poison. I feel the bite of death in its sting."

"Damn it! If you're going to die anyway, let me stay with you." She flung herself down on her knees and kissed his cool lips, his cheeks, and eyelids. "Don't send me away, Hawk. I'm begging you."

"Have courage, panther woman. You can do this."

"And if you die alone?"

"Then all is as the spirits intended, and you will fulfill my destiny."

"I can do this," Kate murmured aloud. "I can do this."

She could not guess how many hours she had walked since she'd abandoned Hawk beside the rocky creek; she knew only that it had been a night and a day and now another night. She no longer felt the scratch of briers or the cramps in her legs, and she had long ceased starting with every rustle of brush or howl of a hunting wolf.

The cool mountain air swirled around her, chilling her cheeks and bare arms, but so long as she kept a steady pace, the cold was not life-threatening.

High overhead, a half-moon glittered in the star-strewn sky. Hawk had warned her to camp at dark and build a fire, but she could not. If she stopped walking, the horror that shadowed her footsteps would find her.

Leaving the man she loved had been so hard. And if she failed him . . . But she would not think about that anymore than she would think about Robert. She'd killed Robert because she'd had to—because he was going to shoot Hawk. She was sorry Robert was dead; she was always saddened by death but didn't regret her action.

She continued walking, keeping the rising sun on her left as Hawk had instructed, and hoping she hadn't gone too far astray when darkness fell.

Strangely, she had no fear of the wild animals. She had faced an enraged grizzly, and there could be nothing more frightening than that. Besides, if she lost Hawk, nothing else mattered. And so long as he lived, she would keep fighting to save him.

He was still alive. She clung to that certainty. And no matter how many times she stumbled and fell, she got up again and kept walking. Her tears had long since ceased falling. Her eyes were as dry as her throat and mouth, and it was hard to swallow.

Kate found the mountain spring by tripping and falling in it. So great was her thirst that she lay on her hands and knees and lapped up the sweet, clear water without even using her hands for a cup.

The rivulet was tiny, barely inches wide, so narrow that she might have stepped over it. But it was sufficient for her needs. The water cleared her mind and made her realize that she needed to rest. She would do Hawk no good if she killed herself by falling off a cliff in the darkness.

With heavy eyes, Kate cleared a space of grass and pine needles. She dug into the rocky soil to make a hollow and used flint and steel to strike a fire. She fed the infant flames with tinder, then added larger twigs and sticks. Finally she dragged a section of fallen log as thick as her thigh to straddle her crude hearth and provide fuel through the night. Then she curled up beside the welcome heat and sank into a dreamless sleep.

An unfamiliar woman's voice came from somewhere above her. Kate sighed and fought against wakening. But the lilting syllables continued to drift around her like a shower of feathers, brushing, teasing, and caressing, until Kate realized that someone was speaking Cherokee.

Her eyelids fluttered. "Oh!"

Hawk's eyes were gazing into hers.

She sat bolt upright. Icy disappointment drenched her. It wasn't Hawk. The copper-skinned face was not male, but exquisitely feminine. Around her forehead, she wore a strip of quill-worked white doeskin with a round disk of polished jade in the center. And from her earlobes hung cascades of tiny silver beads.

The woman stared at her, a woman with a high forehead, night black hair, and riveting cheekbones. She was so beautiful that Kate couldn't keep from expressing her first impossible thought. "Are you Hawk's mother?" It was a foolish notion, and she knew it as soon as the words tumbled from her lips. Surely this woman was too young to be the mother of a grown warrior.

A hint of a smile played over the Indian woman's gently curving lips. She spoke again in what Kate thought was Cherokee, but Kate still couldn't understand the words.

Kate scrambled to her feet and looked around her. Ten, twenty, perhaps thirty magnificently garbed warriors and several other equally handsome women stood staring at her in the soft light of early dawn. "Cherokee?" she asked. "Cherokee?" She used the word Hawk had patiently taught her to pronounce, the word his nation used among themselves, meaning *the real people*.

And then, above her in the treetops shrieked a familiar cry. Kate saw the flash of red tail feathers, and for a few seconds she believed that Starlady might actually flutter down to perch on her arm. Instead the hawk circled three times and flew off north.

Several of the Indian men pointed at the bird;

others made comments. The women whispered among themselves.

"I must make you understand," Kate said. Hastily, she grabbed Hawk's hunting bag from the ground and held it out to the woman wearing the jade coronet. "Please, you must come. Hawk is dying."

The black eyes—so much like Hawk's—narrowed. Kate sensed that her world hung in the balance.

"Fire Hawk," Kate said in stumbling Cherokee.

Incredibly, the beautiful woman's face lit with emotion and she nodded. "We come," she answered.

"Yes!" Kate seized her hand. "Come!" She searched her mind frantically for the Cherokee words Hawk had taught her. "Quick! Fire Hawk waits."

The Cherokee tracked Kate's footprints to find the spot where she'd left Hawk. A party of warriors ran on ahead, faster than Kate or any of the women could keep up, but not swifter than a red-tail could fly.

When she reached him, he was unconscious, barely breathing, but the Cherokee had already cut out the poisoned arrowhead and seared the wound with hot coals. Starlady perched on an overhanging tree limb, staring at Hawk with eyes of living obsidian.

For two days and nights, Hawk did not open his eyes. And in all those hours, Kate did not leave his side or let go of his hand for more than the time it took to tend to her most vital functions.

"I won't let you die," she whispered to him as she held his head in her lap and washed his fevered skin with cool water. "I won't let you."

Hawk had said that his mother was skilled in healing, and so she proved to be. Rainbow Basket boiled the roots of painted trillium and poured the liquid over her son's injuries. The other women helped by cooking broths of venison to give him strength and preparing teas made from willow bark to bring down the fever.

Rainbow Basket showed Kate how to prepare the roots of round lobed hepatica to make a drink that would clear his lungs and taught her how to drip nourishment and medicine into his mouth, drop by drop.

For long periods of time, Hawk's mother sang softly to him, brushed his hair, and wafted smoke from a pipe over his body. But mostly the Indian woman and her companions prayed for him.

In caring for Hawk and in praying that he might live, the women were united. The Indians could not understand English, and Kate's Cherokee was almost nonexistent, but Kate believed that God must welcome prayers in all languages. She was certain that He would hear and realize how this man was loved.

It was Rainbow Basket who forced Kate to eat when she had no appetite and sleep when she was afraid that if she relaxed her guard for even a few moments she would wake and find him gone.

Starlady also troubled Kate. The bird hadn't hunted since she'd returned to her master's side. Now, dull-eyed and head drooping, the great hawk seemed to be dying as well. Kate sensed that the red-tail and the man she loved were linked in some mysterious way, and she feared that if the bird had lost heart then the end must be near.

In the twilight hours before dawn on the third morning, Hawk's skin burned with such heat that it seemed impossible to Kate that any man could survive. Then the terrible fever gave way to chills. His teeth chattered, and he shivered and tossed. He groaned and shouted in Cherokee, and threw off his fur blanket.

In desperation, Kate lay down beside him and wrapped her arms around him, trying to quiet his thrashing body. "Shhh, shhh," she'd soothed. "Be still, my beautiful Hawk, sleep and get well."

He continued to toss, the shivering stopped, and once again, he grew hot to the touch. Finally as the sun was coming up, Kate rose and walked to the creek for another dipper of water, intending to pour it over the inflamed wound on his leg.

She was so exhausted that her eyelids felt heavy and her mind began playing tricks on her. Colored lights danced before her eyes, and the mist that rose off the grass seemed to echo with the faint tinkle of bells.

She knelt beside the stream and took a second to splash cold water over her face. From the corner of her eye, she saw Rainbow Basket go to her son's side. Then Starlady shrieked. The red-tail's head snapped up, and she flapped her powerful wings and rose into the air.

A cry ripped from Rainbow Basket's throat.

Kate's heart skipped a beat, then began to race. "No! No!" She leaped up and ran to Hawk. She tried to prepare herself for his death, but she couldn't. "No!"

Rainbow Basket stood up and called out to the other Cherokees. Kate stopped and looked down at Hawk. Her eyes were so full of tears that she could barely make out his face. "Oh, Hawk," she murmured.

"You found my mother," he rasped.

"Hawk?" Kate flung herself down on her knees. "Hawk?" She shook her head, unable to believe what she had heard.

Rainbow Basket nodded and moved away, leaving Kate and Hawk alone.

Kate touched his forehead with trembling hands. His hair was wet with sweat. "You're alive."

A smile tugged at the corner of his cracked lips. "I must be," he rasped. "A dead man couldn't feel this bad."

"Oh, Hawk, I love you," Kate exclaimed. "I love you so much."

Love shone back at her from his jet-black eyes.

Kate motioned to Rainbow Basket to come.

Hawk's fingers closed around Kate's, and he held her tightly. "Mother," he said in Cherokee.

"My son," Rainbow Basket replied softly. "My beloved son." She knelt at his side.

Hawk sighed deeply. "You've met my wife," he said. "My wife," he repeated in English for Kate's sake.

His mother's mouth tightened in disapproval.

He was tired . . . so tired. His head felt as though it had split in two, and his leg was on fire, but he needed to tell his mother about Kate. "I love her," he said.

His mother shook her head. "Her skin is white."

"She is a good woman," he murmured. "She is—"

"Sleep, my son," Rainbow Basket said. "Rest."

"Kate is my wife," he whispered in English, and then dropped back into Cherokee. "She is English but . . ."

"She is a good woman," Rainbow Basket admitted.

"I love her more than my own life."

"We will talk of this later."

Kate would have pulled away, but he held her fast. "No," Hawk insisted. "If you love me, Mother, you must make her welcome as your daughter."

Rainbow Basket shook her head. "It is not me you must convince. It is the council. You are the Chosen One. Your life is not your own."

"I have . . . kept faith," he whispered. "I have . . . come back."

"What is it?" Kate demanded of him. "What is she saying?"

"She said you . . . are . . . a good woman," he answered in English.

"Painted Stick and the high council must decide," Rainbow Basket admonished. "If they do not accept her, she cannot stay. It is the law."

Wearily, Hawk closed his eyes. He was too tired to argue with his mother. Kate was his wife, that much he knew. The spirits had chosen her as they had chosen him. Now he had only to convince the High Council of the Cherokee.

Chapter 24

During the next two weeks, Kate stayed close by Hawk's side, tending his wounds and coaxing him to eat. "Now you spoil me," Hawk teased. "Both you and Starlady."

The red-tail had resumed her hunting. She brought back a rabbit, squirrel, or bird almost every afternoon and dropped it at Hawk's feet.

Kate found the bird's habit amusing, but the Cherokee, including Hawk's mother, seemed to believe the red-tail was more spirit than flesh and blood.

The Cherokee men and women watched Starlady as they watched Kate. Rarely could Kate cross the campsite or go to the stream for water without feeling the curious gazes burning into her.

"What if they don't like me?" she asked Hawk. He lay in the shade of a beech tree, propped up on a bed of sweet-smelling cedar branches, covered with a throw of soft deerskin.

"They like you well enough," he replied as he squeezed her hand. "They simply aren't sure what kind of medicine woman you are, good or bad." Hawk's voice was still rough and gravelly, but Kate knew he was growing stronger each day.

"I'm not either," she said as she massaged his upper arm with an oil of crushed mint leaves. "I've told you a hundred times that I'm no witch."

He chuckled. "So you have, but you've not convinced me, and I doubt you'll convince them either."

Kate could not have said that Hawk's mother and the other women were unkind to her. Rainbow Basket and her friends took great pains to point out common objects and tell her the Cherokee names for them. Kate didn't need Hawk to tell her how important it was for her to learn his language. Gradually she learned enough to understand a few basic words such as *cook, eat, sleep,* and *water.*

"My mother says that your lessons are going well," Hawk told Kate one morning.

No one else among the Cherokee spoke English, and although she was self-conscious about her pronunciation, she tried to use what vocabulary she had to communicate with Rainbow Basket and her companions.

"What did she say?" Kate asked him.

"She says that you are very bright, and you have good manners, and . . ."

"And?" Kate urged.

He chuckled. "And your accent is terrible."

"I know." She couldn't help giggling. "It must be awful." She glanced across the cooking fire and saw Rainbow Basket looking at her.

"Come, Mother, join us," Hawk called.

She glanced at Hawk and then back at Kate.

"Please," Kate said, motioning to her.

As the woman approached, Kate summoned her courage and greeted her in formal Cherokee. Rainbow Basket nodded solemnly. Hawk broke into laughter.

"What? What did I say?" Kate asked.

His mother covered her lips with her fingers and sat beside them, her dark eyes dancing with amusement.

"Tell me," Kate pleaded.

"You bade her a blessed day and asked if she had eaten firewood," Hawk managed between outbursts of glee and fake groans of pain.

Kate giggled, and all three began to laugh together. "I'm sorry," Kate said, when she'd gotten control of herself once more. "I only meant to ask . . ." But then the humor of the situation set her to giggling again.

Rainbow Basket leaned close and hugged her, then said something to Hawk in Cherokee and he replied in the same tongue. The embrace needed no translation, and Kate returned the warm gesture.

"Mother wants to know what your clan is," Hawk said when they had calmed down enough to speak without chuckling. "As I told you before, there are fourteen minor clans and seven major. Clans are very important among the Cherokee. She and I are Wolf Clan, and the town where we will live is a Wolf Town." His eyes twinkled. "I told her that you are a Bird."

"A bird? What do you mean, I'm a bird?" Kate tried not to let her dismay show. "The English don't have clans."

Hawk shrugged. "No clan, no husband," he explained. "You cannot marry inside your own group. A Wolf and a Bird are well suited, and I think that since the Hawk Spirit chose you, you must be one of their own."

"I have to be a bird if I want to be your wife?"

"No, but it helps."

Kate chuckled. "I'll be a bird. At least you didn't make me a snake."

"If you'd rather—"

"No, thank you. Katherine Miles of the Bird Clan of England, that's me." Then she turned serious. "We are not deceiving your mother, are we? I'd not want to be dishonest."

Hawk shook his head. "No, my Kate, we are not. The clan relationship is sacred. Our children will be of the Bird Clan."

"If we are blessed with any," Kate replied.

Rainbow Basket murmured something to Hawk in Cherokee, and he smiled. "We will be," he assured Kate. "Trust me."

When Hawk recovered enough to make the journey back to his mother's town, they set off south and west into the mountains. In order to keep Hawk's wounds from reopening, they walked only a short distance and camped early each night.

There was little opportunity for Kate and Hawk to be alone together, and sometimes it seemed to her as if Rainbow Basket was deliberately chaperoning them.

When she asked Hawk, he agreed. "Mother has it in her head that Painted Stick and the High Council may object to our marriage."

A shiver went through Kate. "And if they do? What then, Hawk?"

"Then I will not stay." He lifted her hand to his lips and kissed the pulse at her wrist. "You are mine, now and forever. My wife, my soul. Not even the High Council can take you from me."

Kate nibbled at her lower lip. The thought that the Cherokee might reject her made her feel hollow inside.

"I love you," he whispered, laying a hand on her shoulder. "Try not to worry so. There will be a great celebration to honor my homecoming. I will not be able to be with you much of the time. Much will be expected of me." He sighed. "Nothing awful, Kate. The English love their ritual, don't they? I am a warrior. I am the Chosen One. I must follow custom, part of which means that I do not show my feelings. It does not stop me from having them."

"We'll be apart?"

"Only for a few hours. And you will never be alone. As a member of the Bird Clan, you will have many relatives, and all will welcome you with open arms."

"But I'm not a Bird," she protested. "Not really."

"You are. Trust me."

On the fifth day, deep in the mountains, they stopped to rest at noon near a clear blue lake. As Hawk had promised, Kate found the land beautiful.

"Have you ever seen a sky so blue? Or smelled air so sweet?" he asked her.

"No." She smiled at him. "We must be getting close to your home."

"Yes," he agreed. "Wolf Town is just over the next ridge. Mother has sent runners to tell them of our approach and to bring us fresh clothing."

Kate averted her eyes so that he could not see her apprehension. When she had shot Robert, she'd cut herself off from ever returning to the English colony. If the High Council did not approve of her, what would become of her?

Rainbow Basket and her good friend, Robin's Egg, swept down on Kate and led her to a secluded spot where the women were bathing amid an atmosphere of excitement and general high spirits.

"Home," Robin's Egg said to Kate, pointing

south. "Wolf Town." She was a tall, plump individual with a merry laugh, and Kate liked her immediately.

"Home," Kate repeated, hoping against hope that what she said would become true.

Kate now understood enough Cherokee to know that as a group Rainbow Basket's attendants were called *pretty women* or *war women.* Some were the mothers of warriors, and all had distinguished themselves in battle. Once Hawk had told Rainbow Basket that Kate had killed a man to save his life, all the Cherokee began to treat her with increased respect.

These ladies were so graceful and good-natured that it was hard for her to think of them as belonging to a society of warriors. They laughed and chattered as they changed their plain buckskin skirts and short jackets for beautiful garments of the softest fawn skin and woven grass adorned with goose down and bird plumes. They draped their throats with exquisite necklaces, slipped rings on their fingers, and arranged rows of glittering bracelets on their muscular arms.

Rainbow Basket brushed Kate's newly washed hair and twisted it into a knot at the back of her head, then secured it with cedar hair pins in the Cherokee fashion. She presented Kate with a white fringed skirt that hung to her knees, soft leggings, beaded moccasins, and a matching white jacket decorated with porcupine quills.

The men had brought fine garments for Hawk as well. While Kate was bathing, Hawk had fastened eagle feathers in his hair. He hung his silver gorget around his neck and donned a vest sewn with silver and turquoise nuggets. New knee-high moccasins and a painted leather loin covering completed his regalia.

With much discussion, the Cherokee men and women formed a procession. At the last moment, Hawk hurried to Kate and held out a small birch-bark container of red paint. "Among our people, it is considered an honor to mark the returning hero," he said. Kate laughed and streaked his face in the pattern he requested. Finally Hawk called Starlady to perch on his wrist and slung his bow and arrows over his shoulder.

Kate's chest swelled with pride as she saw how impressive Hawk looked. How could she ever have thought he was a savage? She wanted to throw herself into his arms and tell him how much she loved him, but she knew that a public display of affection was not the Cherokee way. She contented herself with silently mouthing the word *husband*.

"Your place is with my mother," Hawk reminded her.

"My place is at your side."

"Soon," he promised.

Nervously, Kate joined the ranks of women. One of the *pretty women* took the lead position. Kate, Rainbow Basket, and Robin's Egg walked close behind her, followed by the others marching three abreast. The braves came next, also in groups of three, and Hawk's place was last.

The *pretty women* began to sing as they walked along a narrow trail that soon widened into a broader lane. Trees thinned out to wide cornfields, and beyond that Kate saw a town containing several hundred houses.

Nothing in the Powhatan village had prepared her for the masses of cheering people now welcoming

Hawk back to his Cherokee homeland. Men, women, and children shouted and clapped. Women sang and danced to the tune of flutes and drums. Children tossed flowers, sweet herbs, and corn tassels in the path of the procession.

The rectangular houses of the Cherokee were made of upright logs plastered with clay. The dwellings were without chimneys or windows, but they were high and spacious with plastered conical roofs. Fruit bearing trees, neat storage buildings, and small gardens surrounded each home.

Kate tried to count the people, but soon gave up. There were hundreds, all healthy and handsome with sound teeth, straight limbs and reddish copper complexions. Even Jamestown could not boast so many citizens. Hawk had told her that this was the time of year for a joyous Cherokee festival, the Sampling of the New Corn, *Sah, looh, stee-knee, keeh steh steeh*. Each and every person looked to her as if they were enjoying a holiday.

In the center of the Wolf village stretched a great square, and beyond that a gleaming white, seven-sided log building more than two stories high with a domed roof.

"That is the Town-House," Rainbow Basket said, pointing. "The High Council meets there." She pointed again to an elderly man seated on a mat of cornstalks beside the door of the Town-House. "Our white chief," she said. "Touch The Clouds."

Hawk had explained to Kate that every Cherokee town had two chiefs: a white, or peace, chief and a red chief for times of war. Kate couldn't understand all that Hawk's mother said, but she did grasp the word *chief* and the name Touch The Clouds.

"Hawk's grandfather?"

"*Agidu'tu*," Rainbow Basket said, as she smiled and nodded. "My father."

The *war women* led the column seven times around the Town-House to spirited applause and the throbbing of a dozen water drums. At last, they came to a halt by the entrance. The drums and flutes grew silent; the crowd hushed.

Touch The Clouds said something that Kate couldn't understand and entered the doorway of the huge structure. The war women followed close behind him. Inside, Kate saw why the Town-House was so large and high.

Tiers of benches rose on all seven sides of a hard-packed center area containing a single fire. When the progression reached the ceremonial court, the men and women scattered to take their places in various parts of the Town-House. Kate quickly assumed that seating was assigned according to clan and status in the tribe. Rainbow Basket led her to a place in the first row of the Bird Clan's section and left her in the charge of an elderly matron.

What had been noisy outside was pandemonium in the confines of the Town-House. Men and women filed inside in small groups, filling the communal hall to overflowing.

When no more could be seated, warriors with wolfskin headdresses signaled for quiet and took their positions at drums on the far end of the center space. Then Hawk walked in to the arena and raised his arms in salute. The crowd went wild, calming only when Touch The Clouds arose from his seat and delivered a long speech, none of which Kate could understand.

Hawk stood immobile beside the ceremonial fire. His shoulders were back, his feet slightly apart, his chest thrust out, the perfect Cherokee warrior. Starlady was no longer with him. Hawk must have decided not to risk bringing her inside among so many people, Kate decided.

When the chief had taken his place again, a thin, gray-haired man with long braids stood up from the front row of benches in Kate's Bird section. The elder wore no facial paint, jewelry, eagle feathers, or regalia of any kind, nothing but a plain leather kilt and moccasins.

A sigh passed among the Cherokee, and Kate heard the name "Painted Stick" repeated over and over with reverence. She stared at the little man. There was absolutely nothing remarkable about his appearance, but she could not take her eyes off him. Apparently neither could anyone else.

He is a powerful man, she thought. The aura of greatness shone from his ordinary, lined face.

Painted Stick walked to Hawk and embraced him. Again the Cherokee screamed out their approval. But when the holy man began to speak, not a foot in the building shifted, not a throat was cleared.

Kate leaned forward, hoping to catch a few words of what he was saying. It wasn't a speech really— more of a song or chant.

"From among you, a child shall be chosen," Painted Stick said.

"It is true," echoed the Cherokee multitude.

"And you shall make of him a man," the shaman intoned.

"It is true," they thundered.

"And you shall send him forth to do battle with evil."

"It is true."

Hawk glanced toward the spot where Kate sat. Be

brave, he wanted to tell her. Trust me, heart of my heart.

"The Chosen One goes forth alone."

"It is true!" The shouts of the people rang out.

"And returns to his people as two halves complete."

There was utter silence from the onlookers.

It took all of Hawk's will not to turn and look at Painted Stick. What was he saying? That was not part of the Song of the Chosen! That line was new.

Whispers spread through the highest tiers of the Town-House. People shifted in their seats and glanced at the clansmen beside them. An old woman began to cough.

"Come forth, Kate-Miles," Painted Stick commanded.

Kate's head snapped up.

The holy man repeated his order, and a woman tugged on Kate's arm. Hesitantly, cheeks burning, she stepped into the center area. Painted Stick motioned for her to come closer.

Be brave, Hawk urged silently. Hold your head high, my Kate. Remembering where he was and why, Hawk kept his own face expressionless, his body taut.

From the corner of his eye, Hawk watched Kate take a step and then another until she was near enough for Painted Stick to clasp her hands and peer into her face. For a long time he stared.

Blood throbbed in Hawk's head as his gut twisted. The life of the woman he loved hung in the balance, and his own life with hers. Painted Stick's word was law. If he rejected Kate, Hawk would have to desert his people . . .

Fourteen clans of Cherokee waited expectantly.

Then Painted Stick smiled. "Come, daughter," he said, and led her to Hawk's side. "Stand here," he murmured. "Be honored with the Chosen One."

"Hawk?" she whispered.

He kept his eyes straight ahead. "It's all right," he whispered. "Trust him."

Painted Stick returned to his place on the far side of the sacred fire and signaled for the drums to sound. Then he began the chant again.

"The Chosen goes forth alone."

"It is true," the people answered.

"And returns to his people as two halves complete."

"It is true," hundreds of voices soared.

"A woman with eyes of sky and sea."

"It is true!"

"And hair of new turned earth."

"It is true!"

"By the Hawk Spirit that called him . . ."

"It is true!"

"Shall you know her—shall you welcome her," the holy man proclaimed.

"It is true!"

"For the Chosen has returned."

"It is true!"

"The battle won!"

Here the drums beat a thunderous tattoo, and the Cherokee roared their approval.

"What did he say?" Kate asked.

"He welcomes you. They all welcome you."

"And?"

"And he says I must make an honest woman of you."

"What?"

"Painted Stick says that we must marry according

to Cherokee custom to set a good example for the young."

"And when did he say all that?"

Hawk winked at her. "He hasn't yet, but he will when I tell him that we're going to have a child."

"Hawk? What are you talking about? I'm not pregnant."

"No, but you soon will be." He could stand the strain no longer. Fire Hawk, Chosen of the Cherokee, perfect warrior, broke the solemn protocol of the council fire by sweeping his bride into his arms and carrying her out of the Town-House amid the screaming jubilation of the Cherokee.

"Hawk, put me down! You'll hurt yourself," she said, as they reached the entranceway and stepped out into the bright sunlight.

"No." He strode away from the Town-House.

Kate locked her arms around his neck. "What have you done?" she asked him. "You were supposed to stand there, weren't you?"

"I'll be a laughingstock among the men," he said, but he knew it would be sympathetic laughter.

"Will it harm your mission?"

"No, my heart. It will probably gain me followers. Men do not like others who are too perfect."

Starlady shrieked a *keer-keer-keer* and swooped over them before soaring up toward the clouds.

"Where are you taking me?"

"To a place where we can be alone."

"I can walk."

"You cannot walk. I've spent too long chasing you, Kate. I will not let you get away this time."

"But where are we going?"

His voice grew husky. "To a spot where this man can make love to you." He stopped and covered her mouth with his. The taste of her made his heart race. "First I will show you a place where living water springs from the rock," he murmured, "and where the moss makes a soft bed."

"And . . ."

"And I will fill you with my love," he promised.

"Always?"

"Always, my heart, so long as Sun and Moon light the sky and this man draws breath."

Her eyes glistened with tears of happiness as she smiled up at him. "Word of a Chosen One?"

He nodded. "Word of a Chosen One to his chosen bride."

"Fire Hawk's bride." She sighed contentedly. "It has a nice sound. I think I'll like it."

She kissed him, and the ringing cry of a red-tailed hawk echoed the joyous singing in his soul.

Epilogue

The Smoky Mountains
Winter 1628

"**B**ut Mama, I don't understand," the little girl called Lynx said, tugging at White Panther's fringed cape.

"You never understand," her five-year-old twin brother protested. "You ask dumb questions."

"Do not!" Lynx protested. "I just don't understand. How did Grandmother Rainbow Basket know where to find you? And how did she know that Father had come back to the Cherokee?"

White Panther smiled at the boy and girl who sat wrapped in furs beside her hearth. Winter was a good time for storytelling and a wonderful time for being with her beloved children. Her log house was snug against the winds that whipped down from the mountain high places and large enough for gatherings of her family and friends. Hawk had even built her a window and a proper fireplace with a chimney in place of a center fire-pit.

"Mama . . ." Lynx tugged on White Panther's skirt. "You forgot to tell about—"

"She didn't forget," Little Elk defended. "She didn't get to the next part yet."

White Panther put a finger to her lips for silence. "I'll tell nothing more if you both don't promise to be good," she chided gently.

These children were her heart's darlings, and she could deny them little. But as Hawk reminded her often enough, Cherokee children must learn respect for their elders.

"I'll be good," Little Elk promised, nudging his sister. His night black hair hung straight to his shoulders in a silken wave of perpetual motion, and his dark almond-shaped eyes were exact duplicates of his father's.

Lynx's eyes—one blue and one green—dilated with passion. "I'll be good!" Except for her unusual eye coloring, she was a proper little Cherokee with a round honey-colored face and crow black hair that White Panther braided into a single, silken plait and decorated with feathers and beads.

Being good was never easy for Lynx. She was full of mischief, always scraping her knees or falling from trees in an attempt to run faster and climb higher than her twin.

"I'm sure you'll both try," White Panther said, handing each a honey corn-cake. "Put these sweets in your mouth and be still and listen."

Little Elk nodded solemnly and sat up as tall as his five years would permit. Lynx giggled and popped the cake into her mouth. Both children were identically dressed in thigh-length shifts of doeskin with beaver-skin leggings that were stitched to waterproof leather boots.

"Mama." Her son snuggled close. "The story."

White Panther ruffled his hair and took a sip of hot herbal tea. "Very well. But you must listen and

remember. This is very important, and you will tell
your grandchildren when I am dead and gone."

"You'll never be dead," Little Elk pronounced as
he licked the crumbs off his fingers.

"Won't let you," his twin chimed in. "Never!"

"Grandmother Rainbow Basket did as she promised your father. She welcomed me to the village
and to the Cherokee nation." White Panther smiled
and took another sip of the honey-sweetened brew.
"In time, both the woman with eyes of different
colors—"

"Like me!" Lynx squealed.

Little Elk elbowed his twin. "Hush!"

White Panther raised an eyebrow warningly and
continued. ". . . The woman with eyes of different
colors and the Lady Rainbow Basket came to love
each other. You remember that both Fire Hawk Who
Hunts At Dawn and this woman had been chosen
by the Hawk Spirit."

"Like Starlady's Child," Lynx cried.

"No, dumbkin," her brother corrected. "Not a
real bird. The Hawk Spirit."

"I'm a Bird," Lynx said.

"Shhh," White Panther soothed. "Your father and
I became honored members of the council, and we
taught the people all we knew about the white
men."

"So that they won't come and take our mountains," Little Elk proclaimed.

"Never," echoed Lynx.

"And the High Council decreed that no whites
could come to Cherokee land," White Panther continued softly. "Not now, and not for many lifetimes
to come."

"But you can stay with us, can't you, Mama?" It
was the question Little Elk always asked.

"Yes, my darling, because I am not English anymore. I am Cherokee. My old name was Kate-Miles, but now I am White Panther—"

"Of the Cherokee!"

"And they lived happily," Little Elk supplied, "among the *People*, and in time, they were blessed—"

"With a son and a daughter," his sister finished. "Us!"

"Yes," White Panther agreed.

"But you didn't tell about Aunt Alice," Little Elk reminded her.

"No, I didn't get to that part yet. The Powhatan married the Englishwoman, Alice, and—"

"A bear ate him!" Lynx cried. "A big, big bear."

White Panther ignored the interruption. "Before Gar captured your Aunt Alice, when she was English, she had another husband."

"When she was white," Lynx put in. "When she was white, and his name was Will-Yun-Ben."

"Will-Yun Ben-Hit," Little Elk corrected. "But when Aunt Alice decided to become a Powhatan, Will-Yun-Ben-Hit married his slave woman, Ed."

"Edwina," White Panther said. "His English name was Sir William Bennett. He did marry his serving woman, Edwina, because she was carrying a child that might have been his. They built a new house in Jamestown, and they live in Virginia to this day. And Alice and the mighty Gar had one child, your cousin Otter." White Panther saw that Lynx was getting sleepy. She put down her tea and pulled the yawning child into her lap. Little Elk lay his head contentedly against his mother's knee.

"Soon," White Panther went on, "the English were driving the Powhatan from the sea. One of the tribes moved inland to the foot of the Blue Ridge Mountains. Your Aunt Alice came with them. She met a Cherokee warrior named Horn and went to live in the Deer Village not far away."

"When Aunt Alice comes to visit, you talk about the English lands far away," Little Elk said.

"Across the ocean," Lynx said, in case anyone forgot where England was.

"But you forgot one thing," Little Elk said.

"Did not forget," Lynx argued.

"Did."

"Your brother is right," White Panther agreed. "I didn't answer Lynx's question. How did Grandmother Rainbow Basket know that Hawk and his wife needed help? And how did she know that Starlady was a spirit bird and not just an ordinary red-tail?"

White Panther nodded sagely. "How did she know? Why would she tell her husband, Woods Buffalo, to gather a party of men and women? And why would they walk more than a hundred miles north?"

"Because Grandmother Rainbow Basket was a Chosen One too!" Little Elk proclaimed triumphantly. "She was chosen before Father was born."

"That's right," White Panther agreed. "Rainbow Basket had special powers like those she passed on to her son. And she used this magic to rescue her son when he was hurt."

"By poison arrows," Little Elk reminded Lynx. "Powhatan arrows."

"No need to talk of that," White Panther reminded them all. "The peace pipe has been smoked between Powhatan and Cherokee."

"Powhatan and Cherokee," Lynx declared, "but not English."

"What is this about English?" Fire Hawk pushed open the heavy door.

"Father!" Little Elk cried.

"Father!" echoed his sister.

The twins flung themselves at him, clinging to his leggings and climbing up him. He hugged them and plopped them down on the rug-covered floor. "Away to your grandmother's with you," he insisted. "Didn't you beg us to let you spend the night with her because your cousins would be there? Soon it will be dusk, and tomorrow certain boys may be invited to go on their first deer drive."

"Just the boys?" Lynx wailed. "It's not fair."

"Oh, I think the pretty women's society may have something special planned for you girls," White Panther said as she tucked her daughter into her hooded winter cloak and mittens. "Bundle up, both of you. It's cold outside," she cautioned.

"Good night, Mama."

"Good night."

"Thank you for the story."

"Give that young lady to me," Hawk said. "The snow will be over her boot-tops. I'll take her to her grandmother. She looks like she'll be asleep before the sun goes down."

Lynx threw up her arms to her father.

"Me too," Little Elk cried.

White Panther kissed them both. "Good night, and be good. Don't forget your prayers," she called after them.

Hawk glanced back at her. "Put on your own warm cape."

"Where are we going?" White Panther asked.

"You'll see."

She was waiting outside for him when he returned. She was glad the children would be away tonight. She had a secret to tell her husband, one that she knew would bring him great joy.

Around them, other lodges were clustered. Just over there was Kate's friend Robin's Egg's house, and there stood the sturdy home of Rainbow Basket and Woods Buffalo. Hawk had been right about that too; White Panther was surrounded by friends and relatives.

Home, she thought. *This was home now . . . these mountains, these people.* She rarely even thought of herself as Kate anymore. She was White Panther, wife to Fire Hawk Who Hunts At Dawn.

"Where are you taking me?" she demanded of Hawk.

His breath made puffs of white in the cold air. The years had changed him little; he was still the tall, powerful man she had fallen in love with.

"There is a sunset you must see, my heart," he murmured huskily. "Will you watch it with me?"

She reached out and took his hand. Together they walked to the top of the ridge and stood in silence as the pale golden disk spread purple-red fire across the western sky.

"I've never seen anything so beautiful," White Panther said when the last of the gilded light had faded to blue-gray.

"I know one thing," Hawk said, pulling her so close that she could feel the warmth of his sweet breath on her face.

"What?" She looked into his eyes, savoring the happiness of this moment in the arms of the only man she'd ever loved.

"Tomorrow the sun will rise over the eastern mountains," he said. "And we will watch it together."

"The three of us?" she said.

"So long as we live."

"And after?"

"And after," he promised. "Forever." He kissed her again, then lifted her chin and looked into her eyes. "What did you mean, the three of us?"

Laughing, she hugged him tightly and whispered her secret in his ear.

"You're certain?" he whispered huskily. "We've made another child?"

She chuckled. "Time enough since the twins were born, don't you think?"

"Not for lack of my trying."

"You're as arrogant as ever," she reminded him.

"And why not?" he demanded. "Am I not the Chosen?"

Their laughter mingled and rolled out over the hills and valleys below, and from somewhere . . . far off beyond the highest peak, she was certain she heard the answering cry of a wild hawk.